MW01717266

Leaving This Life Behind

To Carol,
Best wishes
Howard Levine

Leaving This Life Behind

Howard Levine

Creative Arts Book Company
Berkeley, California

Copyright © 2000 by Howard Levine

Leaving This Life Behind is published by Donald S. Ellis and distributed by Creative Arts Book Company

No part of this book may be reproduced in any manner without the written permission from the publisher, except in brief quotations used in articles or reviews.

For information contact:
Creative Arts Book Company
833 Bancroft Way
Berkeley, California 94710

The characters, places, incidents and situations in this book are imaginary and have no relation to any person, place or actual happening.

ISBN 0-88739-261-X Paper
Library of Congress Catalog Number 99-61096
Printed in the United States of America

For Marian; in memory of Martha

Acknowledgements

MMY, Marian Levine, Raymond Moody,
Evan & Ellen Finkelstein, Jim Fleming,
Kiki Thorpe, Jennifer Malnick.

Leaving This Life Behind

- 1 -
Sharon

I DON'T have any great sympathy for truck drivers, but they really should allow trucks in the left lane of the Major Deegan Expressway. That way, I wouldn't have an eighteen-wheeler two inches off of my bumper, double-barrelled headlights flashing Morse code in my rear-view mirror: Move over, lady, or I'll show you why that car you're driving is called a bug. I can't even see the driver, just, in between blinding flashes, the muzzle-like grill of his truck.

My husband advises braking in such situations. Teach the tailgating bastards a lesson. Having long since lost my faith in my husband's wisdom, I shift over into the left lane, seizing the only available opening. The shift is more like a swerve, followed by a corrective semi-swerve in the other direction. This brings me frighteningly close to the truck, which is already charging by on my right, creating what feels like a miniature tornado. My Volkswagen shudders violently. *Now* I brake, forcing myself to do it lightly. A panic-stop in the left lane of the Deegan can have dire consequences.

The truck, which seems to be about a block long, is finally past. The wind dies down. When I'm safely back in the middle lane, I exhale slowly, releasing what feels like an hour's worth of pent-up air. My heart is fluttering; tremors run through my body, as if the car's earlier vibrations were now rippling within me. I grip the steering wheel tightly with both hands while the tremors run their course. Soon I've settled down enough to chance diverting my attention from the road, long enough to fumble in my purse for a cigarette.

My first puff produces a prodigious cloud of low-tar, mentholated smoke. Through this, and over the sun-lit roofs of a couple of cars now between us, I make out the lettering on the back of the truck: "Wednesday is Prince Spaghetti day." Maybe that's the only time Prince Spaghetti drives like he's not sitting on his brains. Today, unfortunately, is only Monday. Assuming that I arrive at my desk in one piece, I'm looking at nine more trips from Yonkers to Manhattan and back before the weekend. There must be some alternative.

Actually, there are a couple. My husband, Paul, has offered to drop me in the Bronx at the subway station on the way into his garage. But that would mean waking up ridiculously early —he has to pick up his cab by 6:30 a.m. It would also mean leaving my three-year-old son Kenny alone on the steps of the day care center, which doesn't open until seven. Scratch alternative number one. The second option is that I could drive to the Woodlawn station myself (after delivering Kenny to his teacher) and park in a lot. Much as I hate driving, that's still an easier trip than driving into Manhattan, and the parking's cheaper. Also, I can get a seat on the train at Woodlawn, it's the first stop. But seat or no seat, I can't handle the subways—period. Even though they're probably safer during rush hour, this relative safety comes at the price of having stomachs and crotches two inches from my face, and strange thighs and hips gripping me on either side with a spreading, clammy warmth. Quite a bargain.

Having been absorbed in reconsidering these options, I suddenly realize that I'm about to pass 138th Street. Either 138th Street or the last exit of the Deegan, the Triboro Bridge, can be taken to get onto the FDR Drive heading downtown. I should have just continued on to the bridge and paid the $1.25 to cross.

But I'm programmed for 138th Street, it's in my mind that *that's* my exit, as if my name were engraved and studded with plastic reflectors on the sign. In a moment of jittery reflex, still flustered from the truck, I jerk the steering wheel to the right. That's all it takes, an unthinking jerk of my right arm. The Volkswagen careens across the right lane, toward the concrete divider that separates the shoulder of the highway from the exit ramp.

I'm frozen with horror. Then, just as suddenly, I'm beyond that: I'm with my mother in our Queens apartment, learning how to rig up a sanitary belt; I'm marrying Paul in the Bronx County courthouse; I'm visiting my emaciated father in the hospital. These events and others are superimposed upon each other in a timeless instant, a distillation of my life. My consciousness is unlocked from sequence, free from terror.

The Volkswagen smashes into the divider. I'm enveloped in a blackness filled with the awful sound of metal and glass bursting, shattering. Yet almost instantaneously the sound becomes a distant echo. I'm moving at an impossibly rapid speed through the blackness, which has become cylindrical, a vortex. In the next moment, I'm floating above the Major Deegan. I *must* be, because I'm looking down on what's left of the Volkswagen.

Through the crushed windshield, I can see a head hanging limply. Shards of glass are strewn over the dark brown hair, which is streaked with blood. The hair is scattered over an overcoat collar, which is also turning crimson in front. That's all that's immediately visible; twisted metal has encased the rest of the body . . . *my body*?

This initial inkling strikes me as ridiculous: But I'm here! Indeed, I *am* looking down on the wreck, somehow. And I can feel the outlines of my body, as if it were draped in an extremely sheer, full-length nightgown. If I'm *in* a body, though, I can't see it. I try to touch myself, my arm, my head . . . nothing. Absolutely nothing.

Bewildered, I paw the air, beginning to panic. I've somehow been set adrift, banished, become an anguished mind anchored to nothing. Crying out, I gaze at the trapped body within the wreck. I feel myself moving rapidly downward, as if propelled by the force of anxiety and yearning. To my utter astonishment, I pass through the Volkswagen—and through my body—in what seems like the blink of an eye. I feel no resistance, no physical contact. Just like that, I'm on the other side of the wreck, above the shoulder of the expressway.

I hover there, an invisible shadow, stunned. I'm completely at a loss as to what to do and where to go. Should I make another attempt to get back inside of my broken body, or not? What the hell am I doing *out* of it? How *can* I be?

As if mirroring my emotions, the scene below me is chaotic. The Volkswagen is not the only wreck in the vicinity. Battered cars are strewn at random angles across the width of the expressway, as if a bomb had exploded in their midst; a tractor trailer is jackknifed; broken glass is everywhere; steam is pouring from beneath the bent hoods of a couple of cars. Traffic on both sides of the expressway and on the exit ramp is at a standstill.

Somehow what has happened, and my part in it, is at once obvious to me. This realization adds to my distress, but also provides an almost welcome ray of mental clarity, a graspable piece of cause and effect. I'd cut off a car in the right lane. The driver's only choice had been to swerve left, really no choice at all in the heavy morning traffic. He'd sideswiped a car in the middle lane, which started a series of crunching ricochets, sending tons of moving metal out of control. Helpless drivers had been caught in the middle.

Despite my role as the precipitator of this awful, smoking mess, I have (after an initial pang of guilt) a surprisingly clear conscience. I'd been under the influence of nothing other than my own easily jangled nerves, which, Lord knows, I hadn't asked to be born with. And from the looks of things, I've suffered the most serious physical damage of all the crash victims. Several uninjured people have left their cars to try to help. The first two on the scene rush to the Volkswagen.

One of my would-be rescuers is a fortyish black man in a three piece suit. The other is a red-haired woman in her late twenties, about my age. Hugging her coat around her, she encourages the man as he struggles to pry open the bent door on the driver's side. Watching clouds of vapor pour from their mouths, I remember leaving the house this morning, seemingly ages ago, and cursing as the frosty January air sank into my face.

Now I feel no chill at all. I feel no physical pain. I settle down next to my rescuers, intending to impart this information. Maybe they'll find it reassuring. Maybe they'll reassure me.

"Umm, hello?" I murmur from behind the black man, but receive no response. I try again, this time in a voice that sounds definitely louder to me. The result is the same. After a few moments' hesitation, I reach to touch his shoulder. My diaphanous hand just passes through him. He doesn't seem to feel anything, doesn't turn around.

However, he does relax his hands and foot from their exertions against the door and side of the Volkswagen. "Damn!" he exclaims to the woman. "I can't *move* it. And I think she's . . . "

Reluctantly, the woman peers through the cracked driver's window. She gasps and turns away, then forces herself to look again. "You're right," she says in a muffled voice. "I don't think she's breathing."

Now a chill does run through me. I stare at the woman, thinking she must be crazy. But in fact, at least in this bizarre state of disembodiment, I *don't* seem to be breathing. I try to take a deep breath. Nothing happens. Yet I don't feel at all starved for oxygen. Maybe, hopefully, this indicates that my physical body (the only kind I ever thought I had) *is* breathing, despite the woman's snap diagnosis.

Assuming a kneeling position on the compacted hood of the Volkswagen, I gaze through what remains of the windshield. There's no need to confirm what I see by touching. I am looking, undeniably, at a corpse, *my corpse* . . . and yet suddenly, eerily, I feel almost no connection to it. I search the face. Beneath matted hair, there is an ugly gash in the top of the forehead. If not for this and the profusion of blood everywhere, the face would almost resemble that of a doll or mannequin. The eyes are half open and glazed. Only the lower portions of the brown irises are visible, through eyelashes which are stiffening with dried blood. The rouge on the crimson-streaked cheeks highlights the pallor of the unbloodied portions of the face. Perhaps owing to my detached state immediately preceding the moment of impact, the mouth is not agape with horror. The lips are parted slightly; between lipstick and blood, the mouth resembles little more than a red smear. The upper half of the body is pinned between the driver's seat and the steering wheel, the wheel apparently having been bent and pushed inward by the imploding dashboard.

It occurs to me that I might have been squeezed out of my body, much as air is forced from a bellows. I consider this idea almost bemusedly, as if it were an interesting explanation for someone else's fate. Maybe I'm still stunned—I *should* be—or maybe it's the sorry condition of what was my face, or the dream-like experience of seeing myself not as a reflection or picture, but in three dimensions. Whatever the reason, I feel no more attachment to that face and body than a snake must feel to the skin it's just shed.

The black man, after a last, futile attempt to budge the door, turns to the red-head and says in a rasping voice, "Look, if she's really gone, then it's no emergency to pull her out. But let's find out for sure." He rubs his hands together, shoves one into a pocket of his suit jacket, and reaches through the windshield with the other. As he does, his arm runs through me, through the space I occupy. With his fingers he probes the neck of the trapped body, searching for a pulse. He does so gingerly at first, then exerts more pressure at different points on the neck. I'm less intent on his findings than on the phenomenon of his arm passing through me like a skewer. I don't *feel* the arm; I know that it's rotating slightly as he works his fingers only because I can see it. Indeed, the man's arm seems no more tangible than his gaze, which also passes through me.

Feeling increasingly uncomfortable, I disengage myself. This requires no effort; I seem to be able to move at will. I hover slightly above the woman, looking over the man's bent back. After a few moments he straightens and turns, giving up on the pulse. Seeming to look right at me, he says, "I'm no doctor, but unless I missed something, she *is* dead."

According to my understanding of this last word, he's definitely mistaken. And he pronounces it with an air of finality that seems to portend exile for me, isolation from everyone and everything I've ever known.

"That's not true!" I declare, a note of pleading in my voice. I'm standing between him and the woman, talking almost directly into his face. And I could swear I distinctly see his every facial pore, every hair, every curve of bone and skin. But it's his eyes, shining and coal black, that really grab my attention. Even as I shout "I'm *not* dead!" I see in his pupils the woman's reflection, not mine.

She's slowly shaking her head. "I don't think you missed anything," she replies to him, gulping. Vapor from her mouth fills the air where my face is. "It's really a shame . . . and she's probably got a kid. See the car seat back there? God. I'm just glad I don't know her personally. But . . . " After a moment her gaze shifts toward the general wreckage on the Deegan and the people converging around it. "Look, let's see if anyone's called the cops and an ambulance yet. There must be an emergency phone somewhere. It looks like it might take more than one ambulance, too. Why don't we see what else we can do? I don't think we're going anywhere for a while."

"You got that right," he says, nodding. "It'll take them forever to clear this, even one lane. And I'm supposed to be mending my ways and getting to work on time. Hell, what's the difference. Yeah, let's see if we can be of any more use than we are here. But I gotta get my coat out of my car first. I'm freezing."

Walking rapidly back down the expressway into a haze of blue smoke from idling vehicles, he soon reaches his own car. The woman hurries in the opposite direction, toward what appears to be the car I cut off. It's sprawled across the right lane, almost perpendicular to the painted lines. Some kind of long, luxury model, its rear end is well into the middle lane. The front fender reaches halfway across the shoulder of the Deegan and is badly bent on its left side. Other than the dented fender and a smashed headlight, the car doesn't seem to have suffered serious damage. Neither does the driver, who's leaning against the front passenger door. He looks shaken, nothing more. A few sympathetic people surround him.

Two teenage boys have just left this group and are moving toward the Volkswagen—where I remain, visibly and otherwise. The redhead walks over to the two teens and speaks to them briefly. At a distance of several yards, I can hear her with surprising clarity: "Listen, she's dead, and a mess. I don't think you want to look." This, of course, causes them to continue in my direction with quickened footsteps. From force of habit, I move aside as they approach.

"God, *look* at that, will you?" says one, sticking his head halfway through the frame of the windshield.

"Holy shit!" replies the other, gaping.

Feeling a strong need to distance myself from the corpse and these new onlookers, I catch up with the redhead; she seems the closest to a kindred soul that I can immediately come by. I don't bother trying to tell *her* that I'm not dead. I'm becoming less and less convinced of this myself.

The redhead and I join the group around the luxury car driver, a squat gentleman with a trimmed, graying beard. He is ignoring the advice of another man, who strongly urges him to sit down on the ground with his head between his knees, a position that is supposed to forestall shock.

"Dammit, I'm alright!" the driver snarls. "How many times do I have to tell you that!" Having stood up from his position leaning against the side of his car, he now sags back into it. He takes a deep breath and exhales slowly, steamily. "I'm alright," he repeats, this time almost in a whimper. Now he addresses himself to his newest audience member, the redhead, "I'm alright. I swear, I don't know what the hell she was thinking about. Cuts across right in front of me. What was I supposed to do? Go look at the other side of my car, will you? Just look at it. Right in front of me. Idiot!"

I take no offense and feel no sense of betrayal as the redhead nods commiseratively. The man is right, even if he's unknowingly reviling a dead person. I probably would have reacted the same way, or worse. The fear and outrage on his face are all-too familiar emotions to me—and they point up, by contrast, the unexpected peacefulness I'm beginning to feel. From several directions, wailing sirens pierce the air. This sound, which used to thoroughly unnerve me, now has no such effect. And even as it grows louder, it seems increasingly remote to my awareness.

Indeed, not only sound but everything in my immediate surroundings is fading, obscured by a whiteness that appears most concentrated in an oval-like form a small distance ahead. The sense that I'm leaving "this" world is overwhelming. I've never really believed in the hereafter; now, however, it seems to be opening up in front of me. And I find myself looking forward to whatever the next step might be. But then it really hits me, like a second death, that I'm also leaving Kenny and Paul.

The thought of Kenny in particular fills me with anguish. I've always felt guilty about not spending enough time with him, and now . . . I want so badly to hold him. The thought is unbearable; I push it away.

Leaving Paul, on the other hand, is something I've considered doing several times before. But now it seems irrevocable.

- 2 -
Paul

BEFORE ENTERING the Beth Shalom Day Care Center to pick up Kenny, I take another couple of shots of spearmint breath spray, practically gagging on the second one. If I still smell of scotch —or was it rye?—then there's nothing more that can be done about it. Kenny, of course, is familiar with the general smell of liquor, but he's probably too young to have negative associations attached to it. It's the smell of Daddy, that's all, and he still seems thrilled to see me when I pick him up. I get a kick out of seeing him, too, at least at first—which is why I don't want to have to deal with the righteous indignation of Miss Nahm, his nursery school teacher. She's explained to me several times that she's taken a special interest in Kenny. He seems withdrawn, she says, and has difficulty expressing himself, etcetera etcetera. The accusatory tone in her voice is plain enough. When she picks up liquor on my breath, I just know that it's all she can do to keep from notifying social services on the spot.

I return the breath spray to its customary location in the

glove compartment. Before leaving the car I have a look at myself in the rear view mirror, giving a couple of useless pats to my wiry hair. Then I step out and slam the door, annoyed at myself for caring about what Our Lady of Sobriety might think of me.

The day care center, a modern, rectangular building without windows, resembles a large army pill box. The air is supposed to circulate, but as soon as I walk in a fetid smell hits me in the face: the odor of empty milk containers and "poop," as Sharon would like me to call it in front of Kenny. The smell increases the queasiness in my stomach. I nod at the receptionist and make my way down the glaring, neon-lit hallway. The light makes the door displays seem even brighter, garish. Chanukah decorations are still up—a poor substitute for Santa Claus and Christmas trees. A giant paper menorah, which resembles a pipe organ, covers the door to Kenny's room, the last one on the right.

Inside, a number of small heads are bowed over gray globs of clay and coated fingers. It takes me several seconds to pinpoint Kenny, despite the distinctiveness of his bushy, sandy-colored hair. While I'm still scanning the room, Miss Nahm approaches. She's actually not bad-looking; she has a cute ass and pointed breasts, which are outlined nicely by the sweater she's wearing. Her black hair is short and symmetrically rounded. She wears no make-up. The fullness of her lips contrasts with her pert nose, above which her dark eyes now study me.

"Hello, Miss Nahm," I mumble out of the corner of my mouth. The first time we'd met, I'd been friendly (and sober). I gave her a big smile and lingering handshake, introducing myself as "Paul . . . Galdoni, Kenny's father." She'd extricated her hand and given me her proper name. Then she said that she'd been hoping to meet me. Something about the way she said that made me feel like prey.

Now she returns my greeting and holds out some kind of fuzzy wire with what looks like colored tissues attached to one end. She informs me that Kenny made it.

I nod. "Yeah, it's nice."

"It's a pipe stem flower, in case you're wondering. If you have any potted plants at home, you might want to stick this in the dirt. He's proud of it," she says pointedly. "Made it pretty much by himself." Holding it near the blue and yellow "petals," she offers me the stem.

Before I can take the flower, Kenny spots me and comes running over to give my legs a bear hug. Slightly tipsy already, I almost stumble backward. As he releases me, I stifle a curse and brush bits of clay off of my pants. I pick one or two up off the floor and flick them at a nearby garbage pail, missing.

Kenny grabs his creation from Miss Nahm and excitedly shoves it at me. "See, Daddy!" he squeals. "I make dat."

"I see," I reply, my tone turning falsetto. "A nice flower. Mommy will like that." I take the flower from him, tousling his hair with my free hand and flashing Miss Nahm a smug smile. Kenny scampers toward the closet in the rear of the room to get his jacket.

"Mr. Galdoni," says Miss Nahm, "please try to be careful driving home. And put him in a car seat in the back."

I turn and peer at her through narrowed eyes. "Look—"

"No, *you* look," she crisply replies. "You've been drinking. And now you're going to drive Kenny home?"

This female is unreal. "How do you know I've been drinking?" I demand, unable to keep the chagrin out of my voice.

"I don't know—your eyes are watery, you've been sucking on mints or something. I can tell, that's all."

"You'd make a great cop, little girl."

"Oh? Well, speaking of cops, they arrest people for drunk driving around here. Just be thankful I don't make a phone call. Were it not for Kenny, I would. But assuming you make it home, he's probably better off there than in a police station."

"Hey, I'm *not* drunk. Okay?" A brief shot of fear is giving way to almost violent anger inside of me. "And I can drive just fine, even though that's none of your business. Hell, I'm a pro. I do it all day. I could drive through the city—or Yonkers—with my eyes closed."

At this point, Kenny returns with his little fur-hooded jacket and hands it to me. I turn him around and insert one arm in a sleeve. "Tell me, Miss Nahm," I say in a low, surly voice, "You don't have any kids of your own, do you?"

"No, but—"

"But you're a young college grad, I'm sure, so of course you know all about kids. And you want to stand there and tell me how to raise mine."

Her face reddens. She starts to respond, then glances at Kenny. The conversation, as far as I can tell, has gone over his head in more ways than one. Still, Miss Nahm clenches her slender jaw, sighs, then works up a half-smile. Patting his shoulder, she says, "Goodbye, Ken. I'll see you tomorrow morning, okay?"

"Zip, zip," he says impatiently, fidgeting with the bottom of his jacket. I reach down over his back, but Miss Nahm is already squatting in front of him. She zips the jacket with a crisp motion that resembles a right uppercut. After stroking his cheek once and receiving a smile in return, she wheels around toward the rest of the kids, who are still intently pounding and rolling clay.

* * *

Outside, Kenny eagerly scrambles into the car. There is no child's car seat, in the back or the front, a fact that I'd almost thrown at Miss Nahm, just out of spite. Sharon keeps our one car seat in the rear of her Volkswagen—she trusts my driving more than hers. She never fails to buckle Kenny into it, even though half the time she's not belted in herself. When she brings Kenny to nursery in the morning, she often forgets to fasten up again, particularly if she's had to wait around for them to open the place. She's nervous about driving, but even more nervous about getting to work on time. Anxious and dizzy though she is, in general, she still looks out for Kenny. She installs him in his little throne in the Volkswagen first thing. And she's been nagging me to get another car seat, which I keep putting off. As far as I'm concerned, Kenny's fine on the front seat, next to me. It makes him feel like a big boy, and makes me feel like I've quit hacking for the day.

I lean over from behind the wheel and fasten the waist belt and shoulder harness around Kenny's stomach. I notice as I bend over him that his face is looking more and more like mine everyday. Kenny has my puffy cheeks and pointed chin ("Acorn" was my unloved nickname as a kid). His nose is wide and flat, like something made of clay and hurriedly pressed on by one of his nursery mates. When he smiles, his thin lips uncover a nice set of even teeth, which, fortunately, he got from Sharon. My teeth jut slightly in a few different directions. Kenny's eyes are narrow but they have strikingly large, green irises. As I finish strapping him in, I notice they're fixed on me as usual. It's as if a three-year-old me is looking back at me. I'm proud of the resemblance, but now it makes me a little uncomfortable. My responsibility for the kid is written all over his trusting face.

"Go home. See Mommy," he chirps, cued by the rasping whine of my Plymouth Valiant as it starts up.

"That's right. We'll see Mommy a little while after we get home," I say, thinking that I should tape record my response for future use. As we drive Kenny announces our destination and purpose repeatedly, as if this were necessary to keep us on course. I absently bob my head after the first few times, then stop acknowledging him at all. I'm wondering if Mommy is going to be pissed off because I didn't call her to find out what we need from the supermarket. There'll be time enough to check in with her when I get home, I figure, at which point I can truthfully plead fatigue as a reason for not going out again. Besides, I did try to call her this morning, but she hadn't gotten in yet. There was some huge tie-up on the Deegan—I almost got caught in it myself, but heard the traffic update in time—so her uncharacteristic lateness was not surprising. After a few lunchtime beers, calling her slipped my mind. A lot of things do. Not our destination, though. I've got Kenny to keep me straight and narrow. Still, I'd probably get us home anyway. I'm on automatic pilot; the trip from the day care center to our "Riverview" apartment is habit. As I told Miss Nahm, I could probably do it with my eyes closed.

The trip runs through the heart of Yonkers, which has neither the quiet class of some of the more northern suburbs nor the pizzazz of New York. What it does have are hills, the tops of which afford glimpses, to the west, of factory chimneys and the murky Hudson River beyond. We pass a lot of old wooden houses with peeling paint, set well above the hilly streets atop their own private humps of earth. These mini-hills appear to be held in place by high concrete walls topped by guard rails or chain link fences. Only by ascending the steep brick steps to the houses can you see the manicured patches of grass which pass for front lawns. Some of these still contain weathered statues of black footmen, deer, dingy birdbaths, or what-have-you. The birdbaths are mostly concrete; they'll be cracked and chipped even more by the end of the winter. Many of the property fronts are spray-painted with English and Spanish grafitti. On windy winter days like today Yonkers is a target of cold, foul-smelling breezes from the river. Its fences are almost obscured by trapped litter. The snow that fell yesterday has already turned into a gray slush, which fills in the potholes and the jagged cracks in the sidewalks.

Kenny, of course, notices none of this as we rattle along in the Valiant. After several reminders of where we're going and who we'll be seeing, he has settled into picking apart the "flower" and twisting the pipe stem into different shapes. Torn bits of blue and yellow crepe paper litter the seat between us. Along with my looks, the kid has inherited my destructive tendencies. He reshapes the stem several times, sticking each new configuration in front of my face and declaring, "See!" Finally he sets to the futile task of trying to break the stem into pieces. Frustrated, he begins to wail. The sound soon causes my head to start throbbing. I tell him we can cut up the stem with scissors when we get home, but either he can't hear me above his own noise, doesn't understand, or can't wait. I promise him the scissors again, to no avail. Then I tell him, loudly, to pipe down. This causes *him* to get louder.

Desperate, I try to distract him. "Look, Kenny, see the big truck!" I say, attempting to sound thrilled, pointing to an "A&P" tractor trailer approaching from the opposite direction. Kenny cranes his thin neck and peers through the windshield. He sniffles . . . then grins and confirms my sighting. "Big twuck!"

"Right," I say at the tail end of a long exhalation. My anger slowly begins to dissolve. I light a cigarette, briefly releasing the wheel, which I can do because traffic has now slowed to a crawl —a frustrating situation that is endlessly replayed in my life, but which fascinates Kenny. The big trucks and fellow travelers drift by him as if in a happy dream.

Crazy though he is about trucks, Kenny's next sighting brings him even greater joy. It's a "Daddy-cab," the name he gives to any yellow car, anything with a light on top, anything resembling the prison-on-wheels in which I spend most of my waking hours. I used to drive the cab home for dinner now and then, when I was working night shift. Once I made the mistake of taking him downstairs for a look, and after that he always knew what it meant when I came in holding a coin changer and portable radio. I'd have no chance for a peaceful dinner until after he'd climbed around in Daddy-cab for a while. He loved pushing the buttons on the meter and watching the red-lighted numbers flicker on and off. Another absorbing game was seesawing coins in the metal fare compartment which opens alternately on either side of the "bullet-proof" partition. A couple of times (unknown to Sharon), I drove the cab around the block with an ecstatic Kenny on my lap. His legs were too short to reach the gas pedal or power brake, of course. But he did "help" me steer and honked the horn repeatedly, his whoops of delight adding to the racket.

The thrill was gone, for both of us, after I switched to day shift, weekdays. This happened in September, at the start of Kenny's nursery school year. Now, having derived some temporary joy from the sight of a passing cab, Kenny whimpers his customary request: "Bring home Daddy-cab." Needing something to focus on, I take a stab at explaining to him, again, why Daddy-cab doesn't visit him anymore.

"I don't have the cab at dinnertime anymore," I say, trying not to slur my words. "I drive during the daytime now, while Mommy works and you're in nursery school. Mommy had to start working to help pay for our food and nursery and everything else we need. And you like going to nursery school, don't you?"

He doesn't answer. I glance over and see him nodding slowly, his lower lip protruding in a pout. "Well," I continue, as we turn off of Broadway onto McLean, "now someone else drives Daddy-cab at night, like I used to when I was bringing him home for dinner. If I still drove at night, then you and Mommy would be away during the day, and I'd be away at night. We'd never see each other."

This is actually Sharon's concern more than mine. In fact, my switching to days was one of her preconditions for taking a job. She wants to maintain some semblance of family life, for Kenny's sake if nothing else. I readily agreed. I do want to spend some time with Kenny, and the kid needs a male role-model (as it's called by those who get paid for such wisdom). Besides, other than the fact that there's usually more money involved, night shift has little to recommend it.

"Bring home Daddy-cab," Kenny repeats at the tail end of my explanation.

"Someday," I reply, shrugging. Remembering my cigarette, I flick off the ashes and take a drag. "Maybe sometime I'll even take you out for a whole day in Daddy-cab. When you're older," I add, covering myself. Cesar Rosario, a fellow hack-pusher, regularly shows up with one of his many kids. He swears by the tips you receive with a cute-looking dependent sitting next to you. Of course, Cesar has relatives all over the city; if a kid turns fussy, Cesar can get rid of him with little problem. If Kenny went off, I'd be stuck with him for the rest of the day.

Now, he seems pacified, even a little excited, at the prospect of a future day on the road. The odds are that this won't last very long. But whatever turn his mood takes, Sharon'll be home to relieve me in an hour or two.

I park on Nepperhan Avenue; the rip-off rents do not cover garage parking in the Riverview Apartments (an accurate name only if you live on an upper floor, facing west). They do pay for the "security" afforded by the doorman. As we walk into our building, I nod at Flannery, the red-faced day man. Ordinarily he just nods back. He's learned that it won't help his Christmas tip to fuss over Kenny, and that I prefer to open my own doors and be bothered as little as possible. Now, however, he positions himself squarely in front of me, the brass buttons on his enormous stomach and chest glittering like detour markers.

" 'Scuse me Mr. Gull-doni," he says, "But the police was here, lookin' for ye. They said they'll be back—and soon."

"Shit," I mutter, swiveling my head to take a fast look out at Nepperhan Avenue. Flannery's is the only blue uniform in sight at the moment. A cold sensation of fear wells up in my stomach. Then I remember Miss Nahm and her built-in drunk-o-meter. Could she have decided to call the cops after all?

"Look Flannery," I say, feigning nonchalance, "did they say what—"

He shakes his head. "No-sir, Mr. Gull-doni, just that they want to talk to ye," he says with a hint of a smirk. Then his eyes move past me, to Nepperhan. "Why if it isn't them now."

Turning, I see a blue and orange squad car pull up with two of Yonkers' finest inside. I take a step toward the building's glass doors, deciding to discuss matters outside. Whatever the cops want, it's none of Flannery's business. Kenny automatically follows me. I hesitate, wondering if I should leave him with Flannery for the moment, and also wondering if I should try to sneak another shot of breath spray. The breath spray stays in my pocket, and Kenny comes along.

Preceded by their own steamy exhalations, the cops have already reached the fancy awning leading up to the doors. As I'd hoped, they seem touched by my innocent-looking little son. After I introduce myself and respectfully inquire what the problem might be, the younger cop glances at his partner, then pats the top of Kenny's fur-lined hood and invites him to hold a "real nightstick." Kenny takes a fast look at me, then grabs the outstretched nightstick with both hands. Meanwhile the other cop, who introduces himself as Sergeant Morris, asks me to come sit in the squad car with him.

"Now wait a minute—" I begin, looking back at Kenny.

Morris gently places a pudgy hand on my shoulder, but I pull away. "Mr. Galdoni," he says, sighing impatiently and shoving his hand back in his pocket, "just come sit down with me. We're not taking you any place. I just want to talk to you privately for a few minutes. Okay?"

Surprised and mildly relieved by his low-key manner, I make a small show of deliberating. Morris draws another long, cloudy breath. His tone hardens—slightly, but enough. "Mr. Galdoni, it's cold out here. Don't make things difficult. Let's just go sit down."

Kenny, happily clutching the nightstick, is already trailing the other cop back into the building. "See you in a minute, Ken," I call out to the back of his hooded head. As I follow Morris, the effort I have to make to walk steadily has little to do with alcohol. He directs me into the front passenger seat, then slides into the driver's a moment later. The car has been running with its heater on and is warm, almost stifling. Morris turns to me and says, "Mr. Galdoni, your wife is Sharon Galdoni, correct?"

I nod dumbly. Whatever I might have imagined him starting off with, this is not it.

"Well sir, I'm afraid there's been an accident. This morning on the Major Deegan Expressway. She was killed. I'm sorry."

I stare at him, unseeing, for what must be several seconds. I have a vision of myself switching the dial on my portable radio this morning—one eye following the station indicator, the other watching the FDR Drive twist and turn in front of me—after hearing the traffic update: ". . . an accident involving several cars and at least one truck. All southbound lanes are blocked . . ."

The update gives way to the sound of my voice. "Sergeant," I hear myself say quietly, calmly, "look, I've had a rough day. I have a kid that I have to take care of. I know you're a cop, but don't give me this bullshit, alright? She probably just got caught in traffic, she—" Suddenly I can't go on. Morris just looks at me, waiting, a moon-faced cop with a salt-and-pepper mustache and slightly bloodshot eyes. His face begins to fade again; a hazy film passes in front of it, in front of me. I close my eyes and sit back, my head resting against the metal detention grill.

"What am I gonna do now?" My voice is little more than a whisper. A sob works its way up from my throat. "Sharon—" Finally, I force myself to sit up and look at Morris. "You know," I manage to say, "I treated her like shit. I really did. I—"

My voice gives. I bolt from the car. Breaking into a run, I reach and pass through the glass doors. The bright light from the lobby's chandeliers glistens before my eyes. Kenny is entertaining the other cop and Flannery with an earnest attempt to twirl the nightstick. I decide to take Kenny upstairs. Sharon'll be home soon, just like I promised the kid, just like she always is. We'll hang out for an hour or two, waiting; I'll open a beer and turn on "Sesame Street", then spend more time watching it than Kenny, who'll pause in his mess-making only if Cookie Monster happens to come on. Then Sharon'll walk in. She'll kiss and hug Kenny, then sift through the mail. It's just the way things are, simple fact, like our names on the directory behind

Flannery's desk: "Galdoni, P. & S." She belongs here, she's part of this scene, part of me, part of the endless, fucked-up routine that I call my life.

"See, Daddy!" declares Kenny, prancing over to me, jerking the nightstick around by its leather strap as if he were grasping a frisky snake.

I nod. "Nice."

Dissatisfied with my reaction, Kenny intensifies his "twirling", causing the tip of the lead-filled stick to bounce loudly a few times against the lobby's shining floor.

"Now, Kenny, that's enough," says Flannery, glancing impatiently at me. He does a small double-take, and I turn away and quickly run the back of my hand across my eyes, wishing I could lay it across his face instead. Then, wordlessly, I take the nightstick from Kenny and hand it back to the younger cop. Kenny starts bawling. I pick him up and, shutting my eyes, give him a tight hug. Perhaps surprised by this, he stops crying almost at once. I hold him closely for another moment then put him down, struggling to keep myself half-way together in front of Flannery, the younger cop, and Morris, who has trailed me back inside. He now faces me, sandwiching Kenny between us.

"We have to take you down to ID the body," says Morris in a semi-whisper. "Unless you want someone else to."

"Uh-uh."

"Maybe you want to take the kid upstairs, arrange for someone else to look after him. We'll wait down here."

I clench my teeth and swallow. "Where . . . where is she?"

"Harlem Hospital."

"Why—"

"It was probably the closest."

I nod. "Well, what the hell's the difference, now. C'mon, Kenny," I say, removing his arms from around my leg. "You can push the elevator button, okay?"

I stride quickly behind him as he runs toward the open elevator. Standing on tip-toe, he proudly presses the button marked "4", several times. My thumb is jammed against the one that says "close". The doors finally draw together, and I look up to see the three men in the lobby compressing into a blurry line of blue. Again I wipe my eyes, an exercise which proves useless once we enter the apartment. Items which I've barely glanced at in months are now tear-jerkers: the potted plants that Sharon tended so carefully; "Mom's Apron," with its giant waist pockets below the name; Sharon's little feats of needlepoint hanging from the kitchen walls. The trappings of a home, a family. Whatever chance she had at that is shot now . . . as if she ever had much of one, with me.

Kenny, the glue that kept us technically together, is removing pots from the side compartment of the oven. They land loudly on the floor. Ordinarily I would either jump on his case or ignore him, depending on my mood. But now the sight of Kenny's blissful ignorance is almost more than I can take. How am I ever going to tell him?

I bend over and tousle his bushy hair, then, reaching into the cabinet above the stove, I pull out a fifth of Johnny Walker Red. I take a deep slug. The scotch burns at first, but then, as if melting the blockage in my throat, slides down with a comforting ease. After a couple more slugs, I reshelve the bottle. An almost solid fog seems to settle behind my eyes.

"Daddy," says Kenny, tiring of the pots, "I turl stick."

"Uh hmm, yeah, you did," I mumble, nodding a few times. "Yeah, you twirled it real good." The nightstick . . . the cops. Sharon. I lurch toward the kitchen's wall phone, almost stumbling over a large frying pan. The usually elusive pocket address book is hanging, fortunately, from a string next to the phone, where Sharon installed it in one of her recent attempts at organization. "Restani, Carmen" is the only entry on the "R" page. The correct holes in the phone's dial are a little trickier to pinpoint, but I manage.

Carmen is home as usual. She's a television junkie, I'm reminded as she shouts "Hello?" over the background noise of the tube. "Sure, bring him up," she replies as soon as she gets the gist of my request. She quickly hangs up, asking for no explanation and putting off arrangement of payback.

Kenny, predictably, is not as agreeable. When I tell him that I'm leaving him at Carmen's for a while, he sticks out his lower lip.

"Daddy stay."

"I can't. I have to . . . Look, Kenny, I have to go somewhere." I take a deep swallow of air. "I don't *want* to go, but I have to. Understand?"

"Kenny come."

"Uh-uh. You can't, that's all."

He starts crying. I squat and put my hands on his shoulders, blinking away my own tears. "Kenny," I say, tightening my grip on his shoulders to steady myself, "I have to go. I can't tell you why right now. You can play with . . . what's his name . . . Sergio. I'll be home soon, I promise."

Kenny shows no signs of calming down. As I pick him up and head for the door, he struggles to free himself, arching his back, kicking his legs and wailing. I hold on to him with one arm, trying with my free hand to fish my key ring out of my jacket pocket, locate the right key, and lock up. Finally I deposit him on the hallway carpet outside the door, forcing myself to do it gently. He starts rolling around like a dog scratching himself. The noise of his screaming is amplified in the corridor. I'm trying to lock the door quickly but having a hard time, hampered by alcohol and a residue of tears. Finally I smash my fist into the door. The loud bang startles Kenny into silence. He stares at me with wet, wide green eyes, as I bend over and shake the skinned knuckles of my left hand. Infuriated by the pain, I stifle an urge to give the door a kick. Instead I shove two different keys into two different key holes, locking up and muttering curses (all of which Kenny has heard before, none of which he's started using—yet). When I pick him up again, Kenny is only whimpering. The opportunity to press more elevator buttons seems to complete his recovery. Mine will take longer.

Carmen opens the door almost as soon as I buzz. My timing is good: a commercial is on. I can hear it blaring from her living room. As usual, Carmen's hair is up in gigantic pink foam rollers. This always puzzles me, since, according to Sharon, Carmen rarely leaves her apartment except to shop. Now, she asks how I'm doing.

I shrug. She gazes up at me, squinting. "Something wrong?"

"No. Yeah, but I can't talk about it." This is true and has nothing to do with Kenny, who has already eased past Carmen to grasp a toy tow truck which Sergio, her four year old, has left lying around.

"Suit yourself," she replies, her questioning gaze lingering on me for another moment. "Should I give 'im dinner?"

"Umm . . . yeah, sure."

She nods. "No problem." Then she turns to scold Sergio, who is trying to wrest his truck away from Kenny.

I head down to rejoin the cops, whose job it is now to babysit *me* for a while. I take the stairs—ten flights—needing the time and the motion, needing to screw up my resolve to deal with this like a "man." Halfway down, I take out the breath spray, hesitate, then shove it, unused, back into my pocket. On re-entering the lobby, I see Flannery and the two cops conversing near the door. A tenant and her young daughter are waiting for the elevator and looking curiously back at the two policemen. The elevator arrives just as Flannery sees me and hustles over.

"Mr. Gull-doni, I'm terribly sorry. If there's anything I can do—"

I bob my head. "Sure," I reply curtly, then continue toward the cops. But after a moment I stop and turn to Flannery. "In fact, there is one thing. Don't spread the news all over the building, okay? It's nobody's business."

"Of course. But if people ask why the police was here—"

"Tell them anything. A little bullshit, you know how to do that."

He shoots me a look, then seems to swallow a nasty retort. He's dealing with a bereaved man, after all, although my attitude probably doesn't seem any different to him. My armor is back in place—or I have sufficient booze inside of me, as the case may be. I feel like I can do it. I can walk in, look at her body, nod "yes," and walk out. A series of simple actions, starting with a nod at the cops now.

"My kid's with a neighbor. Let's go."

The remnants of tears freeze on my face as I follow the cops back out to the squad car and slide into the rear seat. The younger cop pokes his face inside. "You'll be okay back here?"

The kid (he can't be more than twenty) looks genuinely concerned, like a cop in one of those "Your Friend the Policeman" films they used to show us in elementary school. Even then I snickered under my breath at the idea. But now, I appreciate the support and the opportunity to reassure him—and myself.

"Yeah, I think so. Thanks," I reply. As the junior cop joins Morris up front, I lean back against the seat and close my eyes, feeling myself sink into a numbed, boozy daze. After a few moments, though, I jerk myself upright. If Morris knows what he's doing, he'll be going down the Deegan to get to Harlem Hospital. In fact, I'll tell him to. I need to see where it happened, where she was last alive—as if I could somehow reach her at that point, somehow make time stand still, or roll it backward.

* * *

Sharon and I met eight years ago, as night students at Lehman College in the Bronx. At age twenty-two, she was working toward an elementary school teacher's license. I was three years older and ostensibly interested in becoming a P. E. teacher, which I'd heard was a relatively easy and hassle-free job. I spent my days sorting mail in the post office, a job that drove me crazy with boredom. If nothing else, attending Lehman allowed me to feel like I was trying to make a change. However, I only had about twenty-five college credits; at the rate I was going, I would have wound up teaching Physical Education while leaning on a cane. Sharon, on the other hand, did become a teacher. But she didn't stay with it very long. Even before Kenny came along, a year of teaching fourth grade in the South Bronx had been more than enough for her. As an education major, however, she'd looked forward to teaching as an exciting challenge. And she took her education courses with the utmost seriousness.

The course in which we met dealt with techniques of behavior modification. Sharon and I were both members of a group that was supposed to teach the class about assertiveness training, using oral presentations and role playing. At our first meeting, she told the group that she'd joined because she herself often felt an inability to be assertive, to speak her mind, and also because she felt that it was important for children to learn suitable ways of expressing themselves and their feelings. That's pretty much the way she phrased it. When my turn came, I echoed her remarks about children. My real reason for joining was that she had—she was good-looking and wore no wedding ring.

I managed to arrange for us to work together on one of the group's projects: a role play of two adolescents, one trying to resist the other's pressure to take drugs. The role of the pusher was clearly more suited to me. But Sharon, practicing assertiveness, insisted on taking it. She said that she wanted to avoid sexual stereotyping. I looked at her strangely, then shrugged and agreed. She was obviously serious. Wondering what I had gotten myself into, I began mulling over the three ways of saying "no" that I was supposed to demonstrate: timidly, assertively, and aggressively.

Unexpectedly, Sharon began her pitch. In a conspiratorial whisper she said, "Hey, want some grass? Hash? Top-quality stuff." Her brows were raised, widening her already large brown eyes. Her lips, compressed with secretiveness, began to tremble slightly as she tried to suppress a smile. Sharon's mock-sinister delivery—and the mischievousness underneath it—had caught me by surprise. We looked at each other for a moment, then burst out laughing.

* * *

A smile flickers across my face now, then my teeth clench as I fight back a sob. Foolishly, I try to remind myself that we had a lousy marriage, that more than once I'd *wished* her dead. At this realization, my face sinks into my hands. Other visions of Sharon come up, equally clear and painful: Sharon trying to roll her pregnant body out of bed to shut off the alarm, laughing and cursing as she flaps her skinny arms like a beached bird ; Sharon's big eyes shifting rapidly back and forth beneath her pinned-up hair as she alternately does needlepoint and monitors Kenny's progress crawling across the living room; Sharon lying enticingly naked in bed on a muggy summer evening, her face replaced by that of the sultry model on the cover of the magazine she's reading. Images I didn't know still existed in my brain, yet so vivid, so real, that it's almost a shock not to be able to touch her flesh, after removing my hands from my face.

When I see the metal detention grill and the backs of two cops' heads, I'm all but convinced that I'm dreaming or watching some movie. The notion of Sharon being gone is unreal. It casts doubt on everything else sliding by outside of the window, scenery that's as familiar to me as my own face: the ancient Shopwell where she swore she got bargains, the warehouses and factories of western Yonkers, the Saw Mill River Parkway with its cracked asphalt, rustic green toll booths, and bordering trees pointing at a darkened sky.

A short while after the Saw Mill becomes the Deegan, Morris's partner turns around and asks me, ever so gently, to put out the cigarette. Regulations, he says. I actually don't remember lighting up, but there it is, three quarters of a butt. I mumble, "yeah," and stub it out against the base of the grill. As I roll down the window to throw away the butt, a shot of frigid air hits me in the face, momentarily rousing me from the waking daze I'd slipped into. I quickly shut the window and leave it that way even after noticing that my eyes, already raw from crying, have been irritated by the smoke. I close them, but feel myself drifting off and blink them open. There's a reason I wanted to stay awake, but it half-escapes me now. It has to do with Sharon being dead—or a dream I've been having to that effect. My mind is increasingly hazy, as if infiltrated by the lingering smoke. I lean back into the seat. The traffic heading downtown is thickening as we approach the George Washington Bridge. The northbound headlights are moving much more slowly past us, in six hypnotic rows . . .

"Mr. Galdoni?" I start awake at the sound of Morris' throaty voice, squinting under the toplight that he's just turned on. The metal strands of the grill divide his face into cubes, two containing tired eyes, which are peering at me. "We're here. Harlem Hospital," he says. "It won't take long."

I gaze at him dumbly. Tilting my head to look up through the window, I see the hospital rising above us, a gray building punctuated by countless squares of white light. A giant, flourescent tombstone. It doesn't take much time for me to get my bearings; I look back at Morris and slowly nod. We're here. My fucking life has added up to this. No more games about dreaming, no booze available. Just a short, shivering walk into the Harlem Hospital morgue, flanked by two cops who're delivering me to what I must have earned: the sight of Sharon lying lifeless on a table.

She is being lifted by some kind of elevator up to the window I'm gazing through. The lift stops when she's just below my eye level. Her own eyes are glazed, fish-like. There's a deep gash in her forehead. Her face is a pasty white except for smeared remnants of lipstick at the corners of her mouth, except for the inky discoloration around the gash.

"Sharon," I call out. Except for the fact that my voice is choked, this could be an echo of any one of the millions of other times I've called her name. I half expect an answer. After a moment I lean my forehead against the window, shutting my eyes tightly. I don't open them until I've turned away; it takes almost all of my strength to push against the glass. The attendant, a heavy-set black woman in a khaki shirt, looks at me questioningly. "That's her," I manage to say. The words seem to reverberate before fading into the white stillness of the room.

- 3 -
Sharon

"HOW LONG have I been dead?"

I am given the answer even before the question is fully elaborated inside of me. Unlike what I had experienced with the people who'd attempted to rescue me, communication with the Being of Light is effortless, spontaneous . . . and blissful. My former body now seems to have been a shroud, hiding this lovely brilliance. Impossibly, the Being of Light becomes more dazzling, as if manifesting my joy at the answer: I am not dead. Nothing really dies. But I've passed into another state of existence, from which my previous life can be seen more clearly.

Indeed, I already *have* seen my life, in a panorama which was foreshadowed by the visions I had right before the Volkswagen crashed. And I can't guess at how long ago the crash took place. I had a concept of time only up until the point I "decided" to let go of my earthly existence, or at least the vestiges of it represented by my body and smashed-up car, and by the people and wreckage around them. At that point I could see the whiteness, the light, and feel it beckoning. Simultaneously,

I could see the world below. And somehow I knew that I could leave it at will. But despite the happiness and love that I was beginning to feel coming from the light, this option was at first a painful one.

How could I leave Kenny and never again hold him or see his puffy cheeks, his shy half-smile, his delighted grin? What would he do without me? I felt that I could go home—or anywhere—easily. Movement in my new "body" seemed to require no effort. But I also remembered that I'd been unable to make contact with people right in front of me. And I knew the despair I'd feel if that happened with Kenny, whether or not he yet understood that I was gone. It would've hurt with Paul, too, *especially* if he was grieving for me, and wishing, for once, that I was there with him. When I was "alive," the possibility of seeing him overcome with regret would have appealed to me greatly. But, having left my body behind, maybe I'd also left behind some of the bitterness that had knotted my insides. I had no desire to see him suffering, especially if I could do nothing about it.

But what if I *could* help? While alive, I knew people who swore that they'd had real communications—in dreams, prayers, or otherwise—with departed loved ones. At the time, I'd scoffed at the notion. However, having apparently survived physical death, and being invisibly suspended in midair, my estimation of what was possible was beginning to alter radically.

While I was struggling to decide what to do, or what to try to do, the Being of Light remained visible, on the periphery of my awareness (he—she, or it—was clearly not visible to the people below on the Deegan, otherwise they'd have been staring upward in wonder). Yet filled as I was with concern for and regrets about Kenny, Paul, my mother, and others I'd been close to, the love and peacefulness I could feel coming from the being also grew. My painful confusion began to dissipate. I drew nearer to the Being, who was featureless, oval-like in shape, whose radiance was dazzling but not at all blinding. The Being was more alluring than anything I'd ever experienced. The bliss emanating from the Being seemed to deny the possibility of loss or lasting unhappiness. It was time to move on.

My decision was confirmed by the Being's first articulated communication, which simply arose in my consciousness: "Are you ready?" I had a real idea only of what I was *leaving*. Nonetheless I immediately answered, "Yes." Our communication didn't involve language or spoken sounds, but rather a spontaneous transfer of nascent thoughts and feelings. The import of these was unmistakable. It was as if we were of one consciousness; no barriers existed between us. Yet at the same time I had a sense of being gently guided. When I asked, "Who are you?" I felt a powerful surge of warmth and love. That was the Being of Light's answer. It was more than satisfying. Like a child with her mother, I began to trust the Being completely.

As if to test this trust, he (or she) next asked me, in effect, to evaluate my life. Like everything else in my post-death experience, this came as a surprise, and not a pleasant one. I'd finally accepted the idea that I was leaving earth behind, and evaluating my life there was the last thing I wanted to do. The Being's effect on me was so strong that my usual sense that I'd made a mess of things was now only a vague and distant feeling. I preferred to keep it that way.

"You could have done worse," he told me, teasing me with one of my customary comments.

I couldn't help laughing, if ruefully. "That's true. But . . . why?" I added, referring to the requested evaluation. I simply wanted to bask in the Being's radiance, and to eventually find out from him what else awaited me.

"So that you will feel good about yourself when I am not apparent to you. So that you'll know how to grow."

Much as I wanted to, I sensed that now was not the time to ask the Being to go into more detail. I reluctantly agreed to try to make some kind of assessment.

As soon as I did, the Being of Light was replaced in my awareness by animated scenes from my life, which were so clear, so real, that it was like reliving them. The emotions and thoughts I'd experienced at those times were vivid. Amazingly, I could also clearly experience the thoughts and feelings of the people I was with. The Being, although temporarily invisible, made comments and asked questions here and there, but his presence did not impinge on the striking, three-dimensional reality of what I was experiencing. Rather, he was the heightened awareness with which I reviewed my life, the medium by which I was able to both be "in" the moment and see it with some detachment, some hindsight.

The first scene was probably the only one I wouldn't have even vaguely remembered otherwise: I was in an incubator, having been born a month prematurely. I could sense that the whitish-gray mass I saw through the incubator's wall was strongly connected to me, concerned for me. The lines and projections of this mass, which was my mother's face, were distorted by the film over my undeveloped eyes, by the thick glass of the wall, and the harsh overhead light. But her distress came through clearly. My mother was afraid that I would die, and she blamed herself for my tenuous grip on life. She hadn't wanted a second child. My older sister, Gloria, had been more than enough for her to handle. And the meager salary my father earned driving a newspaper delivery truck could barely support the three of them. Now, convinced that her inhospitable attitude had somehow caused my premature birth, she promised aloud to give me all the love a little girl could want. All I had to do was survive.

As if I were still inside of the womb, her anxiety caused uneasiness within me. In the white world of the incubator, I kicked my tiny legs, flapped my arms, and managed a piteous wail. At this, my mother slowly smiled. I was showing signs of life. Visually, I experienced her smile as a slight shifting of the mass outside of me. My internal discomfort began to abate. I soon drifted into sleep.

This dream-like beginning of my life seemed to pass by in an instant, yet its details were quite distinct. And after I'd relived the rest of my life, in affecting moments, it was apparent that the incubator segment had left a deep impression on me. I'd never before had the opportunity to remember and reflect on those earliest days, and felt almost wistful about my total dependency then. I just *was* at that stage; I reacted innocently and spontaneously to whatever happened, and to my own internal needs as they came up. The feeling of uneasiness had passed through me and was gone, forgotten, a brief disturbance, a ripple in my otherwise untainted awareness. I was not yet worried about anything.

This wasn't true during the next experience that I relived: I was struggling with my sister Gloria over a Raggedy Ann doll. This doll more than lived up to its name. Its cotton insides were exposed at the crotch and right armpit, and its red hair pointed in several directions, a hairdo of which any punk person would be proud. The doll's condition was the result of previous tugging matches between Gloria and myself. She was four years old, roughly twice my age, and on strength alone she would have inevitably wound up with the doll. But *my* main weapon, the scream, was a formidable one. My entire two-year-old body worked to generate a piercing cry. Gloria recoiled, but tightened her grip on the doll's leg. She glared at me with hatred, her green eyes moist and narrowed. Her blondish hair thrashed her chubby face as she shook with rage. One of her front teeth was missing; scowling, she looked both fearsome and pathetic. Her scowl intensified, causing scythe-like furrows to run down from the corners of her nose, as she heard my mother's approaching footsteps.

We both knew what would happen next. Even as my mother hissed "Gloria!", my sister proclaimed her innocence. "But I had it first!"

This was true, as usual. Whatever Gloria had, I wanted. It was instinct—just as it was my mother's instinct to take my side, a protectiveness which she never really gave up, at least not willingly. She chided Gloria for refusing to share with me; after all, Gloria was supposed to be "older and smarter." Then she attempted to snatch the doll away. Both Gloria and I were still clinging to it tightly. Snarling, "Let go!" my mother yanked with all her might. Raggedy Ann tore apart at the crotch, wounded beyond repair. A large part of her fluffy insides descended to the floor. Her remains still connected the three of us—a stunned Gloria held one leg, my mother grasped the head, and I held the other leg.

With Solomon-like wisdom, my mother demanded, "You happy now?" This question was ostensibly aimed at both of us. However, my mother's weary brown eyes fastened on Gloria for a few seconds longer. Gloria, the original owner of Raggedy Ann, began to wail.

"I hate you!" she spat out at my mother. Shooting me a look of disdain, Gloria ran out of our bedroom. My mother gave pursuit, her thick heels clomping on the wooden floor. From behind, her gray-streaked brown hair and her heavy, three-quarter-length skirt seemed to mirror each other in shape and texture; both swung vigorously as she stalked after my sister. I sniffled once or twice, then went looking for something else to play with.

After this scene I was filled with guilt. Had I a physical body, I might have been trembling. The Being of Light, though invisible, attempted to comfort me. "Did you realize, then, what you were doing?"

I acknowledged that I hadn't.

"But you do now. That is most important. It was given to your mother and sister to go through struggles like that with you. And you *all* suffered, then as well as later."

"But—"

"The important thing is to learn—during life if one can, and after. They will have the same opportunity you are having and will continue to have."

More than from the Being's message, I derived some degree of solace from the confidence that flowed from him, from his absolute assurance that all would be well. There was no question of doubting him. Nor did I wonder about the source of his authority or his seeming omniscience. So closely were we linked, so natural was our interaction, that he was like a new aspect of my own self, an expansion of it. This was particularly true during the re-experiencing of my life, which he seemed to direct from within me.

The Raggedy Ann scene was followed by one which must have taken place a couple of years later, judging from the changes in Gloria and me. My mother's appearance also gave evidence of the passage of time; crow's feet were showing in the corners of her eyes, and her haphazardly applied rouge failed to camouflage the jowls that were beginning to form around her jawbone. The three of us were in a supermarket—the A&P, I knew from the large, red, monogrammed coffee-grinding machine which Gloria and I were rolling past. I was sitting in the fold-out child's seat in a shopping cart, and Gloria was seated behind me, enclosed within the basket. It rumbled along on the cracked linoleum floors like a subway train, stopping frequently. Periodically, my mother made the mistake of parking the cart at an angle that placed me within reach of the shelves she was perusing. Quietly giggling, I plucked items off of the shelves and handed them down to Gloria, who hid them under her skirt. When Gloria was finally ordered out of the cart to make room for more groceries, my mother discovered two cans of Campbell's Pork&Beans, a jar of orange marmalade, two boxes of Fig Newtons (one squashed), a few cans of cat food, a box of Nabisco Shredded Wheat, and a six-pack of small raisin boxes.

Her jaw dropped, in a look that was typical of her flair for histrionics. "What the—" she demanded, turning on Gloria, who was giggling beside the cart.

"I did it, Mommy," I piped up, wanting to protect my beleaguered older sister, sensing in her a potential ally.

"You picked Gloria up and sat her down on top of this mess?" My mother was a master of sarcasm. Believing that she was actually blaming me, I was silent, cowed.

In addition to her annoyance at having to retrace her route across the store and shelve the items I'd liberated, she was chagrined at the condition of the Fig Newtons. After furtively reshelving the squashed cookies, she dragged Gloria by the wrist to a checkout line, towing the cart and me with her free hand. It was obvious who she blamed.

After this scene the review of my life branched out, taking in the expanding circle of friends and activities in which I was involved as I grew older. But my mother and Gloria remained central players until I was well into my teens. With the Raggedy Ann and A&P segments, I saw a general pattern which was to hold throughout my life: I would act in a selfish or otherwise negative way, then, a scene or two later, in a more generous, loving manner. Love and the gaining of knowledge were the two values which the Being encouraged me to strive for. Manifesting his own generous nature, he indicated that I'd scored high marks in the A&P. When I protested that my attempt to protect Gloria hadn't endeared me to *her*—I could feel her growing resentment of both my mother and me—the Being indicated that my motivation had been the important thing. I couldn't doubt him, but I still saw in this scene between my mother, Gloria and me the growth of a disharmony that would mushroom into large-scale turbulence in another ten years or so, into rifts that were never really repaired. And although I had access to both my mother's and Gloria's feelings and thoughts, I discovered that I had no ability to alter them. In fact, my desire to do so seemed to coincide with the vanishing of the A&P scene, as if in trying to hold on to it, I'd propelled it more quickly away.

Subsequent scenes, in which I was progressively older, came and went with increasing rapidity. They seemed (like the first three segments) to speed by in an instant, and yet present themselves in the clearest detail. It was as if my life itself amounted to an instant, a point in time, or timelessness, through which any number of events could be run. As these events—or my own internal journey through them—moved toward my teen years, everything became increasingly familiar. Insight seemed more readily available, more acute.

Pre-teenage, I was bouncing around inside my father's *New York Herald Tribune* delivery truck. I must have been nine or ten years old. Both flanks of the truck announced, in bold letters, "Bay of Pigs Invasion Aborted." I had only a dim understanding of what this headline meant, and cared less. My father and I were driving up Third Avenue in Manhattan, swept along in a sea of square trucks and oversized cars with rounded roofs and tail fins. We were singing "Darlin' Clementine." Our harmony sounded joyously perfect to my youthful ears, but laughably off key to my posthumous self, as if I was both singer and audience.

My father slapped the huge steering wheel repeatedly, more or less keeping time. His unusually high spirits were due to that new job with the *Tribune,* after several years of delivering *Newsday* on then-remote Long Island. We'd been living in a railroad flat on the Island. Both the new job and our resultant move to a Queens high-rise were regarded by my parents as steps up in class.

He didn't even mind the fact that he now had to work Saturdays. He preferred driving the truck to chauffeuring his wife and daughters around on Saturday shopping outings. As a concession to my mother, who saw herself about to be stranded for half of each weekend in an unfamiliar—albeit more prestigious—neighborhood, he'd offered to take one of the girls off of her hands each Saturday. He'd have willingly taken both of us, but there wasn't enough room on the truck's only seat, which was practically bisected by the huge stick shift. "One of the girls" quickly turned out to be me. Gloria refused to go, on any Saturday.

She was fond of our father, or at least more kindly disposed toward him than she was toward our mother. But Gloria was also distraught over the move to Queens, which meant her permanent separation from her coterie of adolescent friends on the Island. She blamed my father and his new job for this, and she was not about to waste a Saturday tooling around with him in the truck. Going to work with Daddy was kid stuff anyway. Gloria had made all of this abundantly clear during a huge spat she'd had with my parents the previous evening.

For my part, I was delighted by the opportunity to spend time alone with my father, particularly when he was in such an ebullient mood. Suddenly, though, his spirits dropped, as if he'd downshifted. He fell silent. His handsome, animated face, which had been swiveling back and forth between myself and the road ahead, became a sagging profile. My voice, left alone on "Darlin' Clementine," sounded frail and tinny.

"C'mon, Daddy," I chirped after a moment, picking up the song again with as much gusto as I could muster, giving him a little nudge which he seemed not to notice. Posthumously, I could see the images in his mind of the night before at home: Gloria, her fair complexion reddened, screaming that my parents didn't care about her or her wishes, claiming that any of her friends—and probably their parents too—would be willing to let her stay with them on the Island. My father tried to reassure her, practically apologizing, as my mother, enraged by this conciliatory behavior, told Gloria, "Go ahead and leave, if you really want to." The scene was a maelstrom in his mind, the faces jumbled together.

Even as a child, I'd sensed that he was thinking about Gloria, licking his wounds. Failing to re-interest him in the song, I began prattling about my new school, about the bedevilment of my elderly teacher by some of her rowdy students. I might as well have been talking to the dashboard. Finally I threw a little fit of my own, and demanded to be taken home.

Succeeding segments took me past the milestones of puberty —for which both Gloria and my mother had been anxious to prepare me, offering conflicting pieces of advice—into adolescence. The trip through the living growth chart of my childhood had been, above all, engaging. Even if it was emotionally a choppy ride, the quality of being both in it and witnessing it was a wonder, as was the clarity of vision this afforded.

After his comments on the A&P supermarket scene, the Being of Light offered no overt commentary through several subsequent ones, including the newspaper truck scene. In fact I'd all but forgotten the Being's presence, until the review reached my adolescence. But as I began to relive the self-consciousness which descended upon me then, I remembered that I was not alone. Nor was I anxious to see on display my adolescent preoccupations with my own body, or with boys and the various sexual acts they were rumored to perform. Still, the embarrassment I felt quickly dissipated. The Being was clearly touched and amused by my fledgling womanhood. For convenience— or for whatever reason—I've referred to the Being as "he" or "him". But his personality seemed neither masculine or feminine, rather it was reflective of the most sublime attributes of both. I knew that there was nothing I'd been through that he didn't understand and accept. And this made the teen years I was about to revisit seem less uninviting.

Gloria and I were both teenagers in the late sixties, but the similarities between us ended there. This was never more apparent than in the segment set in Central Park.

I'd gone there with my boyfriend Stuart, who, hoping to bolster his claim that deflowering me was not his sole purpose in our relationship, had suggested an innocent afternoon of walking and talking. Hand in hand, we wandered into Sheep Meadow, a large open field as grassy as its name suggests, overlooked by high risers and skyscrapers. On any weekend afternoon, numerous athletic and artistic events could be witnessed there. The "Be-in" which was then in progress was intended to be neither, but did involve music, dancing, and Frisbee playing. It could have easily been taken for some kind of exotic costume ball, overhung and permeated by a pungent haze of marijuana smoke.

Neither Stuart nor I viewed drugs, at least not marijuana, with the *Reefer Madness* mentality. Despite the warnings contained in that now-campy film from the forties or fifties, grass hadn't yet left us depraved or insane. We doubted that it would, especially since we smoked grass only occasionally—as much to be naughty as to get high. For sure, neither of us saw drugs as the key to a new way of life. We held hands more tightly as we found ourselves in the midst of a crowd of painted, beaded, half-naked individuals with hairdos ranging from Rip Van Winkle traditional to dreadlocks, and variations thereof. Stuart, looking out of place in his jeans and button-down shirt, snickered nervously at the sight of the weirdos around him. His eyes nearly popped out when I was seemingly attacked by a jingling woman who joyously called out my name. Gloria ran over and threw her braceletted arms around me, bringing with her a mixture of odors—sweat, sandalwood, and vanilla oil. I gave her a tentative squeeze in return, then she pulled back to have a look at me.

"What's happenin', Sister?" she said. "It's good to see you here. Real good."

Much to my parents' distress, Gloria had been "crashing" in the East Village for the previous few months. They eventually accepted this (they didn't have much choice, she was over eighteen), or at least they came to realize that hassling her was the surest way to shorten her visits. Since she usually arrived unannounced, I wound up missing her more often than not. But even if she *had* given advance notice, I wouldn't necessarily have rearranged my busy teenager's schedule to see her. We'd never really been close, and the gap had widened of late.

Still, I was glad to run into her in the park. She *was* my sister, after all, and a familiar face in a suddenly strange environment. "It's good to see you too, Glo," I replied. "It *is* you?" I patted her bare shoulder and worked up a laugh.

"Oh yeah," she said, her smile temporarily crushing the purple flowers painted on her cheeks. "I mean, yeah, it's me, more than ever. I'm really starting to dig myself."

The sixteen-year-old me nodded, although unsure of Gloria's

meaning. Peering into my sister's mind with a clairvoyance that had become completely spontaneous, as if my posthumous consciousness was a powerful spotlight rendering transparent whatever it was turned toward, I understood that she had no more of a grasp of the meaning of her remarks than I did. Or, at least, there was no longer any connection between her thoughts and the conversation we were having. Gloria's mind was caught up in the bizarre changes that she saw in my face. She experienced the nodding of my head as an expansion and contraction, which took place in slow motion. The glimmering brightness in my brown eyes flared and receded. Gloria shook her head, trying to dispel the distortions. This action caused my face to fragment, producing several eyes and facial features in a Picasso-like jumble.

Were I able to see, as a sixteen year old, the kaleidoscopic contortions of my face that were taking place in Gloria's mind, it might've unhinged me. What I did see— Gloria's eyes losing their focus, the familiar green irises glazing over—was more than enough to make me uneasy.

"Gloria, listen," I said, "When are you coming home again? The parents are worried about you."

She looked at me blankly for several seconds, then the fog seemed to lift. "Tell them not to worry. I'm fine, okay?" she replied sharply. "They need to worry about themselves more than me. And don't let them fuck you over, either. It's past time for that."

"Umm, I don't feel like they are, Gloria. Some, maybe—"

"You'd be surprised. Took *me* a long time to get my head together, 'til I moved out. All this shit about how I have no shame, and what are the neighbors gonna think? That's where they're really at, you know?"

Gloria didn't wait for my shrug in reply. She abruptly turned toward Stuart, as if finally having felt his gaze on her skin. He'd been standing to the side, surveying her frizzed, dirty-blonde hair, revealing tank top, ankle-length red skirt, and tennis sneakers.

"Hi, I'm Stuart," he offered brightly.

I murmured, "Forgot to introduce him."

"That's cool. Like you to meet *my* old man, if I could find him around here. He's a spade, you know? If he wanders over, don't look all bent out of shape about it, okay?"

He didn't wander over, for which I was grateful, even though I liked to think I had nothing against Blacks. The realization that Gloria was sleeping with one did bend me out of shape some —it didn't take much, straight as I was. Indeed, everything about Gloria—her looks and life style, her attitude, which I perceived to be condescending—struck me as odious, that day and for a long time afterward. Over the next couple of years, I saw very little of her. During my life review, she resurfaced a few segments later, at my father's funeral.

Gloria had helped to hasten this event, at least according to my mother. I couldn't really disagree. My father's initial reaction to Gloria's "dropping out" had been a bewildered compassion. He'd striven to make her feel welcome and loved on those occasions when she'd chosen to visit. When my mother demanded that Gloria be cut off financially—"Let her panhandle, she brags about doing it already, like it's a badge of honor"—my father flatly refused. Later, when he understood the magnitude of the changes Gloria had gone through—the drugs, the shacking up —he'd sunk into despair. This had more or less coincided with the folding of the *Tribune*, his employer for ten years. He subsequently became ill. The origin of the cancer that ended his life at a young age was mystery to his doctors. It wasn't to my mother, who knew all about the debilitating effects of stress. She was often "worried sick." Maybe she'd built up some immunity thereby. My father had not.

His funeral took place in Forest Hills, Queens, at the Riverside Memorial Chapels, a large building that could accommodate a few funerals at once. I sat between Gloria and my mother in the front row of the chapel that was reserved for my father. Gloria, obviously dazed, wore a full-length black dress. Her rouge-covered face looked like a reclamation project; her hair was pinned back and covered by a veil. My mother, who had spent much of the previous few months at my father's hospital bedside, appeared haggard and distraught, but dry-eyed. Next to the podium in front of us, draped in a cloth bearing the Star of David and flanked by glass-encased candles, stood my father's plain wooden coffin. The candles' light swam in my eyes, lending a dream-like quality to the sight of the casket. That, I felt, was all that remained of my father; that sealed box, the very essence of death, of obliteration. It was almost more than I could bear. I leaned against my mother and wept.

The contrast between my pre and post-death experiences was never more pronounced than when I relived that feeling of anguish, cushioned this time by the sense of perpetuity, of unboundedness, which permeated my life review. To my posthumous self, the coffin had no more to do with my father than the wooden benches on which his grieving relatives and friends sat. I wondered about the whereabouts of his soul. I was about to query the Being of Light, when he suggested that I instead listen to the words of the rabbi, who was beginning to speak. This surprised me. Following my parents' lead, I'd never given much credence to the knowledge or authority of rabbis, or any other spiritual leaders. They all might as well have been medicine men, as far as I was concerned. The Being's recommendation, though, was cause enough for me to pay close attention to the rabbi's words, much closer than I had the first time around.

Prior to the service, it had been necessary for my mother and I to fill in the rabbi on the main details of my father's life. After beginning the proceedings with a prayer which was all indecipherable Hebrew except for "Avraham Weiss," my father's name, the rabbi acknowledged that my father had not been "religiously observant." However, from what he'd gathered, my father had lived the essence of religious life. He had been a kind, selfless man, who had steadfastly loved and provided for his wife and two daughters.

The rabbi sounded and looked tired as he issued these remarks. He fidgeted with his beard and spoke in a monotone; even as a bereaved eighteen year old, I'd had the sense that he was giving one variation of a standard rap he used for the legions of the faithless he was obliged to eulogize. He could just as easily have been reading from a sympathy card. Gloria, however, seemed deeply affected by his words. For the first time, she broke down and wept loudly, covering her face with her hands. I almost reached to comfort her, but instead stiffened and redirected my blurred gaze toward the rabbi. Seemingly oblivious to the sound of Gloria's sobbing, he finished his remarks about my father. He then recited a prayer in English, which concluded:

The dust returns to the Earth as it was,
But the spirit returns to God who gave it.

Posthumously, my reaction was tantamount to a start, as I recognized that this was what the Being had wanted me to hear. The funeral vanished. The Being's light again filled my awareness.

"I . . . my spirit is supposed to return to God?" I asked apprehensively. "But I've never believed—"

"Belief is not important. Well, it is not of utmost importance. God is, whether or not anyone believes it. If one has not lived an evil life, one is greeted by an emissary of God, who provides guidance for the journey toward Him."

The embarrassment I felt over my life-long atheism (or apathy) was diminished by the Being's soothing presence. Still, it was with more than a degree of trepidation that I said, "So you're the emissary of God."

"At your service." The Being's amusement was palpable inside of me. "You've heard that men, and women, are made in God's image. That doesn't necessarily mean that you'll see God as some person, some king on a throne. It means that the light of life, the source of *all* life, is always inside of you. Death temporarily frees one's awareness from the limitations imposed by the physical body and by the effects of the way one has lived. Then one has a glimpse of God, a small taste of the fullness and bliss that is really beyond description. It's like knowing the sun only by it's reflection in water. With time and growth, one gains the full light, merges with it, and returns to God, as the rabbi said."

I made no response. Having only a sense of the import of the Being's words, I was trying to formulate a question. However, he apparently felt that this sense was enough. He continued, "I tell you this now so that the rest of your life on Earth can be seen in this way, as part of the growth toward knowledge."

With that, the life review resumed. And the fact that there now seemed to be some redemption at the end of the road made it easier to re-experience the turmoil that ensued in the years following my father's funeral.

My mother, the more domineering of my parents, all but came apart with her husband's death. Since she distrusted the Jewish Family Services and other such agencies, it fell upon me to lend her support and whatever insights I could offer as to how to go about surviving as a widow. Out-of-town college, an idea that had seemed very attractive prior to my father's illness, was now out of the question. I had a mother to take care of.

In one life review segment, I accompanied her to an interview for a sales clerk position at Alexander's in Rego Park (I was a Freshman at Queens College and had taken the day off). My plan was to send her forth on her own and wait for her a safe distance from the personnel department. But as we climbed up from the subway station, she took one look at the outside of the towering department store and about-faced. A mother and a home maker, she'd never worked before. The prospect terrified her. I followed her back down into the station, nearly slipping on the slush-covered steps, and futilely attempted to convince her to proceed with the business at hand. Finally, I unleashed some of my pent-up resentment over the turn our lives had taken. I loudly informed her, "Just because you've always hovered over me like a mother hen, don't expect the same treatment from me now. It won't do either of us any good. It hasn't done me any . . . that's for damn sure. Thanks to you," I added, "I'm turning into a nervous wreck."

To my surprise, this outburst jarred my mother out of her paralysis. She slapped my face, turned, and all but plowed her way through a small group of onlookers that had gathered around us. My cheek stinging, I stood in the freezing dampness of the station and watched her re-ascend the stairs toward Alexander's.

It took a couple of years, after my father's death, for me to finally move out. But even before doing so I began to sow some wild oats. This was partly for my mother's benefit—to make the idea of my leaving seem less unattractive to her. Another reason was college, where drugs were readily available everywhere. I saw no reason to say "no." The plague that had struck Gloria (who was actually beginning to straighten out, in my mother's estimation) now hit *me* with full force. At age nineteen, I cashed in my virginity, my college ID, and most of my other responsibilities.

One of the more ironic scenes from this period involved Gloria's wedding. She'd begun to follow a guru who had sold her on the benefits of monogamy within the confines of marriage. Such a lifestyle was said to further one's "evolution." Better still was celibacy, a state of complete devotion to the Master and to spiritual pursuits. However, if this was not one's natural inclination—and Gloria had quickly seen that it was not hers—then family life could provide a means of culturing the selflessness which was a prerequisite to the gaining of higher states of consciousness. Proposed to by a fellow disciple, Gloria had quickly accepted. The marriage lasted a year.

At the wedding, Gloria looked clear-eyed and optimistic, almost cherubic, in her white gown. Flowers were laced through her hair. She gave my mother a few big hugs over the course of the ceremony and reception, which took place at a Unitarian church on Central Park West in Manhattan. While my sister seemed the prototype of a wholesome young woman, I looked, and was, stoned out of my mind. Prior to arriving, I'd inhaled some powerful hash, and I slipped out after the ceremony to have a few auxiliary tokes. At the reception, I downed several cups of wine. The festivities around me were a blur. I viewed their colorful shiftings with a kind of languid fascination, occasionally closing my eyes and grooving to the strands of folk or soft rock music to which the whole thing seemed to move. A couple of times I lost the strands and drifted into sleep, my head landing on the linen-covered table. My mother jostled me awake each time. That was the only real contact I had with her that day.

I did come to life, finally, when some of our tradition-minded relatives hoisted Gloria up in a chair and began dancing around the room with her. She appeared to me to have been installed on a throne, an effect added to by her flowery crown. I stood, tottering, and proclaimed, "Hail Queen Glor-ay-uh!" My voice seemed to flow out from some cool, airy well inside of me, my laughter reverberating before merging into the general commotion. I quickly gathered up carnations from the vases at each table and joined the surging crowd beneath my sister. "Hail to the Queen!" I yelled, flinging carnations up at Gloria. Screaming, I repeated the salutation, throwing the flowers harder. The effort caused me to lose my balance; I landed heavily on my right arm and shoulder. The crowd fell silent. The tail end of "Rocky Mountain High" was suddenly audible in the room.

Sore (I didn't realize how sore until I came down later) but uninjured, I was escorted by a few family friends and relatives to the ladies' room. There I spurned their help but requested that they reassure my mother, who I could hear fretting at the door. I insisted that they then leave me alone, which they did, wisely towing my mother back to the reception room. I was repeatedly splashing water on my face with my left hand when Gloria came in.

"Sorry to spoil your party, Glo," I muttered.

"Hey, that's okay. Nothing is spoiled. Are you alright, though?"

"Just great. My fucking head is starting to split, but other than that—"

"Listen, Sharon, I don't want to lecture you . . . you're my sister, and I love you and all that. But that's why I'm worried about you, too. You need to check yourself out. Drugs and the rest of it—that's just not where it's at. Believe me."

I turned from the mirror and laughed harshly, then winced as my head gave a throb. "You got a lotta nerve, Gloria. Really."

"Look, I know I've been there, but that's how—"

"Right, you've been there, and now you're saved. I'm happy for you. But meanwhile, I'm still taking care of our mother—yours and mine. I know you've been fawning over her all day. But are you gonna be there tomorrow?"

Finishing this little speech, I felt a small sense of satisfaction at getting under Gloria's freshly scrubbed skin. She looked at me for several seconds with a mixture of hurt, anger, and confusion.

"You're taking care of her?" she said in a measured voice. "Maybe you were for a while, but she seems like she's doing okay now. In fact—and I'm not trying to be nasty or whatever—but you're more or less living off of her, aren't you?"

I shut off the faucet emphatically, causing its handles to squeal, and wheeled around to face Gloria. But my righteous indignation died before I could translate it into words. My sister's face was like my own looking back at me. We both knew she was right. Finally, almost gasping, I said, "You think it's a free ride? You think I don't want to move out? I don't have the guts, Gloria. And I feel like I'm fucking sinking, I swear to God."

Before she could offer a sympathetic response (posthumously, I could feel the impulse inside of her), I stomped out of the ladies' room, brushing against the lace appliques of her wedding gown as I rushed past. The Unitarian church receded behind me as I strode aimlessly, blindly, into Central Park, its carpet of brown leaves crunching beneath my high heels.

I continued living at my mother's (or at least sleeping there most nights) until I landed in the psychiatric ward at Elmira General Hospital—which was part of the setting for the segment that immediately followed the wedding. I was admitted to the hospital a couple of hours after dropping some LSD cut with speed. I'd been sitting in a subway car during the evening rush hour as the acid began to take hold. Francie, a friend I'd kept up with from Queens College, was next to me. She was on the verge of dropping out, too. The acid I had scored was intended to help us celebrate her impending liberation. We'd each swallowed a tab (along with plenty of orange juice, which was supposed to heighten the effect), then boarded an "F" train, hoping to eventually arrive in Greenwich Village.

But in order to do so we had to pass through midtown Manhattan. The train was caught in the tunnel between Rockefeller Center and West Fiftieth Street, delayed by what was announced as "congestion up ahead." After fifteen minutes, people in the packed car began to grumble audibly or curse. Those standing were impatiently shifting position, giving off sighs of exasperation through their clenched lips and pinched nostrils. This heavy breathing, of a man standing above me in particular, became a sinister, building roar in my ears. It seemed to me to be the harbinger of an impending explosion, like steam escaping from a volcano. The grotesque squirming of the standees, I was sure, represented the first tremors of the deadly pressure building within the car. I had to get out. Giving a choked cry, I bolted from my seat. Francie, sensing what was happening, grabbed my arm, intending to reseat and calm me. But her action had the opposite effect. Trapped, I screamed and struggled to wrench my arm free. After what seemed like an eternity, I succeeded. Plowing through the parting crowd of passengers to the nearest doors of the train, I strove to pull them open. Finally I began pounding on the plexiglass window of the door, pounding on my own insanely flailing image.

Afterward, I didn't remember the transit cops removing me from the train at Fiftieth Street. Francie told me—and I saw posthumously—that I'd been rigid, almost catatonic, except for my eyeballs, which were shifting rapidly back and forth. After a couple of heavily sedated days at Bellevue Hospital, I was transferred to the psychiatric ward at Elmira General. There, my head slowly began to clear. The clarity, in fact, was almost more than I could take. It was plain to me that I'd wasted the first twenty years of my life, that I'd gone from being a goody two-shoes to being a pathetic pseudo-rebel who couldn't hold her drugs, who couldn't even live on her own without Mommy's supporting hand. And who now couldn't live without a rotating group of doctors, nurses, psychiatric social workers, and orderlies who were variously sympathetic, condescending or indifferent. An army of caretakers in white, their needles loaded with Thorazine.

There was no doubt that I'd screwed up royally. But beneath the ever-present, dull pain inside of me, a pain that periodically sharpened into despair, I sensed a dormant strength beginning to awaken. I reassured my mother, on her daily visits, that I'd be fine and that she could stop worrying about me. I'd bottomed out. I was ready to pull myself together. By the end of the first week at Elmira General, I was half-convinced of this. Francie's visits were helpful too; she made it easier for me to deal with what had happened on the train. The first time she came, I apologized for putting her through the kinds of changes she must have undergone once I started flipping out. Francie replied that she probably would have freaked out too, if she'd had to sit much longer in the middle of all those "intense vibes." The imperative of looking after me—she'd dealt with the cops, and come along for the ride to Bellevue—had, if anything, helped her to keep her own head on straight. Squeezing my hand, she dismissed my apologies as ridiculous.

So did Gloria, to whom I expressed remorse over my generally negative attitude toward her. She understood completely. She charitably blamed it on drugs, with which she'd been through her own trials. Her support also helped—even when it bordered on magnanimity, providing added incentive for me to demonstrate that I could begin standing on my own two feet.

Shaky but determined, I left the hospital. Shortly thereafter, I found a job as a teacher's aide in a day care center in Co-op City, in the Bronx. The job had been advertised in the *New York Times*, and I applied. I came to actually like the idea that the job was distant, in another borough. It meant that I had one foot out of Queens and my mother's apartment. Eventually I moved to the Bronx and started attending night school at Lehman College, which was where I met my husband.

- 4 -
Paul

I'M OKAY, sort of, while the car is moving. The motion has a numbing effect not unlike booze, my intake of which I've managed to keep within limits this morning. Driving down the Grand Concourse, it's almost possible for me to believe that I'm hacking away as usual, switching lanes on short notice, squeezing mileage out of minutes. Ordinarily on the Concourse, I'd be speeding toward the lucrative terrain of Manhattan with a passenger in tow, grateful both to be leaving the Bronx and getting paid for it. Or, I might be bound for Queens and the airports. Some destination or other—camouflage for the fact that I'm going nowhere.

Any destination, of course, would be preferable to my current one: Sharon's funeral. This is probably the only occasion on which her mother would be found in the car with me. The woman's perfume is all but suffocating. Apparently it doesn't bother her the way cigarettes do. I need a smoke badly, but, as with the booze, I'm managing. It's hardest at red lights, where I usually light up, and where, with the car just idling, I can hear

Sharon's mother weeping softly.

I feel an urge to comfort her, but I don't trust myself to speak, particularly not to Sharon's mother. Until a couple of days ago, we hadn't been on speaking terms for over a year. When we were obliged to be in the same room, Sharon and Kenny had usually provided a buffer between us. Neither one is with us now. Still, other than a couple of muffled complaints about my driving, Sharon's mother has been civil enough today. We share a common grief.

The red light at the Fordham Road underpass seems to last forever. I finally take a stab at offering some comfort, at filling the silence in which her sniffling resounds.

"Look, Clara," I say, "At least she didn't feel anything. I know that. It was over in an instant."

At this the floodgates open. My mother-in-law covers her face and sobs, her black veil bouncing against the liver-spotted backs of her hands. Her crying intensifies, until she sounds as if she's being strangled.

"Clara—" Feeling obligated to do something, I reach toward her with my right hand. She pulls away, leaning into the passenger door just as the changing of the light is announced by honking horns behind us. "I'm alright," she gasps, as the honking increases. "Just go, please."

I comply but only allow the car to edge forward, spitefully gazing into my rear view mirror and muttering curses at the drivers behind me. Then I accelerate, shielding my eyes against the slanting brightness of the winter sun, cursing myself now for leaving my sunglasses in my "work" jacket. Trying to escape the glare, I lower my eyes and look to either side, keeping the road ahead on the periphery of my vision. I catch glimpses of the sidewalks framing the service roads on both sides of the Concourse. They're already filling with shoppers, and commuters hustling toward the "D" train, breathing steam in the frosty air. Business as usual. My eyes begin to water unexpectedly, almost blinding me. The next red light is a gift. My head turned away from Clara, I sneak a few dabs at the tears.

As we begin moving again, clouds cover the sun. One small break, at least. "Paul," says Sharon's mother—she pauses for a couple of seconds—"I want to see Kenny."

"Today?"

"You know what I mean. I'm his grandmother. I have rights."

I sigh. "I wasn't intending to deprive you of them, believe me. You might even get to see the kid more than you care to. I know I'm gonna have to figure out . . . logistics, how to handle things now. I'm not giving him up for adoption, believe me. And he needs to get to nursery and back, to you and back, etcetera. But it's hard for me to think about that now, as you can probably understand. As far as today goes, I didn't think bringing him was a good idea. He doesn't need to be around all that grief. He doesn't need to see his mother in a box."

Clara gives a muffled cry. A lump forms in my throat. "Sorry," I manage to say. "I'm not thinking too clearly right now. As usual."

She blows her nose loudly, then sighs. "Well . . . have you told him yet?"

"Uh-uh. Couldn't bring myself to, but I will. I just said, 'Mommy's away.' Told Carmen, the baby-sitter, to say nursery was closed today. Maybe I shoulda sent him. I don't know."

"If you want me to tell him—"

"Thanks," I say, filtering the sarcastic edge out of my voice at the last moment. "But I can take care of it. Just haven't figured out how yet."

It had taken me a while to figure out how to tell everyone else who needed telling, starting with Clara. I wound up calling Gloria, Sharon's sister. She was the logical candidate to let Clara and others know. Even aside from her position as a sibling, she'd seemed to me to be the best person for the job. She's a tough little cookie. She's told both Sharon and me, more than once, that she'd never take the kind of crap from me that Sharon had. I believed her, in fact I found her toughness to be one of her several appealing qualities. It made me think—particularly given her weird convictions about reincarnation and such—that she'd take the news well, and be able to give it out in the same way.

Not that I'd been that calculating. While the cops were driving me back from the morgue, the idea of enlisting Gloria's help with making the necessary calls and arrangements came into my mind like a ray of hope and stayed there. In fact, I clung to it. I couldn't envision what to do next, or even how to cope, if she was not home when I called. Home she was, though. Greatly relieved, I had the presence of mind to ask her to sit down first before I told her. Of course, this request only turned her surprise at hearing from me into dread.

"What happened?" she demanded.

"Well . . . Sharon's dead." With this statement, even more than with the confirmation I'd given the morgue attendant, the fact seemed final and irrevocable. I shuddered and took a sip of scotch.

"Oh God, no," Gloria said softly, after several moments of silence. "How—"

I'd explained simply that Sharon had died in a car crash. Then I requested Gloria's help with everything, starting with Clara. Before replying, Gloria left me waiting on the phone for a few minutes while she collected herself. When she came back, she agreed to inform the family, but insisted that I make the funeral arrangements. Clara would probably want it to be Reform, Jewish, she told me. She called back about half an hour later to confirm this, sounding more shaken than she had in our first conversation. She asked me to let her know the particulars of the funeral arrangements as soon as they were made. With that, her voice broke.

Scanning the Yellow Pages, I'd found the Meyrowitz Funeral Home, which sounded Jewish enough to me. I tried them and a couple of other places, which were even more expensive. Gloria seemed stunned by the money involved. I assured her that with both Sharon and I working, we'd managed to save a little. I could cover it. I paused to allow Gloria to contest this point. She didn't. Nor did she remember the location of the family burial plot. I would have to get that information from Clara. Gloria knew that Clara and I hadn't been on speaking terms, but she said, "The least you can do for Sharon now is show a little decency toward her mother." Along that line, Gloria requested that I arrange to pick Clara up and take her to the funeral. Gloria lived upstate and would have a long drive in, whereas I was not that far from Clara's apartment in the Bronx.

* * *

We arrive at the funeral home on the Grand Concourse and 167th Street, and I pull into the parking lot in the rear. The lot is bordered, on two sides, by burned-out apartment buildings. A fitting location for a funeral home. Were this a Jewish deli or dairy restaurant, it would have been gone at least five years ago, following on the heels of the Concourse's white residents. But funeral homes, like cemeteries I guess, tend to stay put. It's never really registered before, but suddenly I realize that I've seen it over and over: Jewish, Italian, or Irish funeral homes in the middle of neighborhoods where such people no longer live. But where they return, finally, in coffins.

We're early. Clara gets out, and I tell her that I'll be inside in a few minutes, that I need a smoke. This is an understatement. Having no patience for the car's cigarette lighter, I fumble with a match. After a couple of deep drags, I get out and prowl around the parking lot, continuing to poison my lungs. It's freezing out here, as if the blackened, empty window frames of the abandoned buildings are funneling the cold. I shudder and gaze up at the ice-blue sky, at its puffy white clouds drifting carelessly. Sharon. I let myself cry, getting it out. I'll need to have myself together once I'm inside and the condolences start pouring in.

A Dodge Dart with Jersey plates pulls into the lot: Sharon's Uncle Dave and his new wife, whom I met once, at their wedding. Dave spots me as he gets out. It's useless for me to pretend that I haven't also seen him. Instead I approach, scratching at the freezing moisture on my face, thinking that I might as well get it over with, this particular episode of "I can't tell you how sorry I am." I might as well get used to being the target of gushing sympathy, of evocations of God, of hugs from people who ordinarily would have a hard time shaking my hand.

Uncle Dave falls into this category. He's your stereotypical cigar-smoking blowhard, the kind of guy who would pinch Kenny's cheek at some family gathering, loudly proclaim how much the kid has grown, lay a present on him, then wonder aloud why Kenny doesn't kiss his Uncle Dave "hello," or thank him for the present, or even voice a greeting: "Cat got your tongue?" At such times, I would've loved to see a large cat do a number on Dave's tongue. Now, he seems relatively subdued as he steps out of his car. Wordlessly, he clasps my hand (the one without the cigarette) in both of his thick, leather-gloved mitts. His chunky, reddened face crinkles with grief under his fedora.

"She was such a good girl, Paul," he says finally, in a rasping voice. "I'm so sorry . . . for all of us."

"Thanks," I quietly reply, gripping his shoulder in a gesture that both expresses my appreciation and keeps him at arm's length. Even this amount of physical contact makes me cringe inside. I nod at his wife Marcia and attempt a grim smile. She hesitates for a moment, then her arm encircles my waist and she leans against me silently, her stiff, dark hair and fur collar resting against my upper arm. Dave lays a hand on her shoulder. The three of us form a sort of huddle in the parking lot. I break it and suggest that we go inside where it's warm, where my mother-in-law could probably use some company.

Inside, near the entrance, Sharon's name is arranged in white plastic letters against the black background of an announcement board. A sort of preliminary tombstone. I look away, sucking air and swallowing, nodding as the dark-suited manager of the place directs us toward the "reception room." Clara is sitting inside. As we enter, her reddened eyes turn toward us, seemingly without recognition. Soon enough, though, she's weeping in Dave's arms, moaning Sharon's name, calling her "my baby."

I absent myself from this scene, stubbing out my cigarette and entering the stillness of the adjoining chapel. To the right of a podium flanked by upraised electric candles, I see Sharon's coffin. It's completely covered with a blue cloth. The golden Star of David on top seems a final emblem of our separation. Sharon signed, sealed, and delivered to her grave, if nothing more. Silently, unwillingly, I start crying again. I curse myself for it. The tears hurt physically, as if my eyes are being forcibly drained. In some distant corner of my mind, it occurs to me that the Irish know what they're doing when they get drunk at funerals, or after them, whichever it is. Stone sober now, I wonder how much more I can take. I seem incapable of walking away, of averting my eyes from the shimmering Star of David. In the next instant, though, it's as if I'm watching myself from outside, calmly viewing a one-scene summary of my own history, a frame frozen in time. The moment passes, but leaves in its wake a small sense of relief. I can almost feel Sharon inside me now; I feel a closeness to her that I probably never did when she was alive. And I have a sense that she knows how much I'd give to be able to do it over again. The notion that I'll have that opportunity in a way, with Kenny, is a comfort. I make a silent promise to Sharon, redeemable by our son. Brushing away a new surge of tears, I turn back toward the waiting room.

More relatives have arrived, on both sides of the family. My mother is sitting with Clara, holding her hands, a scene I never thought I'd witness. Sharon and I had managed to offend both of our mothers by marrying each other, despite the fact that neither mother paid much attention to her own religion. When my mother finally divorced my father, the fact that she was violating her supposed Roman Catholicism was the least of her concerns. Yet the prospect of having an even nominally Jewish daughter-in-law had taken her a while to get used to. Her relationship with Sharon had begun to thaw, though, with Kenny's birth. And over the past year, Sharon had discovered a sympathetic listener in my mother, who knew all about being stuck with a boozing, cheating husband. But this shift in my mother's loyalties had done nothing to improve the quality of her occasional contacts with Clara, whom she considered to be a condescending snob. Now all of that has been put aside, at least temporarily.

My mother turns from Clara and studies my face for several moments. What she sees there causes her to stand up and throw her arms around me. I can feel her trembling. Dutifully, I put my arms around her. My discomfort increases as she whispers, almost fiercely, into my chest, "I was just starting to love her, Paul. Just starting to feel like I had a daughter."

I disengage myself. "I'm sorry, Ma," I say, glancing around in embarrassment at others who avert their eyes. "God knows I'd change it if I could." I feel a twinge of annoyance at the fervor in my voice, at the need I have to convince my mother that I'm genuinely remorseful—and innocent. This is probably part of the same reflex that made me vehemently defend myself when my mother would let me have it over my treatment of her daughter-in-law. Now my mother's voice contains only grief. The accusation is only in my head. To some degree it has been since I heard the news, despite the fact that I was nowhere near when Sharon crashed.

My mother is the only person other than Gloria whom I told personally. She was beside herself. I had to convince her not to drive up from South Jersey then and there. Even if she'd made it in one piece, I didn't think her company was what I needed. She wound up staying home and making phone calls all night. The recipients of these calls are arriving, I notice out of the corner of my eye: an aunt and uncle, my mother's cousin who I haven't seen in ages, who I mightn't recognize at all were I not sober. An appearance by my father, who I haven't seen in over a year, would be a major surprise. My mother now informs me that he knows, anyway. She spoke to him on the phone a couple of days ago.

"It would be too much to expect him to fly here, but did he call you at least?"

"Not yet."

"The bastard."

"Ma, let it alone. He wouldn't know what to say anyway."

Almost forcibly, she stifles an angry reply. The lines in her slender face stand out; her penciled eyebrows pull together. She looks at me and nods slowly, dabbing at her eyes with a crumpled tissue. My mother is fifteen or twenty years younger than Clara, and ordinarily she looks even younger than that. The wrinkles in the corners of her eyes are usually less noticeable, upstaged by the brightness of her dark brown irises. Now the light in her eyes is absent. Fine red webs extend across the whites of her eyes. My mother's features are sharp and thin: a long nose, slender lips (their length seems exaggerated now by her bright red lipstick), even teeth. Her shoulder-length black hair has recently had a permanent or a teasing, or something. Except for our pointed chins, we don't look much like each other. As she's often said, I take after my father, in more ways than one.

That includes a chronic distaste for most of my relatives, in-laws (excluding Gloria), and wife's friends. But now I'm almost gracious as I accept the rush of condolences, the offers of help, the testimonials to Sharon's lovely character. These words of praise all sound true. The closeness I felt to Sharon alone inside of the chapel remains—although I'm also having trouble remembering her face, even remembering the main details of her life, which I'm supposed to give to the rabbi when he arrives. My mind and emotions are numb; my eyes are empty. Even if I was willing to cry now, in public, I couldn't. I nod and murmur thanks, return hugs of consolation easily now that the ice has been broken by my mother. I'm gripping cold cloth, fur and leather, that's all.

Gloria arrives slightly late, on the heels of a guy who must be the rabbi. Along with her is Lila, her ten year-old daughter. Relieved that they're here, I move toward them, but they've already drawn a crowd. Gloria is comforted and gracefully comforts in return. Her usual self-possession begins to crumble only when Clara rushes over. Mother and daughter embrace, then Clara tearfully hugs Lila, her elder grandchild. Even if Lila wanted to respond in kind, her skinny arms are pinned to her sides. Meanwhile, I'm buttonholed by the rabbi. I follow him into the privacy of the chapel.

"Mr. Galdoni, I'm Rabbi Hersch," he says, extending his hand.

Briefly squeezing it, I reply, "I figured." He looks the part, even though he's younger than I thought he was after speaking to him on the phone. His reddish goatee and rimless glasses fit my image of a rabbi, as does the black fedora that most men our age wouldn't think of wearing. Hersch explains that he'll be conducting services both here and at the cemetery, and that he needs some basic information about Sharon. I give it to him haltingly, not only because my mind is fogged. I feel like I'm reciting Sharon's obituary. Also, I'm even less comfortable speaking to a rabbi than I would be to a priest. Hersch has registered no noticeable reaction, either over the phone or here, to the fact that I'm (in Clara's terminology) "Goyim," but I'm sure he's not surprised that I don't sound overly bright as I try to lay out the information. I speak in a monotone and repeatedly tug at my tie, a garment my neck is not at all used to.

When I'm finished, Hersch asks me who might know Sharon's Hebrew name. I shrug, then suggest that he try Clara.

Then as an afterthought I say, "Look, I don't know what you're going to say. Probably just a standard religious service or whatever." I pause, but Hersch doesn't reply. Behind his glasses, his eyes are fixed on me, waiting. "But . . . Sharon was a good mother, that's all. Maybe you could mention that. She only started working after the kid was in nursery school, and even then she was all upset about only seeing him in the evening. She—"

Hersch remains silent a few moments longer. Seeing that I'm not going to continue, or can't, he nods and quietly says, "Thank you."

To my surprise, Hersch does include what I've told him in his sermon. After reciting in Hebrew and English—the Lord's Prayer is the only thing that sounds vaguely familiar to me—he clears his throat and says, "Sharon Galdoni was a modern woman. She was a working mother, helping to provide financially for her family while performing all the traditional duties of a wife and mother. Yet in an age where traditional religious and cultural values are being constantly challenged, she showed none of the selfishness which has become a religion to many. And when one so young, so vital, is taken from us, it can make us question God's mercy, His existence even. It can challenge our faith. Yet many of us, paradoxically, find our faith strengthened at times such as this. And that faith, that quiet conviction inside of us, tells us that Sharon will be rewarded—*is* being rewarded—for the goodness she exhibited and shared during her time on Earth."

As Hersch pauses, the sniffling in the audience seems suddenly amplified. Both my mother and Clara are struggling to control themselves. I glance at them then quickly avert my eyes, looking back at Hersch, at the hypnotic shimmer of the electric candles on his glasses. As I do so, Clara lets out a bellow of grief. Gloria quickly puts an arm around her and squeezes her tightly, as if trying to smother the sound. From the row behind us one of Sharon's uncles lays a consoling hand on Gloria's hand, atop Clara's shoulder. Hersch continues, looking directly at Clara.

"So we remind ourselves, in our grief, that we grieve for ourselves, not for Sharon. We grieve at her absence from our lives here, because we miss her—because she possessed, and still possesses, those very qualities that will ensure her happiness in the hereafter." After another pause, he concludes, "And now Sharon's only sibling, her sister Gloria, will speak."

Hersch descends the steps opposite from where Sharon's coffin sits. As he does, his eyes briefly catch mine. I nod slightly in appreciation. I have a sense that he's done a good job, more from his sincere tone than the words, of which few registered in my mind. What *did* register was the bit about making a religion of selfishness. For the moment, I'm convinced that I'm turning over a new leaf. I try to hang on to this conviction, try to stifle my cravings for booze and a cigarette, as Gloria pats Lila's hand and approaches the pulpit.

She moves with that same bouncy walk I've always admired. Unwilling to chance looking too admiringly, I look away until she's standing behind the podium. She surveys the audience for a moment. There must be over fifty people here, I realize. Gloria and my mother have made sure that anyone who even remotely knew Sharon has been informed: old friends of Sharon's, including her Queens College chum Francie, some of Sharon's co-workers, none of whom I'd met before. Gloria clears her throat and begins.

"Sharon and I fought a lot when we were kids," she says, nodding slowly as if in grim acknowledgment of the fact. "We've joked about it over the past couple of years: we said that was the reason each of us only had one kid, out of mercy. You get to that point, where you can laugh about it, when there's nothing to fight over anymore, when you realize that you're really made out of the same stuff . . . that you really love each other." Gloria pauses, gulping, retaining her composure.

"Children can be sort of emissaries in that way. Maybe it's easier to show affection to a kid. It's more . . . expected. But when I recognized the kind of love Sharon had for my daughter, Lila, even after Kenny was born . . . it just wasn't something she could have faked. And it wasn't about giving presents or holding a kid on your knee. It was a feeling of . . . family, of oneness. Of inseparability. That was what we shared during the times we all spent together in recent years, times that seem so precious now, so . . . fleeting. Yet that feeling doesn't die, and doesn't depend on being together or apart. That's what I feel when I think of Sharon."

She looks down at Lila and Clara, who are both weeping, and manages a faint smile before dabbing at her own eyes. "As far as the other stuff, the problems she had—well, most of our generation had problems coming of age in this 'modern world,' as the rabbi put it. Added to that, she was only eighteen when our father died. Not only was she heartbroken, but a new load of responsibilities fell on her shoulders. After a while she had a breakdown, and spent a couple of weeks in the hospital. She could have spent the next five years gulping tranquilizers and feeling sorry for herself. But instead she pulled herself together. She finished up her college degree and taught in a school in the South Bronx, a school which was more like a war zone. But she never gave those kids anything less than the best she had to give them.

"Most recently, she was a 'working mother.' Her sleeping hours were sometimes more like a coffee break between two jobs. But her dedication to her son Kenny never waned, despite the demands of her job downtown, despite the troubles that sometimes cropped up at home—" Gloria hesitates here, maybe wishing she had the last words back. She casts a glance my way, sort of like the pat on the rear end a ballplayer gives an opponent he's just accidentally knocked down. I give the slightest of nods, conveying, "It's okay."

"Watching Sharon with Kenny," she continues, "You saw the real Sharon, shining in those pretty brown eyes of hers. The Sharon that didn't die when her body did."

The strength of Gloria's conviction is unmistakable. It shines from her own eyes, it's written all over her makeup-free face. And I'm probably as close as I'll ever get to believing that a soul is real, not just superstition or a fairy tale invented to help finance churches and synagogues. I'm closer than I've ever been —but not close enough.

- 5 -
Sharon

WITH THE entrance of Paul into my life review, I seemed to lose in the subsequent segments any awareness that it *was* a review. Over the last years of my life on Earth, my sense of self had been so wrapped up in Paul that "seeing" him again was tantamount to a resurrection for me. Had it occurred to me that I was dead—according to the accepted definition of the word— and that my death would soon be acknowledged by all who knew me, the notion would've seemed ridiculous. Even the fact that I could now "read" Paul's mind and emotions didn't seem strikingly unusual. To some extent, I'd always been able to sense what was going on inside of him. More often than not, I'd chosen to ignore it.

This was particularly true when he suggested that we get married. That event occurred at Jones Beach on Long Island, and was replayed during the life review. I was working full time, at the day care center in the Bronx. I was also working toward my degree, attending summer session night school at Lehman College. The living was not easy. But lying next to Paul on an oversized beach towel, soaking up the rays, lulled to sleep by the distant sound of the surf, I felt as if I'd been furloughed from prison. When he tickled my bare midriff to rouse me, I giggled lazily and brushed his hand away. I was wide awake in an instant, though, when he whispered into my ear, "Let's get hitched."

I squinted up at him, using my hand to shield my eyes from the sun. "Repeat that?"

He said it again with an exaggerated deliberateness, as if speaking to someone with a limited command of English. Using the sun as an excuse, I briefly shut my eyes again, hoping to reopen them and find a sly, "I had you going" grin on his face. That would have been typical of his sense of humor. But he still seemed serious when I looked at him again. I was stunned—half pleased, half tempted to get up and run. "You better be careful what you say, sweetie," I finally replied with a weak laugh. "I might fool you and take you up on it."

"That's what I'm hoping." Paul's face, which tapered sharply to a now-set jaw, seemed the embodiment of sincerity and expectation.

I sat up and gazed past the crowded shoreline toward the horizon, where a lone, sundrenched gray ship drifted, looking like a toy. "Paul," I said, my eyes still averted. "We've been seeing each other about five months. We're doing okay so far. Isn't this kind of sudden? What's the rush?" I said this for my benefit as much as his, hoping that this modern-sounding wisdom would help subdue the part of me that wanted to jump at an opportunity to be taken care of.

He reached over me and flicked some sand off of the edge of my towel. "Five months is a long time for me, Sharon. Five months of what d' ya call it, monogamy? And you're right, we've been doing fine. You know, I feel like you don't put on airs, like you're for real, like you're not out to prove what a hip chick you are. And you've been through enough to understand where I'm coming from when I get cynical or whatever. Hell, I just feel good when we're together. Alright?"

"Do you love me, Paul?"

"For whatever that means, yeah. I haven't told you?"

"In bed you have. Otherwise—"

He shook his head, giving a laugh that sounded more like a snort, then stood up and stepped over me, adding several grains of sand to my sun tan-lotioned skin. Squatting next to me, he used his index finger to write I LOVE YOU SHARON in the sand. "Okay?"

I couldn't help smiling. "Very romantic."

"Well, I gotta confess that I saw it in a movie. Doesn't mean I don't mean it, though. But . . . what can I tell you?"

We sat for a few minutes in silence, while I tried to figure out what to say. I was bewildered by the offer. Finally, feeling impelled to respond, I again took refuge in modern-day convention. "Well, maybe we could try living together," I said without much enthusiasm. I clasped my arms around my knees as if huddling against a sudden chill.

"Uh-uh," replied Paul, emphatically waving away this suggestion with one of his large hands. "Look, I need to be committed. Can you understand that?" After a moment he snorted and slapped the side of his head. "Let me rephrase that. I'm ready to stop screwing around, okay? In fact I have, since we've been together. But shacking up . . . I just don't think I could take it that seriously. I need to start living like a man, you know? Going out drinking after work with those idiots I work with at the post office, bullshitting around with Mickey-Mouse education courses at Lehman—I'm just getting too old for that kinda nonsense. I need a goal, a sense of direction, *something*. Getting married, maybe having kids eventually, I think it would help. The responsibility would. I know it."

Having only recently settled on the notion that marriage would set life right, Paul found his conviction wavering near the end of this little speech. As he tried to compensate, his voice grew louder and more earnest, like that of a frightened kid being forced to embellish a lie. That was the way it came across to my posthumous consciousness. But even at the time, I had my doubts about his ability to pull off the promised transformation. And I wasn't sure that I wanted him to; the devil-may-care attitude he'd hitherto projected had always held a certain charm for me. "Paul, if we got married, at least if we had kids, I might want to stay home with them for a while. You wouldn't be able, for instance, to just up and quit your job, like you've been talking about doing. It's—"

"Hey, have you been hearing what I'm saying?" interjected Paul. His voice had an edge to it. Doubting himself was one thing, but my doubt was quite another. "I'm not looking for a free ride, okay? And for sure I'm not looking to work odd jobs, or try for a large killing at the track, or whatever. But I don't intend to spend the rest of my life running envelopes through a machine and sorting them, either. You have any idea how boring it gets to do that everyday? It's no wonder people flip out. It's a wonder *I* haven't, yet. But if we got married now, or soon, and pooled our resources, we'd both have more . . . flexibility. More money, half the rent. We could each just work part time. I could check out career possibilities, maybe get some training, and you could finish your degree in half the time."

Mentioning my degree, Paul paused expectantly. He knew what that degree had meant in the past year and a half, since I'd left my mother's. It was my goal. My single-minded pursuit of it had helped me forget about the debacle on the subway and erase the image of myself shuffling around Elmira General's mental ward in a half-tied terry cloth bathrobe.

Between college and my job, I'd been too busy to sink for long into the loneliness that sometimes afflicted me. Still, hooking up with Paul had added something to my life. Now he was offering me a double validation: a marriage certificate, and a Bachelor's Degree a year or two ahead of schedule. This was a powerful inducement. Still . . .

I exhaled slowly and audibly, at the same time running a hand across my sweaty forehead. The heat of the day suddenly seemed oppressive. In a measured voice, I said, "All of that might be nice, Paul. But can I have some time to think about it?"

"Sure, take all the time you want," he replied brusquely, watching his fingers create a little depression in the sand. "Look, I'm gonna go jump in the water for a while. Appreciate it if you could save my place."

With that he was off. I watched him scurry away on tip-toe across the burning sand, his large body bent like a divining rod, straining toward the water. From behind, he presented a picture of vulnerability which I found surprisingly amusing, almost touching. As if for the first time, I noticed the brown hair that climbed up from the small of his back and seemed to submerge before reappearing at the base of his neck. The sight was endearing. At some level I knew (posthumously, it was quite clear) that I was trying to stir up my affection for him, trying to convince myself that underneath he was really a Teddy Bear and that, as he'd claimed, marriage would bring a hitherto unseen Paul to the fore. As it was, I felt that I did care for him, did need his companionship and his love-making. I wanted to be able to say "yes". I was sure it would be the easiest thing to do.

I scooped up a fistful of sand, then unclenched my pinky and ring finger to let it slowly trickle out. I did this at first for no particular reason, but suddenly I was struck by the symbolism of it, corny yet undeniable: I might not get many chances. Not that I considered my time to be running out, in any sense. Twenty-two was young to get married. I didn't feel emotionally ready for it, or sure that I loved Paul, or that we stood even a chance of staying together until death did us part. But on the other hand, I wasn't confident that an offer of marriage would come my way again. Nor was I convinced that I could manage without Paul. I *was* fairly sure that anything other than an unconditional "yes" would destroy our relationship.

I clutched the sand more tightly, completely stemming its flow. This wistful little action did nothing to quell the feeling that I was rolling along toward a decision I could easily wind up regretting. I flung the sand down, then did almost the same thing to myself, reassuming the position in which I'd felt so relaxed only a short while before.

When Paul returned, dripping wet, I childishly feigned sleep. He shook his head over me once; the shower of cold salt water was enough to end my charade. "Paul!" I gasped, curling up my body. "Was that necessary?"

"Just wanted to make sure you were listening," he snickered. "I meant what I said before. I know this is sudden. Take your time and think it over. Then say yes."

"Aye aye, sir."

Over the next several weeks, Paul dispensed with his bravado. In fact he was unusually considerate, almost sweet. I took the bait, and felt a small sense of relief at finally coming to a decision. I now wanted to tie the knot quickly and get it over with. That had been Paul's idea all along. A civil ceremony suited both of us.

It also suited our mothers: if we were determined to get married despite their feelings, better to do it as discreetly as possible. Both their objections were at least partially on religious grounds: Paul's mother wanted her grandchildren to be baptized and confirmed, mine wanted a briss for a grandson and a bar or bat mitzvah. In addition to Paul's "goyische" origins —or, I thought, because of them—my mother also distrusted his motives and character in general. This, of course, only solidified my decision to marry him.

Gloria wasn't overly impressed with Paul either. She didn't vocalize this, though. She wasn't into "making judgments" or offering unsolicited advice. If anything, I had the impression that she was happy for me, and I was glad that her own failed marriage hadn't caused her to feel that all such ventures were futile. At my request, she was a witness to my wedding at the Bronx County courthouse—much as I was, during the life review.

In this segment, I actually lost my identification with Sharon. This experience involved a feeling of freedom and expansiveness which is difficult to describe. Reliving the wedding, I *was* Paul, Gloria, and Sharon, I was the field of life itself on which the wedding played out. Our concurrent thoughts, feelings, and perceptions were like a pattern superimposed on this field and underlying the physical activity of the wedding: the words, the vows, the kisses and hugs. The contrast between the misgivings each of us felt and our outer expressions of joy and optimism was almost comical—all the more so because none of it really seemed to matter. Any differences between Gloria, Paul, and me seemed trivial, illusory. We were like different waves on the same ocean of consciousness. This experience (unique to the wedding segment) was blissful, as if permeated by the then-invisible Being of Light.

The wedding segment was followed by several from my life as Mrs. Galdoni. The experience of being in Paul's shoes, in the fullest sense of the expression, had had a profound effect upon me. I was able to see his particular brand of suffering, his weaknesses, with the same kind of sympathy and acceptance I'd occasionally felt for my own. And my loathing for my own —and his—was gone. For the first time, I was able to clearly see and acknowledge my own contributions to the ruination of our marriage. Die and learn.

After we became man and wife, it took me only a year to wrap up my degree in elementary education. Shortly thereafter, I was assigned to a fourth-grade class at Dunbar Elementary School, which bordered Crotona Park in the South Bronx. I took this as an exciting challenge, a mission that I'd been given to perform. This attitude had been instilled in me by my professors at Lehman. In this they were abetted, unwittingly, by Paul, whose cynical, semi-racist attitude created in me a backlash of determination. Thus fortified internally, and armed with the most modern technologies for teaching readin', 'ritin', and 'rithmetic, I soon discovered that I was woefully unprepared.

My students were a mixture of black and Puerto Rican children. Many of the Puerto Rican kids spoke only limited English —or, I came to understand, spoke as much as suited them. Still, I actually believed that some of the enlightened principles of education I'd picked up at Lehman would render any problem insignificant. After all, I'd done well enough at the day care center, and without the benefit of a degree. But the day care center's program had mainly been arts and crafts. And the neighborhood it served was milder, by far, than where I was now.

My experience at Dunbar was illustrated by one life-review segment that took place in the fall of my only year as a teacher. Colorful cut-outs of turkeys, Indians, and Pilgrims had been taped up around my classroom. Many of these decorations were strategically placed over the cracks in the walls. Outside, brown leaves, pushed by a strong wind, filled most of the diamond-shaped spaces in the silvery wire gratings that protected both windows. I was gazing down at my roll book and taking attendance, still trying to master some of the names, when cold air suddenly gusted into the room, causing a swirl of looseleaf and construction paper. I quickly slammed my hand down on my desk to keep my own papers from flying off. Looking up, I saw Isidro Goncalves with the damning evidence still in his hands. They gripped the heavy wooden window pole with its brass slot-key on one end. He'd completely lowered the upper half of one of the windows, and was now watching with a satisfied smile as his classmates began to scramble after their works of art and scholarship.

"Everyone sit down!" I screamed. "Now!" Screaming was the technique I'd adopted a few weeks into the term, after realizing that democracy was not working. My kind and sensitive approach had been taken as permission to run wild.

My command to sit down was, predictably, ignored. The students, gleefully caroming off of each other like pinballs, were pursuing their papers with a single-mindedness they'd rarely demonstrated previously. A couple of desks were knocked over. Isidro, grinning maniacally, approached the other window with the pole. I was still rooted to my desk, unwilling to allow my papers—already strewn across the desk in their usual disarray—to be blown into the general maelstrom.

"Isidro!" I barked. "Put it down!" I was referring, of course, to the pole. Isidro's slender, bird-like features took on a look of perplexed innocence: his "No speakee English" look. After a moment, though, a glint of understanding came into his dark eyes. He lifted the pole, intending to "put down" the second window.

"The pole, Isidro," I commanded, lowering my voice some, struggling for self-control. "Put it down." Most of the other students had by then recovered their papers and calmed down to some degree. But they were still standing and laughing over the adventure, watching Isidro to see what new entertainment he might provide. It was fortunate that they *were* watching him, when he finally put down the pole. From its half-raised position, he simply dropped it, shrugging as he did so.

Posthumously, I witnessed myself witnessing the descent of the pole. It had seemed to hang suspended in the air, its brass tip gleaming, reflecting the light from the room's opaque white bulb housings. Inevitably though, time and gravity reasserted themselves. The pole landed with a dull thud against the upraised forearm of Thelma Jones.

Thelma was a relatively subdued girl who was most notable for the colorfully beaded cornrows in which she wore her hair. The shriek she let out, when the pole struck her arm, was more from fright than pain. Despite the mild nature of her bruise, however, I immediately dispatched her to the health room. Isidro followed her out, heading for the principal's office with another discipline referral to add to his pile. He wound up with a three-day suspension, which did not reform him in the least. After ten minutes of sitting with an ice pack on her arm Thelma returned to class, with an accident report form to be filled out in triplicate. Her mother subsequently issued a complaint, which resulted in Dunbar's principal placing me under surveillance. He usually managed to poke his head into my room at an inopportune moment. There were a lot of them. It was a long year.

The year was not much better for Paul. Like me, he started out with high expectations. He was going into business with his long-time friend Rob McClellan. The idea had been Rob's: a pizzamobile to service construction sites, college campuses, special events, evening rush hour depots, and any other promising location. Meals on wheels for everyone, eat on the street in style. With Rob's help, Paul envisioned himself the wealthy co-owner of a chain of these trucks. Even the exhaust fumes would fill the air with the irresistible smells of Italian cooking.

Paul accumulated the money for the first (and only) truck by working time and a half at the post office for over a year; this fact was an indicator of the strength of his determination. Our savings account grew—until the advent of the pizzamobile, which was a flop from the beginning. Paul's hours increased, if anything. His income did not. In his infrequent moments at home, he complained bitterly about the problems involved in his new job: the near impossibility of making pizza in a moving truck, the need to pay off the cops for parking privileges, the doldrums between lunch hour and five p.m., and his partner's unreliability.

Overwhelmed by my own troubles at work, I had little patience or sympathy for Paul's complaints. I came home and buried myself in Harlequin Romances. Paul drank, on and off the job, and occasionally stuffed his cigarettes with marijuana or hashish. He retained enough good sense, or survival instinct, to lay off of the uppers and downers favored by his partner Rob. If Paul couldn't do booze and narcotics together, he'd stick with the booze, thank you.

My last experience with LSD had been negative enough to scare me away from illegal drugs of any kind. And Paul's drinking habits had inspired me to become a teetotaler. But while teaching at Dunbar, I picked up a cigarette habit which was to stay with me for the rest of my life—excluding my months of pregnancy with Kenny. I was determined to do my best for him, as soon as I knew he was on the way.

Kenny's conception was not a result of family planning. Still, I was delighted to be having a child. One life review segment took place on the Sunday morning when Paul and I confirmed my pregnancy. We were standing in front of the mirrored dresser, looking at a miniature test tube filled with my urine. I'd peed into the tube about an hour before, per the instructions for the EPT (Early Pregnancy Test). The test was supposed to be ninety-seven percent accurate. If I was pregnant, some kind of ring would appear at the bottom of the tube. Neither Paul nor I could summon up the nerve to lift it and look. He stood in his boxer shorts and sleeveless T-shirt, idly scratching his scrotum with one hand, while holding in the other hand a cigarette that was at least two-thirds ash. His bushy hair sat on his head in sandy-colored tufts; his face was covered with an uneven stubble a few shades lighter. I was wearing one of his striped, button-down shirts, which I'd adopted as a warm-weather nightgown. My face was flushed with a girlish excitement. Our reflections in the mirror seemed to add an appropriate historical significance to the event, as if it was being recorded.

I picked up the tube. An unmistakable dark-brown ring at the bottom stared back at us like an eye. Unthinkingly, I gave a small jump for joy.

"It's a little girl. I know it!"

Paul took a final drag on his cigarette, then shook his head and muttered, "Shit." After a moment he added, "Your ticket out of Dunbar Elementary School ."

"You really believe that," I replied, in a voice softened by my lingering elation. The feeling quickly vanished. A moist film settled over my eyes. "Like I haven't been faithfully inserting the diaphragm whenever you feel like exercising your husbandly prerogative. Except, of course, for that night last month when you came home late—and dead drunk. You still don't remember that? I was asleep. You practically raped me."

"Sue me. *If* that happened —and I musta been pretty drunk if I don't remember—if I was that drunk, I'm sure you could've extricated yourself real easy, if you wanted to."

"I woke up with you inside of me, *dear*. You were coming shortly thereafter. Not that that matters now. I'm having the kid."

Paul stubbed out his cigarette as if he was trying to eradicate any trace of it. "You mean *we're* having the kid," he said, glaring at me. Over the previous week, with my period distressingly absent, he'd mentioned once or twice the merits of an abortion. But each time he'd nixed the idea almost in the same breath. This was owing to the lingering influence of his mother's early attempts to raise him as a Catholic, in combination with a manly sense of proprietorship toward the new life in my womb. And while the ring at the bottom of the test tube didn't cause him to do an about-face (as I'd thought it might), neither did it fill him with joy.

"Sharon, I'm not making shit on that pizza truck so far. If that doesn't change . . . how the fuck am I supposed to support three of us when you stop working? You haven't changed your mind about that, I'm sure."

"Nope, I haven't. You're not gonna make me feel guilty about it, either," I said, for my own benefit as much as his. "I don't want someone else raising my child, especially not after what I've seen at school. With my students, if you can call them that, it's probably too late to change them. Or maybe I'm just not the person who can do a whole lot with them, or even wants to, anymore. But I want a shot at raising a child—my own—from day one."

With this declaration, my nostrils twitched slightly as I compressed my lips, stifling a sob. On the occasions in my life when I managed to muster some resolve, you'd never have known it by looking at my face. Paul knew, however. We'd been together long enough. He drummed his fingers on the dresser for a few moments, then said, "Well, you've got everything arranged nicely in your head. Now I've gotta figure out what *I'm* gonna do." He stalked out of the bedroom and into the adjoining bathroom, leaving me to interpret his remark. I knew he probably meant that he had to decide whether to stay with the Pizzamobile or cut his losses and find a guaranteed source of income. But the threat of desertion was there; he'd intended it to be. I'd needed no clairvoyance to realize that.

Over the next several months, I might have welcomed his leaving, were it not for the pregnancy. Paul's resentment and my stomach seemed to grow concurrently. While he didn't hint at deserting me again, neither did he show much sympathy or concern on those occasions when he was home. I was sick as a dog during the first few months. I threw up most mornings, often at work (it made little difference to my students whether I was in the room or out on a barfing break). I'd drag myself through the day, then come home and crawl under the covers. Paul's mother began to help out during this period. She cooked, cleaned, took me shopping for baby items, and urged me to stop working early. But I wouldn't give Paul the satisfaction. The fact that the Board of Education was unwilling to pay for maternity leave was almost beside the point.

About three months before Kenny was due, Paul swallowed his pride and asked the post office to rehire him. I gave him no credit for doing this. I'd already concluded, based on what I considered to be ample evidence, that he was a selfish bastard by nature. Indications to the contrary were not welcome. Indeed, I felt a perverse sense of gratification when he found out that the post office no longer had a job for him.

Brenner's Cab Company did, though. Paul reluctantly obtained his hack license. His feelings about this latest turn were apparent in the photograph attached to the front of the license. Even if Paul had shaved for the occasion, his picture would have seemed right at home on a post office wall.

I didn't see him produce anything resembling a smile until Kenny was about to be born. Given my difficult pregnancy, Kenny's birth was surprisingly easy. Paul and I had taken no childbirthing classes together, nor even discussed it. I was quite willing to be drugged if giving birth was going to be painful. However, my doctor was relatively young and a proponent of natural childbirth. I was in labor for two hours, and only in the last fifteen-twenty minutes did it become hard to take. Paul was with me the whole time, looking ridiculous in a light green hospital gown a few sizes too small and a paper cap, which resembled, appropriately enough, an ice pack. But if he was hurting for a drink, you'd never have known it. He held my hand and encouraged me with a gentleness that I dimly remembered from the early days of our relationship.

When Kenny popped out, squirting forth like a pink frog, Paul was beside himself with joy over the male genitalia. He bounced up and down and repeatedly announced, "It's a boy It's a boy!". So much for my feminine intuition. Still, a boy was fine with me, and if he made Paul happy, so much the better. The change in him was abrupt and nothing short of miraculous. Exhausted and relieved, I accepted his kisses with a weak smile and drifted into sleep.

For the first month or so of Kenny's life, Paul was a doting father. He managed to steer his cab over to our Pelham Parkway apartment in the Bronx whenever the opportunity presented itself. He was driving twelve-hour night shifts, and one of his pet diversions, at first, was dropping in to visit his future star athlete. Kenny was colicky, and at any time of night there was a decent chance that Paul would find both of us awake. I had to admit, Paul had a facility for getting Kenny to settle down and go back to sleep. He'd tuck Kenny under one arm like a football and walk him around, making soft, guttural noises, which fluctuated between something akin to a kitten's purr and the sound of a dump truck idling. Of course, Kenny screamed during the day also, but Paul usually slept through that. Between exhaustion and booze, he had little problem sleeping. And if he awoke with the time and inclination for sex, I was willing to oblige him. It took little energy (although almost more than I had), and it was the least I could do to maintain what was now, more than ever, a necessary relationship.

If the care and concern Paul had shown in the hospital didn't last, it was still true that he was easier to live with than during the days of my pregnancy and his pizzamobile. He now had a *son*, as well as a job that paid steadily and in which he had neither a partner nor supervisor to contend with. He was on his own, from six p.m. to six a.m. Occasional stops at bars or racetracks were his prerogative. As for any other dalliances he may have been involved in, I didn't ask questions—at first. Paul was supporting us, and he was clearly fond of Kenny. During my first year or two of motherhood, that was enough for me.

The novelty of fatherhood seemed to wear off concurrent with Paul's diminishing tolerance for hacking. He was living proof that it was possible to drink and drive without mishap; navigating around our living room, though, was another matter. In one of the last life review segments, Paul had just arrived home from work around seven a.m. I was in the kitchen trying to shovel spoonfuls of Cheerios and milk into Kenny's mouth. At two years old, Kenny was like one of those vending machines that reject your dollar bill for mysterious reasons. Most of what I put into his mouth came back out in short order. I'd heard Paul coming through the front door as I was holding my hand to the base of Kenny's chin, trying to stem the flow of the cereal I'd inserted into his mouth a few seconds before. The next thing I heard was a clanking metal sound in the living room, followed by a thud and curses.

Paul entered the kitchen and tossed his fare clipboard on the table. He intended the loud clatter to announce that he was peeved about something. Mission accomplished.

"What'd you trip over?" I inquired wearily, neither expecting nor voicing a preliminary greeting.

"I dunno, why don't you tell me. Some truck, I think. You have any idea what's laying on the floor in there? Or maybe I should ask what *isn't*." Paul's vexation increased as his tongue betrayed him. "What isn't," his finishing flourish, was slurred into something like "wudizzen."

I sighed, and with the deep intake of air a foul, boozy smell hit me in the face. "Paul, I was about to clean up. If you want to take over feeding Kenny, I'll do it right now."

"The kid can't feed himself?"

"Ask him. He's sitting right in front of you," I replied between clenched teeth. "And he understands more than you think he does." My voice rose with this last remark, as if I was trying to jar Kenny into looking the part. He sat with milk dribbling down his chin, giving a good imitation of blissful ignorance.

Paul fairly snatched the spoon out of my hand. "Okay, you wanna feed yourself, Kenny?" he said, proferring the spoon with an attempt at a smile, which was more like a sudden twitch in the corners of his mouth. Kenny pushed the spoon away. Paul took Kenny's hand and wrapped it around the handle, a metal figure of Mickey Mouse. When he released Kenny's hand, the spoon dropped, splashing down into the bowl of cereal.

"Dwop," gurgled Kenny, his green eyes blinking. A few small puddles of milk formed on the table; a splotch of fading white appeared on the leg of Paul's dungarees. Resignedly, I sponged the table, also taking a couple of fast dabs at Paul's pants. Tight-lipped, Paul reinserted the spoon into Kenny's hand, this time holding Kenny's fingers around it and guiding him through the process of ladling a spoonful of mush into his mouth. Ninety percent of the mouthful was rejected; a scummy-looking stream flowed around both sides of Kenny's pointed chin.

Paul loudly sucked air through his nostrils. He released Kenny's hand, where the spoon stuck for a moment. Paul's bloodshot eyes followed its arc as it tenuously dangled, a pendulum dripping milk. Finally he said, "Jesus fucking Christ. Even when he gets it in his mouth . . . do you ever *work* with him?"

"What do you think I do all day, Paul? Is he starving?" Kenny's slop-covered bib, in fact, sat over a miraculously plump stomach. "And as far as getting him to feed himself, I've been trying."

"Have you? The kid's two years old already."

"So he's not a boy wonder. You can't handle that?" I realized that I too was now talking as if Kenny was not present. But I was too tired and too peeved to worry about it.

Losing his train of thought, Paul gazed at me blankly for a few moments. "Boy wonduh?" he mumbled finally. "He's gotta be a boy wonduh to feed himself? Maybe if you stopped hovering over him, and let him sink or swim a little on his own—"

"I thought I didn't work with him enough, Paul," I replied, throwing up my hands. Paul's crack about hovering compounded my exasperation—at some level I'd recognized a germ of truth in it. "Maybe you'd like to switch places, *dear*. Maybe you could do a better job?"

"Maybe." He shrugged as if it was no big deal. I stalked out of the kitchen. Kenny started crying. A few moments later, from the bedroom, I heard Paul command, "Shut up!"

The segment ended at that point, as if Paul's harsh voice had slammed a door on this encapsulation of our family life.

There was one more segment: I was interviewing for my job, reminding myself to sit up straight and look my interviewer in her penciled eyes. Then the life review ended, with the Prince Spaghetti truck barreling past me on the Major Deegan Expressway.

- 6 -
Paul

WE STAND around Sharon's open grave—her mother Clara, Gloria, and I, surrounded by other relatives. Clara repeats after Rabbi Hersch, reciting "Kaddish" over Sharon's casket. Apparently, not even a reform rabbi is empowered to confer Jew-for-a-day status. The demand is probably not that great. I try to push away such thoughts, try to stifle my resentment at being relegated to second fiddle at my wife's burial, try to hold on to the righteous remorse I felt at the funeral service.

Clara, supported by Gloria, has to pause a couple of times during her recitation. She bravely attempts to swallow her sobs, her body trembling with the effort. The steam from her mouth diminishes, as if she's temporarily idling. From what I can tell, her recitation of the Hebrew words is, at best, an approximation of what Hersch says. She's doing about as well as I did at my confirmation, when, I remember with surprising clarity, I recited Latin after a priest. The language had no magical properties. Prayer still seemed like a charade, just as it did in English. If Hebrew's any different, you wouldn't know it from the tears streaming down Clara's face now. She's deriving no comfort. Neither am I, as I gaze, bleary-eyed, over the rim of the grave.

Once Clara has finished the Kaddish, Hersch offers me the opportunity to lay the first shovel of dirt onto the casket. It comes as news to me that any of us will be doing any part of the burying. I pull back reflexively, then stare at Hersch with a mixture of uncertainty and suspicion, as if his offer were more of an accusation. But after a few moments I uproot the shovel from its standing position next to the grave. As gently as possible, I spread the first layer of earth over Sharon's coffin.

* * *

Later, at home, I feel like I made the right decision in turning down Clara's suggestion of a post-funeral reception. Being alone is a surprising relief, even if the apartment itself is practically a monument to Sharon. In addition to memories, the apartment still houses my "liquor cabinet," above the kitchen stove. I move toward it, then hesitate. I'm turning over a new leaf, theoretically. That was the plan as of a few minutes ago. I execute a little buttonhook away from the stove, light a cigarette, then open the fridge and take out some soda to mix with my scotch, rather than having it straight. I'll climb on the wagon a bit at a time. As I'm reaching for my current fifth, the phone rings at the other end of the kitchen, beyond arm's reach. I almost don't answer. Finally, on the sixth ring, I pick up the receiver and mumble, "Hello?"

"Mr. Galdoni?" The sharp, clear female voice sounds vaguely familiar, like an element of a dream. I confirm my identity, and she responds, "This is Miss Nahm. Kenny's nursery school teacher?"

"Uh-hmm." The realization that it's been only a few days since my most recent run-in with her stuns me. It doesn't seem possible.

She clears her throat. "Well, I've been worried about Kenny missing school. I tried you yesterday, and again this morning. I've been meaning to get Mrs. Galdoni's number at work. Is Kenny sick?"

"His mother died," I reply, deriving a small, perverse feeling of satisfaction from the gasp at the other end of the line.

After several moments, Miss Nahm says, "My God. What happened?"

"Car crash. On her way downtown, after she dropped Kenny over to you Tuesday morning."

"Mr. Galdoni, I'm really sorry. If there's anything I can do for Kenny . . . How's he taking it?"

I drag on my cigarette. "He doesn't know yet. I just finished with the funeral . . . the burial. Have to pick him up from the babysitter. Then, he's gotta know."

"Well, he might not understand right away, Mr. Galdoni. Try to be patient with him. He's very attached—to both of you."

"Sure," I curtly reply. I almost add that I'll ask for her advice when I need it, but the bottom suddenly drops out of my gathering anger. I'm feeling shaky. At the moment I need the sound of her sympathetic female voice.

She hesitates, then presses on. "Well, what about nursery? He's been making definite progress recently, with his fine motor skills in particular. You saw that flower he made. I think it's important now for him to have some . . . continuity."

"Yeah, I can see that," I say, after another drag that leaves only the filter. "The problem is getting him there in the morning. I have to pick up the cab way before your nursery even opens."

"Where? Where do you pick it up?"

"Down at the end of the Grand Concourse. South Bronx?"

"I know the place. I've been around, some. In fact I live on Van Cortland Park South. Technically the Bronx. If you take the Major Deegan down, you practically pass by my window."

"Well, then I do. I know Van Courtland Park South. It's a nice neighborhood. But anyway, I'll let you know when I figure out about the nursery. It's—"

"Mr Galdoni, what I was suggesting was that you could leave Kenny with me. I could give him breakfast and take him in to nursery with me."

A small light of comprehension goes on in my brain. "That . . . that's a definite idea."

Previously, I'd have laid odds against being able to keep Kenny in Beth Shalom Day Care Center. I'd more or less assumed that some other arrangement would have to be made, something involving Carmen, his upstairs baby sitter, or his

Grandma Clara. Neither option had seemed like a great favor to Kenny. Now, a viable alternative has dropped into my lap. But given its source, I hesitate. Finally I say, "It would have to be six o'clock, the latest."

"I'm up earlier than that. Mr. Galdoni, it would be no imposition, believe me. I'd like to do it. All you'd have to do is drop him off and be on your way. No problem," she adds, as if reading my mind. "And coffee to go if you like."

"I don't know what to say." I mean this literally, but it comes out sounding as if I'm overwhelmed with gratitude.

"Don't worry about it. It's something I want to do—for Kenny. Maybe it's unprofessional, to get involved outside of school like this, but I feel close to him. And I think he feels close to me. He's just lost his mother," she concludes, her voice giving a little.

"Yeah, I realize that," I snap, squeezing the receiver as if trying to choke off the words. "Look, I don't mean to sound nasty. Really. I appreciate the offer, and I think I'm gonna take you up on it. It's just . . . this has not been easy on me, that's all."

"I can imagine."

I take a deep breath. "Well, anyway, I do appreciate it. Why don't you give me your address, and we can start after the weekend. Also your phone number, in case anything unforeseen comes up."

Hanging up, I mix the scotch and soda (light on the soda), then attempt to drink it slowly. I've never been much good at sipping; I put the glass down half empty. Then I start working on a pile of dishes in the sink, an unusual act for me. I try to draw out the job, stalling. I'm in no hurry to go retrieve Kenny and break the news. Yet I miss the kid, miss his noise in the house, and I need the imperative of taking care of him. I'm rarely alone, awake, and sober in the apartment. As if my unimpaired senses were making up for lost time, Sharon seems to be everywhere. The kitchen appliances, even the curved faucet handles in front of me, seem to be extensions of her, as if her invisible fingerprints on them are possessed of a kind of life.

I dry the dishes and utensils and even put them away. I half expect some indication that she's pleased. On the other hand, she might wonder why she had to die before she could get a little cooperation. In any case, I derive some comfort from these small acts of keeping the faith (or adopting it), even as I've just taken the first step toward replacing Sharon in the daily scheme of things.

Actually, Nahm all but took the step for me. I've got to admit that she solved that one problem surprisingly simply and painlessly, at least on the face of it. But the next step will not be that easy for me, or for Kenny. Breaking the news to him is the kind of job that would have been Sharon's by default. She would have wanted it though, she was that kind of mother. If she were only here now . . . For the first time, I understand the meaning of "ironic." I give a laugh, which catches in my throat. After downing the remainder of the scotch and soda, I head upstairs to Carmen's.

Kenny is trailing behind her son Sergio, who answers my knock—fortunately his ears are still sharp enough to hear over the television. He fetches Carmen while Kenny affectionately tackles me around the thighs. "Daddy!" he squeals. "Go home!"

"You gonna come with me?" I rumple his hair. "Try to say 'let's' first. Like, 'let's go home.'"

"Go home."

I manage a half-smile. "Okay. Let's."

Carmen comes over and lays a hand on my arm, looking up at me with bleary, concerned eyes. "You okay?"

I step back from her. "Yeah, more or less. Thanks. You got his jacket? Diapers?"

As I say this, Kenny is already pulling toward the door against my grasp on his arm. "See Mommy!" He last saw Mommy three days ago. The kid has been practically living at Carmen's. "See Mommy!" he repeats in a louder voice, getting agitated.

Carmen produces Kenny's belongings, offering him his jacket to hold. There are tears in her eyes. I thank her for everything, including her offer to help out however she can, then exit quickly with my son.

"Listen, Ken," I say as gently as possible as he tows me down the hall toward the elevator, "Mommy's not home. I'll tell you why when we get in the house. But just don't be surprised when you don't see her."

"I want Mommy," he whines.

"Okay, look, you wanna push the button?" Reflexively, I move to lift him up, but he's already reached the elevator door button on tip toe. This is the first time he's managed to do so, I realize a few seconds after the fact. "Hey, you did it yourself. Wait'll I tell—" I cut myself short, remembering that Sharon's not going to be around to praise Kenny's little feat.

Pleased with himself, he scoots inside of the elevator when it arrives. The "4" button is an old conquest by now. He jabs it a few times with authority, in time to his chant. "See Mom-mee, see Mom-mee!"

"Kenny—" I start to get pissed, but push the feeling away. He'll believe that Sharon's not home when he sees it. Which he does when we enter the apartment. Earlier I could have sworn that Sharon was invisibly present. Now her absence is a glaring fact. As if we had already moved out, as if the furniture was gone, Kenny's cries for her seem to echo. I sit him down next to me and, placing a finger on his chin, gently turn his face in my direction.

"Kenny, Mommy's gone. She died in a car accident," I say quietly, hopelessly. There's no way he'll believe me, even if he really understood "died." I might as well tell him that he doesn't have a nose. Her recent absence notwithstanding, Mommy just *is*. It's fact number one in his little world. If he's sitting here in the apartment with me and she's not home, then she's about to be. Nothing could be more obvious.

I, at least, had the benefit of two cops, professional, recognizable bad news, intruding on my daily sleepwalk. And I'd seen Sharon's corpse, undeniably lifeless. But still, even after identifying the body, I didn't really believe that she was gone. I do now though, as if the necessity of convincing Kenny has done the trick for me. He needs to know that he's a three-year-old semi-orphan now, but that he's still in good hands. Also, he needs to know that Mommy's death is no reason not to keep on with the daily routine. Living is important. Whether or not he understands any of this, it'll be interesting for me to hear it coming out of my mouth—especially the parts about my good hands, and about living. Maybe they'll sound more believable out loud than when I've recited them in my head.

"I wan' Mom-mee," Kenny whines, as if I'm holding out on him.

"She's dead, Kenny. I'm sorry, but you're not gonna see her anymore." Fond though he is of fairy tales, I can't get myself to tell him that he will see Mommy again, in heaven. "I'll still be here, and so will Grandma Maria and Grandma Clara, and Aunt Gloria and Cousin Lila—"

"I wan' Mom-mee," he insists, but then turns around toward the back of the sofa, wedging his knees between two cushions and bouncing. Kenny is nothing if not distractible. Now is one time when I should be grateful for that. But having run over this scene in my mind several times, I feel like I have to make him understand. It's some kind of father-son venture, this sharing loss. I turn him back around toward me; he squirms and resists, whining.

"Kenny, you have to listen to me," I say, a slight edge to my voice. "Mommy is dead. That means . . . You remember the other day when you stepped on that roach bug?"

He smiles. "Squish," he says, accurately repeating the sound effects I'd supplied. Apparently the episode has stuck in his mind. Sharon would have found that encouraging.

I continue, "Right. And when you squished him, you made him dead. That means he won't walk or run or eat anymore. Well, that's the way Mommy is now. She's dead. We buried her in the ground." I choke on the words. "So you won't see her anymore. Do you understand? You'll still go to nursery—"

"Go with Mommy." He jumps down and picks up the stuffed toy raccoon that he's been carrying around and chewing on a lot lately. "Wacoon," he declares, practically shoving it in my face. Annoyed, I brush it away.

"You can't go with Mommy, Kenny. She's dead."

"Go with Mommy."

"No, you can't. I'll be taking you in the morning to—"

Before I can finish he starts crying, which makes me suspect that I've gotten through. I sit him on my lap and gently bounce him. He squirms, trying to get free. "Go with Mommy," he wails. "See Mommy."

I allow him to get down. He's not letting me play the comforting father, and physical struggles make me angry in a hurry.

There's nothing more to say. He'll grow into Sharon's absence, that's all. In fact, he's only three now; it's likely that he won't even remember her in a few years. The thought is almost more than I can deal with.

If Kenny's mind can't grasp the idea that Sharon is gone for good, there's still no doubt that he misses her. As the day goes on his agitation is clearly owing to the fact that he needs a fix of Mommy. He asks for her often. I stop responding after a while.

Periodically I try to distract him. Usually, Kenny is good at entertaining himself—or, at least, trashing the house occupies him long enough to use up the time until Sharon gets home. But now he follows me around, whining. Much as I hate hacking, it does provide one little goal to reach after another, in effect mapping out my day, creating at least the illusion of purpose. Today, Kenny and me have much more time to kill than we ordinarily would, even if Sharon was coming home. And taking him to a playground is out; it's no warmer now than it was a few hours ago at the burial.

Scotch kills time nicely. I periodically down some with soda, vowing to re-begin my reformation once things are closer to normal again. With a buzz on, I reach into my bag of tricks to amuse Kenny, letting him ride me like a horse, flipping him on the bed, opening my mouth wide and bugging out my eyes as if I've just seen a ghost. Tiring, I read to him. He sits still for this a bit longer than usual. But then he starts squirming and looking elsewhere, and I feel like a jerk trying to sound excited about Scuffy the Toy Tugboat's trip down to the sea.

Eventually, the empty condition of the soda bottle alerts me to the fact that we need to go food shopping. In another concession to Sharon, I attempt to make up a list, hunching my body to keep Kenny away from the pencil and quickly scrawling. But I don't get much past soda before my mind draws a blank. The crumpled list winds up atop the mess overflowing the garbage pail. Time to go.

I start fumbling with Kenny's hooded jacket and mittens. Finally getting him zipped into the jacket, I practically snarl at him to unclench his hand so that I stand at least a chance of inserting his thumb into the mitten. The resultant wailing further aggravates me, but I manage to calm myself. Miraculously, we're soon ready. Kenny's angelic little face peers up at me expectantly from within his fur-lined hood. "Go!" he commands. Then I suddenly realize that he hasn't been changed, I picked him up at least two hours ago, and that Carmen's not real vigilant about diapers either. I quickly decide that it'll keep. According to my anesthetized sense of smell, Kenny hasn't crapped. He confirms this with a shake of his head when I ask.

I get ninety-five percent of the garbage into the incinerator. Kenny gets us into the elevator. We return a while later, with items we've grabbed from every aisle in the supermarket. We *must* have covered our needs, smothered them. With Flannery the doorman's help (he'd insisted, claiming to expect no tip), I deposit seven bags of groceries in the kitchen. Flannery, smirking, then offers *me* a tip. "The boy's diaper needs changing. Can't you smell it?" As he leaves, I rip open a package of Huggies and peel off Kenny's pants, almost gagging as I remove his diaper.

"Dammit Kenny, when are you gonna start telling me when you crap?" I demand. "Better yet, when are you gonna learn to use the potty?"

His face puckers. "Wan' Mom-mee!" he bawls, invoking the holy name. I swallow a curse, then lay him down atop paper towels on the living room rug and silently change him, trying to breathe as little as possible. When I finish, I say, "Look Kenny, tomorrow we'll go visit Aunt Gloria and Cousin Lila. Okay?"

This seems to please him. Gloria invited us near the end of the funeral. I'd told her, at the time, that I wanted some time alone with Kenny, and that I'd get back to her. Now, the prospect of a weekend alone with Kenny brings up the possibility of an alcoholic binge. For his sake and mine I dial Gloria, who I figure must have made it back up to Fishkill by now. She has, and the invitation still stands.

* * *

Fishkill, New York is about an hour and a half up the Taconic State Parkway. The Taconic is a mountain road masquerading as a highway, not really my cup of tea. I'd be more comfortable tearing down Second Avenue, dodging other yellow cabs driven by kamikazes like myself. This would be the case even if the Taconic was not bordered by patches of ice. I'm taking it slow. Kenny is asleep on the seat next to me, hanging limply against the shoulder harness. No car seat, as usual. I never retrieved his from Sharon's Volkswagen. I couldn't bring myself to go look at the car.

At the moment, in the warmth of my Plymouth Valiant, driving into a landscape of bare, snow-tipped trees, I'm feeling strangely good. Traveling does that to me sometimes. It's like stepping outside of things without the aid of booze. It provides a little space, a breather between where I've been and where I'm going. My mood is broken periodically by pangs over Sharon, but they pass. In fact, I wouldn't mind if the trip was longer, particularly since Kenny will awake, like clockwork, when the car is stopped.

I pull into Gloria's semi-shoveled driveway and turn off the engine. This is like ringing an alarm for Kenny, who stirs immediately. Rubbing the slits of his eyes, he whines for a hug to ease him into waking state. "Mom-mee." He repeats this a few times, building up to a fit that I manage to delay by announcing, "We're here at Aunt Gloria's, and Cousin Lila is here too!"

As if on cue, Lila comes bouncing down the driveway, obviously unconcerned with the icy patches of snow, although she almost slips on one. She presses her nose against Kenny's window. Even through the frosting glass, her squashed nose and gap-toothed grin are enough to break Kenny up, his squealing laughter interspersed with whimpers.

I step out of the car and greet Lila, peering up at the house and hoping for a glimpse of her mother. Gloria's house is not a mansion, but neither is it what you'd expect of a single mother who supposedly never cared much about money. It has two white columns in front, supporting a balcony that now holds a rocking chair, bicycle, and other items less recognizable under a blanket of snow. A little column of smoke drifts up from the brick chimney, set to one side of a snow-covered roof that will definitely avalanche when the weather gets warmer.

Gloria can afford this house with the help of her ex-husband, Lila's father. He was some guru's right hand man when he married Gloria, a lesser disciple. Shortly after they were divorced, he fell out with the guru too, and back into the real world. He landed nicely and became a big success in the import-export business by using contacts he'd made in Turkey as a drug dealer (his pre-Swami occupation). To his credit, I guess, he has looked after Gloria and Lila financially. Still, Gloria is not about to live off of him. Soon after the divorce, in a concession to the financial facts of life, she took a six-month course in computer programming. Her timing was good, the need for programmers was exploding.

She works now for the giant IBM plant in Fishkill proper, but lives here in what can still be considered the country. As she answers Lila's pounding on the front door I notice she still wears woolen ponchos and such, a weekend hippie. Seeing the three of us, she gives a sweet smile, which is slightly less gap-toothed than Lila's. I send back a rare smile of my own, under the delusion that hers was meant mainly for me. The truth becomes obvious when she gives Kenny a big hug and kiss, and me a quick peck on the cheek.

Kenny follows Lila down to the basement playroom, negotiating the carpeted stairs on his behind. I trail Gloria into the kitchen, where she starts preparing lunch. "The show must go on," she says, as she tears open a package of Seven Grain bread.

Gloria has never been one for beating around the bush, for small talk, for asking how the trip was. It takes me a few seconds to figure out what she means, then I reply, "Yeah. For kids, it never stops."

"That is the truth." She gives a soft, knowing laugh, which pleases me a ridiculous amount.

"Well . . . still, it's been good to have Kenny around. I know it might surprise you to hear me say that."

"It does, a little. But I know what you mean. It's the same thing with Lila. They live in the here and now. It sort of forces you to do the same thing." She rapidly spreads out several slices of bread, as if dealing cards. "Even so, I miss her, Paul. Not that we saw each other all that much, especially after I moved up here. But knowing she was there—" Gloria's green eyes, moist and clear, fix on me. "Of course, I could tell at the funeral that it hasn't been easy on you either. You're the one whose life'll be affected the most, you and Kenny. How're you holding up?"

Given the concern on Gloria's face, I'm suddenly glad that Sharon is the topic of conversation. This is one of the few times that Gloria's ever acted as if our connection was anything other than the result of bad luck. "Like I said before, I'm doin' okay, sort of," I reply, sincere yet playing it for what it's worth. "I mean, it's only been a few days. The feeling of her is so strong sometimes."

"It is. Especially with you and Kenny here. It's like, she must be in the bathroom, or downstairs with the kids, or something. Speaking of which . . . Kenny's doing okay?"

"More or less. He's fussier than usual, I'm sure 'cause his Mama's not around. I've tried to explain to him what happened, but he doesn't really understand."

"That's probably a blessing," she says, doing a fast re-count of the bread slices. "I mean, Lila does understand that Sharon's gone. But that's it."

"Oh . . . there's something more?"

Gloria opens the refrigerator door, as if unwilling to deal with my reflexive sarcasm, then closes it and turns to me. "You know, this has been sort of an acid test for all of that Eastern wisdom I've subscribed to over the past what—ten years? Well yeah, I still believe in reincarnation, the evolution of the soul, all that wonderful stuff. More than ever."

"Glad to hear it," I reply, swallowing. "Seriously. I could sort of tell when you spoke at the funeral. I just . . . maybe we oughta change the subject. Okay?"

"Sure." She works up a small smile. "Let's see . . . what would you like for lunch?" She reopens the refrigerator and takes out a few cellophane packages, jars of mustard, mayonnaise, and pickles. "Got some boiled ham for you and Kenny."

"Thanks. We could have gone vegetarian for a day, though. I mean, Kenny'll eat anything anyway." I cover my face with my palm. "Look, I didn't mean—"

She laughs. "Don't worry about it, I know what you meant. I've seen him in action. But you must both be hungry. Ham and cheese okay for you?"

"Great. With plenty of mustard."

"Beer?"

"You got some of that, too?" I reply, surprised and pleased. "Ordinarily I don't touch the stuff, but since you went to the trouble—"

"A couple of cans. You might wind up wanting something hot to drink after you've been sitting here long enough. Why don't you go get the kids and have them wash up."

I'm happy to oblige her. I pass through the living room, with its crackling fireplace, and find the narrow stairs leading down to the basement. Maybe it's the contrast with the shot of warmth I felt in the living room, or just Gloria's reference to the temperature in her house, but on the stairs down the cold becomes very noticeable, stinging. The basement itself is freezing, but Kenny and Lila don't seem to notice this, or me. Interpreting his directions, she's drawing large crayon figures standing around a house that's supposed to be hers: the columns in front are a giveaway. The figures are labeled in Lila's passable printing. There's one each of "Kenny," "Lila," "Daddy," and "Aunt Gloria." Then, standing in front of the house, there are several figures labeled "Mommy," which Lila has managed to make look reasonably alike. All have big pink smiles, outstretched stick arms, lots of stringy brown hair.

"See, Daddy!" declares Kenny as soon as he catches sight of me. He points at the huge piece of paper.

"Very nice." I try to sound excited. The resultant falsetto pitch is starting to sound less ridiculous to me.

"Mommies. Lotsa Mommies."

"I see," I reply, nodding, glancing at Lila, who smiles almost apologetically. "I'm sure she would like that."

"Show Mommy."

"I can't, Kenny. Look, you wanna eat? Aunt Gloria's making lunch."

At this, to the relief of Lila and myself, Kenny's made-to-order artwork is forgotten. It remains on the linoleum. Lila shows us into the closet-like basement bathroom where, with her help, Kenny splashes some water on his hands, grips the towel for an instant with both hands, then leads the way back up the basement stairs. Clearly he feels at home, despite the fact that he's only been here a few times. Back in the spacious living room, he pauses at the fireplace, gazing intently at the glowing embers. I'm not sure that he's ever seen an open fire before. Lila and I each place an arm between him and the free-standing metal screen in front of the fireplace.

"That's hot, Kenny," she says in her best imitation of a motherly voice.

I move the screen aside and pick up a stick from the pile of wood nearby, telling Kenny to throw it into the fire. He manages to do this, despite being more tightly restrained by Lila. The stick immediately bursts into flames on the red-hot coals. Kenny watches in fascination until the stick is itself reduced to embers. "All gone," he announces. "Bye-bye."

"Did you make a fire, Kenny?" asks Gloria, who has come in on the tail end of the proceedings. She repositions the screen in front of the fireplace.

"Hot," he replies. He reaches for another stick.

"Lunchtime, Ken." He ignores Gloria, instead grasping the new stick, which is considerably larger than the first, and trying to throw it over the screen and into the fire. It bounces off of the fireplace's brick outer wall and lands short of the fire, propped up against the inside of the screen. Before he can attempt to retrieve the stick, I pick him up and begin hauling him toward the kitchen. He starts bawling.

Gloria croons, "Don't you want to eat?" This doesn't soothe him much.

I flash her a smile. "Think we have a pyromaniac on our hands."

"Looks like it. Maybe you can toast a marshmallow later, Ken." Receiving no response (even if Kenny was willing and able to compromise, he has no idea what a marshmallow is), Gloria turns and leads the way back into the kitchen. Kenny is frantic. I cart him along behind Gloria, while trying to explain "pyromaniac" to the inquisitive Lila.

Once Kenny, cajoled by Lila, finally settles down—about the time my patience is wearing thin—lunch proceeds smoothly. In fact it turns out to be a barrel of laughs for the kids. Lila is greatly amused by Kenny's efforts to stuff fistfuls of ham, cheese, and bread into his already-full mouth. It used to be that whatever entered Kenny's mouth quickly came back out, flowing past his chin and onto his bib as if he had an invisible digestive tract running down the front of his body. These days the food stays between his throat and his teeth for great lengths of time. Some gets swallowed, some splats back down onto his plate as Lila makes him giggle. The age difference between the two of them seems to have disappeared. If Kenny manages to say "foo-foo" through the mush in his mouth, Lila gets hysterical with laughter, causing Kenny to laugh as best he can, on and on. Gloria seems content to let the kids have their fun. In fact she encourages it. And I'm content, at first, to sip Budweiser and watch her enjoying their antics, hear her soft voice set an occasional limit. Once or twice a foolish grin crosses my face. I feel like part of one of those bullshit commercials showing a red-blooded American family enjoying the product and having a great time together. Love to spare. I can remember Sharon watching such commercials and commenting to me, almost bitterly, "Maybe that's the problem—we don't go to McDonald's often enough." The memory causes a shot of pain and guilt inside of me. I growl at Kenny to stop yanking on one of the tassels of Gloria's maroon and white poncho. She has been gently restraining him, one hand on his wrist. "It's okay," she assures me. Kenny, whose fingers have not left the white tassel he's been trying to remove, attempts one more defiant tug, then returns to the mess on his plate. I sit back and drain my glass of beer, deriving a slight but welcome buzz.

After lunch, Gloria shoves the dishes into her washer and suggests a walk in the woods. She asks Lila to help Kenny get on his jacket and boots.

"Gloria," I say, "Isn't it a mite cold to be taking a hike?"

"Once we start walking, our bodies will warm up," she replies. "There's this trail that leads up to an overlook. It's really beautiful. Besides, think how warm it'll feel in here when we get back. We can sit in front of the fireplace. Kenny'll like that."

"Hot," he says, bouncing with excitement, frustrating Lila's attempts to dress him.

I shrug, cold already but not wanting to argue with Gloria, not quite willing to ask her if she's going to carry Kenny when he doesn't feel like walking anymore. "Okay. But Kenny needs his diaper changed," I say finally, trying to scrape together a little authority.

"Oh right, he still wears them. Let me do it, Paul. See if I still remember how."

"Be my guest." I get the diaper bag from the living room and toss it to her.

She still remembers how. In fact, she enjoys it so much that she doesn't stop until Kenny's new diaper has been buried under several layers of clothing. A short time later, the four of us are trekking uphill through the woods, maybe doubling the foot and paw prints on the snow-covered trail. Actually, all four of us are walking only about half the time; the other half I'm pulling Kenny on Lila's wooden "Flyer" sled. This had apparently been part of Gloria's thinking when she'd suggested the walk. When Kenny gets bored with riding, he gets up and pulls the empty sled himself, or walks holding Lila's hand. Eventually he decides to have me tow him again. But right now I don't at all mind playing the daddy who labors in service of his son. I even override Gloria's protests when Lila adds her weight to the sled. Steam pouring from my mouth, I chug upward.

One benefit of this is that, aside from my toes, which are poorly protected, I'm not the least bit cold. Gloria was right about that. When the kids vacate the sled, to chase each other with snow, walk in my large footprints or slide down snow-covered boulders, the opportunity to catch my breath brings with it a definite calmness. I've never been much of a nature boy (my mother withdrew me from the Boy Scouts when she discovered that I'd been playing hooky regularly), but I've got to admit now that I'm enjoying the scenery. As we climb, the trees get thinner, beginning to look like Lila's stick figures. More of the area surrounding Fishkill becomes visible. We're looking down on rolling hills, mounds of pure white, sprinkled with toy houses that give off wisps of smoke. The kid's voices and laughter echo in the quietness around us.

Gloria seems right at home with the silence. As Kenny and Lila, tiring, flop onto the sled for the duration of the climb, Gloria seems to settle into herself. With most women I've ever known, including Sharon, I would have considered that a blessing. But after enough time listening to the kids, and to my own heavy breathing, I start feeling a need for Gloria's voice, a need to remind her that I'm here.

I tell her about the weekdays arrangement I've made with Ms. Nahm, and about the problem with Saturdays, which I've been working more often than not. "I'll probably have to keep on doing that, too," I say, pausing to gulp air. "It depends on how much money comes down from . . . from Sharon's life insurance policy. And if I gotta work Saturdays, then who's gonna take care of Kenny? I mean, he's got a babysitter in our building. She'd probably do it, although I don't like thinking about Kenny hanging around in that musty apartment all day long. It's—"

"What about my mother?" says Gloria. "She'd do it for free. Couldn't you drop him over to her on your way to work?"

"It's a little out of the way, but yeah, I suppose I could," I reply, switching hands on the sled's rope, which is digging right through my leather gloves into my fingers.

"I'm sure she'd like that. With Sharon working and busy on weekends, she felt—" Gloria shudders slightly. "Paul, I was going to talk to you about this, sooner or later. Sharon was my mother's baby. Now she feels like she has nobody, no friends to speak of. That may be of her own doing, but still . . . She loves Kenny. She'll want to see him. If she could on Saturdays, for the whole day, I'm sure she'd love it."

"Yeah, about the only thing she said to me on the way to the funeral was how much she wanted to see Kenny. That she had a right to. And I guess she does. I just—"

Gloria stops walking and turns to face me. With the redness in her cheeks that somehow makes her face look smaller, a woolen hat covering her blondish hair, and her eyes studying me as she measures her words, I could swear I'm looking at Sharon; the green irises seem strangely out of place. "Look Paul, I know my mother can be hard to take."

Stunned by the resemblance, and by the familiarity of her words, it takes me a few seconds to respond. "Yeah? You mean it's not only me?"

Gloria sighs. "Nope. It does take two to tango. And I've tangoed with her myself, plenty. That's why I'm not still down there. By rights I should be, we just buried Sharon yesterday. But when we took my mother home afterward, it was the same old stuff, with variations: she tells me it takes Sharon dying for me to come visit her. Says that I probably would have been happy if it had happened to her instead of Sharon. Asks what would my father think of me? Lovely stuff. She's lonely and bereaved, but still it's not easy to deal with."

"Daddy go!" demands Kenny from the other end of the rope. We start slogging through the snow again.

"She talked like that in front of Lila?"

"Uh-uh. That she wouldn't do. Lila was watching the tube, we were in the kitchen. She almost never goes off in front of the kids. That's to her credit, I guess, although it also shows that she knows exactly what she's doing. Still, she's sweet to the kids, and she's their grandmother. I know Lila likes seeing her. So does Kenny, from what I've heard."

I shrug. She takes this, correctly, as grudging agreement. Kenny does in fact look forward to seeing "Nanny." He used to babble about it constantly whenever Sharon told him that they were going over. Gloria continues, "You know, like this genius I work for at IBM says, you've got to look at the big picture. That's one of the reasons I like walking up here, it helps me do that. She's family, Paul. Mine, Kenny's, and even yours, sort of. There's a reason for that."

I gaze at her blankly for a few moments. "Oh . . . you mean a cosmic reason, or something like that."

"Yeah, something like that. Even if you don't believe in past lives, and karma from them, we've all got things to work out with each other. You can tell that just from looking at the present."

"Maybe. You can try to work things out, or you can just absent yourself. Which is what I've always done with your mother. Maybe that'll have to change a little now," I say, paying lip service to the idea. I reach into my jacket pocket for a cigarette, but then stifle the urge. Gloria would not be charmed. Besides, it's easy to imagine this air cleaning my lungs. Each breath seems to follow a cool, clear path down to the bottom of my heaving chest.

We round a bend and arrive at the overlook. Lila points out to Kenny that we can see all the way to the Hudson River. Even here upstate, the river's too polluted to freeze. I can just make out the sunlight shimmering on the water.

Kenny joins Lila in bouncing echoes off of the hills across

from us. His name and various other sounds, including the inevitable "Mom-mee!", reverberate and die in the valley. Even I cast a few loud hellos out into the air, my baritone echoes sounding enormous after Kenny and Lila's tinny ones.

"Wonder if Sharon can hear us," I say to Gloria, only half joking.

"It's entirely possible."

"I don't know about 'entirely.' But if you wanna believe in life after death, and God and all that—or at least believe that life isn't a bad joke—this is a good place to do it." I indicate the view in front of us with a small sweep of my hand. "Maybe I shoulda brought a camera, so I could stick a few pictures up in my cab. Maybe next time I'm about to lose my temper with Kenny, I'll whisper, 'Fishkill' to myself. It might help. I'm probably gonna need all the help I can get."

"You might." Gloria pauses long enough to irk me some.

"Thanks."

She studies me for a few moments. "Paul, I was just agreeing with you, that's all. Raising a kid by yourself is not easy for anyone. I can tell you that first hand. And I'd guess it's harder for a man, whatever your intentions might be. My ex-husband, he thought that raising a family would help him grow spiritually. Maybe it can, if you stick it out. But when he saw what was really involved, day to day—"

"Hey, you think I don't know? You think I haven't been involved with Kenny?"

"I didn't say that. But I've never gotten the impression, from Sharon or you, that you enjoyed it much."

I suck in some cold air, letting it out slowly as if it was smoke, at the same time watching my supposedly insulated shoe shuffle some snow around. My toes are close to numb. "Well, you got that right," I say finally. "Ninety-five percent right, at least. But now, I'm gonna try my best. Stay sober, try to make the kid feel good about himself. It's the least I can do for Sharon after being such a bastard most of the time." Turning away from Gloria, I take another deep breath and shut my eyes tightly. She indicates no disagreement, makes no move to comfort me, which I appreciate in a weird sort of way. "It's the least I can do for him, too," I say, inclining my head in Kenny's direction and shivering slightly.

With his small hands, Kenny is having no luck trying to make snowballs. A chip off the old block, he flings down a fistful of powder, giving a cry of frustration. Then he begins poaching on the small pile of snowballs that Lila has already amassed. She doesn't protest as he takes one and, with an effort that is hampered by the bundle of clothing he's in, manages to throw the snowball one or two feet. Smiling with satisfaction, he reaches down for another of Lila's snowballs.

Gloria is obviously pleased and amused by this little performance. I say, "He can be a cute little rascal, sometimes."

"He can," she replies, nodding. "You know, he really seems to be doing okay, so far. He calls for her, but it's almost like it's a game of hide-and-seek or something. If anything, he's seemed happy most of the day."

"Sure, with Lila here. And with you." My voice drops slightly on "you," the word wafting over to Gloria like a mating call wrapped up in a little cloud of steam.

"Lila loves him. So do I. I'm sure he feels that," she replies, suddenly misty. "Feel free to bring him up whenever you like. You could even leave him here for a while, if you want some time off. I know it's a long drive, but—"

"Thanks for the offer. It's not that long. And I wouldn't mind hanging out myself, to tell you the truth." My eyes hold Gloria's briefly, then she looks away.

"Well, I guess you're welcome too."

"Am I?"

"Sure, as Kenny's father, Sharon's husband. But if you're thinking about anything else . . . Look, I'm sorry. I'm just starting to get edgy for some reason. Maybe I misread you."

I shiver again. The cold, having numbed my toes, seems to be traveling upward. "Nope, you read me right," I reply. "I just thought I'd put it out there, for what it's worth. I needed to, okay? Just don't think, like, I'm tryna put the make on you or whatever. It's not that cheap." All of this comes out unplanned, which, given my sober condition, is not much like me. "I probably shoulda kept my mouth shut," I add, speaking to the top of Gloria's puffy maroon hat. Her face is tilted down and away from me.

"That's okay," she says softly. "You've just lost your wife. It hurts. I'm her sister. We look and probably even sound alike. I'm a reasonable facsimile."

"Don't sell yourself short. It's not just today—" I hesitate, realizing that my foot is already half way into my mouth. Too far to stop and have it make a difference. "It's not like it just started," I say, gazing out over the valley, trying to imagine myself gliding away. "I probably wouldn't have said anything anyway. But seeing how much Kenny likes it up here, and seeing as how we probably wouldn't get up here much in the normal course of events—"

"Not unless there was a little something in it for you."

"Gloria—"

"You know, what bothers me is not even that only a few days after Sharon's death, you tell me that you've had your eye on me," she says with quiet disdain. "It's not that big a surprise, and what's true is true. But you use Kenny as an excuse to tell me that now? It's for him?"

"Hey, gimme a break, alright?" My voice has a trembling edge to it. I resist the urge to tell her that she's got a sarcastic tongue which seems to run in her family. "I don't need to hide behind Kenny or anyone else. And if I was the kind of selfish bastard you seem to think I am, I'd just put the kid up for adoption. I would have split from him and Sharon long ago."

"Well at least you don't have to put up with Sharon anymore," says Gloria, twisting the knife. Her moist green eyes fix on me. "Paul, if I'm doing you an injustice—and I seriously doubt that I am—but if so, it's probably because you've laid plenty of injustices on my sister. This one is a little hard for me to deal with. You say it's for Kenny? While Sharon was alive, I understand you stepped out on her now and then. Was that for Kenny too?"

"Shit!" I growl, spinning away from her, spraying snow. "Kenny! C'mon, we're goin' home!" From what I can tell, he's been "helping" Lila put together more snowballs to restock the pile he's just wasted. He gives me a look of incomprehension which is accentuated by the fluid running from his nose. The look infuriates me. I stomp over and grab him by the wrist. "Let's go."

I move him a yard or so; his entrenched boots function as runners. Then he starts wailing. Echoes mix with fresh cries to create a torture chamber for my ears. "No home!" he bawls. I start pulling again, my arm extended. Gloria steps between us, her back to Kenny, her side pressed against his arm and my fingers.

"Paul!" she says in a fierce whisper, her face no more than a foot from mine. "Stop it! If you give a damn about the kid, just *stop*."

I stare at her dumbstruck, as if she's just slapped me, then look away and nod slowly. Almost to myself, I say, "Yeah. Yeah, okay." My voice is low and harsh, all I can manage as the rage starts to die away. I let go of Kenny and glance over at Lila, who quickly averts her eyes. "Go ahead, Ken," I say, my breathing starting to settle, the vapor dispersing. "It's okay. Make some snowballs for Lila." I make one myself, hand it to my whimpering son, and give him a little shove in Lila's direction.

- 7 -
Sharon

THE BEING of Light re-emerged, at the end of my life review, much as the whiteness of a screen becomes visible again when the film projected on it has run out. His invisible presence throughout the review had been responsible for the clarity of awareness which I'd experienced, regardless of the particular drama I was reliving. That clarity remained afterward, all but indistinguishable from the Being himself, who shone with a brilliance that seemed a celebration, a culmination of the review. I felt like I'd been through a graduation of sorts, as if I'd died again and been once more "resurrected." The distinction between life and death seemed practically nonexistent. It was out of a blissful, idle curiosity that I'd asked the Being how long I'd been dead. He'd reiterated that I was not in fact dead, but rather living without a physical body. He trusted that I would find the experience enjoyable.

It's only now, sensing the Being's imminent departure, that I become acutely concerned with time again. I'm both wondering what comes next and wishing I could forestall his departure.

He assures me that I'm not being deserted, that I'll receive guidance in the journey I'm about to undertake—toward greater purity and knowledge. He doesn't use any spoken words. But through the juxtaposition of the Being's radiant life with what my life had been, I understand that I have a distance to travel. I also no longer desire to return to earth or to what I left behind there. I'm even looking forward to the trip ahead, whatever it involves. But I'd give anything to be able to take Kenny with me, or at least to know that we'll someday be together again. When I ask the Being about this, he answers that I will indeed be with my son again, eventually.

A thrill of excitement and anxiety runs through the invisible body-in-principle I now occupy. "After he dies," I say. It's more a statement than a question. "But . . . how will I find him? Will I know how, and where to—"

"Don't worry," says the Being gently. I somehow know this is his final benediction to me, and he couldn't have picked one more apropos. Nor could anyone have more of a right to deliver it. His nature, his very existence is the strongest argument I've ever encountered against worrying, about anything. But old habits die hard. And my love for Kenny never will.

In the next instant the Being disappears, or rather his all-encompassing light diffuses, fading into an environment which seems to glow faintly throughout. I find myself standing in a meadow of silky grass, which ripples outward as far as I can see. To one side of me, a forest of trees, their leaves golden and translucent, slopes up from the meadow. To the other is a swift stream, which appears to flow toward me from the horizon. It's water is a sparkling combination of colors, reflecting the grass and blue sky at its origin.

The beauty of this panorama is so stunning that it takes me a while to notice a figure walking toward me across the meadow. It's a man who looks to be close to my age. Impossibly, yet undeniably—I can't be mistaken about this, having just been through the life review—his bouncing gait and curly black hair once belonged to my father. Coming closer, he grins at me, his black mustache spreading over his handsome face, dark eyes lighting up with joy. He could have just stepped off of his newspaper truck twenty years ago, he looks so young.

I'm speechless with happiness, not only at seeing him, but at the fact that he obviously sees me. In the next instant I can see myself, through his eyes. Without feeling it, I've somehow "regrown" a body. It almost exactly resembles the body I had right before the crash on the Major Deegan. The only difference is that this one is slightly translucent and seems all but weightless. I hold my hands in front of my face. There is no wedding ring, no nail polish, but they're definitely mine. I know my hands when I see them. Seeing through them, though, is a first. I can make out my father beaming at me. It's as if he is standing in a flesh-colored fog. Those parts of him visible through the spaces between my fingers, including his smile, seem brighter by contrast. I drop my hands and survey my arms, legs, and clothing, then look again at the figure now standing unobscured and luminous in front of me. My father.

"Daddy?" This single sound somehow seems a composite of every utterance I've made since infanthood. "Daddy!"

"Sharon, my little one." His eyes glisten. We embrace, and I can feel the breeze that fans the meadow move through both of us at once, as if by joining our negligible masses together we've become material enough to provide some token wind resistance. My first "tactile" sensation since dying, this feeling is of a delicacy which has to be beyond the experiential capabilities of flesh and bone.

Tears of joy run in feathery rivulets down my face. Negligible though my father and I might be individually or collectively, our joint consciousness is of a happiness without limits. Embracing becomes superfluous. So does speech. Together or standing apart, our access to one another's thoughts and feelings is complete and spontaneous.

As I'm unable to formulate a question out of the several that I need to ask, my father mentally says, "Sharon, sweetie, I didn't think you'd be the first of our family to join me. What happened to you?"

"I was in a car crash. I must've died," I reply bemusedly, feeling as if I'm talking about someone else. "I know that you died, almost ten years ago. And here we are, together in . . . wherever. It looks like some meadow out of a dream. And you,

Daddy, it's just so good to see you. Especially looking young and healthy again, after what you went through in that hospital. Makes me feel like a kid again myself."

"You can take on whatever appearance you want here." My father says this quite matter-of-factly. Far more amazing to him is the length of time he's been "dead". "It's really been ten years? I'd say time flies, but here it doesn't even get off the ground. I was concerned with it when I first got here, you know, out of habit. But it just started to seem unreal pretty quickly. You'll see what I mean. So, tell me about your mother and Gloria. How are they?"

I feel a pinch of jealousy at my father's immediate concern for them, Gloria in particular. This is an old habit of *mine*. My father, demonstrating that he has not changed that much himself, is about to amend his words and say that I should first tell him about myself and the life I left behind. Before he can, though, I comply with his original request, determined to act like a big girl for once. "Well mother, she . . . Since it doesn't seem possible for me to tell you little white lies anyway, she took it hard when you died. I mean, we all did, but she was almost incapacitated. She finally got herself together enough to start working. That helped. But she was bitter, Daddy. She felt like your dying young was sort of the final evidence that she'd been put on earth to suffer."

It dawns on me that in life I'd never have spoken to my father about my mother with anything approaching this kind of frankness. Now that taboo is not even an issue. Everything I know about my mother becomes my father's knowledge, too. There's one piece of information that neither of us is privy to, however. Were it necessary to talk, I'd have a difficult time saying it: "God, I wonder how she'll take my death. I can hardly bear to think about it, Daddy."

He sighs and slowly shakes his head. This motion, superimposed on that of the waving meadow grass I can make out through his face, makes the grass look as if it's fluctuating wildly, as if hit by a sudden, swirling wind. "I'm sure it won't be easy for her," he says. "At least with me she had some advance notice, although from what you say it doesn't seem to have made much difference. I tried to tell her not to worry about me, that I was going to a better place—"

"What? Daddy, neither one of you ever believed that. You were an atheist, and proud of it," I declare, registering mild distress despite my declining opinion of atheism. I wouldn't have imagined my father to be one of those people who suddenly gets religion on his deathbed. Of course, *I* might have been one, if given the chance.

He replies, "I don't know about proud of it. Honest, maybe. But I've always been a flexible man, too, Sharon." A hint of a grin plays around his mouth. "Especially after getting a first-hand taste. I came here, before I left my body for good. It just happened: suddenly, I found myself floating up near the ceiling of my hospital room, looking down on my body in bed, and on your mother. She was asleep in an armchair next to my bed. Her head and arm were propped up against those upraised sidebars the bed had. It was one of my clearest images of her after I died—her hair bunched up in the crook of her elbow, gray roots showing in her part. Dear woman, she was in that room almost as much as I was. I worried about you, but she said you were getting old enough to take care of yourself. And Gloria already was, in her way."

"I remember."

My father ignores my brusqueness. "Anyway, I don't know what was more astounding, the fact that I was floating up there, or how wasted away my own body looked. I tried to wake your mother, tried to talk to her and to the nurse in the room. But it was impossible."

"God, I went through the same thing, after I crashed on the Major Deegan Expressway. People came running, trying to help. One of them pronounced me dead. I tried to argue with him about that. It's sort of like one of those nightmares when you're trying to cry out and can't. Worse, even. You can hear yourself, but no one else can."

"Sort of what it's like being a parent." As ever, he enjoys his own joke, and despite the joke's poignancy for me, I'm struck by a wave of giddiness. "Myself," he continues, alluding to his pre-death, "I was just so grateful to be awake, with a capital 'A,' and yet free of pain. Nothing could have really bothered me. Stomach cancer is no fun, take my word. Next thing I knew, I was going through this tunnel. I could see a beautiful light at the end. When I got there, I saw my own mother, your grandmother, who died before you were born. She told me she'd been waiting for me."

"She'd known you were dying." He nods. "Does that mean you can somehow see Earth from here, or know what's going on there?"

"No dear," he replies, dashing my hopes. "Some people do remain attached there for a while after they die, before finally letting go. But when you're here, and someone you love on Earth is approaching death, drawing nearer to where you are, you can feel it in your own consciousness. The link to that person is already there. It's always there, and it gets re-awakened somehow. You just *know.* With you, since you died suddenly, it took a little while for me to realize it. I came as soon as I knew."

"I was well taken care of in the interim."

"You must have deserved it, Sharon. And there went *your* Atheism," he adds dryly. "Meeting Hashem directly is very convincing. Actually you met His angel. A chip off the old block."

"Hashem?"

"Hebrew for God, dear."

"So the Being of Light is an angel of God—or Hashem."

"Being of Light? That's descriptive. Yes, an angel of God, or Hashem, or whatever you want to call Him or Her. It doesn't really matter. Not that millions of people haven't been killed over the issue, but—" He gives a philosophical shrug. "Anyway, when I saw my mother, the first time, there was no way I wanted to return to Earth. But wonderful as it was, she told me that my time had not come yet. Next thing I knew, I was back inside of my body, back in the hospital.

"It was sort of like being let out of solitary confinement and given a week on the beach, only to be put back into solitary again, complete with torture racks. But some of the . . . *exhilaration* still remained. I knew without a doubt that I hadn't been dreaming. I woke your mother up. I wanted to tell her about it before my energy ebbed. That was a mistake. She'd never accepted the fact that I was dying, and I'd more or less gone along with her assurances that I would get better. It was the easiest thing to do, I guess. So she didn't want to suddenly hear that I now knew what death was like, that it was much better than mere oblivion. She didn't want to hear about being left alone. I suppose I didn't really understand until that moment how much she needed me."

My father pauses. Wiping at the mist that has settled on my eyes, I notice that the lustre of his body has dulled, literally reflecting the change in his mood and mine. This reminds me of a conversation I once had with Gloria—about auras, the subtle light energy that people supposedly give off, sort of spiritual and emotional ID cards to the few individuals on Earth who can see and read them. I'd scoffed at the idea, naturally. But here it would be hard to. The fields of light around my father and myself, while not approaching the brilliance of the Being, are still plainly visible.

"Well, she always came off as a tough old buzzard," I say, dabbing at my eyes once more.

"True. But she suffered a lot, your mother. Her family was poor, her father was a religious nut who treated her like dirt. But even if she was overbearing herself, it was out of devotion. She wanted the best for you and Gloria."

"Yeah, she said it often enough."

"That doesn't make it less true. She had to live under all those constraints when she was young. She hated it, but that was all she knew. That was where she got her training for raising kids. She expected unquestioning obedience, expected her values to be yours. I tried to moderate that some—"

"You were caught in the middle, especially between her and Gloria."

"Smack dab." My father smiles ruefully. "Of course, even parents who were more liberal-minded than your mother—including Yours Truly—had a hard time accepting drugs, free love, and what-have-you."

"She had a hard time accepting my going out on dates at age seventeen, even with straight-laced young men."

"Sharon, unhappy people find things to be unhappy about, that's all. Like you say, she saw life mainly as misery, with death as the topper. And she took a certain pleasure, if you can call it that, in proving herself right. So you can imagine her reaction when I told her that the old pie-in-the-sky religious nonsense was actually true, that there's an afterlife which is quite lovely. It must have sounded as if I was looking forward to cashing in my chips. Well, I was."

"So she felt sort of betrayed."

"To put it mildly. She told me that it was a sin to want to die—I still can't believe she used the word 'sin'—and that I would be the death of *her*. I finally recanted. I pretended to agree that it must have been some kind of dream, something maybe brought on by all the drugs they were pouring into me. I've since discovered that a lot of people have had those kind of experiences before dying for good. Ah, Clara," my father sighs, his moist brown eyes gazing through me, as if I'd reacquired invisibility. "And now she's lost you. Or she believes she has," he says to me finally. "I hope she gets here soon, Sharon. I may not be the one to judge this, but she's suffered enough for one lifetime."

I half-heartedly concur, which my father picks up. He adds, "The one thing you should understand about your mother is that she had a lot of love to give. She gave it to me, despite the fact that I wasn't religious enough or rich enough for her father. That was not an easy thing to do in those days. She never expected me to wine and dine her; the fact that I could make her laugh, that I treated her like an equal, was more than enough for her. She only needed to have her love returned. Believe me, that was easy to do. She was like a beautiful, wounded bird. But having children, having to raise them, was difficult for her. Understand, I'm not blaming Gloria or you for anything. Most marriages change a lot when the kids arrive. It's not surprising. You learn up here that children are born with their own debts to pay, in terms of the experiences they'll have to go through."

"And will put their parents through, I suppose."

"Right. It's a cooperative effort," says my father, amusing himself again. "Gloria, was willful, rebellious—"

"But she changed a lot after you died."

Surprised and pleased by my defense of Gloria, he does a small double-take, telepathic pantomime. "Well, your mother didn't want it to take that long," he continues. "And you—you were her baby, Sharon. She needed you to be, even after you were too old to play the part. And if she got a little domineering, well, maybe a strong hand was something you and Gloria needed. When Gloria started going off the deep end, I was the one who vacillated. I made it easy for her to have it both ways, to degenerate with Daddy's well-meaning support, financial and otherwise. I just wound up feeling like a fool, utterly useless, especially after I lost my job. I was the one who fell apart. Not your mother."

"Fell apart? You got cancer."

"And what do you think cancer is? The body devours itself. I just self-destructed, that's all. Of course, I didn't really understand that until I was out of my body for good. When I died, it was like I'd shed the grief along with my body. The mind and the body are really the same thing, dear. Here, you can tell that just by looking. These so-called bodies we have now, they're just images, reflections of our thoughts and feelings, mirrors of our personalities. On Earth, the physical is more predominant; here the mind is, consciousness is. Which is why you can take on any appearance you want. Most people, like myself, are not that imaginative. They're happy just to look the way they think they looked their best, usually their youthful looks. But you can be anything you desire, you can go anywhere, create anything. It's really quite nice." He says this as he once might have described some new area to which he was delivering newspapers. "Too bad it's such a well-kept secret on Earth."

"If I can create anything . . . could I clone my son?"

"Into the kind of subtle body you and I have, yes. But you can't re-create his mind or personality, his soul, really. That's—" My father's face suddenly lights up in a delayed reaction, switching from its scholarly demeanor to the radiant visage of a new grandfather. "So how old is he, Sharon?"

"Three."

"You miss him."

"More than I would've thought possible. Still, it's easier being here, easier this way than if I had lived and he died. I don't think I could have handled that."

"He was in the car?"

"No, thank God. He's fine. A lovable kid. He has some developmental lags, as they diplomatically call them, but he's a sweetheart in his way. I just hope my husband can manage to take care of him now." A shiver of grief runs through me. "He had a hard enough time taking care of himself."

"Him you don't miss so much."

"Well, more than I'd have guessed. Most of the time, I would have welcomed the prospect of not seeing him for several weeks —or years. Not that . . . I mean, he probably did the best he could. At least it seemed that way during this sort of instant replay of my life—"

"With the Being of Light, as you call him. After you died."

"Right. Starring you, among others," I reply, smiling briefly. "Mother didn't consider Paul to be a great catch. Neither did I, after we were married for a while. He drank a lot. Wasn't thrilled about having Kenny, either, although I've got to admit that he stood by us. He brought home the bacon, if not much else."

"Kenny? Not a bad choice, considering some of the names people were giving their kids around the time I got sick. Menachem, Ezekial . . . Can you imagine naming a baby—"

"Well, this one would have been Abraham, after you, but Paul vetoed the idea. Said his mother would be upset. So his name is Kenneth Abraham Galdoni, your half-Jewish, half-Italian grandson. Daddy, one of the first things I felt after he was born was that I wished you were there. I wanted you to see him so badly." A lump forms in the area of my throat.

"Show him to me then."

"Daddy, how can I do that?"

"Picture him, standing right here." My father points to a spot between us.

This suggestion produces an image of Kenny in my mind which, to my amazement, manifests itself. Standing in the grass at my feet, looking literally angelic, is my son. But my astonishment and the joy of having miraculously, immaculately rebirthed Kenny, soon give way to an equally powerful sense of disappointment. Kenny is life-sized but obviously lifeless, three-dimensional yet almost transparent, as if he's been fashioned of tinted air. His beautiful smile and the pale twinkle in his green eyes become depressing in their fixity. I discover that I can move him, alter his expression at will, even have him mouth "Mommy" like some ethereal Barbie doll, an exercise that moves me to tears. I bend to pick him up, girding myself for the effort from force of habit. No effort is involved, of course. He's as light as I must be, indeed he is a visible extension of my own mind —and one which my father enjoys immensely.

"Such a handsome little fellow," he declares, taking "Kenny" from me and holding him up at arm's length. "I love you and Gloria—my love knows no bounds—but I would've liked to have a son. Of course a grandson would've been better still. None of the responsibility, just *knochas*, enjoyment."

"Daddy, that's not Kenny. It's a mockery. He might as well be in a wax museum."

He puts Kenny down, standing him in the grass and rumpling his hair, which shifts back and forth above Kenny's frozen face. "A wax museum? Now *that's* a mockery. As if a person is a body, and he can be immortalized by replicating it. All we are —you and I, and Kenny, and anyone or anything else—is life, consciousness. In different forms, but it's the same infinite consciousness, everywhere. That's why, with the physical barriers between us gone, you and I can read each other's minds. But you and Kenny exist on different planes now, and as you've already experienced, the barriers are even greater. But it's temporary, sweetheart. "

"You talk like it'll take a few days."

"Sharon remember, time has a different value here. As in timeless. And the barriers I was talking about are real from one standpoint, but from another it's not a question of when Kenny will get here. He *is* here, in essence. If that sounds like some empty philosophy or rationalization, believe me it's not. Coming here is like coming home, coming to the place where you started, where you've always *been*. On Earth it's forgotten, hidden from us. Well, not entirely. That love you've always felt for your son, that's just the bliss of infinity peeking out. The kind that surrounded you in the presence of Hashem's angel. Here, you grow toward Him, toward God, Hashem. After a while, there's no question of lacking anything. And whenever Kenny does get here—well, I can tell you first hand how blissful you'll feel." My father beams at me.

Feeling uncomfortable over the already-discernible diminishing of my sorrow for Kenny, I come up with a concern: "Will he remember me? He's so young."

"His body's young, that's all. You know that expression 'kindred souls?' Here you learn the real meaning of that. He'll remember you, don't worry."

"I'll do my best, Daddy. Just . . . be available."

"Always."

Glowing like Tinkerbell, I smile back at my father, who is living proof that death has its rewards. He'd always been kind and gentle, even as his world started caving in around him. But the unrestrained love I feel from him now is something new. The level-headedness that had characterized him on Earth, which I'd come to regard as weakness in the face of my mother's bluster, has evolved into an undeniable wisdom. If he was once an atheist, he now speaks of God as of an old friend and mentor. One whose powers, apparently, are unique.

Having been averting my eyes, I now glance over at Kenny, who appears to be gazing across the meadow like a sentry. "You know, Daddy, I was half joking when I asked about cloning. The joke's on me, I guess. Can we make him—or it—disappear?"

My question is answered in the next instant: to my amazement, the Kenny-doll vanishes.

"Well, it was better than a photograph," allows my father, who, on Earth, had faithfully recorded with his camera anything that could be remotely construed as a family event. "As you see, anything you can create you can destroy. Of course, it's not matter we're dealing with here. Matter, and souls, are the province of Hashem."

I nod dumbly, staring at the now-empty space, both relieved and stunned. "Just like that?"

"Just like that. It's a lot easier here than on earth to fulfill your desires. Still, depending on what you desire, that can be a mixed blessing. Some people—"

"Daddy," I interject, still gazing at the spot where "Kenny" had been, "I'm starting to have a strong desire to move away from here. I'd really like to walk through this meadow, holding your hand like I used to."

"Easier done than said." He extends his hand. I take it in mine and the two become virtually indistinguishable, their separateness blurred by their translucency.

Our walk across the meadow seems more like a glide. My feet, liberated from both the high heels I'd been wearing when I crashed and the weight of my body, leave no prints, no impression on the shimmering grass. Yet my feet are touching the ground; I can see the grass beneath, around, and through them, as if it was growing out of me, rooted in my soles. Seen through my pants, the knee-high grass appears darker but no less visible. I suddenly realize that my blue jeans and maroon sweatshirt (I'd arrived wearing only these, the kind of clothing I prefer) are translucent but show no "flesh" beneath them. It's like looking through tinted glass. Both intrigued and mildly alarmed, I roll up a sweatshirt sleeve. Lo and behold, I find translucent skin, complete with wispy blonde hairs. My "arm" vanishes again as I roll down the sleeve, appears again as I roll it up.

"This is too much!" I say, giggling, as I exhibit this phenomenon for my father, who is amused mainly by my fascination with it. "And it's like, I know there's no real material in the sweatshirt, it's just—"

"An image."

"Right, but I swear I can feel cloth."

"Well, your eyes are not the only senses you can use here. You can have any sensory experience—and I do mean any—without having to be in the physical world."

"You know, it's almost as good as the real thing," I declare, stroking the "denim" of my jeans, literally sinking my fingers into it.

"It's better than what you call 'the real thing,'" replies my father, stooping to caress a blade of grass. "You can experience more deeply. With any of the senses, you feel like you become whatever you're touching, hearing . . . seeing, tasting or smelling."

"Sounds sort of like what happens when you take certain drugs."

He gazes at me in disbelief. "You too?"

"For a while. I gave that up years ago, Daddy. I flipped out once on LSD. That was more than enough for me."

"Oy, Sharon. You had to put poison in your body?" He shakes his head. "Well, at least you gave it up. Is Gloria still—"

"Uh-uh. Like I said before, after you died, maybe *because* of your death, she changed dramatically. Became a model citizen, and then some. No drugs, no alcohol, no tobacco, no meat, no negative thoughts let alone words, you name it." I pause, chiding myself, surprised at my own resurgent cynicism. It's as if I'd turned back several pages of my life for my father to read. "I don't know, she did get herself together, I guess . . . and I fell apart. Our usual see-saw routine."

"Sounds like by dying I did better by her than I did when I was alive."

"You did *fine* when you were alive, Daddy. I think she just appreciated it more afterward. And you wouldn't have believed it. She became a disciple of this guru, Swami . . . something, and she was as obedient as you can be."

"A guru?"

"That's—"

"I know what that is, sweetie," he interjects, steering me through the grass so that we're now heading toward the stream. "They were starting to come to America while I was still an earthling. Of course, not everyone who claims to be a holy man is one. But up here, I've met a lot of people from the East, India in particular. It seems that in their traditions there's a lot more understanding of what's really what than there is in the West."

"Well, I guess those traditions also include swamis who double as matchmakers. Gloria's marriage was more or less arranged by her guru. And part of the deal was obedience to her husband."

"That must've been hard for her. She couldn't have changed *that* much," declares my father, hopefully.

"No, she did have to sort of subjugate herself. For whatever reason she thought it was the right thing to do, part of her atonement or something. She was almost like a servant." I smirk despite myself. "At least she was until her husband left her. Shows how appreciative he was. Part of the problem was that he couldn't deal with having a child carrying on in the house, even though Gloria was the main caretaker. Lila, their daughter, was a frisky kid, colicky at first, but still—"

"Lila. A very pretty name. Here stands a grandfather twice over." He grins and brushes at his chest as if polishing a medal. "So how old is this Lila?"

"When I died, which couldn't have been that long ago, she was ten. And a sweet kid, though I'd prefer not to have her jumping out of my memory in front of us."

I can feel my father enjoying this little concern of mine, and can see the hearty amusement on his face, which is incongruous in the absence of sound, as if he were instantly breathless from laughter. "I can wait dear," he replies. "So how did Gloria make out after her husband left?"

"Oh, fine. The pendulum just swung in the opposite direction. In fact, at one point I tried to convince her to take child support money from the guy—Phil was his name, although he liked to call himself 'Bhagwan.' I'll give him that, he did help them financially. Decided that material wealth was the answer after all, and made a bundle. But at first Gloria wanted nothing more to do with him. I think the only reason she wound up accepting the money was so she could go to computer school and eventually support herself."

"She became a scientist? Gloria?"

"Daddy, where have you been!"

He gives me an offended look, which he manages to maintain for a moment before the irrepressible smile shines on his face. "In another world, dear," he replies.

"Well, you've obviously been absent from Planet Earth, U.S.A., New York City for many moons. Half of the people there work in computers now. Gloria lives upstate, in Fishkill, and programs computers for a nice living. That was her concession to financial necessity. She and Lila have a nice house with a fireplace and everything. I'm sure you'd love it. Mother does. Of course, she'd like it much better if there was a man living there, lawfully wedded to Gloria. Gloria did live with another guy for a while; last I knew she was still involved with him on and off. She's just real reluctant to get married again. And my marriage didn't do anything to make her think differently. She didn't care for my husband much."

"So you and Gloria kept in touch? You spent some time together at least."

"We got a lot closer," I reply, feeling a wave of sadness for which I'm almost grateful; it's an admission that indeed I loved Gloria and looked up to her. There was a bond between us which at some level I'd always recognized, and resented. Now the resentment is gone. "She was getting divorced around the time I was recovering from that breakdown I had. It was good to talk to her. I think for a while I was a project for her, something to help her forget her own troubles. I don't mean that to sound negative. She was helpful, that's all. Even though she was falling out with her husband and moving away from that whole circle they'd been involved with—swami, friends and followers —she still swore by the basic beliefs. She told me that if I was suffering, it was because my karma was being balanced, that I was really something much greater than the day-to-day changes I was going through. I mostly thought it was baloney, but at the time her presence and her support really helped. And she understood about drugs, completely.

"After she moved up to Fishkill and I got married and started working as a teacher, we didn't have much contact with each other for a while. When Kenny was born, Gloria and Lila both sort of took a shine to him, and vice versa. We had some good times together, although that happened less frequently after I went back to work. The four of us would get together with mother sometimes, too. She liked seeing the kids."

Against a backdrop of waving grass and trees with leaves at once green and golden, my father nods, satisfied that his family has remained relatively intact during his absence. He's also proud of me. "So you became a teacher? That's an exalted profession," he says.

"Not in the South Bronx it isn't, Daddy. If Hashem is truly present everywhere, He must be taking a long siesta there. For a while I tried, but the kids were ridiculous. *Wild* fourth-graders. I needed either a whip or a magic wand, and neither was available. Throw in the fact that I was pregnant for most of the year, and you get the picture. It was a zoo. Maybe I should've stopped working. Maybe being in that environment wasn't good for Kenny. I know it wasn't good for me. It could've had something to do with the way he turned out. Actually," I add, "I'll never know the way he turned out."

My father affectionately touches my chin. Although I feel no pressure, the sight of his fingers penetrating my jaw is enough to cause me to jerk my head upright. "That's not true," he gently reminds me. "It's not even true that he'll 'turn out' to be some kind of person and that he'll stop evolving after that. There are no wax museums up here. I get the feeling that you very definitely did your best for Kenny, both before and after he was born."

"It could be. Lord knows I tried. It's just that there was this sort of new age wisdom, which Gloria espoused, that said practically everything affects the embryo."

"Well, the main thing that affects the embryo is the soul that enters it. I'm sure Kenny's soul had already been through a lot more than the second-hand influence of a bunch of wild kids."

I gaze at my father dumbly for a few moments. "Reincarnation?"

"So it's called. But Sharon, there's plenty of time to learn about that. I'm not much more than a beginner myself. Right now I'd like to learn more about the details of my daughter's life. How old was Kenny when you went back to work?"

"Almost three," I answer, detecting no criticism, implied or otherwise, in the question. "He started nursery school, an extended day program. It worked out much better than I thought it would. He has this sweetheart of a teacher who takes a real interest in him. He used to practically run into her arms when I dropped him off. I guess I wouldn't have minded if he was a little more reluctant to leave me," I add, smiling. I have a very clear image of Kenny awkwardly propelling himself down the neon-lit corridor toward Cheryl Nahm's room, struggling to unzip his jacket while lurching ahead. From behind he looked as if he'd had one too many. On him, it had looked precious.

My father nods slowly and doesn't speak until the recollection is gone from my mind; clearly he's shared it. Finally he says, "And how did *this* sweetheart of a teacher like returning to the classroom? Was it any better?"

Briefly, I'm surrounded by a pinkish hue, my afterworldly blush. "My principal used less complimentary adjectives on my evaluation," I confide, actually amused by the memory. "Regardless, I wouldn't have gone back to teaching. I had learned my lesson, no pun intended. Of course, the job I took instead, the one I was in a rush to get to the morning I crashed, was no great bargain either. I was an administrative assistant with this economics research firm. It was either high pressure or utterly boring, depending on the time of the month.

"I went back to work for financial reasons, period. Then again I wouldn't have wanted to wait forever, and wind up like mother. I practically had to drag her kicking and screaming to her first job interview after you died. But motherhood . . . it was about the only thing I ever did that I felt really comfortable with, like, 'This is where I belong.' I didn't even mind the solitude. If reincarnation is for real, maybe I was a hermit in a past life; and maybe Kenny and I go back longer than I think. In retrospect, I could swear that sometimes we almost communicated the way you and I do now, with some kind of telepathy. I miss him, Daddy." My lip trembles. "But somehow, I also have the feeling that everything will work out alright—and positive thinking has never been my forte."

"It's not positive thinking. It's just knowledge."

We reach the stream. It looks pristine, with a sparkle that seems to radiate from its pebbly bottom. This is probably the first stream I've ever seen that I'd have no qualms about drinking out of. The aquamarine water rushes around and over various protuberances without really seeming impeded, as if the roots, boulders, and mini-islands are part of the substance of the stream itself, at once solid and liquid. I roll up my pants and step in, feeling the water flow into and through my legs, a giddy, cleansing sensation. My feet on the bed of the stream look like jellyfish that have ingested myriad pebbles.

On a large rock that appears to be quite solid, my father sits and watches me splash around in the coolness. Although I hadn't been aware of any weather before, it now seems an agreeably warm day for the activity. I feel and notice the sun for the first time. It must have been shining right along; the sky is cloudless. Maybe the sun's brilliance is diminished by the faint glow that seems to radiate from everything here. Little beads of "sweat" begin to form above my eyebrows and upper lip. I sprinkle water on my face and arms. By way of helping out, my father reaches down from his perch and splashes the rest of me. My clothes are soaking wet. He laughingly assures me that if my drenched state is not agreeable, it can be remedied at once. But the cool wetness against my skin is delicious and exhilarating. I feel as if I'm wearing only water.

The exhilaration becomes more intense as I bend down to take a drink. If pleasure in drinking is concommitant with the depth of one's thirst, I would have to have been seriously dehydrated. As long as I drink, the sense of relief and fulfillment, of being anointed by the stream, remains unabated. When I stop after what seems like a long time, I have absolutely no feeling of being full or bloated, or even of having drunk anything. As before I dipped my face in the stream, I feel no thirst. I gaze quizzically at my father, as if to say, "What else can you show me?" Grinning, I take a pratfall into the water, kicking up my legs, sending a glistening shower over him. He remains dry.

"Spoilsport," I tease, sticking out my tongue, splashing him again to no avail. I take his hand and attempt to drag him into the stream, but it's like trying to pull a shadow. Giving up, I take another drink, with similarly lovely results. Then I say, "Tell me Daddy, is this Heaven?"

"Sharon, my late daughter, that is a good question. Heaven by whose definition? Certainly it doesn't resemble the heavens described by those geniuses who run religions on earth. There are lower planes than this, where souls don't have the kinds of . . . choices they do here. They don't have the freedom. And there are higher planes than this. The lower ones you don't really want to know about, believe me. One difference between earth and here is that there's no fascination with evil here, even on the lower planes, where those who've willfully lived evil lives reside. They simply reap what they've sown. The truth that one's body here is a reflection of one's personality and character is even more apparent at the lowest levels. The people, if you can call them that, look grotesque, beastly.

"On the higher levels, on the other hand, there's not even the appearance of physicality that there is on this plane. If the word Heaven has to be used, that's where it really applies.

There's just pure bliss. You got an idea of it from Hashem's angel. We try to move in that direction as quickly as possible, but without worrying about it, of course. One step at a time. Or maybe I should say one flight."

- 8 -

Paul

I ACTUALLY hung Kenny's picture up in my cab this morning, my first back to work. It dangles now from the base of my rear-view mirror, encased in a little oval frame—an amulet that's supposed to remind me of why I'm still hacking. Even as a picture, the kid can't sit still. As I rattle over the cobble-stones on Second Avenue south of Fourteenth Street, I have to hold on to the metal frame to keep it from repeatedly smashing against the windshield. My passenger, a twenty-something black guy wearing a suit and tie and carrying a briefcase, finds this touching. "Cute kid. He's also a ringer for you, although you'd never know it from that mug shot on your hack license."

I do a small double-take and glance in the mirror, trying to figure out if the guy is wising off or just being friendly. His smile looks mocking to me, although that could be my imagination.

"Hell, with that picture hangin' under your face in the mirror, looks like a family tree if ever saw one."

I shrug. Unless I'm either hard-up for tips or drunk, I usually don't talk much to male passengers. That goes double for black males, who ordinarily don't make it into my cab in the first place. But now I'm surprised by the quavering sound of my own voice, as I answer the guy. "Well, he's got his mother's smile." I almost add, "She's dead," but catch myself, wondering what the hell I'm thinking.

"He got lucky," the guy says with a laugh. "Hey, just kiddin'. Far corner'll do it," he adds as we arrive at Fourth Street. He reaches through the sliding "bullet proof" partition, which I'd forgotten to close when I stopped for him, and hands me three dollars and five cents, plus a fifteen cents tip. In the past, I've tossed such tips back at people, sarcastically informing them that they probably needed the money more than I did. Now I just enter the fare next to "2av-4" on my trip card, extending the job until the guy has thanked me. I give the barest of nods, without looking up. The slam of the rear door as he steps out is like a starter's gun for me. I dart back out onto Second Avenue and take a right at Houston. Below Houston there are slim pickings unless you want to go all the way downtown to the Wall Street area, which I hate even more than the rest of Manhattan. I could get around Wall Street faster on Kenny's tricycle.

Flagged by a red light, I screech to a halt at Houston and the Bowery, cursing. This intersection is forever manned by winos and derelicts looking to "clean" a few windshields in exchange for booze money. One of them smears my windshield with a rag that looks like it was rejected by a grease monkey, then knocks against my window with a filthy hand: pay up. I'm even more disgusted by the guy than I would be ordinarily, since I haven't had a drink yet today. I'm definitely feeling the need. Multiply my habit by two or three and you have his, him.

These guys were freezing to death regularly during the cold spell that started the week before Sharon died. It's warmed up in the last few days, but the wino in front of me, who is actually blocking the cab now, pissed off that he hasn't been paid for his services, looks like he has a terminal cold. His face seems to be composed of mucus, blackheads, and bristly hair, with a few patches of red skin peeking out. As I back up, intending to pull around him, he takes a swipe at the hood, misses, and falls on his face in the middle of Houston Street. He stands a good chance of being flattened into a puddle of booze by one of the cars or trucks coming from Second Avenue. I pause for the several moments it takes for the guy to roll into a semi-sitting position. This is long enough to cause a couple of cars to have to brake behind me, honking to announce the now-green light ahead. It's unclear whether this noise is for the wino's benefit or mine. He gives his opinion of it with his middle finger. The thrust of the finger seems to somehow help pull the rest of him upright. Having done my good deed for the day, I steer around the guy as if he were a large pothole. Those, at least, sometimes get fixed.

I take a right onto Third Avenue and light a cigarette. The terrain improves slightly as I head uptown, past Cooper Union and Saint Mark's Place, where skid row is a game played by teenagers, past high-risers and gentrifying tenements, past the whores at the corner of Thirteenth Street, each looking like she could transmit several diseases just by touching you. I would have to get seriously desperate before partaking of anything I've seen streetwalking around New York. I'm not that bad off yet, despite the fact that I'm now without even the minimal sex life I had with Sharon, to whom I was nonetheless faithful for what turned out to be the last four or five months of her life. Good timing or dumb luck. And I could swear that now I miss having her sleeping next to me more than anything else. That much of what I told Gloria in Fishkill was true. I wasn't just trying to get into her pants . . . although I probably wouldn't have turned down the opportunity.

As it turned out, that mess in Fishkill wasn't a total fiasco. On the way home, an unexpected shot of pride jerked me upright: I couldn't be *that* much of a schmuck. Or if I was, that would have to change. In the past, this kind of resolution has usually been triggered by my getting thrown out of a bar or some other kind of ridiculousness, and by the suspicion that I was headed for the Bowery myself, that Sharon's mother's opinion of me was not off by much. My determination to be a good boy has typically lasted no more than a couple of drinkless days. There are bars on nearly every block in every borough of the city. It's hard to resist the double temptation of getting out of the cab and into the "Blarney Stone," or wherever. Currently, I've been on the wagon for maybe a day and a half.

I'm sure that Cheryl Nahm could see the difference in me this morning and was seriously impressed. I entered her apartment at five-thirty, stone sober, a respectable working man towing Kenny in one hand and a new car seat in the other. Actually, it's only new to Kenny. Gloria had offered it unasked, Lila having long since outgrown it. Were it not for this donation, I'd most likely have forgotten that I'd promised to bring a car seat when I arrived at Nahm's on Monday morning. I was amazed at Gloria's intuition, until I realized that my inadequately furnished car had been sitting in her driveway all weekend (we'd stayed over Saturday night; I slept downstairs at what Gloria considered a safe distance).

Correctly or not, I'd taken the car seat to be an indication that I was not permanently implanted on Gloria's shit list. This morning, I handed the seat to Nahm as evidence that I meant business where Kenny was concerned. I made a show of ascertaining that he understood the new procedure for getting to nursery, and that he felt comfortable with it. This was unnecessary, of course. As soon as he saw Nahm, he was more than happy to ditch me. Both of them had big smiles for each other. One actually formed on my face too. It was a touching scene, the more so when she hugged him and gave me a moist-eyed little glance. I nodded and looked away, uncomfortable to find myself wondering at that moment what she had on under her floor-length bathrobe; it had parted to reveal a bare calf and knee as she'd squatted down to Kenny's level. Politely declining her offer of coffee-to-go, I rumpled Kenny's hair and took leave of him for the first time in three days, breathing a sigh of relief on my way out the door.

Despite my mother's unsought assurances that "getting back into the old routine" would do me some good, I felt the usual disgust when I arrived at my garage. The place is like a giant concrete outhouse for cabs, stinking of carbon monoxide and gasoline. The drivers' room features the odor of piss from a continually stopped-up toilet, mixed with wall-to-wall cigar smoke. By comparison my cigarettes smell like perfume.

That sitcom "Taxi" was one of the biggest crocks of bullshit I've ever seen on TV, which is saying a lot. Taxi garage as social club. Right. Aside from the day dispatcher and the guy who drives my cab at night, I know only a couple of guys by name. The day after Sharon died I called Rico, the night man, and told him not to worry about bringing the cab back for me until Monday. That was it; no one at the garage knows or cares that my wife just died. There's no sunshine fund, never has been. Aside from the general apathy, alienation and what-have-you, most cabbies (the lifers in particular) love to curse the stinginess of their passengers, but are themselves chronic skinflints. Even when one of the garage's cabbies was killed in a holdup, it didn't inspire a whole lot of generosity or togetherness. His picture in the newspaper was taped to the wall in the drivers' room (he looked vaguely familiar, a fortyish long-hair who drove at night), and a slotted metal box was left under it for donations. One or two guys talked about organizing a strike for more police protection. In a week the whole thing was forgotten.

Of course, that's life in the Big Apple, as some genius must have once said. At the intersection of Fourteenth and Third, I'm hailed by a heavy-set woman who flags me as if she were hand guiding a cargo plane down onto a runway. "Bloomingdale's," she grunts, heaving her fur-coated self into the back seat. She spends the trip up Third teasing her "red" hair, using the plexiglass divider as a makeshift mirror. At least she's taking me back into midtown, theoretically where the money is. On the way up Third the bodegas become gourmet food emporiums. We pass yuppie restaurants with foreign names, doormen wearing white gloves and whistles, all of this maybe two or three minutes from the Bowery, if you make the lights. Making the lights, or running them, is one of the big thrills involved as I pinball around Manhattan, launched by the important people who can afford cab rides.

I drop the woman—literally, the way she gets out of the cab—in front of "Bloomie's" and head down Lexington, jockeying for curbside position in a sea of yellow cabs. Rush hour ended over an hour ago, so pickings may be slim for a while. I usually have a little nip around this time, but now I light another cigarette instead, exchanging one poison for another.

The smoke backs up in my mouth as I pass the Graybar building near Grand Central. This is where Sharon worked. Once in a while I used to surprise her for lunch. I was always amazed at how happy she was to see me, despite the fact that she knew I'd be losing money by missing the lunchtime rush, the martini shift. She hated her job, and I guess I became a friendly face, an ally, evidence that she had a life outside of the office. I can almost see her face the last time I popped into her little cubicle. Her lips pressed tightly together, she was gazing with a mixture of attentiveness and disgust down at this enormous IBM Selectra. Her hair, pulled back and above the rear of her head, pointed up at me like a periscope. I was almost surprised she wasn't aware of me at once, even though I'd entered quietly.

I cleared my throat. "'Lo, Mrs. Galdoni. I've come to take you away from all this. How's pizza sound?" (I'd finally gotten to the point where I could eat the stuff again after blowing all my money on a pizzamobile.)

She looked up and, after a moment's worth of shifting gears, gave me a smile. It shone through her rouge and lipstick like an unearthed jewel. "What a nice surprise. This is an offer I can't refuse, even if it means I have to work a little late. You buying, sweetheart?"

"What? You make more than I do." This was a lie. Despite her fancy title—Research Specialist-Administrative Assistant—and her college degree, she was making peanuts. "Okay, I'll spring for the drinks," I said.

"Soft ones, right?" She smiled again and pantomimed a kiss, then stood up, petite and pretty in a blue skirt and silky blouse. She stroked my cheek. "You wouldn't believe how good it is to see a man around here with some stubble on his face."

I nibbled on her fingers, for some reason more turned on by her than I'd been in a long time. "Look, maybe we could close this door."

Sharon laughed. "There's not enough room, unless you want to do it standing up. Besides, I don't bring my diaphragm to work."

"Glad to hear *that*."

"Paul—"

"Just kidding, dear," I quickly added, looking away to hide an involuntary smirk. I took her hand and towed her out the door, willing my prick to deflate so I could walk instead of waddle. This was especially important in order for me to negotiate the mobbed lunch-hour sidewalk on Lexington Avenue. I usually get a little crazy in that kind of scene; at least in a traffic jam I'm in the cab, I have a little space around me, a little armor. But with Sharon clinging to my arm, I didn't much mind the curb-to-wall crowd of humanity. I ran interference for her and we talked, about her asshole of a boss, and about the various anuses who'd sat in the rear of my cab that morning. Pushing through three mobbed blocks, we doggedly carried on a conversation as if some principle was involved, as if our little time together was inviolable.

For a moment I could swear I see her on the sidewalk now: we'd just been momentarily separated was all that had happened. I hit the brake. The cabbie behind me somehow manages to stop without ramming me. He leans on his horn and curses me out. Even in my rear-view mirror, reading his lips is no problem. Hell, I could recite along with him. I actually wave an apology; I probably caused a chain reaction of red brake lights for twenty blocks back. Besides, maybe I deserve to be cursed, for being a sentimental schmuck if nothing else.

Smoke fuming out of my nostrils, I hit Forty-second Street and make a squealing right turn. This causes the picture of Kenny, which had bounced against the windshield when I braked for "Sharon," to swing wildly from side to side. It also forces my next fare, an old gent who'd been standing waving his arm in front of one of the Grand Central exits, to jump away from the curb. I pop out of the cab and toss his luggage into the trunk while he stares open-mouthed. Luggage is a good sign. This might turn out to be a long trip. The longer the better: one of the airports, maybe Brooklyn, or even Staten Island. Maybe the guy's going to Canada.

* * *

At close to five P.M. I pull up at Beth Shalom Day Care Center, having exchanged the cab for the Plymouth Valiant. I sit for a moment with my head tipped back against the head rest and close my eyes. Getting out seems like more of an effort than I can manage. For once, I can dispense with the breath spray. I don't think there are any laws or moral objections to smoking and driving, although with Nahm you never know.

To my surprise, she gives me a smile as I enter Kenny's room. This has to be a first. Showing great faith in the kids, she leaves ten or twelve of them slicing away at colored paper with scissors. She still looks glad to see me even when she gets within sniffing range. Given her good looks, this could be a hallucination borne of wishful thinking and fatigue. Or maybe it has to do with our brief impersonation of a family this morning. Whatever the reason, I muster a little smile of my own.

"How's he doin'?" I ask, sending a concerned glance over in Kenny's direction. Kenny is clumsy with his hands, and the scissors might as well be chopsticks. But still he's hacking away, oblivious to me, probably lacerating whatever lines he's supposed to be following.

"Not bad," Nahm replies, setting her full lips and nodding slowly as if in testimony to the kid's courage. "Clingier than usual, which is maybe to be expected. At first, I practically had to show him where his coat hook is again, and walk him around from one activity to the other. A couple of weeks ago, I got him to the point where he'll tell me if he has a poop. But—"

"Right, Sharon told me that," I interject, feeling like an overgrown kid, squirming ever so slightly despite Nahm's matter-of-fact tone. "Still, you don't need to be changing diapers. I'm gonna have to toilet train him somehow, I guess." Naturally, I'd always considered this to be Sharon's job. But aside from getting Kenny a little potty (which he wound up using as a helmet), she took the attitude that he'd use the john when he was "ready," whatever that meant. I don't know if she expected him to announce it or what, the kid's not a big conversationalist. My own contribution to the process has been to yell at him now and then, usually if he crapped his diaper when Sharon wasn't around.

Nahm replies, "Well, now more than ever, I wouldn't push him on it. Besides, he's the only one here left in diapers, so peer pressure may do the trick. As I started to say before, today was the first time in a while that he didn't say anything to me after the fact. Finally one of the other kids started teasing him, calling him 'Stinky Pants.' Kenny threw a small fit about that, rolled around on the floor, which made cleaning him up a bit more difficult. But once I finished and calmed him down, he was pretty much okay."

My eyes flick over toward Kenny again, but I don't whistle or call his name. I'm trying to be polite; detailed descriptions of his day have never fascinated me and this one is no exception, despite my having dutifully asked for it.

"Didn't eat much of his lunch or snack," Nahm adds. "Of course, he's always been a picky eater."

"Sometimes. It depends," I reply, a bit of an edge to my voice. "He eats enough to keep growing, that's for sure. Hopefully he'll be able to survive on my cooking." For the moment, Kenny seems to be doing fine, wielding his little snub-nosed scissors with the concentration of a diamond cutter. I start wondering why the hell I'm in such a hurry to leave. Nahm is nicely put together, I'll give her that, and all I have in front of me is a Sharon-less evening with Kenny. As soon as this question enters my mind Kenny, the little wise guy, looks up and spots me. A surprised smile crosses his face. He drops everything and hustles over, stopping about a yard from me as if suddenly shy.

"Hey chief," I say, rumpling his springy hair. "How you doin'?"

"Do good work."

"Yeah, I saw you. Got anything to bring home?"

"Show Mommy!" he declares, then dashes back to his work table, not giving anyone the chance to set him straight. He returns with a paper "snowflake" which is shaped like a lop-sided stop sign and looks as if it's been attacked by mice. I make the appropriate sounds of approval while Nahm, who'd departed along with Kenny, returns with his new car seat. I accept it with thanks. It would be unwise to suggest that she just leave it in her car.

After sending Kenny off to fetch his jacket (and chewing out one of the other kids for trashing the floor with paper scraps), Nahm says, "Look, if there's anything else I can do . . . I mean that."

"Yeah, I don't doubt it." It would be hard to, given the

earnest look on her smooth, pretty face (could it have changed that much in a week?). I just thank her for the offer and keep my sinful thoughts about what she *could* do for me to myself. Still, the stirring in my crotch is a big improvement over what she used to inspire in me. Zipping Kenny into his jacket, I tell Nahm that I'll see her in the morning. I give her a smile. She beams a goodbye as if delighted to see me finally coming out of my crusty shell. This is probably the kind of look she gives her kiddies to help build their self-esteem.

Outside, Kenny dashes up to his home-mobile, the Valiant. It takes a moment for me to decide what to do with the car seat and another few to figure out how to install it in the front.

"No seat!" protests Kenny, probably wanting no deviations from the little routine that ends with Mommy walking in the door and hugging him. As I half-heartedly explain to him why he needs to be kiddie-seated, I have the uncomfortable feeling that both Sharon and Nahm are somehow monitoring this process. I try to sound more convincing, but Kenny, arms folded across his chest in a pose he must have picked up from me, is obviously having none of it. I start hooking up the seat, and he starts screaming. Wordlessly, I yank the car seat back out, causing the freed-up shoulder harness to dive back into its launch pad. I fling the seat into the rear of the car. "Fine, Kenny," I say, taking a deep breath and hoisting him into his usual place on the front seat. "Just, let's not scream. It's hard for me to listen to that, okay?" I pull the shoulder harness across his stomach and stab it into "locked" position.

I slide in behind the wheel and notice the peeved look on Kenny's face: his lower lip sticks out like a visor for his pointy chin, and his upper lip is tucked in. I have to restrain a laugh, leave the kid some dignity. He probably sensed that I was pissed —it's usually not hard to do—and he's returning the favor. He probably feels freer to do so given the unusually gentle treatment he's been getting from me lately.

"Go home, see Mommy!" he demands, the pout deepening. He says this with an air of defiance, as if Mommy's absence were the result of a command of mine, as if I'm holding out on him.

I stick the key in the ignition, but decide to wait on starting the car. "Look Kenny, we've been through this. You can't see

Mommy. She's gone. I know that's hard for you," I say, looking for a light of comprehension in his eyes. His lower lip has retracted some, maybe that's a good sign. "It's hard for me too, Kenny. But I can't do anything about it. It's not my fault, believe me. It's no one's fault. It just happened. Mommy's car crashed, and just like if you drop a glass hard enough, it breaks . . . it's like Humpty-Dumpty. You understand, Kenny?" A note of pleading creeps into my voice. I need the kid to cooperate, to fake it, whatever. But he's no longer looking at me. He's concentrating on trying to fit his pinky into one of the mice holes in his snowflake. I cup his chin in my palm and turn his face toward me, then lean in as if trying to get closer to his brain. "Just don't expect to see her when you get home, that's all. You gotta get used to it, Kenny."

The car takes a while to start. It finally does just as I'm about to throw a fit of my own. I thought I was in a halfway decent mood before I picked up Kenny, but he's the acid test. I pull out of the parking spot, double-checking for oncoming cars. My vision is a little blurry.

Kenny is strangely uninterested in the various vehicles we pass on our way across Yonkers. He shreds his snowflake (standard behavior, it doesn't mean he's given up on seeing Mommy), then spends most of the trip kicking the underside of the dashboard with his sneakers. The thudding is just one more noise the car makes, it's fine with me as long as I don't have to listen to fussing. I'm free to disbelieve, like Kenny, that I'm going home to an apartment permanently devoid of Sharon. That she's gone and I'm still delivering Kenny along the same route, still tracking along through the suburban slums. I was the one who mentally reserved the option to split, maybe when the kid was old enough or when Sharon and I got sick enough of each other, whichever came first.

Flannery the doorman nods at me and I return the favor, towing Kenny along with a tight grip on his hand. Since his nightstick juggling act in our lobby last week, Kenny has developed a thing about cops. If he sees anyone in anything resembling the uniform, he declares "Po-weese!" and charges over, grasping and patting the blue cloth like he's dealing with a stuffed cop. He's done this to Flannery a couple of times. Not that the phony bastard doesn't like kids, at arm's length, but with Kenny the novelty wore off quickly. You could tell that Flannery put Kenny's onslaught in the same category with being pawed and licked by a dog. There are similarities, but he's still my kid.

Still Sharon's, too. Once we're in the apartment, I try to distract him from the plans he's making for her impending arrival by having him "help" me make some chopped meat into patties. Standing on a chair, he takes a few whacks at the burgers-to-be. Then the novelty wears off and he slithers down, wiping bits of pink meat on his shirt. I try not to get pissed, the thing needed washing anyway. Paul the Housemommy.

Dinner, ordinarily cooked by Sharon, is passable, although the burgers are black on the outside and almost raw in the middle. I chase them down with a couple of beers and try not to watch Kenny, whose grease-covered face looks as if he just emerged from the womb. As I'm wondering if the sight would gross out Gloria the Vegetarian, the phone rings.

It's her. I must be getting psychic or something. She's civil and to the point: Clara wants to come over and go through Sharon's things, hopefully on Saturday. She wants Gloria to come along for moral support, and maybe to try on some clothes. I don't have to be psychic to tell that Gloria is not thrilled with the idea. Neither am I, although I guess it has to be done, and I'd probably feel better about going into the closet without Sharon's dresses hanging there like so many ghosts. I cover the receiver and burp, then say fine, name your time. Gloria does so, then asks to speak to Kenny. During conversations with Aunt "Gwa-waw" and "Why-wa" (Lila), he says "fine", "pway", "help daddy," and a few other words, finishing with "bye." With his usual soft touch, Kenny slams down the receiver. I assume that this was according to instructions received from the other end of the line, although with Kenny you never know. I can't get a straight answer out of him when I ask. I'm sure that if Gloria wants to chat with me, she'll call back.

We finish dinner and I actually clean up, thoroughly. Even with Kenny helping me, though, washing dishes and sponging surfaces only takes up so much time. Taking up time is more or less what life with a kid is about. Unfortunately one of our main machines for this, the VCR, needs repair. But even if it didn't, part of my supposed resolve to do right by Kenny involves "interacting" with him, and sneaking in some education in the process. Rummaging around in his "book box" (a name that comes out of his mouth like a short burst of machine gun fire), I pick out a book called *Preschool Learning and Discovery*. One page features a large grid with pictures of edible and non-edible items. The idea is to find the yummies and color them, which presupposes finding the crayons. This takes a while. Kenny follows me around as we look for them, the blind leading the blind.

One of Kenny's blinder spots has always been a confusion about what belongs in his mouth and what doesn't. So I guess I shouldn't be surprised when he points to the first picture, a rowboat, as being good to eat.

"Uh-uh, Kenny," I say with a small laugh, "You'd break your teeth on that, and put splinters in your belly. You can't eat that. Point to the ones you can eat, the ones that taste good."

He points to the banana in the next box.

"Okay, good. Banana. What else?"

He points to the next box, a picture of the sun.

"Look, just the ones you can eat, understand?" I'm starting to get pissed. This should be simple enough. He gives a whimper and tentatively points to a strawberry. Before I can praise him for this, and for passing over a picture of a ladybug, he points to a tree.

"Aw, shit. What is that, Kenny?"

"Twee."

"Can you *eat* that?"

He looks at me, at the scowl I can feel on my face, and starts bawling. Within a couple of seconds he's reached a serious decibel level. I curse again under my breath, get up from the living room rug and stomp off toward the kitchen. The only problem with this maneuver, recommended by Sharon as preferable to losing my temper, is that she is not here to take over. Kenny hustles after me. His crying intensifies. Feeling slightly ridiculous being chased, I make myself turn toward him, slowly. "Kenny, it's okay," I say between clenched teeth. I rumple his hair, simulating affection. If anything he gets louder. Through a remarkable act of will, I pick him up.

Fortunately, this comes across as reassuring. He starts to settle down. We continue into the kitchen, where I take out a beer and a cigarette. "Look, Ken, why don't we just color that stuff in," I say, putting him down in order to light the cigarette and rip the tab off of the beer. "Okay?" I take a drag followed by a sip, playing hot and cold see-saw with my throat.

"Gimme," he sniffles, reaching for the cigarette.

I hold it away from him. "Uh-uh, this is something you do when you get older. Unless you get lucky." The son of two smokers, his chances are not good. He reaches for the beer.

"You know you can't have this," I say, then realize that he's drunk out of soda cans several times. The ability to tell Coke from Budweiser is not something he's developed yet. Rejected twice, he starts wailing again. I cut him short with the beer, practically sticking it into his mouth. One taste should be enough. As he sips, some dribbles down his chin. He grimaces at the taste and gives me a questioning look with his green eyes. Then he asks for more.

So much for strategy. I can't help laughing, and feeling some pride in the kid. Obviously he's a chip off the old block. I let him hold the can this time, for a sip which turns into a guzzle. Kenny is not happy when I take back the can, especially when I save him from further temptation by draining it. I can sympathize this time when he turns on the tears. Also, I'm wondering how getting drunk would affect him. If it turned out to be a sedative . . . as I'm unwilling to try out this little experiment, the best way to get him to settle down these days seems to be to pick him up. I carry him back into the living room, leaning my head away as he tries to pluck the lit cigarette from my mouth.

If Kenny handled the cigarette the way he handles a crayon, he'd look like a torture victim in no time. After I deposit him on the living room rug, he starts trying to color the boat, the one he thought would probably taste good. Holding the crayon like an ice pick, he covers the boat, water, and half of the banana next door with streaks of red. As usual, he's nowhere near the lines of the pictures he's supposed to be coloring. I guess I should understand; the lines on my taxi trip cards get very shifty when I'm drunk enough. But as far as I can tell Kenny is unaffected by the few drops of beer he had. He's no more clumsy than usual. When my instructions to try to stay inside of the lines prove useless—his brown crayon moves like a lie detector needle all over the box with the tree—I stick the red crayon back back in his hand and try to guide him in coloring the picture of the strawberry. Maybe I squeeze his hand too tightly. Maybe he senses my disgust, or maybe he's just in a more fragile condition without Sharon around. Maybe I am too. As soon as the whimpers start, I snatch the crayon out of his hand and fling it across the living room, shouting, "Fucking shit!" The crayon bounces of the flower framed wall mirror, leaving a lipstick-like smear.

Next I kick a couple of sofa cushions that Kenny has thrown on the rug. They bounce harmlessly away. Although I'm enough in control to keep from doing real damage, I can feel my anger building, as if these acts of "release" are just releasing more rage.

Fuming, I turn toward Kenny, who, stunned into silence, is cowering on the rug next to the *Preschool Learning and Discovery* book. I've never really hit the kid, aside from occasional whacks on the behind. Even though they were blunted by his diapers, Sharon got seriously angry the couple of times she saw me do it. I got even angrier in return, defensively I guess. I don't want to be hitting on the kid; my father used to kick my ass and I never enjoyed it much. I can understand the impulse, though. Swallowing more curses, I pick Kenny up at arm's length and let him drop on the couch.

"Look, I can't deal with the fussing, Kenny. You have to understand that." I'm talking almost directly into his face. He's used to my booze-and-tobacco breath, so it's probably not the smell that causes him to turn away. He's just at the end of his attention span now that I seem halfway sane again and am delivering the same old rap. I turn his face back toward mine with two fingers on his chin, as if flipping a switch. "Just try not to cry so much. It'll make it easier on both of us."

"Like a broken record" doesn't come close to describing the despair I feel as I recite these words: he doesn't understand them, and I don't really believe them. Most of the things that would make life easier would also land me in jail. The weight of time—of the rest of the evening, of the next God-knows-how-many years until Kenny can take care of himself—sits on me like death.

Twenty minutes later Kenny is sitting on my shoulders, cushioned by a new diaper (the old one contained at least five pounds of piss) as we head down the steep hill leading from Nepperhan Avenue to the Hudson River. He's still light enough that it's almost like walking alone, except for the two grimy little sneakers I'm clasping, except for the fact that he squirms all over my neck and shoulders as I walk. On this cloudy night the river can be smelled more than seen. Essence of sewer. We pass through a hole in a rusty chain-link fence—Kenny, even in his winter jacket, strolls through, while I have to contort my body a few different ways—then we park ourselves on a couple of boulders. They are part of a narrow patch of shoreline between two metal loading docks belonging to Standard Coal Co. The sound of the water (and whatever is floating in it) lapping against the base of the rocks seems to have a calming effect on Kenny. He idly scratches at the boulder beneath him, humming in a monotone and bouncing the backs of his sneakers against the dried green slime along the boulder's side. A few small chunks of ice drift by under the docks, testimony to the single-digit temperatures we were having around the time Sharon died. It takes serious cold to form even a cube in a chemical river like the Hudson.

I light a cigarette and gaze out into the blackness, hoping for some revelation about how to be a single parent and keep from going nuts. Not that I especially feel like thinking; the usual fog in my brain isn't going to vanish just because I'm sitting by a river smoking a cigarette, striking a pensive pose. Even if it did, there are probably no easy answers, as some wise person must have said. But an idea, a possiblity, does occur to me.

"No, uh-uh," I say aloud, even as the idea—unthinkable a week ago—starts to seem worth pursuing. Desperation? I decide to sit on it for a day.

Make that half a day. I bring Kenny to Nahm's apartment again on Tuesday morning, and this time I accept her offer of coffee-to-go. While I'm adding milk, siphoning some off into a cup for the suddenly thirsty Kenny, I clear my throat and say, "Look, Miss Nahm—"

"Cheryl," she says. "Miss Nahm to you," she adds, addressing Kenny with mock sternness followed by a smile. Intent on licking at his new white mustache, he pays her no attention.

"Okay . . . Cheryl," I reply, feeling my edginess lessen slightly. I study Nahm, aka Cheryl, for a few moments. With her high cheekbones, dark eyes, and page boy haircut, she looks vaguely Asian, an effect somehow added to by the floor-length bathrobe. She also looks fine and fresh for six A.M., bright-eyed, undoubtedly bushy-tailed. Gulping down a swig of coffee, I say, "You told me yesterday, when I picked up Kenny, that if there was anything else you could do—"

She nods, waiting, evidencing neither eagerness nor mistrust. I plunge ahead. "Well, I've been having a hard time, just . . . taking care of the kid, being patient." I glance at Kenny, who's roaming the other end of the kitchen, chewing on the lip of his styrofoam cup, oblivious as usual. "There's a woman in our building I could leave him with sometimes. She doesn't charge much. But all she does is watch the tube, which does him no good. And besides, I don't wanna just dump the kid. Evenings I can manage, sort of, but when I think about a whole weekend of just me and him . . . you get the picture."

"Yeah, I get it."

"Look—"

"Mr. Galdoni . . . Paul, is it?" I nod, grab a cigarette, then stick it back into my jacket pocket. "Before we start getting . . . before you jump to the wrong conclusion, I meant yes, I do understand what you're saying. I don't have my own kids—at least not that I can deduct on my income tax—but I think I can relate to the need for some time away. Or at least some time when you can hear your own thoughts."

"Right, you oughta be able to. But you should also understand that I'm not tryna dump him on you. I, um, was thinking about the three of us, you know? Spending some time together." This feels more like an admission than an offer or invitation. I look away, feeling the back of my neck get warm.

"That would be fine with me."

It takes a few moments for this reply to register, for my mind to realize that it doesn't have to come up with some kind of retort. "Yeah?" I venture finally.

"I kid you not. And just for the record, I'm not trying to be a good samaritan. I am sympathetic to your situation, in particular your need to have other adults to be with and talk to. My calendar is not exactly crammed with social engagements these days. And since your wife . . . Lately, I get a different feeling from you, that's all. Like you might be worth getting to know."

"Thanks."

"I didn't mean that as faint praise."

"Well, I'll take what I can get."

"I'll bet."

I do a small double-take, giving a laugh that's more like a snort. At this point Kenny wanders over with his now-smeared milk mustache. His lips are flecked with bits of styrofoam, and a large piece of it protrudes, beak-like, from between his teeth. I look at Nahm and break up. She joins in, at the same time giving Kenny a hug, then wetting a paper towel to remove all the white matter from his face. She opens his mouth and peers in like a dentist, taking a couple of swipes at his tongue. I am amazed by the way he cooperates with her. I can understand the female touch and all that, but if it was Sharon trying to perform those operations, she, like me, would've needed a firm grip on Kenny's skull to get him to stay still. Nahm now holds up the large piece of styrofoam with his teeth-prints on one end. "Is this food, Kenny?" she asks.

"Sounds familiar," I murmur.

Kenny replies, "No," dutifully shaking his head, while eyeing the styrofoam as if thinking that maybe it just needs a little chocolate syrup or something.

After Nahm and I make arrangements for Saturday—some park, weather permitting—I rumple Kenny's hair and say goodbye to "Cheryl," feeling like the ice has been officially broken with my usage of the name. It's an easy one to whisper, I discover while driving down the Deegan toward my garage. I even close my eyes once to imagine saying it in the dark.

It occurs to me that Sharon would never believe that I have a date, or whatever it is, with Nahm, Cheryl, or anyone fitting my usual description of Kenny's teacher. Nor would Sharon believe—check that, she wouldn't be surprised at all—that I made this arrangement for the same day that her mother and sister are coming over to go through her belongings. I slap my forehead when I realize this.

Gloria doesn't seem too annoyed when I call her and request that she and Clara come on Sunday instead. Nor does she bother suggesting that I call Clara myself. Gloria calls me back the same night and says that the new plans are okay with her mother. Even so, I assume that I've again confirmed Clara's opinion that I'm a shithead. It doesn't take much to offend the woman.

* * *

On Saturday morning, Cheryl is ready when we arrive. Evidencing no wear and tear after a week of her kiddies, she's already packed lunch for the three of us. She'd insisted, despite a half-hearted argument from me. The fact is, I'm quite willing to let her assume all adult responsibilities for the day (except maybe driving).

My week, of hacking and watching Kenny, included several moments when I thought I was about to lose my grip, such as it is. The worst of these occurred last night, when Kenny dropped the mayonnaise jar. Lately he's taken to exploring the refrigerator—I don't know why, maybe he's just checking to see if I'm keeping it stocked—and last night he took out the Hellman's, then lost his grip. The jar exploded all over the floor. It was no big loss, the mayo was ancient, but still . . . It was right before his bedtime, and I had just enough energy left to get him ready. Period. Or so I thought. Confronted with a floor covered by yellow gunk and broken glass, I found enough energy to smash a few dishes. This is called "channelling your violence" or "picking the lesser of two evils." I couldn't physically harm Kenny, I'm just not willing to sink that low. He was crying as it was, maybe demonstrating enough intelligence to realize that he'd screwed up. Probably the tears weren't owing to fright; he was fascinated by the sight and sound of the dishes smashing on the kitchen floor. His eyes were dry by the time he took a cup off of the table and smashed it down onto the linoleum. My jaw dropped. Then I started laughing, and couldn't stop. I didn't finish cleaning up until midnight.

Now, I'm more relieved to see Cheryl Nahm than I would've ever thought possible. And Kenny's psyched for the trip. He tugs at Cheryl's front door knob and repeatedly shouts, "Go!"

"Just a minute, Ken," she says, firm but friendly. Cheryl seems attuned to both my needs and his. She's already changed his diaper, asked if he's hungry, and wiped his nose. I protest, though, when she slides into the back of the car next to Kenny.

"Cheryl," I say, "This is my day off. Could you sit up here? He'll be fine."

She complies, buckling herself in front and saying, crisply, "Tallman State Park please." This despite the fact that we're in the Valiant.

I laugh. "Lady, this is gonna be a serious fare, and I do expect a tip. Used to be I could've shut off the meter in the cab, saved both of us a little money. Charge less but not have to give half of it to the garage, you know? But now that I work for myself, everything on the meter comes to me anyway."

"You have to pay for your own gas," she says, showing a quick, impressive grasp of the finances of hacking.

"Of course. Between that, the fifty bucks I give the dispatcher in the morning, and not being able to skim money off the meter, the garage makes more and we make the same or less. These guys are not in it for charity."

"I'm sure," she replies as we pass under Fordham Road, heading for the George Washington Bridge. "Especially since they're not doing the driving. It must be . . . tedious. And dangerous."

"Well, the danger is probably overdone, and the tedium is . . . underdone, or something. I'd say it could drive you to drink, but I won't. And I don't . . . anymore, hardly. Lately." Gently, I tell Kenny to stop kicking the back of my seat. "Driving days, I'm sacrificing a little money for a little more safety and a little more sleep, I guess. Although guys have gotten it in daylight too."

"What made you start?"

"Bwidge," says Kenny, pointing in front of us.

Cheryl replies, "Right. That's the George Washington Bridge."

"Wash bwidge."

"Got a sponge, Ken?" I say, earning a laugh from Cheryl.

She says, "Do you think you could wash that with a sponge, Kenny? It's a big bridge, isn't it?"

"Big bwidge," he repeats, pointing at it again as we approach the exit ramp off of the Deegan. "Big twucks." He cranes his head, trying to keep the bridge in view as we circle up and around the ramp. "Big bwidge, big twucks" turns into a chant. Hopefully he'll be asleep soon.

"Anyway, you asked why I started hacking? Masochism." Glancing over at Cheryl, I'm almost startled to see her eyes fixed on me, her face in Sharon's seat. "Actually, the main reason is sitting behind us. Although maybe I shouldn't lay it on him. Maybe I shoulda tried harder to finish college. I dunno."

"How long did you go?"

"A whole twenty-five credits worth," I reply, my voice dropping. "I was trying to work full-time and go at night. That's a hard road to hoe. The only alternative was moving back in with my mother, which I was not about to do, fond of her though I am. Having a college grad for a son would have made her proud, too. It'd be a family first."

We cross the invisible line that separates New York and New Jersey. We're actually on Martha Washington, the lower level of the bridge. Kenny is quiet now. In my rear-view mirror I see something like awe on his face. Open-mouthed, he's gazing at the tractor trailers, buses, and other vehicles moving toward New York through the smoky dimness of the lower level, each briefly eclipsing the sunlit Hudson below. Cheryl says, "Well, I've known at least one Ph.D and one medical doctor-to-be, neither of whom was worth the weight of his degrees—minus the frames. Basically education expands your options a little bit, that's all."

"Yeah, and kids decrease them. Not that . . . I mean, I know that's what a lot of women say these days. Sorta like Marlon Brando in *On the Waterfront* : 'I coulda been somebody.' 'Cept his problem wasn't that he got stuck with the kids. Ever seen that movie? It was on Channel Five the other day."

"No, I haven't. But I'm glad Marlon Brando didn't get domesticated. At least some things are still sacred," says Cheryl with a dry laugh.

"Yeah, Clint Eastwood, Sylvester Stallone, all those tough, loner types. I'd like to see one of them stand up to a poopy diaper." Gratified by her obvious amusement, I flip down my sunglasses with a little flourish as we emerge from the shadows of Martha Washington. "Anyway, part of the problem is that there's never been anything that I've really been interested in doing, at least nothing that paid money instead of costing it."

"Well, that's one problem I haven't had. Once I realized that I probably wasn't going to be a movie star—about age nine—I pretty much always wanted to be a teacher. I—" Cheryl is interrupted by a wail from Kenny. A glance in the mirror tells me that the sun is bothering him.

"Close your eyes, Ken," I say, giving him one of my standard pieces of advice. The ramp onto the Palisades Interstate Parkway now curves in a different direction, putting the sun at our backs. His eyes tightly closed, Kenny doesn't notice this. Cheryl, to my surprise and gratification, doesn't clue him in. "Yeah, you seem good at teaching," I inform her.

"Thank you, Paul. It just sort of seemed an obvious choice for me. Even in elementary school I thought I knew more than my older brothers and sister, parents, teachers. I've always been pretty sure of myself. Opinionated, outspoken, ready to give advice."

"Can't say as I've noticed that."

"Ha ha."

"Okay, maybe a little. But why'd you pick preschoolers? How much do they understand?"

"It varies," she replies. "But at that age they're more open, less . . . formed. You can do a lot with them, if you do it the right way. I had to learn to mellow out a little bit, let them discover things for themselves. They're also vulnerable, which forced me to work on saying things more gently, being kinder. It helps develop your feelings, it really does." She glances back at Kenny.

He's nodding off. The car is working its magic.

"Yeah, when he's asleep like that, Kenny's a pretty lovable kid. He's—I don't mean to sound cynical or whatever. I do have feelings for him."

"I know you do. And I also know it's not easy. Kids I mean. Even one, full-time."

I start to ask her if that's why she's smart enough not to have any of her own, then think better of it. Instead I nod and say, "That's true. Although, believe it or not, I actually thought about becoming a teacher myself. Older kids. Phys. Ed. That's what the college was about. Thought I wouldn't mind throwing out basketballs at the beginning of a period, collecting them at the end. A minimum of hassles."

"There's probably more than you think. High schools are no picnic nowadays."

"Yeah, you might be right. Even while I was going to Lehman College, I wondered if I'd really do it if I ever got the degree. I mean, when I was in high school, gym teachers seemed like overgrown camp counselors to me, running around in shorts with whistles around their necks. Only reason we didn't laugh in their faces was that most of them were *big*. Big and dumb, at least that was the way they seemed. Hell, back then you could find something to laugh at about anyone, and we did. Drink beer and sneer. It was easy to do."

"I remember the kind; they were a large percentage of the student body at my high school."

"And *you* sneered at *them*."

"Right. Discreetly, of course," she says, laughing. "So, I guess you didn't have any idea then about what you wanted to do."

"Yeah, I wanted to be Marlon Brando." I look over at Cheryl and flash her a smile. It's becoming apparent that she believes in eye-to-eye contact; every time I glance to my right, she's looking back at me. By the time this trip is over she'll be very familiar with the right side of my face.

She smiles back at me. "Wiseguy," I hear her say as my eyes shift back to the road.

"That's exactly what I *didn't* want to be," I reply with a throaty laugh. "My father was a small-time Mafioso. Collected protection money for the big boys. He also boozed, made my mother cry a lot, and kicked my rear end. Took a while before I understood what he did for a living, but even before that I knew I didn't want to be like him. Besides, my mother might've taken his piece and shot me first. 'Course, I am like him in certain ways, or I have been. I wasn't all psyched up to make a success out of myself, to get a good honest job, say 'yessir' to my supervisors, and bust my rear end for peanuts, hoping maybe they'll pay me some serious money after ten years. So now I'm working for peanuts anyway. No supervisors on my back, hacking has that over the post office. But the money seems to go down instead of up."

As I say this I catch a glimpse of the Hudson through the leafless trees that border the Palisades Parkway, sticking up like sprouts of hair on top of the cliffs. These sheer cliffs, the Palisades, are probably the only part of New Jersey worth seeing. Far below the river glitters. I point across to the other side, at New York State. "You see Standard Coal over there?"

Cheryl gazes over her right shoulder. "Uh-hmm," she replies, her tone indicating puzzlement at the sudden turn in the conversation. "It's hard to miss. The letters look like they were set forth by God, or maybe the same guy who did Mount Rushmore."

"Yeah, well, right up from there, there's this high riser?" I jerk the steering wheel to the left as a loud horn informs me that I'm straying into the right lane.

"There're several of them."

"Right. One of them is where we live. 'Riverview ' they call it."

"For obvious reasons."

"Sure, if you live on the top five floors, facing west. But they charge the same rip-off rents if all you can see is Yonkers or just the high rise next door. And now that we have just one salary coming in, paying that rent is not gonna be easy. Assuming I wanna stay there now anyway, which is questionable."

"Was there life insurance?"

"Yup. The cash amount's still pending, but at least there'll be *something*. Maybe. Even in death Sharon proves herself right again. I laughed at the idea of getting the insurance, thought it was one more example of this super-responsible attitude she had. She . . . I dunno if I wanna talk about this," I say, shaking my head. "The initial shock has kind of worn off, but the problem is, I still feel like I was a bastard to her." I dig in my pocket for a cigarette. "This is called confession, I guess. My mother used to recommend it before she became a lapsed Catholic."

"Paul, there's nothing wrong with wanting to talk about things. Sometimes it helps."

"Right," I say, almost thanking her, sarcastically, for the words of wisdom. "You don't mind if I smoke."

"No, go ahead," she replies, making a little show of giving permission despite the fact that I've already pushed in the car's cigarette lighter. "Maybe roll down the window if it's not too cold."

"Sure." I roll it down, light up and take a drag, then add my smoke to the pollution on the Parkway. "Well, being blessed with enough intelligence to see bullshit everywhere, I thought getting married and having kids might make things a little more meaningful. But what it meant was . . . Shit, I don't wanna talk about this." I take a fast check on Kenny. He's softly snoring, draped over one side of the kiddie seat with his head against the right rear door.

Cheryl says, "Fine, I understand. Believe me, I hear plenty of stories as it is. Usually around six p.m., when the mothers are dog-tired and picking up their kids, getting ready to exchange one job for another. They talk to me. I'm like a way station, a coffee break or something. It's like, 'How are you? You won't believe what that S.O.B. did last night.' A few of them are divorced, two are fighting with their exes over child support. Maybe I get a skewed picture of the pros and cons of marriage, I don't know."

"Well, at least I never bent your ear like that."

"No, I usually bent yours. Almost literally."

"Cheryl, anytime you wanna bend my ear, feel free." I refrain from any clever remarks about the availability of the rest of my anatomy, instead saying, "So you've never been married yourself." I'd gathered this fact from Sharon. Despite Nahm's relative youth—twenty five years—I'd remarked that her single status figured, that any man who wanted to keep his balls would keep away.

"No I haven't," Cheryl replies.

"Fine-looking as you are, I assume that's by choice."

"Yes and no. Fine-looking as I am." She performs a mock primping of her page boy haircut. "Not to mention personable. I haven't yet felt the need to put an ad in the *Village Voice* personals. Close, but . . . I *was* once engaged. The guy was an intern at Montefiore Hospital. It turned out that his long hours involved some gynecological research at the apartments of a couple of the nurses. Maybe I should've been grateful when he owned up to it. He said he'd thought he would 'get it out of his system'—"

"An overload of sperm."

"Right. I would have preferred not knowing, despite my supposed belief in forthrightness. Not that I wish he would've gone ahead and married me, definitely not. But he could have just made up some lame excuse about his fear of commitment or whatever. Nothing kicks you in the ego like getting cheated on." I nod sympathetically, dragging on my cigarette and letting the smoke out of the left side of my mouth. Cheryl's story has kicked me in the conscience, even more than Gloria's well-founded accusation that I'd cheated on Sharon. And whether Sharon would have preferred knowing or not (probably not) she had the misfortune of finding out not from yours truly, but from the little tyke who more or less bound her to me.

I used to get laid occasionally in the cab. I'd get drunk and proposition any half-way decent-looking female I picked up. I figured, what could I lose? A fifty-cent tip? A few of them got pissed and copied down my name and hack number. I didn't even bother covering up the license; the Taxi and Limousine Commission is not made up of gentlemen who get irate about sexism. And sometimes I scored. I figured it was harmless, and if I had to hack I deserved a little treat once in a while. Made me feel like a teenager again, doing it in the back seat. Whoopee.

Once myself and this nubile Puerto Rican chick got surprised by the cops. They'd decided to check out the cab they saw parked on a deserted street—not that cops usually worry much about cabbies, at least about protecting us. My fare and I had to get up in a hurry. She just pulled down her dress, and forgot her panties in the back seat. Apparently, when we were rolling around they got wedged between the seat and the backrest. Later that night, I stopped home with the cab, and Kenny was still up. His sleeping habits were all screwed up at the time. Naturally, he wanted to go down and play in the cab. First I said, "No." I was too tired (and drunk, which fortunately the cops had chosen to ignore). But Kenny kept bawling about "Daddy-cab." Finally, Sharon took him down. She always had a hard time saying no to the kid. She buckled him into the back seat after he requested a spin around the block.

Kenny has never been able to keep his hands off of anything. His roving fingers turned up the panties. Sharon discovered the little pervert chewing on them. The experience radicalized her. When she came up and showed me the panties—they were green lace, I still remember clearly despite being stewed at the time—I said somebody had probably been shopping, and the panties fell out of a bag or something. Sharon threw them in my face and told me to take a whiff, which I did. It almost knocked me over.

Sharon never forgot this, and she never forgave or trusted me again. This was evident about a year later, when we were discussing her starting work and me switching to day shift. "Aside from the other benefits involved, it'll probably be easier for you to keep your pants on in the cab in broad daylight," Sharon said. Despite the sarcasm, her eyes betrayed an undiminished hurt. It was hard to miss, even for me.

* * *

As we approach one of the Palisades Parkway's many toll plazas, I refuse Cheryl's offer to pay. "It's on me." Big spender. I whip a single out of my jacket pocket as we coast up to a toll booth. The collector, a green-uniformed woman whose body looks like it would have to be deflated for her to get out of the booth, takes a side-long glance at me, grunts, and snatches my dollar. Her usual friendly service, probably. But it's easy enough to imagine that she somehow knows who she's dealing with. I might as well have a sign on my forehead reading, "Adulterous Asshole."

I leave a little rubber as I pull away from the booth. But I quickly slow down. There's usually at least one cop hanging around a toll plaza (waiting for his cut, I'm sure). Besides, Cheryl is pressed back against her seat by the squealing exit. She says, "You can take the boy out of the cab—"

"Right, okay." I give a laugh which sounds more like I'm clearing my throat, then ease the Valiant up to sixty. I almost flick my cigarette butt out the open window, but manage to short-circuit this usually reflexive action. Cheryl would probably think nothing of it, but—"So," I say, snuffing out the butt in the car's ashtray, "When did you break up with this guy?"

"Doctor Strangelove? About six months ago. I've been out once or twice since then, but mostly I'm staying in."

"I think he must have been crazy to cheat on you, Cheryl." Read that "Sharon," judging from the intensity in my voice as I make this declaration, staring straight ahead at the road. Some belated atonement.

I'm mildly startled, in the next instant, to feel Cheryl's hand on my shoulder. "Thanks, Paul," she says, her lips curving up at the corners. She lets her fingers slide lightly down the arm of my jacket before she removes them. I can hardly feel this, but I get a ridiculous charge out of it anyway, as if she'd sprinkled magic dust capable of instantaneously tightening one's pants. "Your opinion of me seems to have changed alot from what it used to be," she adds.

"You could say that," I reply into the windshield. "It's been weird, but I swear, seeing you in the morning this past week has sorta recharged my batteries—and not just because I was dropping Kenny off. I actually don't mind getting into my car in the morning now. That's a major change, believe me."

"You have metamorphosed."

"Isn't that what butterflies do?"

"Caterpillars. Also tadpoles."

"Well, I've been called worse, I guess. 'Snake in the grass'—"

She laughs. "I don't know if that's accurate. If anything, you usually seem pretty up front to me. Anyway, it's been five mornings that you've left Kenny off, and I really wish I had one of those cameras trained on my door. Each time you seemed a little different to me, a little more relaxed. The first morning, it was like you had one foot out the door even before you came in, like you were about to enter a minefield or something. You sort of sent Kenny in ahead of you."

"Figured I need my legs more than he does."

"Ha-ha. Seriously though, the reason I said metamorphosis —metamorphosed, I mean—is that it's characterized by stages. And just seeing you in the doorframe five consecutive mornings, if I could put each frame next to the previous one, it would make a perfect picture of . . . metamorphosis. Tell me Paul," she adds after a moment, "Am I imagining this, or do I sound like a fool?"

I slip my hand over the back of hers, more than doubling the weight atop her left thigh. "Never," I reply with quiet conviction. Placing my hand back on the steering wheel, I'm grateful for the necessity of having to pay at least a little attention to the road. It distracts me from the uneasiness I'm starting to feel. Obviously, I'd never felt much reluctance about cheating on Sharon. But now it's easy to imagine her watching us, even to imagine her alive inside of me, as I did at the funeral. Or maybe I'm just developing a conscience, a few years too late. And, wonder of wonders, I might also be developing some foresight. It occurs to me that even if Cheryl and I hit the sack just once, it couldn't be a one night stand. We see each other too much. And Kenny's involved, blissfully ignorant or not. If the pendulum of my relationship with Cheryl swung the other way again, the distaste we used to feel for each other would be peanuts, given my remarkable talent for making things go sour.

Still, the possibility that Cheryl is now having reservations of her own seems to bother me more than any of mine. After a period of silence, broken only by Kenny's snoring, I jump-start the conversation with a little white lie. "You've never sounded like a fool to me, Cheryl. Not even when you were talking about stages of inebriation. I didn't really wanna hear it, but I sorta knew you were lookin' out for Kenny . . . and tryna save his daddy from Demon Rum."

"Well, think of all the money you'll be saving on breath spray," she cracks, causing my face to get warm and pink. "Seriously Paul, please don't think I'm some kind of prude. When it's . . . appropriate, or when I feel like it, I've been known to raise a glass or two."

Which she demonstrates later, over dinner at an Italian restaurant called Sorrento's. We'd figured that we had earned the privilege of being waited on after several hours of towing Kenny around Tallman State Park. The young fella had woken up on the wrong side of his car seat. Little squirt though he is, when he decides he's not walking, it almost takes a "toe-toe truck" (one of his favorite vehicles) to move him. He'd finally consented to travel around the park using one of two modes of transportation. The first was having Cheryl and me each hold his hands and together jerk him up off of the ground whenever he counted to three. This exercise can dislocate your shoulder and/or your elbow after you've done it a few hundred times. Unfortunately Kenny's joints all seem to be made of rubber. The only alternative he would accept was riding in Cheryl's arms or on her shoulders; mine were suddenly unacceptable. If I seated him on my shoulders, his usual perch, he started screaming and throwing himself toward her, dangling his body parallel to the ground, apparently confident I wouldn't let go of his feet.

He also loudly refused to let me push him on the baby swings in one of the playgrounds in Tallman. I had to resist giving him one hard shove that might've sent both him and the swing hurtling back up and over the horizontal bar they were hanging from. I could see them twirling like bolero balls, the two lengths of chain wrapping around the bar until Kenny himself was fastened to it high above the ground, draped upside down over the swing's safety belt, bawling. I could see it all clearly.

Whatever the reasons for his behavior (I'm sure a Kiddie shrink could come up with a few), it afforded me the opportunity to show Cheryl what a patient daddy I can be. I humbly accepted her compliments. And despite "Special K" we had some fun, chasing and tickling each other with these giant cattails that grow along the Hudson River. We also made a fire a little ways back from one of the cliffs. Kenny was mesmerized by the flames. We toasted marshmallows and gorged ourselves on them. Later we pulled into the first restaurant we came across on Central Avenue, the main shopping strip in Southern Westchester.

* * *

Fortunately Sorrento's lays a basket of breadsticks on you, which I've been using to plug up Kenny's mouth. Soon he takes over this job himself. Cheryl is working on her second glass of predinner Chianti. Her face is aglow. Even after her veal parmigiana arrives she can't stop sipping and talking about herself: when she was a kid her family ran a hotel in the Catskill's Borscht Belt; her older, teenaged brother and sister hated having to help out, but she, a precocious kid and the apple of her father's eye, loved the place. She loved showing off her smarts and maturity to the elderly guests, easily downshifting to play with the kids of the occasional younger vacationers. She informs me that the whole Borscht Belt is almost dead now, that her father sold the hotel at a loss to some guru and his followers who still use the place as an ashram; her father now wholesales gourmet foods . . .

I nod my head, sip scotch, chew overdone meatballs, and occasionally wipe Kenny's face, feeling a perverse sense of satisfaction at the obvious loosening of Cheryl's strings under the influence of a small amount of wine. This last is a hopeful sign. Conscience or no, I've decided on my place. Hers is a studio, and Kenny's used to his own room and still sleeps in a crib. The gleam in Cheryl's eyes and the flush around her high cheekbones fade slightly when out of the blue I suggest that she stop up after we pay the check and help me put Kenny to bed. He'd like that, I add, not bothering to check with him on this.

"Then how would I get home? What are we really talking about here, Paul?"

She asks this question with more amusement than accusation, as if appreciative of my having come up with a truly ridiculous pretext.

A smirk flickers across my face. "Well—"

"Because I'm willing," she says abruptly. "At least I think I am. And I don't want to think about it too much—or any more than I already have. Just . . . romance me a little first, Paul. That way I won't feel like I'm a substitute."

Substitute or not, physically she is the genuine article. And romancing her turns out to be no problem. Kenny cooperates for once, falling asleep on the way home from Sorrento's and barely stirring as I change his diaper, slip on his Batman pj's, and lay him in the crib. Leaving his door slightly ajar, I return to Cheryl in the living room. I stroke the side of her face, tentatively. I'm a mite hesitant now; this *is* still Sharon's house, even though she's dead, maybe more so because she is.

Possibly reading my tentativeness as an attempt to be gentle, Cheryl responds in kind. She brushes her lips against my palm, my fingers. Maybe there's something to be said for trying a little tenderness after all. This soft, shy contact between us is enough to inflame me. Cheryl too, apparently. We step back from each other, but in the next instant are wound up together, sucking on each other's tongues like schoolkids in heat.

- 9 -
Sharon

"WOULD YOU want him to die before his time?"

I look at my grandmother, my father's mother, who died before I was born, and shrug helplessly. "I really don't know. On earth, I would've said I'd have to die with him. Not knowing, of course, how lovely that might've been. Now I'd say yes, send him right up, except maybe for the grief it would cause my mother. It would probably kill her. Which might be the best thing that could happen to her anyway." I glance over at my father, who gives me a non-commital smile. Talking to myself as much as to the others, I conclude, "I don't know. I just don't."

My father, my paternal grandmother and grandfather, and I are discussing my recurrent longing for Kenny. I've already been given to understand that his "time" to die doesn't necessarily have much to do with his biological age. And that I in fact hadn't died before my time; there's really no such thing.

Be that as it may, the time and place in which a person most recently lived is usually quite apparent here. My grandmother is wearing a "cotton" summer dress, circa 1945 or thereabouts.

It's white with blue stripes running horizontally on the bodice, and running vertically on the skirt and sleeves. This cotton really breathes. Through it I can see the backrest of the square wooden chair on which my grandmother sits, part of a visual reproduction of the dining room set she owned for thirty years in Oceanside, Long Island. Only the dress and the arrangement of her dark hair— pulled back from her forehead and temples and hanging down in a fan shape behind her ears and neck— give any indication that she is of a generation other than mine. She looks no older than me, having chopped ten or fifteen years off of her appearance after she died. In fact, she could be some lost sister of mine. We resemble each other as much or more than Gloria and I did. Several of my grandmother's genes must have been funneled down to me through my father. This is much more apparent than it ever was in the black and white photographs I'd seen.

We share more than dark hair and eyes, however, more than diminutive stature. She can relate very directly to my feelings about Kenny.

"After I died," she says, sipping tea from a fine china cup (this is a posthumous addition to her kitchen, part of the kind of fancy set she'd craved but couldn't afford on Long Island), "I couldn't bear the thought of deserting my family. I actually stayed around for several days—"

"I could tell," says my grandfather, winking. "For about a week, I'd get this terrible feeling of guilt whenever I threw my dirty underwear on the floor."

My father, clearly his father's son, enjoys this little joke immensely. Even I can't resist the giddy feeling transmitted by the two of them. Not so my grandmother. "I knew I was dying," she continues, ignoring them. "At age forty, with my children just teenagers. I built up such resentment about it, such an unwillingness to leave them . . . and my husband," she adds grudgingly. "I just carried that feeling with me right out of my body. People on earth have fantasies of attending their own funerals, to see how much everybody loves them. You'd be surprised at how many wind up doing it."

"I couldn't have stood that . . . even assuming my husband had the good sense not to bring Kenny."

"My *kinder* were there," she says, smiling, sending a little beam of love in the direction of my father, who responds in kind. "Abraham and your Uncle David, they were so brave."

"*Nu*, I was what, fourteen?" says my father. "In those days, a man wasn't supposed to cry. It was hard."

"I knew, *tattaleh*. I could see, I could feel it. It was terrible. Especially with Papa over there crying his eyes out. My loved ones grieving needlessly. I knew I wasn't really dead, but I could do nothing to make them feel better. As if my heart wasn't already broken. There was nothing I could do."

"You could've at least kept the rebbe from ripping my good suit," my grandfather tells her. A torn collar symbolizes bereavement.

"Oh, *shah* !" She throws a cube of sugar at my grandfather. He dissolves it in mid-flight, as if playing some astral video game. At this, he and my father are silently convulsed again. The two of them are like rambunctious kids. Cheering me up is a responsibility they accept with glee.

My grandmother sighs. "As you see, the family gets reunited anyway. It happens over and over again. Here, and on Earth." She looks at her husband and son with an exaggerated weariness. "You'll be with Kenny again . . . When he dies, or even before," she says, alluding to my father's pre-death visit from his hospital bed. "In the meantime, it's good to let him work out what he needs to down there. There are reasons he must grow up without you, reasons you died when you did."

* * *

It's just dawn, but already the heat is unbearable. Sweat pours from beneath my helmet. Dust kicked up by Vitellius' hooves sticks to my forehead, pains my eyes. I named him Vitellius after the emperor candidate of the Rhine Army, whose legions we are bound to meet in combat. The stupidity of the horse Vitellius approaches that of the man. I have to jerk the reins as we ride to avoid collisions with the chariots to either side of mine. Vitellius the horse might consider this to be my failing more than his. My brain is still thick from last night's wine, and my head pounds as if the hooves were landing on it instead of the cracked ground. Only my clenched teeth slow down the stream of curses from the foulness of my mouth.

Through the dust and almost blinding sunlight, I can barely see the roofs of Cremona near the horizon. The thought of whores, and food, sickens me now, but that will change by the time we reach Cremona. That's if we get there ahead of the barbarian dung that Vitellius employs as his soldiers.

It means nothing to me who becomes the emperor of Rome. If Vitellius offered more gold than Vespasian, I'd be running my sword through the men wearing the same helmets and breastplates as I am now. Or one of them would run me through. That means less than nothing to me. If it meant more, I'd be pissing on the floor of my chariot; I'd have been dead long ago.

Looking at the warriors around me, it's hard to imagine dying. We are like a thundering, deathless herd of gods, the fanning crests of our helmets like wings across the plains. But like the gods, most of us would betray each other in an instant if it suited our purposes. It suits us now to fight together, in order to remain living men.

Soon we are close enough to Cremona that the village's huts now stand as separate from one another. From this distance, they look like round arrowheads planted in the ground. The pointed roofs seem to grow higher as we approach. Still, they may soon be levelled, depending on the mood of our general, Galba. It must be a sad life, living in an unwalled village, waiting to be crushed beneath the hooves of one army or another. Yet these peasants deserve what befalls them, if they are stupid enough to believe even for a moment that a government, and the laws that it makes, can protect them. The government can no longer protect itself. That job, and the gold that comes along with it, may soon be ours. Onward for the glory of Vespasian.

For now, whatever pitiful riches Cremona possesses will have to do. As we enter the village, Vitellius almost plunges the chariot into one of the drainage ditches these peasants have dug. I swerve at the last moment, cursing the sons of whores.

My curses are echoed by Cestus, the soldier to my right. Our hubs brush before he swerves away from me. A fast reaction only possible because we were slowing, scanning Cremona through the dust and the troops before us. We rein our horses in front of a hut where fenced-in pigs are squealing in fright. This sound, and that of horses neighing, alone ring through the village. One would think no people live here. Surely they are no longer asleep, but cowering behind their clay walls.

Finally a young boy, perhaps seven years, runs from the hut as Cestus and I step over the fence. Its slats will do nicely for a fire. Ignoring the boy, I draw my sword as Cestus, on all fours, pins down a fat pig. The boy, screaming, "No!", sinks his teeth into my forearm. The sword falls from my hand as I roar in surprise and pain. I bring my clenched free hand heavily against the side of the boy's head. He collapses on the ground. Blood is oozing from the bite wound on my arm. Enraged, I bend down for my sword, just as the boy's mother rushes shrieking from the hut. I grasp the handle of the sword. She reaches me, bent on pleading for her son, as I bring the blade up from the ground. I hear Cestus yell, "Hold your sword! We'll take them!" His voice seems to come from a great distance, even as the point of my sword tears another hole in the woman's tattered robe and plunges into her breast.

* * *

"I didn't do that." I manage to get this across only because it's not necessary to speak here. "How could that have been me?" I evaporate the tears streaming down my face, but more appear. Suddenly I can do without being able to manifest whatever my mind desires, I can do without the knowing via direct experience, or re-experience, that prevails here. My grandmother had only been trying to comfort me when she'd mentioned that there were reasons for my death. But how could I not want to know them? The desire had been enough.

"That was you, princess," says my grandmother, stroking my cheek with a transparent hand. Although she looks my age—the whole notion of which is starting to seem absurd—I definitely feel like her grandchild; I'd enjoy being a babe in her arms. "The soldier was a lesser version of you," she tells me. "All your lives were. Even the lovely Sharon. They're all steps on the ladder back to Hashem. If one of the steps gets rotted—or if several of them do—some of the repair work must be done on Earth, some here."

My grandfather informs my grandmother that she's spoken well. Their native tongue was Yiddish, once incomprehensible to me. Now, it seems for a moment that I understand my grandfather better than my grandmother does. Accustomed to his teasing, she reflexively shoots him a look, then half-smiles as she realizes that he's serious. Meanwhile my father's attention has not strayed from me. He beams at me with a love which is almost palpable, which warms me inside, which I need now more than anything.

"But, even though it was so real," I say, "That must have been two thousand years ago."

My grandmother replies, "A blink in the eye of Hashem. And besides, payments—*nu,* it sounds crude, but that's what it amounts to—can be deferred over a few or even several lifetimes. You've had at least one incarnation between your lives as a Roman soldier and Avraham's daughter, Kenny's mother. There've probably been more."

"I don't want to know about them," I quickly answer, eliciting gentle laughter all around. It produces a tentative smile on my face. "Not now, anyway. And why . . . why is it that on earth people know nothing about anything? Nothing about afterlife, nothing about their pasts, really. People trace their roots, or think they are, that was fairly popular when I died. What a joke."

My father says, "It wouldn't be so funny to have that kind of information by itself. That woman you killed, for instance. Think how you'd feel if you were aware of it without knowing that she in fact didn't die; her body died, that's all. It's something you really only understand by going through it yourself.

"I do know that, don't I."

"You do, sweetie. And also that there was some reason she needed to die then. You were just the agent."

"No, Daddy. Uh-uh. I was a filthy son of a bitch. Son of a whore, as I might have brilliantly put it in Latin. I had no idea that language could be so vile."

My father concedes the point. "Okay, maybe you weren't the nicest person in the world then. Still, it was not an accident that you were visited upon the woman."

"Avraham, you're starting to sound like you just stepped

out of the bible," interjects my grandfather, feeling that serious conversation has gone on long enough. His greenish eyes fall on me. "Have some more of this cake, beautiful. We've met several women here, mostly Americans, who refused to believe that they weren't in highest heaven when they realized that they could eat anything, forever, and never gain an ounce." He slides a luscious-looking chocolate layer cake across the fine linen table cloth. My grandmother had elected to manually embroider this table cloth, in a pattern of flowers that almost seem alive. She stands now waiting for more tea water to boil on the range, an activity which is unnecessary but which she finds comforting. I find the exquisite taste of the cake comforting, to say the least, despite previously feeling that I had no appetite for anything. When the first forkful of cake crosses my lips, a creamy chocolate thrill runs through me. To everyone's amusement, my aura temporarily turns a rich brown.

Still, it takes a while for me to really relax, to recover from my little trip to Rome. I rearrange my hair several times; repeatedly, I glance over my shoulder at the stately grandfather clock in the living room. Its hands and pendulum haven't moved since the early stages of my residence here in the family house, which is a somewhat embellished replica of the house where my father grew up on Long Island. The clock is one of the embellishments: a monument to timelessness. My grandmother intentionally created this piece of nostalgic decoration so that it cannot be set in motion mentally, rather it must be wound. She only vaguely remembers the last time she wound it prior to my arrival.

After joining my father in his parents' astral abode, I tried to help out by ordering things a bit (hanging loose was never a skill of mine; witness my dismal failure as a hippie). The others humored me in this; my grandmother helped me to plan laundries and meals. Eventually I saw how ridiculous this was: not only does no one keep time, but time doesn't keep itself. It's night outside of our kitchen window only because that suits our collective mood. Thus are day and night determined here. Unless, of course, one is reliving part of a past incarnation on earth.

We eventually do this together. When my grandmother said

that I'd had at least one incarnation in between being a Roman soldier and being Sharon, she wasn't just figuring the odds. She'd in fact recognized an old acquaintance. We'd been together before, at different periods of history—including the late 1700's, in Virginia.

I am lying near death in an old woman's body. Gazing upward through the smoky air, I see stalks of corn alongside slabs of salted pork hanging from the ceiling. Frigid air seeps through the logs of our cabin, despite the clay packing and the fire kept roaring by my grandchildren, Jane and Thomas. It occurs to me that I will soon amount to nothing more than those slabs of pork, in fact less, since I'll be not salted but slowly rotting. And yet this time (unlike Rome), there's an element of awareness that extends, briefly, beyond the immediate situation. Far beyond. Maybe this is because I'm so close to dying. Maybe it also has to do with the fact that my companions from my "current" sojourn in the afterworld are re-experiencing past lives of their own along with me: I recognize the souls of Jane and Thomas, my colonial grandchildren, to be those of Sharon's twentieth-century paternal grandparents. This recognition comes not from sight or any other sense. Rather it's a quiet yet unmistakable knowing, one which fades back into the haze of my sickness but leaves in its wake an unfamiliar feeling of comfort.

Despite repeated promises made to their father, who is out hunting pheasant, Jane and Thomas are unable to keep from taunting each other. Thomas calls Jane a "sow's arse", and in turn Jane wonders how he knows the end of a pig so well. This is how the children amuse themselves. In the absence of my son, their father, their taunts get more ribald. Understandably, they have little faith left in my alertness.

I've had to be more of a mother to them than a grandmother. Their mother—may she rest in peace (if her religion earned her that)—died of the consumption the same year that it took my sister Emily and my husband Joseph. Has it been eight years now? The years run together, yet moments from long ago stand out as if they'd happened yesterday. I remember my first sight of Viginia's verdant shoreline, after what seemed to be years of seasickness, years of salted beef, years of thirst. At least we survived the voyage. Many did not, including my mother. Father never recovered from her death. That is the excuse I've given him for deserting Emily and me, another moment that could have happened yesterday. How old was I? The same age as Jane now, or younger? Nine? Somehow I knew—I can still see his broad back, blunderbuss over one shoulder, sheepskin sack dangling from the other hand, swinging as if he was scything wheat. Had I driven him away? Surely it was not Emily, his little lady-in-waiting, cursed with a boyish sister who has legs like a wolf's, hands like a wolf's claws. Emily looks up at me now, the little dimpled face suddenly turning down and flinching as acorns rain down from the tree I'm in . . . but then I had the heart of a frightened rabbit when it came to canings. And how could he have spared the cane, finding me with clumps of Emily's hair in my fingers, and her screaming? My screaming soon replaced hers. Had Joseph, whose family took us in, not taken a shine to me . . .

A cold wind prickles the skin of my cheek. Dimly I recognize my son Seth as he pushes the door shut behind him. He has three bloodied birds dangling from his hand, itself reddened from the cold. Inclining his head toward me, he hushes Jane and Thomas as they loudly greet him, the way children should greet their father. My father.

* * *

"Daddy—?" Even as I gaze stupefied at my father and grandparents, a smile begins to spread across my face.

"Yes Sharon, my sweet daughter. Or should I say mother? You raised me well. You even taught me how to read, which was unusual back then."

"You taught us, too," adds my grandmother. "*Nu,* it's no wonder you were a teacher in the Bronx."

"If you can call what I did there teaching. I was your mother," I say, turning back to my father. "If I didn't know it, I'd never believe it."

He shrugs. "Well, believe it. It's a balancing act, I think that's what they might call it on earth."

"They would call it a fairy tale, or maybe some hokum cooked up in Hollywood. Although, come to think of it, Gloria might say 'I told you so.'"

"She might say, 'Let's stop pulling each other's hair already.'"

"She was Emily?"

"Maybe," my father replies. "Probably. We can say for sure once she gets here. Understand, in the long run these things are not that important. And they're more complicated than they seem at the moment. You're dealing with many lifetimes and interrelationships."

"Interrelationships seems like the right word, Daddy. Can you tell me anything about Kenny?" I cast pleading glances at my father and his parents. "I'm sorry if I sound like a broken record, but—" I pause. Satisfied that no one feels put upon, I continue, "Maybe he was my father in Virginia who deserted us? And maybe that's why—"

"Again, it's possible. It makes sense. Well, at least he's got your husband to take care of him."

"That could be a mixed blessing."

- 10 -

Paul

SEX IN the morning is not something I've engaged in much, although this has not been by choice. Most mornings during the past ten years I've woken up hung over to one degree or another, with breath that could repel a bear. Also, on any morning when it hadn't been necessary to wake up via an alarm clock and Kenny had found it in his heart to let us sleep, Sharon was out of bed before I woke up. She claimed that if she didn't hear Kenny by nine A.M., she all but assumed that the worst had happened.

So I was a mite surprised this morning to open my crusted eyes and see a sleeping face on the pillow next to mine, especially when I realized that the face, topped by a short mop of swirled brown hair, was not Sharon's. After a brief start I sighed and flopped my head back onto the pillow. Sharon was gone. I recognized Cheryl and recalled our trip to Tallman State Park yesterday.

A drowsy smile crossed my face as I remembered our first bout of sex last night. Moaning and groaning, we'd actually rolled around on the living room rug, as if challenging ourselves not to lose for even a moment the unbelievably sweet, slippery connection between us. Afterward, we had spent a fair amount of time and laughter plucking bits of shag carpet from each other's skin. She'd then accepted the beer I offered, which she sipped while I tossed down a couple of stronger drinks. After that, it was easy enough to continue the festivities in the king-sized bed that Sharon and I had bought after we'd gotten married.

Now, watching Cheryl's breasts rise and fall beneath the sheet, tantalizingly outlined with each inhalation, there's no chance of my dozing off again. It's 9:43 a.m. according to the digital clock on the night table. Through the paper-thin walls, I can hear Kenny playing in his crib, honking the red nose of the "Honkee" clown doll he sleeps with (it's actually labelled "Honkee" and dressed in a confederate flag. Kenny found the thing in a park, and Sharon's desire to toss it out had only increased his attachment). This activity sometimes occupies Kenny for a while, and keeps him in the crib. I'm hoping I'll get lucky now.

Cheryl barely stirs as I slide the top sheet down to the foot of the bed. I lightly run my tongue over her pink nipple. It brightens and swells, practically inserting itself into my mouth. Sleeping Beauty now awakens or stops playing 'possum, as the case may be. She reaches down and strokes my organ, which needs no encouragement, then guides me inside her. This is like slipping back into a dream. I wrap my arms around her. Then, piercingly, the doorbell rings. Not the downstairs buzzer, the doorbell. Either Flannery has Sundays off or he's being his usual useless self. The bell rings again, longer this time.

With a whimper of frustration, Cheryl lays back, dropping her arms to the bed and removing her legs from around my rear. Then a light goes on in my brain. I freeze. "Jesus Christ!" I bite off. I push myself up on my elbows and pull out of her.

She sighs in protest, "Oh, don't," then notices the alarm on my face and gives me a quizzical look. "Just don't answer it," she says, shrugging. "Or if you feel like you have to, put on a bathrobe—then come back here and take it off, as soon as humanly possible." Her lips part in a breathy smile.

In the next instant, the first option is gone. Kenny has climbed out of his crib and is fiddling with the locks. I could run out naked and tackle the little so-and-so, but he's known how to unlock the door for a while now; it doesn't take him much time. And I'm sure Sharon's mother would be offended by the sight of my uncircumsized prick first thing in the morning. I vault out of bed, find my bathrobe and throw it on. "Cheryl, get dressed. Take my word for it, it's necessary."

"But, why?" she asks, a hurt tone creeping into her voice. "Besides, my clothes are in the living room."

"Christ." I reach into the closet for one of Sharon's robes to give Cheryl, think better of it, then dash into the living room as I hear Kenny yell, "Nanny!" Snatching up Cheryl's things, I catch a glimpse of Clara in the foyer, hugging my son.

"You're glad to see me, *tataleh*?" croons Sharon's mother. Behind her stand Gloria and Lila. I fucking forgot they were coming. I don't believe it. I'd told them to come around ten figuring that if I forgot, I'd be here anyway.

Tucking the clothes into the fold of my bathrobe, I hustle back to the bedroom and toss them in. "It's my ex-mother-in-law, my sister-in-law, and my neice," I say, surprised that I have the clarity of mind to lay out the relationships. "I forgot they were coming. I'm sorry. It'll be alright, I'll take care if it."

Before she can reply, I close the bedroom door. I'll take care of it. Right. I could have told her to just stay in the bedroom, even asked her to hide in the closet, but the ladies will be heading for both places. The closet contains much of what they came for. It occurs to me as I move toward my visitors that strictly speaking I've done nothing wrong, have nothing to apologize for. But even I don't believe it.

Gloria is now taking her turn hugging Kenny, whose pajamas are all askew from the affection and from rolling around in his crib. I position myself in front of Clara, who is advancing toward the living room. "Hello, Clara," I say, nodding, trying to shake loose some reason why she and her cohorts should come back later. "How you doin'?"

The slack skin near the corners of her mouth puckers as she looks askance at me, her filmy brown eyes narrowing. The unspoken message is obviously, "Since when do you give a shit?"

So much for the tiny bit of thawing I thought had occurred between us during the drive to the funeral. Finally she replies, "As well as can be expected." She starts to unbutton her overcoat.

"Um, maybe you shouldn't do that," I say. "I'm sorta embarrassed about the condition of the house, didn't get a chance to um . . . maybe the three of you could go downstairs, have some coffee for a few minutes, lemme clean up."

The skeptical look on Clara's face deepens. Gloria, who has deposited my son with Lila, says, "Don't be ridiculous, Paul. Besides, if you really feel like you have to clean, six hands are better than one. I mean two." She glances from me to Clara and back again, hoping for a cheerful response from someone.

As if jerked by the same string, our three heads swivel toward the bedroom door which, with a slight creak, has just opened. Fully dressed, Cheryl steps out.

For once, Clara and I are on the same wave length. Her mouth drops open in horror. I want to scream, either at Cheryl or life in general. I have an urge to just turn and walk out the door, leaving the females to sort things out for themselves. Both of these notions flash in and out of my mind in the same instant, short-circuiting each other. Dazed, I wait for someone to take charge.

"Hello, I'm Cheryl Nahm." This introduction so completely overshadows the sound of Kenny babbling "Why-wa"—the only sound there had been for a few extremely long seconds—that Kenny's voice might as well be coming from another planet.

Clara finally turns to me, her haggard face now alive with rage. "You son of a bitch," she snarls. "You goyische son of a bitch!" I study the hair on my bare toes. My hands are clasped behind my back as a safety precaution; slugging Clara would not solve anything, although it might feel good. "Ten days Sharon's been dead, and you bring home this, this—"

"Ma, don't blame her. She probably didn't know," says Gloria, placing a calming hand on Clara's shoulder, taking pity on the red-faced Cheryl.

"I knew," says Cheryl, after clearing her throat. "I mean, I knew about Sharon passing away. I barely knew *her*. She was always in a hurry in the morning, she . . . Look, I'm Kenny's nursery school teacher. Believe it or not, I've been trying to help out. At least that's the way it started." Her voice cracks ever so slightly. "I didn't expect . . . I didn't know you were coming, Mrs. . . ."

"Weiss," Gloria fills in for her mother, whose jaw has dropped anew on learning the identity of my bed mate.

"Cheryl, I'm sorry. I swear I just forgot." The note of pleading in my voice disgusts me almost as much as the situation itself. I start to whirl away toward the kitchen and my stash of booze, but then stay put. Something tells me that if Cheryl has not already written me off, leaving her even briefly alone with my in-laws would do the trick.

"Kenny's teacher?" repeats Clara dumbly. She gazes over at her grandson, then at Lila. Lila's been wearing a little gap-toothed smile, a look of stunned fascination at the goings-on. Now, trying to feign ignorance, she fixes her face and looks away from Clara, who repeats to no one in particular, "Kenny's teacher. That surprises me a little. The fact that he's got a woman here," she continues, addressing Gloria now, "even with Sharon's family coming over, that shouldn't surprise me. Should it? He cheated on her when she was alive. He—" Clara's voice gives. Her face seems to crumble, wringing out tears. They run down her rouged cheeks. Even after her sobbing is partially muffled by Gloria's sweatered breast and shoulder, the sound is almost unbearably loud.

Meanwhile Cheryl, having retrieved her jacket from the foyer closet, quietly asks if I know the name of a cab company she can call. The look she gives me is icy.

"Look, they'll be here for a while. Lemme drive you," I reply almost under my breath, seeing both a way to escape from my own apartment and a chance to explain to Cheryl . . . to explain what? I'm sure I could come up with something.

"I think you ought to stay here."

"But—"

"Let me put it like this," she hisses, glancing over at the trembling Clara. "I don't want to be with you right now, or discuss it for one more second. Is there a cab company?"

I give her a name and she proceeds to the kitchen telephone. Clara disengages herself from Gloria and starts searching for the bathroom. She's been here maybe once before in her life. Sharon and Kenny always went to her house. I call out directions and a couple of seconds later the bathroom door slams shut. Now it's Gloria's turn. Even Lila, I notice, is looking at me with disgust.

"Paul, you really need to get your shit together, you know?" Gloria says with quiet contempt (Lila seems as flustered as I am: her hand flies up to cover her mouth when she hears her mother use the "s" word. Kenny imitates the gesture. In another situation this might be amusing). "How the hell could you forget? You forgot once, changed the day, then forgot again?"

"Paul, what's your address?" Cheryl asks from behind me, re-entering the living room. Apparently she's too classy to just yell from the kitchen. Visual daggers are now coming at me from two directions. I give her the information and she hustles back to the phone. Slowly I turn again to Gloria. "How could I forget? Good question. I did, that's all. I'm a fucking asshole. Okay?"

"You got that right," replies Gloria, not the least bit fazed by my surly attitude. "And you should apologize to my mother, Paul. You owe her that, at least."

"Fine. Clara!" I shout toward the bathroom door, "I'm sorry. Alright?" This is of course not a bonafide apology, but it's the best I can do, a disgusted, childish plea to everyone in the house to leave me the fuck alone.

Cheryl takes me up on this first. The loud silence which follows my "apology" is broken by the sound of the front door closing behind her. Shortly thereafter Kenny comes over and tugs on my bathrobe.

"Poop," he announces. I'm actually grateful, even though the diaper I'll be changing contains at least twelve hours worth of piss to go along with the crapola. I haul him off to his room and slap him down on his changing table, which he's long since outgrown. His calves dangle over the raised edge, which to me is the cut-off point: if the soles of your feet extend past here, son, you oughta be in underwear already. But Kenny's not a bit embarrassed about this. Nor does he give a shit (no pun intended) about the soap opera-ish goings-on of the last twenty minutes. Usually it doesn't take much to set him off. But now he just lays there and talks gibberish to himself as I remove the diaper that holds a little sea of piss around a turd island. The diaper thuds into the wastepail atop a few day's worth of dried-up ones. I push back Kenny's legs so that I can wet-wipe his bottom. A nauseating job, but I'd do it for an army of kids rather than walk back out into the living room. Maybe I should ask Kenny to teach me how to crawl again; that might be a more fitting re-entry. I make a half-hearted attempt to get him dressed, then let him squirm free. He's the one ally I have left, and that will change very quickly if he starts fussing. In a new diaper and nothing else, my ally charges over to the other side, heading for Lila. He's intercepted by Clara, who lifts him up in a huge, proprietary hug. Her body starts shaking with sobs again. Kenny squirms in an attempt to get loose, creating the brief impression that they're dancing together. In order to dry her reddened eyes, she finally puts him down.

"Listen Gloria," I say, inserting myself into the space between her and Clara, hoping to ease things along. "Maybe you and Clara could start looking through the stuff. I'll show you where, you can just take whatever you want." I almost add that none of it's worth much, but hold my tongue. Still, it's true. The only thing of real value that Sharon owned has already been hocked: over the next month or so I'm supposed to be receiving a large amount of life insurance money.

Leaving Lila behind to play with Kenny, Gloria and Clara follow me into the bedroom. I point out Sharon's dresser drawers and our huge walk-in closet, one of the features that had sold her on the apartment. Gloria and Clara march into the closet as if they owned its contents, maybe a third of which are mine. I hang around to monitor the proceedings. For a while I listen to them sliding hangers around and to Gloria protesting that she has all the dresses and sweaters she needs. Clara, for some reason, has a strong desire to keep the clothes in the family. She even calculates how long it will take for Lila to grow into some of the stuff. They finally stagger out of the closet, each practically buried under a pile of clothing. Gloria invites me to leave so she can try a few things on. I grab a pair of boxer shorts, shove them under my balled-up blue jeans and flannel shirt, and slink out of the room.

Using Kenny's blocks, Lila has erected what must have been a spiffy-looking castle. Kenny is in the process of wrecking it as I pass by his room, headed for the john. Judging from her increasingly irritated tone of voice, he's probably wrecked several of her creations by the time Gloria and Clara come out of the bedroom. Clara's eyes are wet again. She hands me some pictures of Sharon, which she must have found in the dresser: Sharon in different hairdos, clothing, and surroundings, but always with the same cheesy smile. Sharon hated taking pictures as much as I did—and still do. Clara asks if she can take some of the photos. I'm surprised that she's asked my permission. I look through the photos first so as not to seem like I don't give a shit, like I'm mainly interested in forgetting Sharon. But that *is* what I'd like to do, and not just because I feel guilty for having been a lousy husband and for sleeping with another woman in Sharon's bed. I'm not used to getting choked up, and it doesn't help much with staying sober.

I come across an instamatic of Sharon and me, pre-Kenny, hamming it up in the snow. I'm sitting on this gigantic snowball we'd rolled up. Sharon is sitting on my shoulders. Both of us are dusted with snow. Our arms are extended outward from our shoulders, bent at the elbows with palms held out as if testing for more precipitation, as if shrugging, "What, me worry?" We look like a cross between The Abominable Snowman and Buddha. The smile on her face here is genuine, whiter and brighter than the snow around us. The picture was taken in the back yard of some friend of Sharon's from teaching. Her name escapes me now. But I do remember that despite the fun Sharon and I had playing in the snow, we had a fight afterward. She'd wanted to return the invitation, invite the friend and her husband up to our place for dinner or whatever. I nixed the idea. The husband was a good photographer but otherwise a jerk. As usual, I had my way. And even before Sharon quit teaching, her friendship with the wife began to peter out.

The picture gets blurry as I look at it now. Turning away from Clara and Gloria, I wipe at my eyes with the back of my hand. "Take them," I manage finally, handing the stack of photos back to Clara without looking at her. "Take the clothes, too," I add needlessly, referring to the pile they'd exited the bedroom with. "Whatever's left over I'll give to Sal's, as in Salvation Army."

"What about Kenny?" says Gloria, her mother's mouthpiece. "You were supposed to arrange for him to spend time with my mother. On a regular basis."

"Take him too," I reply without hesitation. I'd anticipated the question, in fact I was hoping it would come up. "I'll pick him up tonight around seven, Clara. Take some diapers." I take my leaky eyes off to the kitchen; the conversation is over. Bye-bye time. Gloria and Clara follow me, along with Lila and Kenny, who've just re-joined the adults.

Gloria says, "Maybe you ought to get him dressed, Paul. Has he had breakfast?"

I give a little snort. "Surprise, I forgot. Coming right up." I feed and dress Kenny in record time.

"You'll pick him up at seven. You remember where I live?"

"Sure Clara," I respond, not bothering to return the acid in her tone. "And we can discuss future arrangements when I pick him up. You ladies are free to hit the road now."

Alone in the apartment for the first time since Sharon died, a wave of relief washes over me. It's been a point of honor not to just shuck Kenny off to Carmen upstairs—also a point of finances. Until the life insurance money comes down, times will be tight. I'd rather not have to plead poverty to Carmen, even though, given her sympathetic, emotional Italian nature, she'd probably offer to watch him for free, or adopt him if necessary. Of course, nothing's free. And I'm sure the time I'll be getting from Clara will have some grief attached to it.

But for now I'm not worried about that. I'm free to chase after Cheryl and try to explain myself to her. Hopefully I'll be able to come up with something. The shot of grief that hit me when I saw Sharon's photo somehow made me more desperate to salvage things with Cheryl. I pour a glass of Johnny Walker, chase it with a beer, then toss down some more of the scotch. A nice little buzz starts to spread around my head from between my eyes, probably helped along by the fact that I haven't eaten anything since last night. I stumble over to the telephone. It beats me to the punch and rings, the sound echoing inside my skull. The sound of reprieve. It's got to be

Cheryl. I pick up on the third ring and discover that I'm wrong as usual. It's my mother.

She's been calling every Sunday morning for years. Usually she has spoken to Sharon, who knew that as a rule I wouldn't answer the phone unless she was away from home or on the can. I almost tell my mother I'll call her back. But when she asks me how I'm doing, I hesitate long enough for her to know something's up, something aside from Sharon's death. She promises that I'll feel better if I talk about it. Maybe she's right. For sure, she's the only person left on the planet I can spill my guts to. But I want her to convince me to do it, as if that'll take some of the blame off of me for the story I've got to tell. Instead, she takes my little game of hard-to-get as an opportunity to urge me to go to church. "Believe it or not, I've been a couple of times since Sharon passed. It helps, Paulie, it really does. I've even confessed," she tells me.

"To what?"

"To whatever. It helped. And the sermon I heard this morning, it made me feel like maybe there's a God after all. It helps. Just try it, Paulie."

"I'm glad it helps you, Ma," I reply, trying not to sound like I'm humoring her. While I was growing up, my mother's Catholicism was strictly for show. After my father split, she packed in the church for good, or so she claimed at the time. But before that, like most mafiosi wives, she'd been obliged to go to services with her husband. I guess this was the Mob's way of seeking forgiveness before going out to murder and plunder some more. Publicly she was Catholic, although I'm sure it was fear, not religion, that kept her from divorcing my father. Privately, wanting no more attachments to him than she already had, she religiously practiced birth control. She'd correctly figured that my father, having produced a son on the first try, would have no objections. His disdain for the church was at least as great as hers.

I'm no different in that way. I turn down my mother's invitation to drop by the old church with her. Then, slurring some of my words, I lay my latest troubles on her.

"Your name is not Galdoni for nothing," she cracks when I'm finished. "Your father never tried very hard to hide it either.

He—"

"Ma, for Chrissakes, I wuzzin' screwin' around. Sharon's *gone*. Unfortunately, her mother and sister are not."

"Paulie!"

"Okay, that came out the wrong way. I screwed up, not them. I forgot they were coming. It wuzzin' that I didn't give a damn. But what worries me now is how to make it up to her. Cheryl, I mean, Kenny's teacher. Believe it or not, it wuzzin' just a roll in the hay. I'm startin' to like her almost as much as Kenny does, which is sayin' a lot."

My mother, who probably liked Sharon as much—or more—than I did, says nothing. She doesn't have to. Knowing what she's thinking, I beg out of the conversation. "Look Ma, I gotta go."

"So go."

"Hey, don' be mad."

She doesn't reply for a few seconds. Then she sucks air and says, "Paulie, I'm not mad. You're a big boy, you do what you want. It's your life. Sharon's gone two weeks. You coulda waited a little time, but . . . If you can wait a little time now, before you dial Miss Whatever-her-name-is, lemme speak to Kenny. And maybe bring him down here next weekend. Then I won't be so mad."

"Well, I can't do the first thing. My in-laws cleaned me out, even took Kenny. Just for the day. But before you start complainin' about bein' low grandma on the totem pole or whatever, yeah, we'll come down next weekend."

"Paulie, don't do me any favors." Even over the phone, the hurt in my mother's voice is obvious.

"Ma, I didn't mean it like . . . Believe me, if you didn't live so far away, you'd see plenty of Kenny. And me," I throw in as an afterthought. "Next Sunday, we'll get on the Turnpike."

After a little more conversation—I tell her how much I'm looking forward to her home cooking, which seems to soothe her feelings some—I hang up, just long enough to locate Cheryl's number. After dialing, I jam the phone between my head and shoulder, so I can speak and have my hands free to rip the tab off of a can of Bud. On the first ring, the receiver slips up to the bottom of my nose. I get a whiff of my own breath. It's fortunate that this conversation is going to take place over the phone. Or is it? After six rings, I hang up and dial again. No answer. She must have gotten home by now. I quickly brush my teeth —something I'd forgotten to do while my in-laws were here— then stick the unopened can of Bud in one pocket of my jacket and the breath spray in the other.

I manage not to speed on the Saw Mill River Parkway. Since drunk driving became a major issue about a year ago, I take pains not to attract cops. Drinking has made me a more careful driver. The highway's white lines zip by me like they're being sucked in by some giant vacuum cleaner, or like *I* am. Sucked in again. Life could be described as a process of getting sucked into one mess after another. It takes tremendous concentration now to keep the Valiant between the lines. I'm forced to snuff out my cigarette: the smoke in my eyes isn't helping any. Still, I've polished off a couple of cigarettes and the beer by the time I somehow arrive at Cheryl's.

I buzz from her lobby as I've done every other day this week. This time I get no answer. I hang out until some grandpa exits to take his terrier out for a crap. The old geezer eyes me suspiciously as I catch the lobby door. Can't blame him, I'd eye me suspiciously, too. But that's all he does. This is New York, and I'm big and scruffy enough to discourage even a polite "Can I help you?"

I could swear he makes a mental note of my license plate number when he passes me sitting parked in front of the building ten minutes later. Having rang, knocked, and banged, I'm convinced that Cheryl's not home. Fine, I'm in no hurry. I sit and watch some kids playing touch football across the street in a playground. I watch them because they're less boring than the trees. Except for a period of weightlifting in high school, which I did hoping to become more of a hunk than I already believed I was, I've never cared about athletics. Part of that might've been that I was uncoordinated, one of those guys with muscles that looked impressive but got in the way of each other if I tried to dribble a basketball or whatever. After a while even the muscles were gone, replaced by a small beer belly, sunk into a slouch developed from bending over sorting machines, steering wheels, and bar counters.

After another fifteen minutes or so of dumbly watching the kids score touchdowns in between arguments, it occurs to me that I might be in for a long wait. I try to decide whether to get some food and drink or take a little nap. I'm leaning back against the headrest while I'm thinking about this, and the decision gets made for me. Amazingly, I wake up at just the right moment, opening my eyes to the sight of Cheryl pulling a two-wheeled shopping cart up the sidewalk toward me. It takes a few moments for me to realize that I'm not dreaming. She looks like she's coming out of some bright haze, the way the sun glints off of her cart and the mohair in her pullover hat. Only when she's a few yards from me can I really see her face clearly. This is about the same time she notices me.

She looks only mildly surprised. Her mouth tightens, then relaxes into a sigh, which sends a faint cloud of steam out in front of her. Her body seems to stiffen then relax, too, as if she was about to speed up her pace and then thought better of it. I pop out of the car. Looking away, I open my eyes wide. This is supposed to make me look awake and sober when I turn around.

"Help you with the groceries?" I say, in my best imitation of a perky voice. She doesn't answer. But there's enough indecision on her face to encourage me a little. Before she can decide to tell me what I can do with my help, I turn humble. "Look Cheryl, will you please hear me out?"

She sets her shopping cart back on its small rear legs. It groans as the bags of groceries settle. "I'll try," she says.

"I wasn't tryna embarrass you," I say from a small distance, hoping to leave enough outdoor air between us to blunt the smell of my breath, which I forgot to spray. "Believe me, I feel like a jerk. I set it up so I wouldn't *have* to remember, like a week in advance. I set it up for a time I figured I'd be there regardless. Didn't expect you to be. That part of it was a lovely surprise for me. And I really hope it wasn't the last time."

Her face tightens, making her look more Asian—and more angry. She says, "Paul you know what 'chutzpah' means?"

"Yeah, I've heard it before. Several times. If you could market chutzpah, I'd probably be a millionaire. But, like, I'm not tryna put the make on you again. I mean . . . shit, I can't say anything right."

"Booze might have something to do with that." I look at her with my jaw dropped. "I can smell it, Paul. It's hard to miss. But that's beside the point, now. It wasn't a 'lovely surprise' for your relatives. Or for me. Paul, I felt *low,* like an accessory to some kind of disgusting crime. And I've been trying to figure out what the hell I was doing in your bed—*Sharon's* bed—in the first place. The only reason I can come with is that I wanted to be there. I was being impulsively romantic. Hell, I was even happy to be there in the morning, up until the time the doorbell rang. I mean, I'd mainly known Sharon by sight, like I told your relatives—"

"Ex-relatives."

"Whatever. That's almost beside the point too. I can believe that you forgot. You couldn't have done that on purpose, although God knows you should've remembered. But, especially after that rap you gave me in the car about how my ex-fiance must've been crazy to cheat on me, I hear from your mother-in-law how you used to cheat on your wife."

When Clara had made this accusation, I hadn't seriously considered denying it for Cheryl's benefit. With Clara standing there bawling (and Gloria to back her up), I couldn't have mustered much righteous indignation. Probably it was wise not to try. Somewhere in my fogged brain I know that to try it now, even to issue a quiet, polite denial, would not play well at all. "Cheryl," I say, "That was not a line I gave you in the car. I meant what I said."

Fact is that I did, but that doesn't seem to come across. "Right. You meant it at the moment. You were horny enough."

"Dammit, if I just wanted to get laid, whaddya think I'm doin' here now?"

It might be my imagination, but her voice softens ever so slightly. "I don't know. Why don't you tell me."

While driving over here I'd thought of a few serviceable reasons why she shouldn't permanently throw me out of bed. Of course, my mind draws a blank now. What I finally tell her seems to originate from someplace like my heart. "Because I care about you. Okay? And um, believe it or not, I didn't ask you to spend the day with me—and Kenny—figuring that we'd wind up in the sack. I didn't rule out the possibility, but, if that's what I was plannin' from the start, I probably would've remembered that little appointment I made with Sharon's family. I'm not that stupid. But, I see you everyday, and you're the only person I feel like I can talk to, okay? I don't wanna sound like poor little Paul or whatever, but I don't have many friends. You know, it's been in and outta the cab, in and outta the day care center, then home. Bingo. And I'm not a real sociable guy to begin with, so . . . you understand what I'm sayin'?" I hope she does, because I'd have a hard time running it back for her.

She nods slowly. "Yeah, and I pretty much believe you, or at least I believe that you mean it now. But Paul, if you were so dedicated to work and family, where did you find time to cheat?"

"I didn't, not recently. Not that I was really lookin' . . . Cheryl, you think I feel good about it? Proud?"

"I don't know. A lot of men think it makes them real men, you know, like notches on a gun in the old days. Given . . . what happened to your wife, yeah, I can believe you regret it now. That doesn't mean you wouldn't do it again, though."

I throw up my hands. This is probably for my benefit as much as hers. If I act exasperated enough, maybe I'll convince myself that she's wrong. "Look, it's just something I did while I was driving night shift. Maybe a couple of hours one night, maybe a coupla nights. I was driving twelve hour shifts, and I guess I figured I was entitled to a little fun. None of it meant anything. And I never meant for her to find out, there was no way she should've. What was really wrong was that she did." I have a vague sense that I'm cutting my own throat as I say this, but it's too late to stop. "We had a lousy relationship. I guess that was my fault, too, although we both agreed to get married. But I never wanted to hurt her." This last part comes out in a little sob, choking off more words. I grimace as some of this morning's scotch backs up on me, stinging my throat and filling my mouth with a nasty taste.

"Paul, it's *wrong*, that's all," she declares, unmoved by the sorry sight I must be in front of her. "You snuck around behind her back while she was home with Kenny? Speaking of which . . . where is he?"

I take a deep breath. "Spending the day with Grandma. I think she'd take him permanently if I let her."

"Would you?"

"No way," I reply, suddenly pissed. "I'm not a complete schmuck."

She gives a sharp-edged laugh. "I never said you were a complete schmuck, Paul, although I seem to have a talent for getting involved with men who fit that description. They're not much different from most of my kids at nursery: they get bored with one toy, toss it away, and find another. Not that I've been looking to marry every man I meet, but I want something that has a chance to last. Maybe I got more involved with you than I should've, or more quickly than I should've, especially given the involvements you and I already have with Kenny. But if I can't trust a guy, forget it."

"Look Cheryl, what I did is in the past. And at least I haven't tried to deny it."

"I don't think you could've pulled it off. You didn't look real surprised when she said it."

"For Chrissakes, gimme credit for something."

"You want a pat on the head?"

Furious, I spin away from her, then whirl around again, almost losing my balance. "Dammit, I want *you*. Alright?" She stares back at me defiantly, as if I'd just told her to go fuck herself. I had practically snarled my little mating call into her face, wrapped up in the smell of beer and regurgitated scotch. We stand glaring at each other, frozen that way for a few long seconds, like we're posing for some cartoon about the war between the sexes. Then I suck in some air and let it out slowly. "Cheryl, look, I can change," I say quietly, dropping my gaze. "It might not seem like it, but I've changed already, since Sharon died."

"Maybe. But to be honest, I have all kinds of advance warning with you. If I wound up getting hurt, I'd have no one to blame but myself." She reaches back and grasps the handle of her shopping cart. "I need to go upstairs," she says, swallowing. "I need some time to think. Tomorrow morning when you drop Kenny, I'd appreciate it if we could talk about the weather or something. Don't even give me any meaningful glances."

I nod, eagerly. "Time to think" strikes me as a small victory. I reply, "Aye aye, sir," mustering a smile to soften the sarcasm. "See you tomorrow." I slide into the Valiant, but I don't start it until I've watched her squeeze through the door into her lobby.

- 11 -
Sharon

I WAS much prettier in the mid-1800's. Even now, as I relive a segment of my life as Chava, in my mind I am still a *shayne maydele.* Years ago, I was surely as beautiful as any young woman in our *shtetl*. I was not concerned with the ones who lived outside of it, in the village. I rarely saw them. The goyim I did come across were usually men, mostly police and Russian peasants who fancied themselves Cossacks. These men knew immediately that I was Jewish, even if they encountered me outside of the shtetl, but it never occurred to me that this knowledge had anything to do with my prominent nose, or with my almost pointy chin, which, in retrospect, recalled Paul's. I assumed that I was identified by the stretch of road I walked on, by the food-laden straw basket over my arm on Friday afternoons, and by the small triangular kerchief over my close-cropped hair. Of course, I presented an attitude of deference at the approach of goyische manhood. My dark eyes were kept downcast, awaiting whatever lewd comments the clods chose to bestow on me—they were inevitable, even from a lone yokel with no one other than his horse to show off for. Their filthy speculations about the treasures residing beneath my drab cotton dress frightened and sickened me, yet I felt a strange pleasure as well. My convictions regarding my own loveliness and desirability were undiminished.

These convictions seem to have carried over to Sharon-of-the-hereafter. I am gradually making friends with the memory of the person I was most recently. I'd liked very little about myself as Sharon Galdoni (nee Weiss). If I had, I probably wouldn't have spent half of my brief life making up my face (a job I temporarily gave up when I became a full time mother to Kenny). As Chava, on the other hand, I used the one mirror in our house mainly for self-admiration. Rougeless and unadorned, I had no real ego problems, concerning my looks or anything else. But the evil eye did eventually look my way in the form of serious discord, involving myself, my second husband Yankel, and my son Mottle. The latter were to be known some hundred years later as, respectively, Paul and Kenny Galdoni.

Once I re-inhabit Chava I have total access to her memory. Internally and externally, I *am* Chava, as she faces her impending separation from Yankel. In a rare moment of introspection, I stand shredding potatoes and trying to understand God's reasons for this latest rearrangement of my life.

I was married for the first time at age fourteen—to Senderl the Shoemaker, as he was called by almost everyone in the shtetl. His surname was his profession, as if he'd been born for the job like a hen is born to lay eggs. In fact he'd been apprenticed soon after his bar mitzvah, some fifteen years before. He turned out to be fit for his occupation in the same way his shoes fit their owners, perfectly. Customers began to urge Moyshe, the long-time proprietor of the shop, to take a well-earned rest and let his assistant do the work on them. Moyshe laughingly obliged, his gray beard bouncing on his ample stomach.

Senderl provided not only comfortable shoes, but comfort. He handled feet with the same reverence he accorded all the works of his Creator. No "Beard Without a Jew" was Senderl. If he knew less Mishna and Gemora than the men who sat at the eastern wall of the synagogue, he had nonetheless attained that which such knowledge is supposed to bestow; he was truly a pious man. To him the mitzvot were offerings to God, rather than duties to be performed in case there was such a place as heaven. It was this piety that made my father (who fancied himself a tsaddik in his own right) see Senderl as a perfect match for me. He thought I was in need of such an influence.

Senderl had recently lost his wife. Their marriage was childless, and he sought a young woman with many child-bearing years in front of her. An arrangement was made between my father, Senderl, and the matchmaker. I had no objections, though it wouldn't have mattered if I did. My looks were considered to be part of the bargain. I was surprised to hear that my father thought I was beautiful, but I was willing to believe in his sincerity. I was also willing to believe that Senderl and I would learn to love each other. Surely marriage would be better than life as the elder sister to five siblings, a second mother but without the respect, a target of my own mother's complaints.

She stopped complaining so much when I presented her with her first grandchild, Mottle. Senderl, never a complainer, was filled with bliss. Even before his previous wife took sick, he'd never considered exercising his option to divorce her on grounds of barrenness. In such cases many considered divorce to be more of a religious imperative than a personal choice. Not so with Senderl—even though "Be fruitful and multiply" might have been the commandment he wanted most, in his heart, to fulfill. The boundlessness of his loving gratitude made me almost uncomfortable. It was my unfulfilled duty to reciprocate. I admired and respected Senderl, looked up to him, and hoped that the "love" part of the marriage contract might yet show itself.

I had no problem loving Mottle, the little *mentsh* who suckled at my breasts for what seemed like hours at a time. During his first few months, I spent a large part of my time gazing down with contentment at his rosy, fat cheeks. But there were also moments when I could have sworn that I saw payess, even a beard, growing on him before my eyes. This distressed me. I wanted him to somehow remain a free person, unfettered by endless mitzvot. I wanted his hair to remain soft, wispy, and available to my fingertips, uncovered by a skull cap. Still, these misgivings usually passed as suddenly as they had come. Mottle was so much a part of me that it seemed impossible that things would ever be otherwise.

But when he was three, Senderl bundled him in a prayer shawl, intending to carry him off to Hebrew school. The prospect of beginning his Jewish education appeared to frighten little Mottle. Or maybe it was me who started screaming first.

"Senderl! He's too young, he's just a baby!" I cried, grasping my husband's broad shoulders, my fingers sliding on his caftan. Unperturbed, Senderl brushed me off. The wooden hinges of our door creaked as he stepped out with our son.

"Shah!" Senderl admonished with a quiet sternness as I screamed again and our neighbors craned their necks. "He is not too young, Chava. He's a smart boy. And old enough to begin to know his real father."

"What about me? I'm his real *mother*."

"The Lord is that, too."

My husband's determined strides stirred up dust at his heels. I stood at the edge of our yard weeping, holding out my arms. Mottle managed to work his arms free of the prayer shawl and reach back for me, crying, "Mammeh! Mammeh!" His struggles were no problem for Senderl. They turned a corner and were gone . . . as Mottle would be gone now for ten hours a day, five days a week, and half a day on Friday, spending more time in school than with me. If I was not his "real mother," surely his real mother would not force him to spend his days in drudgery, at the mercy of a cranky teacher.

I wiped my eyes on my apron and turned back toward the house. The yentas I had for neighbors would have much to discuss, I knew. It was obvious where their sympathies lay. They'd all suffered similar losses, assuming they'd even considered them as losses. Not a woman moved to comfort me. They averted their eyes, practically turned their backs. I stepped inside and slammed the door behind me. Miraculously Gittle, my eighteen month-old daughter, had slept through the racket.

It turned out that both Senderl and I had strong intuition where Mottle was concerned. By age eight, Mottle was known as an *iluy*, a young genius who knew all of the prayers and half of the Pentateuch, the five books of Moses. And the adulation he was beginning to receive from his bearded elders was making him "stiff-necked with pride," a sin he would have to repent on Yom Kippur (and then probably commit again the following year). If he detected some slight violation of the kosher laws, or found a few crumbs of bread undisposed of during Passover or clothes left hanging on the Sabbath (when they could no longer be folded), he would actually scold me for these things. Slaps across the face did not deter him. Indeed, they hurt me more than they hurt him, as if each smack had bounced back with greater force against me, driving us further apart.

Senderl, who didn't believe in striking anything other than the heel of a shoe, was typically silent at such times. Only once do I remember him intervening. Mottle was approaching ten, and he considered himself to be only slightly less than a talmudic sage. The rebbe of our synagogue and his wife had come to our house for Sabbath dinner. I'd taken pains to have the house clean and ready. Yet, after sanctifying the house by lighting the Sabbath candles, I committed what Mottle judged to be a terrible oversight. The blessing of the wine was about to begin and the challah, the twisted bread that I'd spent half the day baking, had been left uncovered.

After drawing everyone's attention to this dereliction, Mottle said, "Mother,"—he'd long since left "Mammeh" behind—"how could you forget to do this? Especially on this Sabbath, with the rebbe here?"

Feeling my face redden, I stared at Mottle with anger. Finally I took the white embroidered cloth and flung it down on top of the challah. After what seemed like a long silence, a soft, guttural laugh issued from beneath the rebbe's gray beard. Placing a hand on Mottle's shoulder, he said, "Nu, so now the challah is covered . . . and your mother's made a beautiful Sabbath table, has she not?"

Mottle hesitated. Senderl, with a firm hand on Mottle's other shoulder, turned him away from the rebbe. Father and son stood facing each other. "Mottle," Senderl began, pausing for a moment to make sure he had his son's attention. "Maybe you are not yet aware of the reason we cover the challah. It symbolizes our desire not to hurt its feelings, to shield it. It shouldn't feel unappreciated or ignored while we are blessing the wine. This symbolizes the care we take with other people's feelings. And yet, you speak unkindly to your own mother, whom you are commanded by God to *revere*. And this you do in front of our honored guests? In front of your brother and sisters?" Senderl's eyes fell briefly on each of his three younger children, ascertaining that the message had been received. Mottle, his eyes brimming, ran from the room.

After that evening, Mottle's attitude changed: he became more aloof. This was in part a consequence of the time he spent away from home studying (already, at the age of ten, he was rumored to be the target of more than one rich father, who saw a chance to marry off his daughter to a future *talmid khokhem*, a wise scholar). Still, when Mottle was home, he was polite to me and tolerant of the gushing affections his siblings bestowed upon him. As they crowded around him, seeking his approval, I felt almost jealous of them. They could give him their love so easily, and cause him to act like a child again.

This brief period of peace ended with the passing of its architect. Senderl's sudden death from pneumonia turned me from a skeptic into a non-believer: here was a man who was practically a saint, yet buried before he was forty years of age. What good had his religion done him? We all wept for him. Mottle cried for the man who had taught him by his very way of life.

Perhaps Mottle's grief was extended by the knowledge of who his father's likely successor would be: Uncle Yankel. Senderl's younger brother was his opposite, a schemer who tried to live on odd jobs and possibilites. They didn't even *look* like brothers. Senderl had been hefty and full-bearded, a bear of a man with a gentle heart; Yankel was tall and thin, with curly black hair pushing out from under his cap like a bustle and a short, coarse beard that clung to his face. It had been no problem for Yankel to remain a bachelor. No prospective fathers-in-law were beating down the door of the house in which he still lived with his parents.

As Senderl had not died childless, it was not Yankel's obligation to marry me. But marry me he did. He liked the children, excepting Mottle, and they, excepting Mottle, liked him. Before

Senderl's death, Yankel had been a frequent visitor in our home, inviting himself to dinner and an evening of roughhousing with the children. Wine inspired him. Even the girls loved to be twirled through the air by him, to be chased as he clambered on all fours and barked like a dog, to hold on to his *tzitzit*, his fringes, and be pulled around as if he was a horse. But Mottle was mortified by such usage of the fringes, which are meant to be a reminder of God's commandments. Senderl was quietly amused. If he ever noticed the gleeful looks that sometimes passed between Yankel and me, he never said anything to either one of us.

Regardless, I did share my younger children's fondness for Yankel. And while we were not hungry while Senderl was alive, neither were we rich. We would need whatever help Yankel could provide now. He was a *balegoleh* by trade, a coachman who took people from one shtetl to another. Between his earnings and the sewing I could do at home (a talent I'd picked up from Senderl), we would manage. If Yankel's travels were sometimes interrupted by ventures into business, trying to work as a middleman, cadging what he could from both seller and buyer, that was alright with me. Behind his back, most called him a *luftmentsh*, a man who tries to live on the air produced by the big plans emanating from his mouth. But I'd affectionately considered him a dreamer, even before we were married.

I had also found a certain romance in his travels as a coachman. Some nights after the children were in bed, Yankel would tell Senderl and I of the goyische excesses he'd seen: drunken dancing (in public!) between men and women, prostitution, and drunken brawls. In taverns where he sometimes stayed overnight, he'd heard of priests chasing women and even each other. I believe that Senderl let me hear these things as cautionary tales, as evidence of what life became in the absence of Godliness. Yet I took them as proof that there was indeed some excitement beyond the invisible walls of the shtetl. So I had come to welcome Yankel's unannounced visits, especially since I knew he would not be inspecting the house for signs of things unclean or unkosher.

With Senderl's passing and my marriage to Yankel, my main motivation for being a good Jewish housewife was gone. My younger son cared little if the unwashed dishes made it necessary to serve meat on a dairy dish, or eat it with a dairy utensil; his suffering at school, where he showed none of Mottle's brilliance, was almost enough to make him an antisemite. And Mottle's censurious eyes were increasingly absent. After Senderl's death, Mottle often finished a day of studying by eating and sleeping at the rebbe's house. But the time Mottle spent at home did not cause me to mend my ways. My love for him was mixed, regrettably, with a desire to spite him.

In this I was encouraged by Yankel, who considered his eldest nephew and stepson to be a pompous little donkey. "Fine," Yankel would tell me, "Let him go and tell the rebbe. The yentas gossip about us anyway. We'll give them more to discuss. Let it be our contribution to the life of the shtetl." I couldn't disagree with him, at least about the yentas, meaning most women in the shtetl with a little time on their hands. Who were they to judge us? I felt that raising three children, as well as being a part-time mother to the demanding Mottle, was all that any just God could ask of me. Yet we were becoming outcasts, the more so because we were thought to be defiling the memory of the pious Senderl. I spent more than one night weeping over that accusation, usually delivered by neighbors as they passed on the street. Most of my neighbors would no longer set foot in my house. They never knew when Yankel would be home, his working hours were irregular and so were his social habits, and they feared him. He would look directly at a woman, even compliment her on the way she looked, which a pious Jew was not even supposed to notice.

Nor was a pious Jew supposed to think of sexual intercourse as anything other than a means of procreation. That had been Senderl's attitude. While he thoroughly enjoyed our excursions into baby-making, he'd had no trouble abstaining during the proscribed half of each month during and after my menstruation. Nor was he interested in love-making during pregnancy: the seed had already been sown.

Yankel, on the other hand, had always found me alluring, or so he'd informed me when he proposed marriage. He'd been somewhat embarrassed to say it, but I'd set him at ease by thanking him for the compliment, surprising myself with my own sincerity. And he turned out to be as good as his word. On nights he was home, he wound up in my bed as often as not. He always returned from his travels with a healthy appetite for my body. He'd even lewdly discuss his intentions beforehand, a practice unheard of among the pious. I'd shush him and giggle. If his arrival home had occurred during my monthly "unclean" period, that usually didn't deter us.

In order to keep an outward appearance of observance, I continued my monthly visits to the mikva, the ritual bath taken to make intercourse kosher again. Another result of visiting the mikva was that others knew that one had menstruated and therefore was not pregnant. I wanted no rumors that I was with another child. Nothing turned the yentas vicious more quickly than discovering themselves to have been mistaken. For whatever reason, Yankel and I never conceived. It wasn't for lack of intercourse.

Mottle probably was not aware of our "excesses" and violations in this area. Or he may have been. In any case, he wouldn't have confronted us about it—not because he was technically still a child, but because of the base nature of the subject matter. He did feel free to criticize Yankel and I about most other things, Yankel in particular. The arrows were delivered directly, I'll give Mottle that.

One evening in particular stands out clearly in my memory: Yankel and I had been married about a year, Mottle was eleven. He came to the door looking haggard for someone so young, his brown eyes slightly bloodshot from studying late, his dirt-blonde payess scattered by the wind across both of his thin cheeks. The ends of the payess fell below his jawbone; it looked as if slender vines were overgrowing his face. The other children were asleep in their bedroom. Yankel and I were sitting at the wooden table in the one large room that served as kitchen, dining room, and social area. We were sipping wine. Mottle stood dumfounded in the doorway. Only Mottle's front foot was inside as he said, "Good evening, Mother and Uncle Yankel. Where is my dinner?"

"It's warm on top of the oven, Mottle," I replied.

"Will you get it for me?"

"Your mother is finally resting a little after a hard day," said 'Uncle Yankel' (Mottle steadfastly refused to address Yankel otherwise, even after Yankel became his stepfather). "Why don't you get your own dinner? There is room for you here at the table."

Mottle stepped all the way in and closed the door loudly behind him. "Mother and Uncle Yankel, you are drinking."

"Nu, no wonder they call you a scholar, Mottleh," said Yankel, his eyes shining in the candlelight. "But don't worry. At least we are drinking kosher wine."

"So? You drink what is here. And when my father was alive, my mother drank only on Sabbath and holy days. You are destroying his memory, even as you live on what little he left us."

"Mottle!" I yelled. "How dare you! Your uncle . . . your *stepfather*, with no thanks from you, has been working to support all of us." In fact, a desire to support the family had been another of the reasons Yankel gave for wanting to marry me. And he had proved (mostly) as good as his word. It was true that Senderl had not left us destitute, and that our parents and the community had made donations after he died. And while he'd been alive, it had not been necessary for me to earn money in order to keep us all in clothing, food, and school. But it was also true that Yankel was now our chief breadwinner. And he was proud of it.

"Tell me, Mottle," he said, intentionally belching, "What do you know of the finances of this family? Almost nothing," he declared, answering himself correctly. "You sit all day squashing a chair with your snotty nose in a book. And you have the nerve to suggest that I am trying to live on your mother's charity? What *khutspeh* ! In a year or two you'll be a *kest kinder*, paid by some rich father-in-law to study all day. He'll show you off to his rich friends: his son-in-law the scholar. You'll be his evidence that he's a righteous man—even if he got most of his money by cheating people."

Mottle stood with cheeks flushed with chagrin, his eyes about to overflow, obviously trying to think of a retort. Watching him, this wounded, enraged child, my heart felt as if it would burst. I wanted to rise out of my chair and hold him, protect him. But I was torn. And I knew that Mottle would all but push me away if I came too close to him then. Finally he said, "I'll be studying God's law, doing His will. There is nothing greater than that. But you, you'll keep neglecting the mitzvot, violating the laws, living like Goyim. You—both of you—it's Jews like you who destroy our faith, destroy our covenant. There is no greater sin."

Yankel snorted. "Oh? In case you haven't learned this, Mottleh, the Goyim themselves are more than willing to destroy our faith. You've heard of pogroms, maybe? How many so-called pious Jews—who would rather have died than stray one hair from the letter of the law—wound up dying anyway, by the sword of some peasant, some Cossack? I'm talking about Jews who did the will of God. What good did it do them? It makes me wonder about God.

"But assuming we want to believe in Him, and that He cares about what we do or don't do, it might be instructive to remember the story of the second temple," said Yankel in a high-pitched, mock scholarly voice. "According to the rebbes, God allowed the Romans to destroy the temple not because some Jews forgot to wind straps around their arms every morning, or started milking cows on the Sabbath, but because they'd become hypocrites. They forgot about treating other people kindly, and dealing with them fairly. They forgot about honesty. Also, they forgot about respecting one's elders . . . one's parents. Little trifles like that."

Nodding his head thoughtfully, almost as if he was davening, Mottle replied, "The part about elders and parents I have not been taught was part of their sins." He paused, and the thin "smile" that formed on his face chilled me. "But nonetheless, I'm impressed, Uncle Yankel. I didn't think you knew anything."

Yankel grabbed the neck of the wine bottle, lifting it like a dagger. Then, after a moment's indecision, he slammed the bottle's square bottom back down onto the table. Fortunately the glass was heavy. The bottle only cracked, but enough for wine to begin to seep out. "Chava," he said in a voice which seemed to come from his chest, "I'd better go out now. If I don't, I may commit an even greater sin than those we are already guilty of." He pushed his chair aside and stomped toward the door, causing Mottle to scramble out of his way. Yankel was quickly gone.

I stood as if paralyzed. Mottle, avoiding my eyes, moved toward the oven, where his dinner sat atop the hot stones. I took a step toward him, then turned and ran out the door, pursuing Yankel. My husband was walking away with long strides, his back receding into the dark night as if he was an apparition. After several steps I gave up the chase and returned to the house. Mottle had taken his dinner into his bedroom, where the other children lay asleep. He knew I would not want to risk waking them. Nonetheless, I almost entered the bedroom where he ate in darkness. Instead I sat again at the table and buried my head in my arms, remaining there even as the wine began to flow down onto the floor.

* * *

Roughly three years later I stand shredding potatoes for pancakes and listening to Yankel banging around in our bedroom. I'd refused to help him pack his trunk. It is not his fault that he has to leave, but helping him to pack would somehow be helping the Czar to stock the Russian army. It seems His Highness doesn't hate Jews so much that he won't allow them to die for Mother Russia. But Yankel seems to think that he is going off on some adventure. He is almost eager to go, another reason he can expect no help from me in packing. It isn't a big job, really, but he acts as though he is helpless. He's gotten used to having me pack his bag for his trips as a coachman, when I'd known he'd be coming back. Now, however, I am convinced that I will never see him again, and convinced, too, that that possibility does not really disturb him. A few years of life as a father and husband have been enough for him, even with the time spent away traveling. The fool actually embraced the call from the Czar, took it as a chance to really get away from the shtetl and live. He's already rid himself of his beard and other vestiges of Jewish appearance. He'd never considered not reporting and fleeing instead. For that, and for the chance of a reunion someplace else, I would have helped him pack.

The clod finally accomplishes it himself. As I mix the shredded potatoes with onions, I know that I am resigned to his leaving. I will manage, perhaps nicely. I am still a handsome woman, and it likely will not be a very long time before even my youngest child has a family of her own. Mottle already does. As Yankel had predicted, my eldest son has been married into money and now attends a Yeshiva in another, larger shtetl. I was surprised that he had found time to impregnate his young wife, whom he saw so infrequently, but I am hopeful that with the birth of my first grandchild, I will get to see more of Mottle. But if I don't, I will survive that, too. I'd begun losing him a long time ago. Maybe it still hurts, but it hasn't been fatal. And if that is true with Mottle, then surely I can also manage without Yankel.

I make sure to dry my onion-teary eyes as Yankel, dragging his trunk, approaches to take his leave. Yet I am surprised to find myself weeping as he kisses me and says, "Chavalleh, I know what you think. But I promise you, we will see each other again."

* * *

Little did I know. With that farewell, I find myself back in the hereafter as Sharon. Somehow it is crystal-clear to me that Yankel and Mottle have been reincarnated as Paul and Kenny. I sit alone on my grandparents' lawn, and marvel at having just passed from one world into another without so much as blinking an eye. Or rather, it's more like the worlds have passed through *me.* It is as if my "I"-ness, my consciousness, is the only constant, a screen on which perhaps anything I desire to know can be played. Except, of course, what has transpired on earth since my death.

If there seemed to be no time involved in my metamorphosis from Chava back into Sharon, there did seem to be a blending. I feel as though I've arrived back in the hereafter as both women, or as something more than both of them: the consciousness they shared. Sharon's personality eventually returns to the forefront. But as it does, I'm surprised to find that I suddenly feel the loss of Senderl more acutely than I had as Chava. He seems the finest person I have ever known, certainly the finest I've ever been married to. But unlike with Yankel/Paul and Mottle/Kenny, I know nothing of his current fate. I assume he is someplace on earth—until he suddenly appears on the lawn in front of me.

At first I don't recognize him, surrounded as he is by brilliant light. But Senderl it is, full-bearded and robust (if transparent), wearing a cap and a vest with fringes showing from beneath. For a moment he looks out of place, a nineteenth-century Russian Jew on a suburban lawn. But then it's as if the surroundings conform to him, they become his aura and take on the light of godliness that he radiates. The thoughts and feelings he conveys only add to the bliss that arises inside of me.

"Chava . . . it is Shah-run you are known as now?" he asks in precise, accented English. "You were once my wife and the mother of my children, and it delights my heart to see you here in the beyond . . . again." He pauses and I smile, recognizing the significance of "again." Senderl continues, "I have not returned to Earth since dying as Senderl the Shoemaker. Tell me, Shah-run, how long has it been?"

"Over a hundred years. Well over." I look at him with amazement.

His beard parts in an amused smile, as if my reaction is endearingly quaint. "Nu, this is the closest I've been to Earth since the last of our children left to return there. Usually I am someplace closer to the fullness of God's light, God's love. It is called in English, I think, 'a higher plane.' Souls remain there for a very long time. Indeed there is nothing *but* the souls, and the light which borders infinity. I took on my old appearance so that you could see me. But at some time I must return to earth. It is only in a human body that one can truly gain union with God."

This is news to me. I've believed since dying that the body I've left behind had been more or less a prison. But I can't doubt that Senderl knows what he's talking about. I am eager to hear his explanation. It soon becomes apparent that I will not be hearing it alone.

We are joined first by my father and grandparents. They are greeted warmly by Senderl, the five of us being part of the same karmic chain. We are also part of what turns out to be a large, multi-national gathering on the lawn. As one former native of

India puts it, all have been attracted by Senderl's "darshan," his aura of holiness and knowledge. No announcements or advance notice were needed, and space to accommodate everyone is no problem; the space is adjustable and so are our "bodies." No public address system, interpreter or facilities are necessary. And if Senderl hadn't originally come for the purpose of discoursing, he obviously takes great joy in doing so.

"Only on earth can we truly come to know God," he repeats for the benefit of his enlarged audience. "Only there, where He seems most absent, where everything appears as solid and each person dies a little each day, where many suffer much—only knowing God there is knowing Him to be everywhere. Here, we are resting. We are relieved from the fear of dying; we come to understand the reasons we may have suffered on Earth; we can have those things we wanted there but could not have, then we understand them to be only toys of the mind. And after enough of this back and forth between here and earth, hopefully one time when we return to earth, we are finally ready to know God, who is the substance of everything. Only the human body, physical and yet having the . . . quiet history, the imprint of all that has gone before; only the mind, with its roots in the infinite; only these are able to return to their source. Finding God within, one finds Him without. Then one is never without Him. Never." Senderl pauses. I have the feeling that the absolute silence attending this pause would have continued for some time, had he not invited questions.

"Are *you* ever without God?" The woman who asks this first question draws a mild rebuke from the same Indian fellow, who points out that traditionally holy men are not expected to speak about themselves. Senderl modestly expresses his doubt that he himself fits into such a category, then goes on to say that his own case is instructive for all, and that one's "self" is ultimately no different from anyone else's. He proceeds to explain how it is that he himself has not yet gained permanent God-consciousness.

In his last life on Earth, he'd come close. He'd found that sometimes while praying with his eyes closed—a habit he'd picked up from the Hassidim—his mind would slip away from the prayer, away from everything. He'd experience a pure, blissful awareness. Invariably, coming back to himself, he'd be surprised, even startled, by the length of time that had passed. He knew he hadn't been asleep. Quite the contrary. He came to understand the experience as fulfillment of the command to "Be still and know that I am God." The experience was infrequent, though, and others he spoke to did not have it at all. And if the stillness within him lingered, even in the midst of making shoes or family activities, it nonetheless would eventually fade.

His relatively young death had occurred because it was necessary for him to spend some time in heaven, soaking up the reflection of God, before going further. This would ready his soul to return to earth and gain the eternal freedom of God-consciousness, which would happen when the right family and situation became available. Supposedly, a great many "openings" would be occurring before long.

In the meantime, he's happy where he is, sharing knowledge with other souls. When all questions have been answered, everyone sits together in silent contentment. Gradually people leave, directing their attention elsewhere. When it is just the five of us again, Senderl wants to know what I can tell him about his relatives on earth. None of the particulars surprise him. Kenny's apparent learning difficulties, for example, were the result of his mind/heart imbalance as Mottle; the scales are now tipped in the opposite direction. Before reincarnating, Mottle had known that the body he'd be entering would contain a somewhat defective brain. He'd wanted to become Kenny. In the afterlife, the soul sees what it needs to evolve and eventually seeks a suitable incarnation. Of course, once the "River of Forgetfulness" (as Senderl, quoting the Greeks, described it) is crossed, the person on Earth remembers nothing, but lives hampered—or bolstered—by the fruit of actions performed in past lives. Or dies young because of them.

I'd known before being born as Sharon that it was time for me to repay the debt incurred during my murderous incarnation as a Roman soldier. Once I was born to Clara and Avraham Weiss, that knowledge resided deep within me, consciously unavailable but responsible for some of the "free-floating" anxiety

I'd carried around. I'd had some subconscious difficulty with the idea of dying violently as a young mother. Also, as a teasing Senderl points out, I'd been a mite haughty (if lovable) as Chava. That had been a contributing factor to Sharon's cigarette-puffing insecurity.

Yankel / Paul, on the other hand, demonstrated the truth that some traits are carried over (until ultimately balanced) from life to life. After dying, Yankel had been reunited with Senderl and other family members before eventually returning to earth. Senderl now informs me that my intuition as Chava had been correct. Yankel had died in the Crimean War. He'd been mistreated beforehand by his "fellow" soldiers, led in their abuse by their commanding officer. Yankel hadn't advertised his Jewishness, but his circumsized condition and last name had been dead giveaways. He'd died young and bitter.

The Paul I'd known on Earth wasn't an especially happy person either. Between his ongoing restlessness and the child he now has to raise by himself, it seems that Paul has his work cut out for him. Assuming he accepts the responsibility. I'm hopeful that he will. Somehow I don't believe that he'd give Kenny up for adoption, or try to pawn him off on my mother or Gloria. Given their past history together, Paul and Kenny may be in a situation in which each can make some evolutionary strides. Maybe. Senderl, at least, sees it as a positive opportunity for both of them.

Senderl returns to his higher plane, despite all of our entreaties to stay a while longer. Travelling in a more horizontal direction, I go jogging on a path through the woods. This is something I'd have been loathe to do on Earth. But here, it's like gliding through a womb of sunlight and shadow, sheltered by whispering trees. I feel no fatigue. And whenever I want to I can go back home, directly. Or, if home is where the heart is, then as close as I can get, given the absence of my son.

- 12 -
Paul

"AH . . . YOU haven't gone home yet."

Gloria graciously refrains from complimenting me on my powers of observation. Instead she gives me a look of distaste, her eyes lifting to briefly scan my face, then tells me that Kenny should be about ready to go. This is the best news I've had all day (with the possible exception of Cheryl's no-decision regarding the future of our relationship). It looks like I might be able to retrieve Kenny and make a fast exit.

Given both her limited tolerance for her mother and the long trip back to Fishkill, I'd expected Gloria herself to have exited by now. Or maybe I'd just have preferred it that way. Clara's opinion of me was merely confirmed this morning, but in Gloria and even Lila's eyes I've surely sunk to a new low. Gloria actually checks behind her, as if making sure everybody's decent, before stepping aside from her mother's doorway and allowing me to enter the apartment.

I can see Kenny standing in the kitchen, squirming under Clara. She's bending over him, giving his face a post-dinner wipe-down. "So, how'd it go?" I ask Gloria, feeling obligated to say something.

"Oh, fine. He had a good time."

"Yeah? Good. Well—" I make myself move toward Clara and Kenny. If either of them is aware of my arrival, you wouldn't know it. Her back to me, Clara starts attacking the mess around the high chair she keeps for Kenny. My son, still wearing a filthy bib, charges over to Lila, who's washing dishes. She helps him climb up on a chair that she'd apparently brought over for that purpose. He's about to "help" her with the dishes.

Regardless of how charming this sight might be, I'm more than itchy to leave. I stroll over to Kenny and give his bushy hair an affectionate rumple. "C'mon, Ken," I say. "We gotta go."

Absorbed in watching a soapy glass fill up with water, he gives no response. I repeat the instruction, then attempt to lift him off the chair. He tries to wriggle free. "No!" he declares in a sharp, squeaky voice—the voice that Sharon used to just laugh off or ignore. I don't think I've ever managed to do either. Grabbing Kenny around his little pot belly, I heave him up, trying not to be rough but almost knocking the chair against Lila. When I try to set Kenny down on his feet, he does his collapsible legs routine, hoping to get his behind onto the floor. I pull him upright.

"Get your hands off of him!" shrieks Clara, rushing me and grabbing one of my arms. Reflexively I jerk it back and away from her. But I'm in control. I don't swing the arm forward again, even though the urge is there. I'm not such an asshole that I'd punch an old woman, even Clara. Gloria doesn't seem convinced of that, though. She hustles over and inserts herself between me and her mother.

"Unnecessary, Gloria," I hiss into her face. "You can stop playing hero now. I'm not about to swing on Clara or anyone else."

We stand glaring at each other. I have a quick feeling of deja vu, something to do with the mountaintop in Fishkill. The feeling is broken when Lila, apparently satisfied that I'm not going to go nuts, solemnly steps over to her mother in a gesture of solidarity. This makes me feel seriously foolish. Embarrassed. "Look, I'm not a violent person, okay?" This is addressed to everyone in the apartment, but my eyes are locked on Gloria's. I take a deep breath. "In fact, hurting anybody, in any way, is the last thing I wanna do. I'm really sorry about everything that's happened today. I'm sorry about everything. Okay?"

This unplanned apology is greeted with a deafening silence. Clara, spent from her kamikaze attack on me, tightens her lips in a look of outrage, then gulps more air. Meanwhile I still have hold of Kenny's rubbery wrist, despite his twisting and pulling like a hooked fish trying to get free. Finally, to demonstrate my benign nature, I let go. He pitches forward onto the linoleum and starts bawling. I can't win.

Lila and Clara, unaccustomed to his death-cry, rush over to him as if he's suffered serious damage. Or maybe they just prefer his company to mine. Feeling like I ought to show some concern, I turn to check on my son. He starts crying louder when he sees the freaked-out look on Clara's face as she bends over him. Shaking my head, I study the ceiling for a moment; there are several cracks in the plaster, but nothing I could fit into. Stifling a sudden urge to laugh, I'm turned around again by the sound of Gloria's voice.

"Try to take it easy on him," she says in a tight little whisper. "I'm hoping you want to. If you don't—"

"Gloria, save the threats, alright? Kenny's doin' alright, and I would never harm a hair on his head. I'm doin' my best with him, not that I need anybody watchdoggin' me. If I make it through this day, I'll probably be alright."

Her green eyes show no sympathy, but she seems to decide that she's said her piece. She spins on her heel and returns a few seconds later with Kenny's jacket. "You'll bring him again next week?" she says. It's as much a directive as a question.

"Sure." This answer earns me the jacket, which Gloria now hands over. "Clara," I say, "Figure ten A.M. next Sunday."

She grunts in acknowledgement. "I gave him a bath. How often do you bathe him?"

"Often enough. Why, does he smell?"

Clara glances down at the sniffling, oblivious Kenny, then gives me a look of greater disgust than usual. She must think

I'm insensitive. "No, he doesn't smell," she replies, gently pinching his wet cheek. "But he's got diaper rash, and his, um, his penis has an irritation."

I stifle a perverse smile at her difficulty with mentioning Kenny's organ. Obviously she's not bashful with him. I can tell that she's inspected every inch of his bottom thoroughly. "Yeah, well, I'll try to change him more often, and use some . . . what is it? Desitin? And I gotta get into a routine with the bath." This may not be easy. Bathing him after dinner usually takes more energy than I've got. "C'mon Ken," I say. "Put this on."

I hold the jacket open for him to slip in his arms. For no reason that I can see, he's now as cooperative as he was contrary five minutes ago. Not only does he slip right into the jacket (even figuring out which arm goes in which sleeve), but he starts walking toward the apartment door. Lila and the ladies are forgotten. Seeing an opportunity to pick up a few badly-needed Brownie points—it's ironic that I'm probably going have to deal more with my in-laws now that Sharon's dead—I catch up to Kenny and turn him around. "Aren't you gonna say goodbye to Lila and Grandma Clara and Aunt Gloria?"

"Come give Grandma a kiss," says Clara, all of a sudden dripping sweetness.

She holds out her arms. Encouraged by a gentle shove from me, Kenny goes over and plants a wet one on Clara's puckered mouth. This kiss would not get points for form, he just sort of opens his mouth and makes contact, the same method he uses to leave his mouthprint on window panes. A forward little fella, he performs the same trick on Lila and Gloria. Sharon taught him to "kiss," it was one of her last accomplishments, and her absence now is conspicuous. I almost expect her to put in an appearance at this gathering. And I wouldn't half mind. For a few seconds a shot of grief, of regret, takes the place of the edginess I've felt since walking in Clara's door. Walking out with Kenny is a definite relief.

"Twain," he comments as the Number 4 pulls into the Mosholu Parkway station a block down from Clara's building. It's one noisy twain, especially when it brakes, which sounds like metal strangulation. After a brief stop it rattles away from the station, its yellow-lit windows heading . . . which way? It's important that I figure this out in order to find my car. I'm only vaguely familiar with this neighborhood. Mosholu Parkway runs between two "Els," or it used to before they tore down the Bronx remains of the Third Avenue El. The Jerome Avenue El, on which the "4" train runs, frames the parkway on the west. I parked uptown from the station, I think . . .

No one in his right mind would risk imprisonment to rip off a heap like the Valiant, but after several minutes of searching for it I'm starting to wonder. I'm also starting to understand why over the last year Sharon urged Clara to forsake the apartment, cheap rent notwithstanding. From what I remember of the few times I've been here, this was never Park Avenue. But neither was it El Barrio. The streets to either side of Jerome Avenue are dark and grungy, and the avenue itself, in the nighttime shadows of the elevated tracks, gives me the creeps. Probably the Transit Authority built these things with the idea of discouraging other forms of transportation. Driving under an El at night is no great thrill either. It's like a motorized sobriety test, threading the cab between the iron pillars and the glaring lights of opposing traffic, which is almost squeezed into your lap by the pillars across the street. And the pillars don't bend; on more than a few nights I've been amazed and grateful that I didn't wrap my cab around one of them.

"Daddy-cab!" announces Kenny, as if reading my mind. He's spotted some cabbie cruising down Jerome, with no off-duty light on. The guy is either a fool or as oblivious to the dangers as Kenny, who is predictably tickled by the sighting. It starts him bugging me about taking him to work. "Out wi' Daddy!" After he repeats this a few times I'm ready to jump all over his case. But then, wonder of wonders, I spot the Valiant up the avenue. It looks as good as a limousine. I actually scoop Kenny up and run the giggling young fella half a block to the car.

After clicking him into the front seat and pulling out between two pillars, I have to cut back to the right in a hurry to avoid an oncoming bus. This accomplished (with maybe an inch to spare on either side), I remember that I *have* promised to take Kenny hacking sometime, and that I've heard that one should keep promises made to a kid. Like tomorrow. I could use a day and a half of not having to look into, or away from, accusing female eyes. That means calling Cheryl tonight, but I can probably make it fast.

Kenny falls asleep on the way home and barely stirs as I slip off his jacket and sneakers and deposit him in his crib. The diaper will have to keep until morning. I pop a beer then dial Cheryl, who picks up on the second ring. My reluctance to speak to her seems to have vanished; I answer her "Hello?" with a small avalanche of words.

"Hi, it's Paul. Before you get the wrong idea, I'm not callin' to ply you with sweet words or anything. I'd feel like a jerk doin' that over the phone . . . but anyway, I'm not droppin' Kenny off in the morning. He's got, I dunno, a little pink eye or something. I'm gonna take him hackin' with me, then to the doctor around four," I add, embellishing the lie as I go along. "If it fades, I'll bring him Tuesday."

There's no reason for Cheryl not to believe this little lie. Still, the silence at the other end of the line causes me a small shot of anxiety. "Well, I hope it turns out to be just a minor irritation," she says finally. "Let me know tomorrow. And you don't have to apologize about calling me. I've thought things over. Sunday is a good day for doing that. I just think we ought to cool it for a while, Paul. And it's not just because of that mess with your in-laws. I mean, we got hot and heavy in a hurry, especially considering that not long ago we weren't exactly each other's favorite people."

"That happens," I say, trying to sound like I know something about life and love. "All that energy we put into hating each other, we just sort of turned it in the opposite direction. Maybe that's why it was so hot and heavy."

"We hated each other? Disliked, maybe. We only saw each other five minutes a day. And Jesus, where do you get these ideas? Right, they do that in the movies—one minute they're at each other's throats, the next they're tearing at each other's clothes and panting. Hollywood bullshit. But Paul, this is not a game. Which is sort of what I'm trying to say."

I take a fast swig from the can of Budweiser. "Yeah, well why don't you go ahead and say it then. I don't mean . . . I'm not tryna get nasty, it's just that you oughta know that I'm about as far from hating you as I can get. And I wanna know what's what."

"When I figure it out, you'll be the first to know. I'm just leery. I've been lonely, and I have my needs, emotional and physical. And you just lost your wife. We see each other every day, and we're now the two main adults in Kenny's life. We could wind up just sort of falling into a serious relationship, by default. I don't know if that sounds right, but you know what I mean."

"Yeah, I believe I do. Still, I thought a serious relationship was what you wanted." I'm not sure that's what *I* want—in fact, if I never hear the word "relationship" again in my life, I won't mind—but, being described as a candidate for seriousness is a lot better than I've done lately.

"It is what I want. But I'm willing to bet that if I told most people what happened the morning after our first date, and then told them that I thought this could develop into something serious, they'd probably say, like . . . are *you* serious?"

"Well, they can say what they want. And if that sounds Hollywood, too, or pop-music corny or something, I'll have to take the rap."

Cheryl doesn't seem impressed. "Right. Still, at the very least, I need to proceed with caution now, not be over-eager . . . until I get to know you a whole lot better."

"Or trust me more." I feel like a hypocrite as I say this, having just fibbed to her about two minutes ago.

"That's definitely part of it. A big part."

"And how's that gonna happen if we don't see each other except to pass Kenny back and forth?"

"I didn't say that would be the case. I just need a little space right now, Paul. That's about all I can say. So, call me tomorrow, and let me know about Kenny and Tuesday morning. Okay?"

"Yeah. Sure." We exchange goodbyes, and I make myself hang up gently, like a big boy. I don't exactly feel like I've eaten humble pie, but my ego is having a problem with the fact that Cheryl is obviously in charge at the moment. I think about looking for the phone number of Denise, this female I hooked up with a few times last summer, but then decide against it. I need to be able to look in the mirror, and I'd like to be able to look Cheryl in the eye tomorrow morning. Also, Denise had a hungry crotch, she screwed lots of men. I was probably lucky that I didn't come up with a social disease. AIDS is the last thing I need now. Besides, one disease is enough. If alcoholism classifies as a disease, I may be enroute. I pour the rest of the beer into a paper cup (there are no clean glasses available), then add a shot of scotch. I hear that this is a big combination in Pittsburgh, a favorite of steelworkers and other real men. Count me in.

* * *

Early Monday morning Kenny and I head down the Major Deegan to pick up Daddy-cab. I'm suffering a mild hangover, sipping black deli coffee, smoking and cursing to myself. Kenny is fighting sleep. When we pass Van Cortlandt Park South, Cheryl's exit, I could swear that he gives a little start. Maybe the kid's starting to learn his way around, developing his hacking skills. Could be that it's in the blood. I wouldn't wish it on him, but at the rate he's going it's hard to imagine him as a doctor or whatever. Of course, he's still young, but looking at him now—he's nodded off, and a line of elastic drool is moving down toward his jacket collar—it's hard to imagine him even getting toilet trained.

If he is a future cabbie, he'll probably enjoy it about as much I do, judging from his reaction when we arrive at the garage. Maybe he thinks he's woken up in a dungeon. For whatever reason, he starts bawling loudly. I could swear his screaming dissipates the smoke in the drivers' room, as if the air is purged by the sound waves bouncing insanely from wall to wall. Even though they must have heard us coming through the garage, the few cabbies waiting in the room still look startled—it's not possible that their smelly sanctuary has been invaded by a little kid. One guy almost spits up his coffee. "Jesus, man," says another, holding his ears. "Take 'im outside!"

I'd rather not do this. It's cold in the garage, there's no place to sit, and besides, I have to crap. I'd hoped to be able to do that alone for once, hoped to pawn off Kenny on one of my fellow cabbies for a few minutes.

"Kenny, *zip* it," I hiss. For some reason I don't want to get loud with him in front of these bozos. I do give his arm a little squeeze, which only makes him get louder. I'm about to haul him outside (in fact, I'm thinking about running him back to Yonkers and his babysitter Carmen, where maybe I should've just left him in the first place), when one of the cabbies picks himself up from his bench.

"Whatsa matter, kid?" he asks Kenny. The old guy bends down and lays a pudgy hand on Kenny's cheek, stroking it once with his fingers.

Kenny gazes up at the chubby, smiling face with its wispy goatee. The guy is your struggling-artist-driving-a-cab type, except he seems a mite old for the part. He's bald on top with white hair fringing his head, covering his ears. He's also smoking a cigar. He's unusual-looking enough to make Kenny forget that he's supposed to be crying. When he remembers again, he's down to a whimper. His new friend chuckles.

"Just like my grandson," he tells me. "Wants to grow up to be a siren on a fire truck. What's your name, little fella?"

He sniffles. "Kenny."

"I'm Sol. Wanna shake?"

Kenny slaps him "five," a trick Carmen's son taught him. Sol gives a yellowish smile and returns the favor.

"Um, listen," I say, "You think you're gonna be here for a few minutes?"

"At least. My partner's probably parked somewhere using the steering wheel for a pillow."

"Well, I really need to use the can. Think you could—"

"No problem," he replies. "C'mere Kenny, have a look at my coin changer." While he's unhooking it, I duck into the bathroom. I hear no loud sounds from outside while I'm in there. Nonetheless, I try to be as quick as I can without risking a hernia. Kenny's unpredictable. Also, I'm nervous about him showing his ignorance, or underdevelopedness, or whatever he's got.

What he's got when I come out is a handful of quarters, which he'd managed to eject from the coin changer while Sol held it. Getting the quarters back into the slot at the top proves more difficult for him, though, sort of like he's playing pin the tail on the donkey, only he doesn't have a blindfold on. But Sol seems to be in no hurry. He uses his finger to steer Kenny's hand when a quarter gets too far afield, and makes a big deal out of it each time Kenny succeeds in making a deposit. Kenny's obviously enjoying this game. A couple of the guys waiting on the benches have started cheering him on; I guess they're bored with reading about the latest murders in the *New York Post*. Still, I'm relieved when I see Rico, the night man on my cab, pull into the garage. Perfect timing, Kenny's just plunked in the last quarter. I grab my clipboard and Kenny's hand, then thank Sol. As I make my way over to the dispatcher, it occurs to me that the next time I see Sol I ought to introduce myself.

Having forked over fifty dollars for the privilege of driving my cab all day, I buckle Kenny into its front passenger seat. He's obviously tickled. So am I, strangely. Not only am I proud of him (now that we're at a safe distance) for charming the guys in the drivers' room, but this is a milestone of sorts. The kid's growing up, he's going to work with his old man. Hell, my own father didn't take me along with him until I was seven or eight years old. And even then, when he was really conducting business I was left outside.

He'd only taken me once. I was on summer vacation and my mother was too sick to watch me herself. We drove up to a crowded bakery in some city. It could've been Trenton or Philly, my father was a "collection agent" in both places. He double-parked in front of the bakery and told me he'd be back in a few minutes. For awhile I watched him standing at the door, opening it for exiting customers and waving away new arrivals. No one really questioned his authority. Despite the fact that he was nicely dressed in a suit, tie, and fedora, there was something about him—his size, or the way he indicated with a flat wave of his hand that the bakery was temporarily out of business—that made it obvious that he was not a person to argue with. That fact had always been obvious to me.

Still, after he'd drawn shades and stuck a large "Closed" sign on the door, I decided to disobey his order to remain in the car. I was too antsy to stay. Other cars were getting stuck behind ours and honking loudly, the drivers cursing me as they finally pulled around and passed.

I walked into the sweet-smelling bakery to find my father with two fists full of shirt collar. His back to me, he stood with one knee braced against a glass case displaying chocolate cakes and other goodies. The case was topped by a wooden counter, and its edge more or less bisected the owner of the bakery. His fat stomach was jammed against it, his face about an inch from my father's. Next to the baker, an aproned, gray-haired woman stood wringing her hands and crying. My young brain understood her to be his wife. After a few seconds of surveying this scene undetected, I also understood enough about my father and the way he earned his living to make me feel as if my own throat was the one being squeezed.

The baker's bulging eyes alighted on me. My father, noticing his prey's shifting focus, released him and whirled. For an instant I saw fear on my father's face. This was quickly replaced by a look of anger and disbelief. "Paulie!" he barked. "Didn't I tell you t'stay in the car?"

In a trembling voice I answered, "Yeah, but—"

"Here, kid," rasped the baker. He extended toward me a large, thick round cookie, topped half with chocolate and half with vanilla: a "Black and White." In his desperation, he had grabbed the perfect offering. I loved Black and Whites. Yet I knew instinctively that if my father was seriously pissed at someone—and already pissed at me, too—it would not be a good idea to go running over to the enemy.

Dusting off one of the puppyish whimpers I'd given up along with diapers, I said, "I want it, Daddy."

My father glared from me to the baker and back again. Surrounded by pleading faces, his own face softened for a moment. His thin, sneering mouth seemed to relax, as if someone who'd been pulling back on his cheeks had suddenly let go. "Take it Paulie," he said, cursing under his breath. "You want it, take it," he added, trying to cover himself, trying to turn this moment of kindness into a lesson on manly self-assertion. Nonetheless, some of the air had seeped out of his puffed-up chest. When he turned to the baker again, he almost sounded like a reasonable man. "Look, I really don't wanna hafta raise your rates, smash up your windows—or your person. You understand what I'm sayin'?" The baker nodded rapidly. "Next week," said my father. "Have it for me next week. As in Monday."

"We'll have it," said the baker's wife, her now-dry eyes fixed on my father. "Even if it means we have to work overtime to stay in business. After all, we have our own children to feed."

My father's jaw tightened, then he spun on his heel and left the bakery. I stood for a couple of seconds looking at the baker and his wife, my mouth stuffed with cookie. Then I turned and scurried after my father.

As we drove away in the car, my father explained to me that people have to pay their bills, that it's like stealing if they don't. I wasn't about to argue with him, but even at my young age it was hard for me to believe that he'd been the good guy in the bakery.

We never talked about what happened there again, but I never forgot it. Sometimes I like to think that my father didn't either, that that was when he began to see what an asshole he was. But maybe I'm wrong. Maybe that had nothing to do with his eventual split from the mob. Probably they just didn't pay their goons enough money, especially since a lifetime commitment was expected.

In my father's case this requirement was somehow waived. Or maybe he violated it. It was never clear to my mother what the story was. It's safe to say, though, that it was no accident that my father left his mob family and us at the same time. I was about fifteen years old then. Even before he split, he was cheating on my mother regularly. And with impunity as far as she was concerned. I guess that was one of the perks of being a tough guy by profession—your wife didn't complain much if she valued her health. My mother shed no tears when he finally headed west, putting a safe distance between himself and the South Jersey mob. He has a liquor store and a wife in Arizona now (where he got the capital for this is another mystery), and he actually sends me Christmas cards. My mother remarried a couple of years after he left. She found another jerk; she really knows how to pick them. This one, long since gone, inspired me to split to New York, where I hooked up with the post office.

* * *

Kenny spends his first hour or so in the cab fascinated by the picture of him that is hanging down from the base of my rear view mirror. I make the mistake of taking down the picture so he can take a closer look ("See!" is the way he puts it). The kid must have eyeballs in his mouth: he sucks and chews on the "gold" frame and plastic covering until I finally take the picture away, inspired by my second fare, a chunky black nurse. After several minutes of talking with Kenny about how much fun it is to go to work with Daddy, she asks me if Kenny is an especially self-centered child.

The question seems to come out of left field, but I shrug and reply, "I dunno, I hear they all are."

"Wellll . . . if he swallows that picture, he's really gonna be full of himself." The woman guffaws for about five minutes. She has an interesting laugh, sort of like a subway train barrelling through a tunnel. I can't help joining in.

In fact, this turns out to be my most social day ever in the cab. With Kenny in front, I have heads poking through the open partition, smiling and chatting as if a cabbie taking his kid to work with him is just the dearest thing in the world. One elderly gentleman, in the course of a stop-and-go ride down Fifth Avenue, actually narrates to Kenny the entire story of "Lady and the Tramp," complete with some impressive snarling.

The first person to ask Kenny about his Mommy is a good-looking brunette in a business suit. She gasps when he replies, "Mommy dead." He seems to have finally accepted this idea on Friday, when he said, "Mommy dead" to Cheryl several times at nursery. She thought it was a breakthrough. After hearing this announcement countless times, usually out of the blue, the thrill is gone for me, if it was ever there. The brunette in the cab doesn't believe Kenny until I confirm that he's telling the truth. She lays a fat tip on me. This happens a few times over the day. No one seems willing to believe that I'm running a scam, even if Kenny makes the announcement unasked, which he does a couple of times. In fact, whether or not the topic of Sharon comes up, serious tips are the rule rather than the exception. Kenny has earned his keep today.

That's true even if you subtract the price of a few items, like the pen that he chewed up as if it was beef jerky. At least he chewed on the top of the pen rather than the tip. But even if his tongue had turned blue and his taste buds were grossed out, I doubt that he would've learned much. These days he seems determined to stick anything and everything into his mouth, except maybe vegetables. Of course, I'm not a real good example there, unless tobacco can be considered a vegetable.

Also subtract from my earnings today the price of several cans of beer and a few shots of whiskey. I was forced to take a lot more breaks than usual; after about eleven o'clock, Kenny got very squirmy. Like a good daddy, I kept my temper, parking the cab and walking him around Midtown and in and out of a couple of bars.

Although he was bewildered in the smoky darkness of bars, where no one fussed over him (except for one clever bartender who wanted to check his ID), Kenny did enjoy tracking around Midtown. I let him walk, even though he was all but swallowed up in a jungle of legs, hips and crotches. Undeterred, he held on to my hand and plowed his way down the sidewalks. He likes bouncing off of things, which he manages to do even in relatively uncrowded spaces. But after a couple of near-accidents, including getting his head grazed by a swinging briefcase, I carried him on my shoulders, holding onto his hands to prevent him from snatching at any of the hats or interesting hairdos passing by below him. The kid doesn't understand the principle of private ownership. What fascinated him most, though, was the statue of Atlas holding up the world (while gazing down on Fifth Avenue).

"See!" Kenny yelled, pointing up at the bronze mass of muscles. "Like Daddy!"

"Whaddya mean?" I said against my better judgement, knowing that his answer would probably nullify the boost he'd given my ego.

"Carry," he replied.

"Yeah, that big ball on his shoulders, that's supposed to be the whole world, Kenny. The world is like everything you see around you—me and you, and all these buildings and cars and people, and a lot more."

"Carry like Daddy."

"Well yeah, but I'm just carryin' *you* on my shoulders. He's got . . . actually, there are similarities," I said with a laugh which jostled him into some giggles of his own.

Now, smoking and driving home in the Valiant with Kenny asleep next to me, I'm still amazed by that little conversation. It's got to be the best we've ever had. My son may be developing a brain. In fact, with the exception of my day and night with Cheryl, this was the best day I've had in a while. Just the fact that I remember so many details distinguishes it from the usual ten hours of living death.

However, the day may be about to end on a lousy note. Kenny wakes up cranky and whimpering from his second nap of the day. I carry him into our building. Flannery makes a big show of opening the door for me: he can put aside animosities for the sake of a child, even though he knows I can manage fine with one hand.

"Afternoon, Mr. Gull-doni."

"Yeah, afternoon Flannery." I slip sideways through the door and around his brass-buttoned potbelly. He hustles ahead of me and presses the elevator button. Kenny starts wailing. He wants to push the button, and his job has been usurped.

"Okay," I say with enforced calmness, depositing him on the lobby's maroon carpeting and shooting Flannery a look. "You can still push it, Kenny." Unfortunately, the doors slide open before Kenny can put his little index finger into action. I try to get him to push the button anyway, but he's inconsolable. We almost get snagged by the closing doors as I drag him into the elevator. Inside, the volume of his screaming is unreal. I manage to stay somewhat detached from it by imagining Flannery's amusement as the sound recedes up the elevator shaft.

Even if he's no longer under the illusion that Mommy will be waiting for him inside the apartment, the fact that she's not adds to Kenny's list of grievances. Another problem is that I promised to take him to a pizza joint for dinner, but then decided not to wake him up on the way home. Or at least that was a good excuse to renege. Taking him out to eat is always a risky operation. Even in a fast food joint you never know what he'll knock over, or when he's going to decide to exercise his vocal cords. He wails pretty much the whole time I'm making dinner. By the time the burgers are ready (I'm getting the hang of it, they're cooked on the inside, too), I'm ready to kill Kenny. I wind up leaving a greasy spatula-print on the kitchen wall, smashing the thing into the wall as if trying to kill a monster fly. This finally quiets Kenny down. I've heard somewhere that the survival instinct is inborn.

After dinner and a couple of beers I'm ready to sack out, but Kenny's usual bedtime is still an hour away. That should be covered by the cartoon special we start watching at 7 o'clock. Tired as I am, I get giddy over Woody Woodpecker's jackhammer laughter. The closing credits are accompanied by that insane sound, which now seems directed at me. After sitting in cars most of the day and doubling his nap time, Kenny is obviously not about to fall asleep. He's been bouncing all over the couch, as if the cartoons were an exercise tape for him. I have to pin him down to get him to hold still long enough for me to double-diaper him. I put him in the crib, listen to a minute's worth of screaming, then take him out and let him run loose. He messes up the living room while I clean up the kitchen, even Brillo-ing a blackened pot from a few days ago. That takes care of my last shred of energy. Kenny is still going strong. Finally, after kicking off my sneakers and snuffing out my cigarette, I lay him down in bed with me. This seems to settle him. Maybe it's the novelty of being in my bed. When Sharon was alive, I'd have slept on the couch rather than try to sleep with Kenny.

I must have dozed; I'm awakened by the bony pressure of the little bugger's elbows and knees snuggling against my midsection. Is he out? I squint down at the side of his bushy head and pray that he is. Then I feel myself sliding back into sleep . . .

Kenny is hanging on to the string of this balloon. We can't be in our apartment, the balloon's way too high. The balloon is huge, semi-round, tan, with windows and wheels, a double-barrelled tailpipe, even an antenna, all painted on. It's a swollen Volkswagen bug, the way the car might look during a near-sighted LSD trip. And of course it's Sharon's bug, she's the silhouette in the driver's window.

The balloon is rising, taking Kenny with it. I try to yank him down but can't seem to get a grip on him. I do grab hold of the string, in time to be lifted off my feet. We move up into a flat, white sky, if that's what it is. The string has stretched out considerably. Kenny, in diapers only, is having no problem crawling upward, he doesn't even seem to have to hold on. I barely manage to inch up the string after him. I try to yell at him to come down but produce no sound. As we move up the string, the shadow in the driver's window takes on more detail: a fixed brown eye, a bloody trickle of tear, a gaping hole where the mouth should be. If he sees this, Kenny's undeterred. I try a last grab at him as he reaches the balloon, tries to fit his arms around it, bites it with his huge teeth. The balloon explodes . . .

I wake up with a start, giving a yell that seems to come from someplace else. My sudden movement rolls Kenny off; he must've been right on top of me. He settles onto the mattress and goes on sleeping without missing a beat. It takes a short while for me to get my bearings, to remember what Kenny's doing in bed with me, to realize that I've been dreaming. Usually my sleep is alcohol-black. *If* I have dreams, I never remember them.

I get out of bed and strip to my underwear, dropping my pants and flannel shirt on the rug. It's then that I notice how cold it is in the bedroom. I'm shivering by the time I finish pissing, get myself into long johns, drag the blankets out from under Kenny, and cover us both with them. Damn it's cold. And the apartment never seemed so empty.

- 13 -
Paul

"HI, KEN!" Beaming, Cheryl bends over and gives her favorite student a hug that curls him backward like the letter "C". Maybe it's just by contrast that the greeting she gives me seems lukewarm at best. Her smile goes slightly limp, the "hello, Paul" is issued with a leftover cheeriness that evaporates in the air between us. Dropping her eyes, Cheryl informs Kenny, "You went to work with Daddy yesterday. Did you have fun?"

"Uh-hmm," he replies, having discovered recently that this is adult jargon for "yes" and less trouble to pronounce. She waits a few seconds for him to elaborate, but his attention has already gone to the cloth belt of her bathrobe. He yanks on the ends of the belt, then starts pulling them apart as if trying to open the robe.

"A chip off the old block," I comment, working up a laugh.

Ignoring me, she gently removes the belt ends from his grasp.

"Yes indeed, Cheryl, we sure did have a good time. Doubled my usual tips, too. Maybe I oughta take him with me everyday."

"No you *don't,*" says Cheryl in a mock-childish voice, possessively hugging Kenny again, laying it on thick. Releasing him, she steps back and peers into his eyes, then looks up at me. "Which one is it?"

I gaze at her dumbly for a moment. "Oh, it's um, the left eye. It was pretty much better by the morning. I didn't wanna take any chances, plus I'd already promised him—" I shrug and exhale slowly, relieved at having recovered in time from my case of liar's block.

"Well, it looks fine now," she says, lifting the eyelid as Kenny squirms.

"Yeah. Look, Cheryl, I gotta go." She looks fine too. Finer than I care to admit, since the next move is up to her. Or, at least, I have to give her a week or two. I've got my pride, theoretically. I tell them both goodbye, rumple Kenny's hair, and make a fast exit.

The week or two turns out to be a few days. Thursday is a fairly rotten day in the cab. My second passenger is a painted lady who at 7:30 A.M. is aglitter with enough jewelry to resemble a chandelier. When we reach her East Side destination, she informs me that she's misplaced her purse. She does, however, have money upstairs. Could I wait a minute? I wait ten before finally admitting to myself that I've just eaten a seven-dollar fare. I drive away cursing like like a lunatic. When later in the morning some asshole wants to pull the same number on me, I tell him he'd better give me something of value before he leaves the cab, or I'm going "upstairs" with him. My delivery would've made my father proud. Finally the guy, who is fiftyish and relatively small, admits that all he has is the clothing he's wearing (which doesn't look like it'd bring much). He took the cab because he had nothing left for a bus or train. On hearing this, I tell him to get out before I kill him. Scratch another five dollars.

The final straw is a trip to Kennedy Airport that takes two hours owing to some overturned tractor trailer. Thirty-dollar fare, fifty-cent tip. The young couple's suitcases produce a series of small thunderclaps as I snatch them from cab's trunk and dump them on the sidewalk in front of the TWA terminal.

On the way back from Kennedy, I stop in at some red-neck bar in Howard Beach. I feel right at home. I'm still fairly drunk by the time I arrive at the day care center to pick up Kenny. But I retain enough good sense to go nowhere near Cheryl, especially since I'm not in possession of my fool-proof breath spray. Fortunately, she's at the far end of the room helping some of her charges fingerpaint. Also fortunately, Kenny is not one of them. We can split quickly. I call him from the doorway, telling him to get his jacket, cursing myself as I stifle a boozy burp. God bless him, the kid cooperates, bringing me the jacket straight away. We'll put it on outside. I give Cheryl a fast wave, but she's not looking my way. This bugs me.

In fact, by the time we exit, I'm convinced that she doesn't give a shit—or maybe she thinks I don't, the way I checked in and out without really checking on her. Kenny gives me a strange look as I stand on the sidewalk outside of Beth Shalom, inclining back toward its door then leaning away again, rotating ever so slightly like a weather vane in a shifty breeze. He hustles over to the Valiant parked a few yards away and tugs on the front door, saying, "Open!" I realize that I forgot to get the car seat from Cheryl, and that I now have a legitimate excuse to go back inside and chat her up a little, see if I *can* tell which way the wind is blowing. My anxiety is enough to get me pissed at myself, to make me wonder where the hell this juvenile bullshit is coming from. Maybe I should've had a few more drinks. Well, that oversight can be remedied.

"Open!" yells Kenny again. He actually has his hands on his hips, like he's about to demand the keys if I don't get a move on. I grant his wish, then practically toss him into the front seat, belting him in before he's even stopped bouncing. He gets upset about this, and for once I can't blame him. I feel like kicking myself in the ass. Instead, I slide in behind the steering wheel and apologize for the rough treatment, explaining that I had a rougher day. I might as well be talking about physics, but my gentle tone and the rumple I give his hair—Daddy's usual signal that he's feeling kindly—seem to neutralize an oncoming tear-storm. Just to make sure, I offer to stop on the way home for some cheeseburgers and fries. Fries are a new favorite of Kenny's. It's an offer he can't refuse.

"So how wuz your day, Ken?" I say, the slurry sound of my voice blending into the noise of the engine turning over. "Whatd'ja do?" Silence. "Didja make anything?"

"Uh-uh." This probably means nothing that he hasn't already destroyed.

"Nothing? Well, neither did I, pardner." Yuk yuk. I can't even enjoy my own cleverness, since in this case it cuts a little too close to the bone. Worrying about money was always Sharon's job, or obsession; I've been trying not to sweat it. Still, shelling out six bucks at Burger King's drive-up window (even there I get stuck in a line of cars) is something I do reluctantly. The life insurance check is supposed to come sometime this century, but I'll believe it when I see it. Something has to give, because I can't start working weekends again, not if I want to remain sane, not if I want some time to hang out with Cheryl.

As we drive up Broadway-Yonkers, I actually have an urge to pump Kenny about his teacher and her current mood. Desperation? Of course I wouldn't sink that low; it would be useless anyway. In fact, the notion of asking Kenny for his observations and advice brings a stupid grin to my face. I glance over at him while we're stopped at a light. His foot is playing pitty-pat with the glove compartment door, which doesn't close flush against the dashboard. Lately he likes to rectify that with his sneaker, letting the door fall back again (there's about a quarter of an inch of play), then repeating the procedure. Over and over again. His lower lip is sticking out as he intently watches his foot in action. I'm getting absorbed in watching him. A honking horn behind me snaps me out of it—the light's changed. As I start driving again, I have an image of Kenny sitting cross-legged in a diaper, smoking a pipe, pondering his advice to the lovelorn. He looks like a little guru, or maybe Sitting Bull Jr. I break out laughing then look over at him again, as if double-checking on who's riding next to me. His attention drawn by the loud laughter, the little innocent is beaming back at me, green eyes lit up, big smile showing me a handsome set of baby teeth. He doesn't know what I'm laughing about and doesn't really care; he's happy just to join in the party.

Bringing my attention back to the road, I'm suddenly choked up. I put a cigarette in my mouth and tell Kenny to push in the lighter. Even with his seat belt on he can reach it now, and he's proud of that. Notch this achievement above the elevator button.

Flannery is absent from the premises when we arrive home, it's probably one of his days off, although I wouldn't say there's a big difference between those and his days on. His replacement, a black gentleman with a gray mustache, seems to get a genuine kick out of Kenny feeling up his shiny "gold" buttons and reaching for his hat. Before I can pull Kenny off, the guy gives in. Kenny's ears and eyes disappear into the gold-trimmed "poweese-man" hat. The only problem with this is that he pitches a fit when he has to give it back. The doorman shrugs apologetically and I tell him not to worry about it, it's nothing unusual. Holding the hat behind his back, he gamely smiles at Kenny, then sends us on our way, informing me that the mail arrived an hour ago.

Towing my son, I dutifully trudge over to the boxes to pull out the usual catalogues and requests for donations addressed to Sharon, the usual bills addressed to me. But today I am informed via a green card that yesterday the mailman attempted to deliver a registered letter, which I can now pick up at the post office. I'm about to put this off until tomorrow when I realize what might be inside the letter. Kenny gives a confused whine as I pick him up and hustle him back outside and into the car.

It does turn out to be the life insurance check. A twenty-five thousand dollar present from Sharon, who's been dead over three weeks. She'd picked up the optional life insurance policy from her job despite my comments that it was a waste of money, that the only way we might wind up cashing in would be if she worried herself to death. The letter from the insurance company is short and not real sweet: "Please find enclosed a check constituting the benefits payable on the death of your wife, Mrs. Sharon Galdoni. We offer our sincere condolences. Please be advised that the continuance of coverage for yourself and your son, Kenneth Galdoni, necessitates your renewing the policy as an individual, since Mrs. Galdoni is no longer employed at Research Institute of America. This continuance must be effected within the next thirty days . . . "

At a substantial increase, I'm sure. Sharon was always the person in charge of finances, insurance, etc. In fact, the only dealing I can remember having with life, health, or auto insurance was three weeks ago, when, all the time not believing I was doing it, I'd xeroxed her death certificate and mailed it in along with a copy of our policy and a cover letter typed up by my mother. I must've done something right. I'm now looking with blurred vision at the reward for those little actions: $25,000. I dab at my eyes. I feel like I'm holding Sharon's remains in my hands. Or one hand, since the other is occupied fending off Kenny. Having observed my teary fixation with the little rectangular piece of paper, he's trying to snatch it away to have a look.

No way Jose, or Kenny, or whomever. This is one item I'm not about to let him tear, chew, or otherwise mutilate. Twenty-five *thousand*. I scan the numbers, then the letters, then back again, double and triple checking. Finally convinced, I carefully insert the check back into its envelope, then fold the envelope and stick it into the breast pocket of my jacket, beyond Kenny's reach. When he starts complaining, I grab a change of address form from a nearby shelf. It's about the same shape as the check, and paper is paper to him. He's happy with his, temporarily at least, and I'm starting to feel grateful for mine. My eyes are still ever-so-slightly fogged by the time we reach the car, but mixed in with the sadness is relief. This check means maybe a year's worth of freedom from money problems. For one thing, we can now go home to Riverview knowing that we're in no foreseeable danger of getting evicted. Moving out is an option I've thought about on and off since Sharon died. I'd like it to stay an option and never become a court order. Maybe I can stretch the money via interest on savings. I'm not even *tempted* to take a few thousand to the racetrack and see what I can do. I must be growing up or something.

Kenny almost nods out by the time we get home again. This is not a good sign, but we have a bag of goodies from Burger King which might keep him in a decent mood for a while. When we get upstairs, I discover that the check has not vanished from my pocket since I last felt for it in the car. I hide it away in my booze cabinet above the kitchen stove, a convenient place to look in on it until I can get to the bank.

My son doesn't seem to mind that his cheeseburger and fries are long since cold, and I could care less about the temperature of my food. I wash down the once-flame-broiled slop with a colder beer; it all tastes fine to me. I'm hungry enough, in fact, suddenly I'm famished. Wanting to chow down undisturbed, I almost don't answer the phone when it rings. But on the off-chance that it's Cheryl, I finally pick up after six or seven rings. I immediately wish I hadn't.

"Hello, Paul. It's Gloria. Am I interrupting something?"

I can't tell if this is politeness or sarcasm. "No, nothing real stimulating is going on," I reply. "We're eating dinner. I was in the middle of a bite. Didn't wanna chew in your ear, so—"

"I can call back." As she says this, I hear some music—Michael Jackson?—start up in the background.

"That's okay, I'm about done. What's up?"

"Lila, turn that down!" she yells, with immediate results. To me she says, "I just wanted to confirm for this weekend. What time are you bringing Kenny over to my mother's on Sunday? You said ten A.M."

I think this over for a few moments. "Um, actually I was thinking about maybe late Saturday afternoon. Let him sleep over, then I'll pick him up Sunday afternoon." This more or less confirms my snap decision to call up Cheryl and offer my company this weekend. Hope springs eternal, or my organ does.

Gloria sighs. "Were you going to inform anybody? It's Thursday night already."

"Sure, I would've."

"Sure. Well, I'll call up my mother. It'll probably be alright, although she doesn't react well to changes in plans. I'll call you if there's any problem. Just . . . be sure you get him there, alright?"

"Of course. And I'll be sure to pick him up before he gets on her nerves too much. My mother has dibs on him for Sunday night. We're going down there for dinner." I glance guiltily at Kenny as I say this. With cheese, ketchup, bread, and beef crumbs spread all over his face, he's obviously ignorant of the fact that he's being spoken about in an unkind way.

"I'm not worried about him getting on her nerves, Paul. I'm just worried about him getting to her apartment. It's about the only thing she looks forward to anymore. She's just . . . She's been seriously depressed since Sharon died. She's taking antidepressants now. Just the fact that I could even get her to go to a doctor, let alone take medication, shows how bad it is."

"Yeah, I remember Sharon talking about how she refused to go to doctors. Didn't trust them." Not only do I remember hearing that from Sharon, but if I didn't know better I'd swear she was telling me again now. With the agitation in her voice —unusual for her—Gloria's a vocal ringer for her sister. And she's inherited Sharon's half of the job of complaining and worrying about Clara.

"At least she's got her job, thank God, although ringing up lingerie in a department store gets kind of old after a while, even part time. She's never had many friends, has maybe only one now, this woman who kvetches constantly about her operations, among other things. Just what my mother needs. But last weekend, when she was with Kenny, she actually seemed happy. She—"

"Look, Sharon—I mean *Gloria*—believe it or not, I sympathize. Kenny likes going over there, and I guarantee I don't wanna keep him all to myself. If you're worried that I'm irresponsible or whatever, I can also guarantee that I'll get him there. I mean, we're all playing on the same team, you know?"

Her silence makes it obvious that this is news to her. In fact, I was surprised to hear it come out of my mouth. But at that moment I meant it. Now, feeling like half a jerk, I sputter a question about Lila.

"She's fine. She's coming down with adolescence, but she's a good kid. How's Kenny?"

"I'll let him tell you himself," I reply, seeing an easy out from the conversation. "You can hang up after that. Tell Clara to figure around four o'clock Saturday. See ya'."

Kenny and Gloria have what's got to be the longest phone conversation he's ever had with anyone. He "Mommy deads" her a couple of times, pausing in between to listen for several moments, itself a major feat for him. Then he says, "Daddy-cab." This is followed at intervals by "Go work," "Go work w'Daddy," and "Fun," as Gloria gets the story out of him. When he says, "Check!" it takes me a few seconds to understand what he's talking about. My first notion is that he's come across some CB lingo or something on television. Then I realize that I was going on in the car about the *check,* half to him and half to myself. It's fine with me that Gloria doesn't succeed in doping out what he's talking about this time. Finally saying "Bye," he bangs down the phone.

I figure I should get him in bed before calling Cheryl. Otherwise, even if she's interested in talking to me, staying on the line will be chancy. I take off a dirty diaper, get crap on my fingertips, then run a bath for Kenny, letting him flop around with his ducky and boat while I straighten the kitchen a bit. I return to the bathroom to find him chewing on a bar of soap.

"Kenny, what the hell are you doing!" I demand, although I can see what he's doing just fine. I use my fingers to brush bits of soap off of his lips and teeth, none of it's really gotten inside his mouth yet. He's probably crying because he's been deprived of his snack, not because he's had a taste of it. It occurs to me that maybe I should've let him have a good taste; it would teach him a lesson. Instead I use a washcloth to soap him from neck to knees, holding him still with one hand and scrubbing with the other. The pressure of my hand on his stomach is enough to make him gasp, interrupting his crying. After this, his new cries, amplified by the bathroom's close walls, are *loud.* I dip him back into the water then lift him out again, rinsing him off like a plate. Then I wrap a towel around him and lift him out of the tub, all the time resisting murderous impulses that would take only half a minute, max, to carry out.

Skipping his bedtime story for once—he's rarely gone to bed without one—I diaper and pajama Kenny, then make myself give him a little hug before depositing him in his crib. After a few whimpers, he quickly falls asleep.

Cheryl picks up on the second ring. She says "Hello?", then "Oh . . . hi," after finding out that it's me. This double greeting is followed by a long silence, an invitation to come out with whatever it is. The clever beginning I've planned doesn't wind up sounding real clever.

"Look, Cheryl," I say, "I've got a proposition. I mean, a suggestion." I manage a moment's worth of laughter, then plunge ahead. "Could we please get together this weekend? We don't have to sleep together if you don't want to. We don't have to go anywhere near my apartment. I'd just really like to see you. Okay?"

"Well—"

"Look, if you don't want to, it's cool."

"Really? Thank you, but I want to. Or at least, I'll take my chances."

"You sure?"

"You want to argue about it?"

"No thanks," I quickly reply. "I mean, I was prepared to. I thought I'd hafta convince you . . . Maybe I should just shut up. Quit while I'm ahead."

"That is a good idea," she says, and I don't need a picture phone to know that she's not smiling. Neither am I, although the mission seems to have been accomplished. "Is Kenny going to chaperone us again?"

"Nope. I'm dropping him over to his grandma's Saturday afternoon, and he's sleeping over."

"Well, he wasn't such a hot chaperone anyway. What time should I be ready?"

"Six-thirty. Dinner, a movie. My treat."

"Sounds nice. Are you sure you can afford it, though?"

"Easily." I'm reluctant to put my foot in my mouth again, so I don't elaborate. Instead I say, "See you then. Actually, see you in the morning."

Hanging up, I turn on the tube and catch the beginning of "Cheers". Happy doings at the bar. Making a quick trip to the fridge, I take out a couple of beers, intending to join the celebration. Instead I wake up in the armchair halfway through "Nightcourt," my hand still wrapped around the first, half-empty can. Turning off the tube and flopping into bed takes all the effort I can muster.

* * *

I'm sure Gloria's description of her mother's suffering was not made up. But it's hard to feel much sympathy for her. Clara, alone, sneers at me when I drop Kenny off Saturday afternoon. She looks like death. Still, it's amazing the way that sagging, tired face can tighten with hatred at the sight of me, then beam at Kenny in the next instant, as if someone was changing slides inside of Clara's head. I hand her the diaper bag at arm's length, and inform her that Kenny had a bath the night before last. Then I tell him to have fun, reaching back to give his hair a quick rumple as I exit.

With time to kill, I pick up the *New York Post* and sit in my car catching up on the latest murders and rapes. Flipping to the back, I look through the racing charts. I notice that Caesar's Salad, a horse I won on a while back, is running tonight at Yonkers Raceway. There's an OTB, as in Off-track Betting, on Jerome Avenue. I open the car door to take a walk over, then think better of it. Just to make sure, I drive away, parking ten minutes later near Cheryl's. I lean back against the front passenger door and close my eyes. I'm hoping not to get much sleep tonight, so . . .

I wake up with a start, wondering where the hell I am. There's a newly fallen dusting of snow on my windshield which doesn't help. For a second I could swear I've been packed in mothballs, that I've slept for several days, ála Rip Van Winkle. But I get the time from my car radio and discover that sure enough, I'm still early. I never nap for long. As usual, I'm just as tired, even after the cobwebs have worn off. The only change is that I'm a lot hungrier. A cigarette helps with this some, but it also ups my pulse a few notches. After stubbing out the butt and taking several hits of breath spray, I'm too antsy to kill any more time. It's getting dark as I walk the couple of blocks to Cheryl's. Along the way a few late-arriving snowflakes land on my head. This is better than birdshit, I guess.

Cheryl takes a while to buzz me up. By the time she does I'm starting to get nervous, starting to smell a rat, starting to run a catalogue of bars through my mind. It turns out that she was in the shower; she didn't hear me buzzing until she turned off the water. Obviously wet, she opens the door in her robe, waves off my apology, and tells me to make myself at home while she dries off and dresses. I do my best. Her apartment doesn't look a whole lot different in the P.M.; it's neat enough. Clearly Kenny only spends a few minutes a day here.

When Cheryl finally rejoins me in the living room, I suck in air. She's wearing a silky blue dress that comes down to her knees and either stockings or pantyhose (I'm sure I'll figure it out). "You look good," I tell her. "*Very* good."

"Thank you," she replies, smiling and doing a playful pirouette. "Ready?"

I return her smile. "I've been ready." On the way out I explain my early arrival. "I was fleeing temptation. There's this OTB on Jerome Avenue, near my . . . near Kenny's grandma. I thought I had that out of my system, the old horse-playing disease. But I happened to look at the paper, and this horse I won on once is running tonight. I just hope he doesn't win . . . or place . . . or show."

"Do you have to find out?" she says as I open the car door for her. She slides in with that knees-together daintiness that females are probably born with.

The Valiant, still warm, kicks off on the first try. "I suppose I could live without that information."

"No newspaper for you tomorrow," she says, leading me to wonder if she's planning to be around. "From what I've seen of OTB, 'horse-playing *disease*' is an accurate term. I pass by the one down near Broadway and 238th when I go shopping. Seedy-looking. That's if you can see through the haze. Looks like a cross between . . . an opium den and a bank. And an adult bookstore, maybe."

I laugh, and flick on my headlights. "Yeah, there are guys who practically live in those places. I've never liked them that much myself. I was more into going to the track, seeing the action live. Used to go with this ex-buddy of mine, the one who went in with me on that pizzamobile I told you about. Never go into business with a friend, especially if it's his big idea, you're laying out most of the money, and the business isn't gonna make it."

"Sounds like another kind of gambling."

"Well, yeah. Maybe it cured me, too. I had nothing left to gamble, and a family to support, although that doesn't stop a lotta people."

"So I've heard, from one of the mothers at Beth Shalom in particular. You should feel proud that you're that responsible."

We're driving down Van Cortlandt Avenue East, a long, curvy hill that leads toward the Deegan. Conditions are still a mite slippery, so I'm taking it slow for once, and only chance a quick glance at Cheryl to see if she's serious. "Well thanks," I reply, deciding to believe that she is. "It's true, I never bet the rent money. Or the alimony and child support I woulda had to pay if I bet the rent money. But, still, I understand how people do it. You're sunk in far enough, you figure it's the law of averages or something, you convince yourself that your luck's about to change. You can *feel* it. It's easy to do."

We make a decision about a restaurant and a movie. Actually Cheryl had figured those items out in advance; she more or less lets me know to make sure I head north on the Deegan. Then she says, "But still, you quit. Horse playing, I mean."

"Yeah. One bad habit down, a few more to go. I quit after Rob McClellan—my ex-pizza buddy—and I were no longer buddies. I got tired of going to the track alone, and leaving with less than I came with. Plus, I could probably be described as a cynic. With the kind of luck I've always had—not just with horses, with everything—I didn't believe that Lady Luck was gonna suddenly start smiling on me." I decide not to tell Cheryl that quitting the track for good was a promise I made to Sharon and decided to keep, a token peace offering around the time she discovered the panties in my cab.

"Although," I continue, "Who needs Lady Luck? A smile from you, Cheryl, and I'm in good shape. I gotta say, though, that if I was still a betting man, I'd have laid odds against you agreeing to come with me tonight. Life is full of surprises, I guess. Occasionally they're pleasant ones." It's also a surprise to be sober and hear all these words coming out of my mouth. Maybe this is a side effect of living with only a three year old, or of having a job in which the only other adults I encounter are strangers sitting behind me on the other side of a partition. Or it might be some result of the affection I feel for Cheryl, which seems to be growing.

We're stopped at the last red light in the Bronx. I look over at Cheryl. A smile is playing at the corners of her mouth, as if she's in on a private joke. It's a sexy look, possibly owing to her pink lipstick, or my imagination. She says, "Well, you're *my* gamble, I guess."

I'm trying to figure out how to respond to this when I'm

informed that the light's turned green by a honking horn behind us. This is happening more and more these days. I must be getting senile. Toeing the gas pedal, I reply, "I'll try not to disappoint you, kid."

She's unimpressed by my sarcasm. "Just be yourself," she says. "With some modifications."

"Such as?" I reach into my pocket for a cigarette, which I hold unlit.

"Don't lie to me. Ever. That's if we last long enough to justify using the word 'ever.' Although, somehow I feel like we already have. Maybe that's because it's been so intense."

"That it has."

"Well, I can live with that. I think," says Cheryl as we pass 233rd Street, where the Deegan becomes the New York State Thruway. "I've had more than enough of yuppie men with their textbook sensitivity. You know, they're trying so hard to be real, like they've taken a few courses in it. And of course, if you don't want to go to bed with them right away, that's cool. But bye-bye.

"I went to bed with you right away because I wanted to. And I know that over the phone I said, or at least strongly intimated, that I didn't want to sleep with you again so quickly. But, since the ice has already been broken between us . . . I think that if we develop something lasting, it's not going to be about sex, about having it or not. It'll be about the way we relate to each other as people, or some cliche like that. Besides . . . the sex was nice," she says, almost bemusedly. "Very nice."

I burst out laughing. "What?" she says.

"I don't know . . . just the way you suddenly shifted gears. Caught me by surprise. Quite pleasantly, I might add." I give her a sly grin.

She reaches over and pinches my cheek. "Yes Paul, the earth moved."

"Oh, that was just Kenny thumping around in his crib," I say, even as my face flushes with pleasure. "He's a restless sleeper."

"Ha-ha. Anyway, speaking of Kenny, and of why I decided to take you up on your invitation tonight, I love him so much that I figure if he has some of your genes, you must be alright."

"I'll have to thank him," I reply, although Sharon's genes

probably deserve more of the credit. Not that I've ever thought there was that much credit to be taken in the first place.

I cut my speed as we approach Yonkers Raceway, which looms over the Thruway like a giant, beckoning whorehouse—the last gasp, or grasp, of metropolitan New York before you start getting into the more countrified 'burbs over the Tappan Zee Bridge. Just outside the racetrack, the service road is packed with headlights and winking taillights. I catch sight of harnessed horses cantering down one side of the track. The ultraviolet floodlights are intense; the horses and jockeys look like they're trotting around in a giant, hazy white fishbowl. The light bounces off of the lower levels of the grandstand, the yellow and orange sections. These are filling up with people who can afford expensive seats along with whatever they might drop at the windows. Masochist that I am, this glimpse is enough to whet my appetite. I curse under my breath and push in the cigarette lighter.

"Doesn't it get cold in those stands? I mean, even the football season ends in early December."

"Football is child's play, my dear," I say, mildly impressed by her knowledge of the sports calendar. "Not that people don't bet on football or anything else, but this is a second *profession.* Or the only one for some of these bozos, between the track and OTB. You take a little nip now and then and the weather's no problem. Of course, neither is anything else, depending on how many nips you take. Eventually, if you don't wind up wiping windshields on the Bowery, you wind up telling it to Alcoholics Anonymous or Gamblers Anonymous. You can get real anonymous. Maybe I'm lucky."

After several moments of silence I reach over and take Cheryl's hand. She gives mine a squeeze and runs her thumb over the back of it. This is soothing and then some.

So is the pre-dinner wine, some Chinese stuff that Cheryl orders at the Mandarin Gardens. Dinner—various once-crawling sea animals and strange looking vegetables—turns out to be delicious. Things are going so nicely that I even have high hopes for the fortunes in our cookies. But mine turns out to be typically irrelevant: "Still Waters Run Deep." Crumpling it, I say, "Maybe if it said 'distilled liquors'—"

She laughs and takes a last bite of her lo mein, deftly using her chopsticks to pluck a few lone strands off of her plate (I'd quickly given up on the chopsticks; among the more dominant genes that Kenny got from me is probably the one for eye-hand coordination). Cheryl then breaks open her cookie and reads, "Fame and fortune are yours for the asking."

"Sounds good."

"Yeah, but who do I ask?"

"Sweetheart, if I knew that—"

She sighs. "Vital information is left out. Paul, let's trade fortunes. At least yours is poetic."

"Hey, you can have mine for free. What's mine is yours."

The movie,*Witness*, is both a thriller and a love story, with a few suitably steamy scenes. Afterward it's my place. This is Cheryl's suggestion, and I take it to be a demonstration of her faith in me. Also, my apartment is closer. We're both tired; this is the latest either of us has been out in many moons.

My fatigue vanishes immediately when we get inside the apartment. And Cheryl's only having a little fun with me when she lays back and insists that I undress her, claiming to be too tired to do it herself. The stockings turn out to be pantyhose, which are less of a turn-on but easier to remove. This is a decent trade-off, since I need no turning on. The only problem is knowing where to start. I want all of her at once. She's not holding anything back—she couldn't be; after we both come, it's almost a surprise to roll off of her and discover that we're still in separate bodies. I lay for a while rubbing her back, nuzzling the light peach fuzz under one ear. Finally I whisper, "Whaddya thinkin' about?"

She answers, "Kenny."

It takes maybe half a minute for me to stop laughing. "Kenny?" I gasp. "I'm layin' here thinkin' about how much I love making love to you, and you're thinkin' about Kenny?"

She gives me a quick kiss. "Oh, don't get your male ego all bent out of shape. The feeling is mutual, dearie, believe me. I have not wanted to open my eyes for fear of losing such a lovely afterglow. But inevitably other thoughts start to creep into my mind. It's something I've been wanting to talk to you about for a while."

"Okay, fine," I say, placated. Laying back, I realize that some heat is finally happening in my bedroom, but the result is the same as always: a conversation about Kenny. The recognition causes a few left-over giggles to fizzle out in the area of my throat.

"Have you thought about having Kenny evaluated?" she asks. "I'm concerned about his speech development and his motor skills, both fine and gross."

"Not to mention toilet training. But why get him evaluated? I can see for myself. He's clumsy, he hardly ever puts together a sentence or even more than a few words at a time. Hopefully he'll grow out of it."

"Maybe. But he'll have a better chance if he gets help at a young age. He needs a lot of stimulation, a lot of support. And now with his mother gone . . . even though he might be adapting, and even though he's still got you—"

"I understand, Cheryl. Believe me."

She ignores the slight impatience in my voice. "Good," she says. "If we get him evaluated—Westchester County will do it free of charge—then there are preschool programs he might be eligible for."

I prop myself up on one elbow and gaze down at her. Smart girl—she's covered herself up with the sheet in the name of keeping me focused on the conversation. "But he's already at Beth Shalom," I say. "That's preschool, and it's fine with me. He can go there next year, too."

"Right. With a different teacher and fifteen or twenty other kids who are basically focused on playing. In a Special Education program, he'd be in a small class with a teacher and an aide, speech and occupational therapy available, working specifically on the skills he needs to develop. Also free of charge, I might add."

"Special Education, Cheryl?"

"If he qualifies. They have their criteria."

"Well, criteria or no, even I know that Special Education is a code word. You know, like calling a janitor a 'custodial engineer.' Like calling me a transportation expert. Even when I was in school, everybody knew it. You were in Special Ed. if you were retarded, seriously dumb, or liked to throw chairs while the teacher was speaking. You might as well put a sign on the kid."

Cheryl sighs. "Paul, according to this friend of mine who teaches elementary Special Ed., there's no real stigma attached to it. The kids are too young to know the difference, up until about the fourth grade, anyway. Also around the fourth grade, the die is pretty much cast in most cases. Special Ed. for life. That's why it's important for him to get help now. The younger the better."

"Okay, I'll think about it." Before she can reply, I gently place my index finger over her lips. "And I'm not tryna brush you off, patronize you, or whatever. If you could get me the necessary information, help out with it, translate if necessary, I'll probably go along."

"Well, good. At least getting him evaluated won't hurt."

"Right. I trust your judgement, sweetie. I didn't always, but—"

She gives me a half-smile, which softens the outlines of her high cheekbones. The woman is lovely. "After I showed such good judgement in men—"

I laugh and kiss her. "Look, you're gonna hafta stop reading my mind."

"Why? Makes you feel naked?" She moves closer to me, lightly stroking my chest. This is enough to wake up my organ, which begins to inflate again. Cheryl helps it along by sliding her fingers down with a tantalizing slowness.

Neither one of us is in a hurry to finish our second round of love-making. By the time I come, she's come twice and we're both exhausted. I wake up a while later still partially inside of her. I raise myself slightly and my shrivelled organ slips out like liquid. The desk lamp, which had provided a little subdued lighting, is still on. There is enough light to remove any doubt about the identity of my bedmate. Yet now, as with our first time together, the recognition that those parted lips and the rhythmic breathing don't belong to Sharon brings a momentary shock. Regaining my equilibrium, I cover Cheryl with the blanket, piss, check the time—it's 12:30 A.M.—click off the light, and sink back into bed.

Around 9:30 I'm awakened by the telephone. But it's the

sound of Gloria's voice that really jerks me awake. She apologizes for the hour and an alarm goes off in my head. I'm sitting upright by the time she says, "There's been an accident with Kenny. He swallowed some of my mother's antidepressants."

"Jesus Christ."

"Paul, I'm sorry. She got sloppy with the pills, she's been distracted. You need to get over to the hospital. Jacobi. They took him there in an ambulance. Both of them. She called 911, and gave them my number at the hospital. She was too distraught to talk to me herself. You know where Jacobi is?"

"Of course. Where is he, in the emergency ward?"

"That's right."

"Fucking *shit*."

"Paul, I'm sorry. They wouldn't tell me much about his condition. Just please get over there. I'm coming down myself. We're about to leave."

I hang up and turn to find Cheryl, wide-awake herself, staring at me. "What happened?"

I tell her. "I gotta get over there," I finish.

"I'm coming with you."

"You're gonna see my inlaws again," I say, in a daze; part of me is amazed that I'm not already throwing on my clothes.

"Paul, they can see me like *this* for all I care. Let's *go*."

I'm about to ask her who the hell she thinks she's talking to in that tone of voice. But then, as if the answer dawns on me, my body clicks into gear. We both jump into our clothes, dash past Flannery in the lobby, then pull out in the Valiant, leaving rubber on Nepperhan Avenue.

I run a couple of red lights, barely checking the intersections for oncoming traffic or cops. After the second time, Cheryl says, "Listen, it might be better to get there a minute later—"

"I know what I'm doing."

"Right. Famous last words."

I shoot her a look, necessarily a quick one given the speed at which we're moving forward. After a moment, maybe figuring that pacification is the best way to go, she sighs.

"Sorry. I'm upset."

I nod, slowing to take a right down toward the Deegan, screeching the tires anyway.

"Did she say how many pills he took?" Cheryl asks.

Replying, "Uh-uh," I light a cigarette, then hand one to Cheryl at her request.

She manages to light it on the fading orange coils of the car's lighter. I'm halfway through mine when I realize that Cheryl doesn't smoke, or didn't. I also suddenly realize how much easier my life could be if Kenny doesn't make it. But this notion practically makes me double over, as if the kid were inside of me, gnawing at my solar plexus. Kenny is not supposed to die now. The feeling is overpowering. We're supposed to be together, I know that beyond a doubt, as if it's been ordained and I'm suddenly party to the information. This knowledge provides a brief sense of relief, almost happiness, followed by near-panic: he's not supposed to die now, *but what if he does*? What if whoever did the ordaining didn't factor in Clara? "That fucking woman," I snarl, gripping the wheel tightly.

"Paul, I really don't know her, but I'm sure she'd give anything for it not to have happened. Hopefully, he'll be alright."

I accelerate onto the Deegan. "Cheryl, they don't rush you to the hospital in an ambulance for nothing. She must've left the whole bottle out. If I did that, the whole fucking family would say, 'I told you so. You know him, he's a drunk. Whaddya expect?' They'd have me locked up." I take another deep drag, then try to go on about Sharon's family while there's still smoke in my throat. This results in a coughing fit at 75 miles per hour. I slow down, bent halfway over between the seat and the steering wheel, heaving, pounding the dashboard in disgust with my free hand. She pats me between the shoulder blades then massages the same area, repeating a few times "It'll be alright." This turns into a soft, pleading chant.

Finally I say, "Cheryl, he's gotta be. I don't know how I'm gonna be able to handle it if he's not."

We get off of the Deegan at Fordham Road, by which time I've settled down some. It's now a straight run across Fordham into Pelham Parkway and Jacobi Hospital. But even on a Sunday morning it's hard to run lights on Fordham Road, one of the Bronx's main commercial strips. Gypsy cabbies and other uninsured immigrants are still finishing off their Saturday nights, and cop cars are around, looking for easy prey. Even so we make good time. Fordham Road zips by in a blur of locked gratings, garish signs, and garbage.

A guard at Jacobi directs us to the emergency ward. I think I may have dropped one or two fares there in the past. Cheryl and I may eventually be leaving in a cab, since there are no legal parking spots immediately visible and I'm not about to waste time looking. I park illegally about a block away from the emergency ward entrance, figuring the area right around the entrance is a guaranteed tow-away zone.

Having run a block, Cheryl and I are both breathing hard, holding hands as we push sideways through the hospital's double door. Inside, it takes a few seconds for my eyes to sort everything out. The scene is not unfamiliar: flourescent lighting, white coats and uniforms, a faint, sickly smell of ammonia, muffled sounds of crying. Take away one or two of my senses and there'd still be no mistaking the fact that I'm in a hospital. I know I'm not dreaming. On the other hand this shit can't be happening again. It just can't.

We locate the emergency desk. A second later I locate Clara. There are a few rows of hard plastic chairs, half-full with people waiting to be helped. Clara's sitting in a corner at the back, bent over and trembling, her face in her hands. The sight chills me. I stare at her, trying to decide whether or not to approach her and see what I can find out about Kenny, see if I can keep from exploding at her. Or from crying myself.

Cheryl, mystified by my hesitation, starts dragging me in the direction of the desk. I dumbly trail along behind her. By the time we reach the desk I've snapped out of it, but the problem now is that there's a small line. At the front a semi-frantic mother is going on in Spanish. The emergency nurse, a dumpy black woman, obviously has no trouble understanding her, even with the senora's baby wailing. The conversation doesn't seem likely to end in a hurry. After about half a minute I walk to the front of the line and interrupt. "My son . . . Kenneth Galdoni?"

The nurse tells the woman, "Momentito," then comes out from behind the desk. I can see my face, haggard and puffy, reflected in her glasses. "Mr. Galdoni . . . Mrs. Galdoni," she begins. Neither of us bother to correct her. "Your son swallowed some antidepressants, enough to interfere with the electrical impulses that regulate his heart. Doctors are working on him now. One of them will come and speak to you as soon as possible."

"How is he?" Cheryl asks.

"At this point I can't really tell you anything about his condition. Again, one of the doctors will—"

"I wanna see 'im."

"Mr. Galdoni, it's important now that the doctors remain—"

"My son, dammit. I wanna see Kenny. Now. I won't interrupt anything. I just wanna see 'im *alive*."

My eyes home in on a double door at the far end of the room. I push past the nurse, jerking my hand away from Cheryl's. Before either of them can try to stop me I'm through the door. There are white-curtained cubicles lining both sides of a wide aisle. The outer curtain of one of the cubicles is bulging, pushed outward by the backs of one or two people. I hesitate, then, as the nurse, the guard, and Cheryl come through the door, I yank aside the curtain. It's the right one. I can see Kenny through the gaps in the huddle around him as a few gloved and gowned figures turn to gape at me.

"I'm his father," I announce, which seems to freeze most of them for a long moment. Kenny is laid out on his back. His eyes are closed, his mouth hanging open. There's a tube running from some kind of machine into his neck. A doctor—the only person who did not even pause when I entered—is leaning over Kenny and pushing on his chest.

- 14 -

Sharon

"DADDY, TELL me again how you knew I was coming? Here, I mean. The afterworld."

My father, who'd known what I meant, looks up from his fishing pole. He hasn't had a bite in a while. Of course, he could remedy that at once, but that would be cheating. Half of the fun, he's explained to me, is being surprised. The other half is relaxing as the waves gently rock your boat. As a boy on Long Island, where he loved to fish the Sound, he'd have gladly used his present powers to fill up his boat with fluke, porgies, blackfish, bluefish, maybe even some tropical varieties. Now he's content to "go with the flow" (he took a shine to this expression after hearing it from me recently), to set up typical Earthly odds and wait. He smiles and nods at other sea-faring souls who occasionally drift by in sailboats or yachts. A rowboat is fine for us. To my question he replies, "Sweetheart, earth is the afterworld now."

"You know what I mean," I answer impatiently. "You told me you could just feel it."

"That's right." He gives his line a jiggle, hoping to attract some attention down below.

My grandmother looks up from her knitting, which she's been doing in a flawless rhythm, a counterpoint to the rocking of the boat. "You see that seawall over there?" she says, pointing toward the shoreline. "If it were removed, the water would flood the shore. When someone you love on earth dies, the barriers between you and that person are gone."

"Hopefully they can swim," cracks my grandfather.

"Shah!"

My grandfather, lying on his back with his feet and fishing pole against the side of the boat, chuckles to himself. My father, predictably, is also amused. No one has yet shown any intolerance for my ongoing longing for Kenny, though by now, regardless of their ability to "read" my mind, they'd all have known immediately where my line of questioning was leading.

Actually, the longing has abated somewhat lately. I've felt that I've made a peace of sorts with my separation from my son. But now the feeling of Kenny is overwhelmingly strong. I could swear that I'm about to be with him.

I'm sure of it when I suddenly find myself in what seems to be the meadow where I was reunited with my father. It has the same swift, sparkling stream, the same radiant landscape, the same storybook horizon—a horizon which appears to be neither an ending point nor a beginning; it's a seam of infinity. There is no difference between this and the bluish-gold horizon of the sea, or sound, on which I'd been bobbing in a rowboat with my father and grandparents. The sound is now the meadow; if there was a transition point, I can't remember it. Nor am I concerned about that as I scan the meadow, feeling as if my heart is about to burst. I start running when I see, a distance away, what appears to be an oval gathering, an intensifying of the general brightness. Kenny.

As I run I'm aware that the running is unnecessary, archaic. But this is the way I've been envisioning it, each stride filling me with joy.

But will he remember me? How "old" is he now? I can't really approximate the length of time I've been "dead." It must not be that long, though: suddenly I'm as nervous as I ever was.

This feeling gives way to bliss as, right before I reach the oval light, Kenny emerges from it. Just as I had left him, albeit transparent. My little Kenny, not a hollow reproduction but filled with *him*, his sweet and lovely soul. Which I am filled with as I hold him to me, finally, impossibly. I hold him out from me and feast my misty eyes on his smile, on the green sparkle of his eyes. Then I wrap my arms around him again. With my eyes closed, all I experience inside is his silent exultation. "Mommy!" Like an echo across time, like a validation of my being.

"Sweetie," I say, stepping back from him, chancing letting go. "You can feel how happy I am to see you."

"Yes, Mommy." His face lights up in a smile. Gratified that he's understood me, I grope for something else to convey that he might be able to understand and respond to. "You must have hurt yourself, Kenny. You know that Mommy died in a car crash, and that's why she's here now. What happened to you?"

"I was with Grandma Clara. I think I swallowed some of her pills. The doctor called them . . . antidepressants. I heard him talking in the hospital. I saw him and another doctor and some nurses trying to wake me up. I was above them. I mean, I was laying on this bed, but I wasn't at the same time. I was looking down at them and me. You understand, Mommy?"

As Kenny asks me this, he realizes that I do. He literally beams with pride at my astonishment. "I grew up. Just like you said I would." Then he surveys his body and clothes, still those of a three year old. But he forgets this disappointment when it registers that he, too, is transparent. He superimposes one hand on the other and peers through them both, pokes a finger through his leg, then grins at me with a familiar, childish delight.

"Kenny, you can talk," I inform him. "You can understand. I don't believe it, sweetie. I'd pinch myself, but what good would it do here?" We both giggle. "You can actually talk."

"This is better than talking," he replies. "A lot easier, too."

"And more effective . . . Kenny, Kenny, Kenny. Probably nothing should surprise me anymore. But not only are you here, you're *talking*, Sweetheart. Will you still let me kiss you?" Not waiting for an answer, I plant a kiss on the deliciously smooth "skin" of his cheek, hug him again, get misty again. His receptiveness to hugs and kisses had actually fluctuated a great deal on Earth. Now, he responds to my affection in kind and then some.

"You look wonderful, Mommy," he says as his bare feet settle back down into the lush, undulating grass of the meadow. "And it's so beautiful here."

"It is. Did you see the Being of Light?"

"*That* was wonderful. I remembered him! He said that was because I'd only been on earth a short time, I wasn't far removed from my last stay in afterlife. He said I was about to see you, and that you'd explain everything."

"He said that?" Kenny slowly nods. "Well, maybe we can find your grandfather. He can explain . . . and I know he'd love to see you."

Grandpa Abe finds us. He simply appears, still wearing his fashionably dilapidated fisherman's hat. With him are his parents. "We thought you'd want some time alone with Kenny," he says, smiling at his grandson.

"You knew where I went?"

"Of course. And who you were going to see. Hello, Kenny, I'm your Grandpa Abe." Kenny manages a half-smile, astonished at the way my father and company have just dropped in.

"Grandma Clara's husband," I add. "My father."

"And I'm *his* father, which makes me your great-grandfather Moishe. This is my lovely wife, Sarah." She beams at Moishe with surprise and pleasure. "Your great-grandmother," he continues. "Four generations of ghosts."

Everyone laughs at this. Kenny is delighted to meet his ancestors, and they him (one ancestor he doesn't meet is Senderl, whose uplifting presence I sense. Senderl remains an invisible onlooker, not wishing to confuse his one-time son at this point). I say to Kenny, "Your great-grandparents are my grandparents, sweetie."

"I know that, Mom," he chides.

"Well excuse me, Mister Bigshot." Smiling, I reacquaint my fingers with the thick, springy texture of Kenny's hair. I turn to my father: "He's pretty much the way I left him, his appearance is anyway. I couldn't have died too long ago. But Daddy, he could barely talk. I'm amazed. It's like he's grown up twenty years," I say, aware as I finish that I'm talking about Kenny as if he wasn't standing next to me, wasn't capable of understanding what I'm sending out. I used to jump on Paul for this, and he was doing it to a kid who probably *didn't* understand diddly-squat, as Paul would have said. But Kenny never seemed to mind then, and he doesn't now. He's too busy basking in the glow of everyone's love and admiration.

"He's grown up more than that, Sharon." My father winks at Kenny, who effortlessly returns the wink. "Here he's his soul —or his soul is out of its latest wrapping. You understand what I mean. We are not looking at a three year old, but someone who's been through many lifetimes. If he doesn't remember them right now, he still has access to what he learned. And access to us. Tell me, Kenny . . . to what do we owe the pleasure of your unexpected arrival? You had some kind of accident?"

Kenny explains, and when he's finished my father almost resembles the devastated person he was the last year of his life. "Clara," he says as if addressing her. "Clara . . . what does she have now? She lost Sharon, she was taking pills for depression, and now this? She'll blame herself." A tremor runs through him. Obviously on the edge of tears, he turns to his parents. "How much does one person have to suffer?"

My grandfather shrugs helplessly. "It depends, Avraham."

The faintly glowing atmosphere of the meadow becomes a golden, fluid haze as my own eyes fill with tears. Except for conversations with my father, whose fond memories of my mother are a continual source of wonderment to me, I haven't really thought much about her. Worrying about her from here would be pointless, and Kenny's been the only Earthling I've seriously missed. But now I share my father's grief, and harbor a worry of my own: how is Paul going to deal with this? Will it crush him? Unlikely, but imagining him stricken with sorrow is still easier than the alternative, in which he is rejoicing at being freed, in short order, of both of the albatrosses around his neck. The truth is probably somewhere in between, but my feelings about Paul have always tended toward extremes.

When I get the first inkling that Kenny is about to be returned to his father, that we're about to be separated again, I refuse to even entertain it. But the inkling rapidly becomes a certitude. And I suddenly feel betrayed, shattered.

The reason for this is a mystery to no one but Kenny, who nonetheless is aware that something has gone wrong with Mommy. I scoop him up, as if by clasping his transparent little body to my bosom I could prevent the departure of his soul. This brings me little comfort, and only heightens Kenny's confusion. I put him down, and dry my eyes. "Sweetie," I say, "Sometimes people almost die, or their body stops working, but only temporarily. Sometimes they come here, but they don't stay. Instead they go back into their bodies and continue to live on earth. And they're very happy, because they know what death is really like: it's something wonderful. They're not afraid like other people are. That's what's going to happen to you. It's not your time to be here yet, sweetie. I'm not sure why, but—"

Feeling me falter, my father adds, "It happened to me, Kenny. And it was for the best, even though I didn't want to leave your great grandma and grandpa to return to earth. But I had to, and the time I had left on earth became a time of peacefulness, despite the fact that I was in pain. You, on the other hand, will have a long and happy life, like your mother says. This experience will stay with you. You'll always remember this."

Kenny gulps. "But Mom, I don't *want* to go back. Please. I want to stay here with you." He reaches up for me and his lip trembles as if in prelude to one of his earthly crying fits, as if he were beginning to revert before my eyes. This is almost more than I can bear.

"There's nothing Mommy can do," I tell Kenny, embracing him again. "We'll be together again, we just can't be now. I love you, sweetie, and I'd love for you to stay, but there are reasons . . . Some things we have to learn here, others on Earth. Like Grandpa says, you've already learned about dying. But Daddy and Grandma Clara don't know about that, and they probably think you're gone forever. They must feel terrible. They need you, Kenny. Think how happy they'll be to see you alive and well."

Kenny brushes at his eyes and peers around him at the

meadow. A few birds fly by, looking as if they've just come to life from stained glass. Unabashedly, he studies my grandparents and father, finally turning to me. "You're right, Mom," he sniffles. "I saw Daddy right before I saw the Being of Light and came here to you. It happened when the doctor was pushing on my chest, trying to bring me back to life. I could hear the doctor saying, real quietly, 'C'mon!' Only he was looking in the wrong direction, down. I was up. Then Daddy pulled aside the curtain and said, 'I'm his father.' There were tears in his eyes, Mom. I could feel that he loved me."

There are tears, astral ones, in our eyes too. A wave of powerful love seems to envelope the five of us. The light emanating from each of us forms a field of dazzlingly pure white.

"And Grandma Clara loves you, too," says my father.

"She does. And we had a good time together before I swallowed those pills. She takes care of me sometimes, and Aunt Gloria does. So does Miss Nahm."

"Just like she did before I died."

"No, now she takes me to nursery school with her, too. And sometimes she's with Dad and me when school is over."

I look at my father and grandparents with raised eyebrows, then slowly shake my head as if to deny what I'm thinking. "Paul and this woman don't get along very well," I inform them. "She's Kenny's nursery school teacher. She's very nice. Nice-looking, too. I guess she and Paul must have put aside their animosity for the sake of Kenny." How far aside they've put it is something I suddenly don't want to know. Or, at least, it's not something I want to pursue with Kenny, regardless of how grown up he may temporarily be. He's apparently grown up enough to understand my sentiments, and to wish that he hadn't raised the topic of Cheryl Nahm.

"Don't worry about that, Ken. You can't help what comes into your mind. It's fine," I assure him. "And if Daddy's getting some help now, that's a good thing. As for Miss Nahm . . . well, I'm sure she's happy to be able to spend more time with her favorite boy."

Kenny smiles. Neither of us wants this precious visit to end on a sour note. The fact that it will end momentarily is now plain to all of us. Hashem's will is a lot easier to fathom here—whether or not one is trying to.

I say, "At least this time we get to say goodbye, sweetie. Or, see you later." I wrap my arms around my son and hold him until he vanishes.

- 15 -
Paul

THEY DON'T allow smoking in the emergency ward waiting area. That is ridiculous. If smoking should be allowed anywhere, the emergency ward waiting area is the place. Unless we're in the waiting area for "Intensive Care." The difference is not real clear to me. Intensive Care is where, according to the guard and nurse, I'm not allowed to be without a doctor's permission. They'd informed me in no uncertain terms that I was in violation of that rule, which apparently applied even though my son was lying in there near death. Somewhere in my brain I'd recognized that the best I could do for Kenny was to avoid making any more of a scene. I'd let the guard lead me back to the waiting area. It was actually a good thing that the guard, who was stronger than he looked, had a tight grip on my upper arm. I'd developed a case of blurry vision and weak knees. But I forced myself to overcome both as I passed back through the double door. People were staring, temporarily diverted from their own troubles. They'd seen the guard, the emergency ward nurse and Cheryl chase after me into

Intensive Care as if pursuing a kid who'd just liberated some candy bars from a newstand. Or we could have been playing follow-the-leader, since the three of them were still behind me when I emerged. The least I could do was to try to look and act like half a man—particularly since Clara had lifted her face out of her hands in time to witness the proceedings.

I kept myself together until Cheryl and I got outside on the sidewalk (where smoking is permitted). Cheryl hadn't seen Kenny getting CPR, or the tube in his neck. The curtain had been drawn again just before she'd arrived. After the nurse reasssured me that the doctor would speak to us as soon as he could, Cheryl and I ducked out of the waiting room for a smoke and some privacy. I managed to tell her what I'd seen, then I started blubbering with sorrow and rage. "How the fuck could she leave the pills out? How am I gonna handle this shit?" Cheryl, quivering herself, wrapped her arms around me.

We were standing like that when Clara walked out onto the sidewalk. The shock of seeing her actually approach us seemed, strangely, to calm me some. I knew I wouldn't kill her. I couldn't even feel that much righteous anger, standing there with the same woman Clara had "caught" me with a week before. And Clara was obviously sick about Kenny. After Cheryl and I disengaged, Clara asked to know what I'd found out about him. Her voice was a hoarse whisper, and her eyes looked like red sores in a shrivelled face. The sight of her didn't move me enough to tell her a white lie. But if the voice I used was not gentle, neither was it accusatory. The news was enough, though. Clara gave something like a dry heave, a strangled cry. Probably she would've fallen had Cheryl not embraced her.

Now, the three of us sit together, waiting. The only clue to how much time has passed is that I have one cigarette left in what was almost a full pack. By now I must have worn a groove in the sidewalk outside, with help from Cheryl, my angel of mercy. She's dividing her time between me and Clara, who doesn't seem to be in great shape. Clara's face has not emerged from her hands since we re-entered the waiting room. Her responses to Cheryl's concerned inquiries are barely audible —when she responds at all.

Some hope for rousing Clara arrives in the form of Gloria and Lila. Cheryl and I are standing outside sucking on cancer sticks when Gloria's Chevy Camaro screeches up to the yellow-painted curbside. She jumps out. Lila steps out on the passenger side, still wearing Walkman headphones, one in front of each of her straw-colored braids. Gloria says, "Sorry it took me so long."

"Did it?" I reply. "I wasn't really keeping track." This is not intended to sound nasty; it's not intended to sound like anything. I'm half numb. But Gloria's green eyes narrow for a moment.

Sighing, she says, "How is he?"

"He's, um, he didn't seem to be doin' real well. I only got a quick look at him. That was—" I glance over at Cheryl.

"About an hour ago," she fills in, checking her wrist even though she's not wearing a watch. She and Gloria briefly study each other. "I'm Cheryl Nahm," she adds. "We've never been . . . formally introduced, I guess. We—Paul and I and your mother —we've been waiting to hear from the doctor who's been working on Kenny."

At this point the guard strolls over. He hasn't been far from view since evicting me from Intensive Care. "You can't park here, Miss," he tells Gloria.

Cheryl says, "Let me take care of it . . . Gloria, is it? Your mother's inside, and I think it might do her some good to see you."

Gloria hesitates, then smiles tentatively. "Thank you," she replies, handing Cheryl the car keys. Cheryl gets behind the wheel. Lila, her headphones now encircling her skinny neck, trails Gloria into the waiting room. I take one more deep drag on my cigarette, stomp it out and bring up the rear.

"Mom?" Gloria lightly jostles Clara's shoulder. Clara removes her hands from her face and squints up at Gloria, her mouth hanging open in a look of surprise or confusion. Clara slowly shakes her head. Her small jowls twitch as if she's chewing Jell-o. Finally she rasps, "I killed him, Gloria. I killed little Kenneleh. I killed him." She lets out a long, low moan. Her body shaking, her head drops against Gloria's pelvis.

Gloria gulps and says, "Mom, he's not dead. The doctors are working on him now. He'll be alright." She strokes Clara's gray hair.

"No, Gloria, no. He's dead. The doctors were pushing on his chest."

Gloria looks up at me. I shrug helplessly and nod. "They were giving him CPR." Gloria closes her eyes, takes a deep breath. Lila starts crying. "But that was a while ago," I add. "I'm starting to hope . . . If he was dead, they'd have told us by now. There'd be no reason for them to delay." There may be some truth to this. The waiting area has almost filled up. There are casualties left over from Saturday night, men and women with bandaged heads, faces hidden by ice packs. There are kids, whimpering into their mothers' coats, who'd probably awakened crying in pain. It occurs to me that maybe I should feel lucky that Kenny received prompt service; but that, of course, was owing to his condition. I refrain from voicing these dim-witted thoughts and instead stand watching Gloria, a bastion of strength. She's seated with her arms around Clara, rocking her like a baby. On the other side of Clara, Lila sits listening to her headphones and dabbing at her eyes.

For some reason I feel obliged to hang around for a while, rather than escaping to the sidewalk again. I am relieved when Cheryl finally returns. I inform her that there's been no news yet, and she hands the car keys back to Gloria. Unsuccessfully, she attempts to explain how to get to the lot where she parked the car, then offers to just take Gloria there when the time arrives.

"Thanks, I'd appreciate that," Gloria replies, her arm still around Clara. "I'm not much good at finding my car in parking lots, even if I've parked it myself. That's one of the reasons I'm not crazy about going to malls. They don't really have them in the city, but when I moved upstate, to Fishkill . . . It's suburban sprawl, and giant malls."

Cheryl nods sympathetically. "I know just what you mean. I once spent an hour in a mall in Westchester, looking for my car. Now I hang an American flag on my antenna if I venture into a mall parking lot. I think I know now how Francis Scott Key must've felt."

Both women laugh, quietly. They proceed to carry on a conversation about a variety of topics. Each looks fascinated with what the other has to say. This is some kind of female ritual, I know. Still, watching and listening to them, I'm dumbstruck.

Neither of them is into chattering, and you wouldn't think they'd be real eager to talk to each other anyway. Especially not here, one step from the morgue.

Gloria is telling Cheryl about her last experience in an emergency ward, almost eleven years ago. She'd planned on giving birth to Lila at home, and had made no hospital arrangements. But after a day's worth of heavy labor, she'd demanded to be taken to the nearest hospital. Her husband and the midwife reluctantly agreed. They'd taken a cab to Beth Israel Emergency. "I almost gave birth to Lila at the intake desk," says Gloria, shaking her head ruefully. "The nurse insisted on obtaining every conceivable fact and figure of my life. She had her forms to fill out."

If Lila hears any of this through her headphones, you'd never know it. Once or twice Clara seems interested in the conversation, but each time her face sinks again into her hands. Gloria intermittantly whispers words of encouragement to her. I'm about to head off in search of a cigarette machine when the nurse approaches with a doctor. This is probably the guy who was giving Kenny CPR. He's tall, at least as tall as me—in a flash I remember that as he bent over Kenny, his head was more or less level with the others surrounding my son. I'd only glimpsed the top of his head then. Now, I see sleepy brown eyes, longish brown hair, a bony face with veins showing at the temples, thick lips. I take unusual notice of the doctor's face because he will be delivering The News, and because his approach seems to occur in slow motion. I've been waiting for the S.O.B. for what feels like forever, but now I am not ready to hear what he's got to say.

All I can do is nod when he asks, "Mr. and Mrs. Galdoni?" When neither Cheryl nor Gloria indicates that she is the "Mrs.", the guy plunges ahead. "I'm Doctor Lenzer. Along with several other staff members, I've been treating your son. I can say now that he's going to be fine."

A cry of joy goes up from the females. I'm shuddering inside. I have an urge to give Lenzer a hug. Instead I stand and keep nodding dumbly, as if my head is attached to a spring. Lenzer continues, "For about a minute there I thought we'd lost him. He had no heartbeat. The antidepressants had seriously interfered with the electrical impulses that regulate his heart. But we got it beating again. He rallied. He seems to have stabilized now, although he'll need to stay in Intensive Care for at least the next day or so. If you'd like, two of you—no more—can go in and see him. Briefly. Nurse Borkoski will accompany you."

I turn around and am immediately hugged by Cheryl. Gloria's arms are already around Clara and Lila; it's as if the five of us were bracing for the bomb. I nuzzle Cheryl's hair, then, not trusting myself to stay together, step back from her. "C'mon, Clara," I manage to say. "You and me are the most directly related, I guess."

This earns me misty, approving smiles from Gloria and Cheryl. Lila, too. Even Clara. Her sunken mouth turns up at the corners and she nods agreement with more energy than I thought she had left in her body.

As we slide through the curtain of Kenny's cubicle, I notice that the tube in his neck has been replaced by one running into his wrist from an overhanging bottle. According to the nurse, they're feeding him mainly sugar water. Not surprisingly, he's flat on his back and seems barely awake. But a few moments after we enter his green eyes open wide, as if he's startled by the sight of Daddy and Grandma Clara together. Clara, sobbing, practically falls on him. Nurse Borkoski, who I imagined had been sent along to make sure *I* behaved, winds up having to pull Clara off of Kenny.

"Clara, he's gonna be fine. Remember?" I say as Borkoski releases her and holds out some tissues. Then I turn to my son. "You hear that, Kenny? You're gonna be as good as new." I'm grinning like an idiot. I actually give the kid a kiss. As I do, I could swear there's some kind of shine coming off of him, as if he'd been polished or something. This worries me; I glance at Clara and Borkoski, neither of whom seems to think anything's amiss. I take his hand. "How do you feel, Ken?"

"Fine." After a moment he adds, "I saw Mommy."

"You had a dream."

"No, I saw Mommy in afterlife."

I do a double-take. Not because I believe him, but because he's talking in sentences. I'd expected him to be groggy; I *didn't* expect him to be flashing improved English skills. Or an enlarged vocabulary: I'd be surprised if he ever heard the word "afterlife" before, let alone used it. "Kenny, you were probably dreaming," I repeat. "Or maybe you were hallu . . . maybe you were seeing something that wasn't there, because you were sick. Mommy's dead."

He sticks out his lower lip, a mannerism I never thought would bring joy to my heart. "No," he insists. "I saw Mommy. And Grampa Abe."

Clara gives a little shriek of delight. She gently pinches Kenny's cheek. "Nu, you remember your Grandpa's name. Such a smart boy." It's unclear to me whether or not she thinks Kenny actually saw the ghosts of her husband and daughter. I'm just tickled that the kid has obviously sustained no brain damage, even if his brain played some tricks on him when he was in bad shape.

"And I saw Great-grampa Moy-sa. And Great-gramma Sarah."

At this Clara gasps. "Abe's parents. Did Sharon ever tell him their names? Or did you?"

I shrug. "Clara, I don't think I ever *knew* their names. And I doubt that Sharon told him, either. Her father's name, maybe, but great-grandparents? I doubt it."

Clara bends over Kenny. "Tell me, tattaleh. What did Grandpa Abe say? How did he look?"

"Mrs.—" says Nurse Borkoski,

"Weiss," I fill in.

"Mrs. Weiss, Kenny needs to rest now. We'll have to end the visit." She places a hand on Clara's shoulder.

Clara kisses Kenny, tells him, "Grandma loves you," then allows Borkoski—a sweet-looking young thing—to gently move her away from the bed.

I plant a kiss on Kenny's other cheek, tell him to get some sleep and that I'll see him a little later, that we'll be going home together in no time.

On the way back to the waiting room, Borkoski says, "I couldn't help overhearing your conversations with Kenny. Please don't worry about his mental state, or about the 'visions' he reported. These kinds of experiences are not uncommon. And whatever we make of them, they seem to cheer patients up, at least."

What Gloria makes of Kenny's story (as related by an animated Clara) is that his soul left his body, had a little visit with the souls of Sharon and company, and then returned. "It's called a 'near death experience'," she says. "Ask him later—maybe before he went to the beyond, he heard things the doctors and nurses said while he was supposed to be totally unconscious, or even lifeless. Maybe he saw things he theoretically *couldn't* have seen, like he was watching himself and everyone else from a separate vantage point. These kinds of experiences have been documented, Mom . . . Paul. They're real."

I shrug and glance over at Cheryl, who gives me a warm smile. If she's bothered by the specter of my wife, you wouldn't know it.

Nor would you guess that about fifteen minutes ago, Clara looked like a woman with one foot in the grave. Her head bobs in agreement with Gloria. Clara claims that her husband, Abe, had the same kind of experience as Kenny. If I remember correctly from Sharon, this woman thinks that religion is bulldingy. Clara may finally be coming unglued.

On the other hand, I may not be wrapped very tightly myself. I'm starting to think that maybe Kenny did take a trip to heaven or wherever. At the least, the things that he said are hard to explain. And I've got to believe that the kid knows Sharon when he sees her. He was probably closer to her in his three years than I ever was in our seven together. Maybe that would've changed if she'd been here to go through this with me. Maybe not. It'll give us something to talk about, if I ever see her again.

- epilogue -
Paul

ABOUT TEN days after Kenny's release from the hospital, he's back to his former self—but with some interesting modifications. Food and drink are still insufficient to fulfill his "oral needs," as Cheryl sometimes puts it. At her suggestion, I bought him a rubber giraffe and told him that when he wanted to put something in his mouth that wasn't food, he should use Jerry Giraffe and nothing else. So far, so good. Given the condition of Jerry's neck, I may need a herd of giraffes before Kenny is weaned onto edibles only. Still, we may be getting someplace.

Kenny's speaking ability is only slightly improved from his pre-accident days. He still doesn't put together sentences. But he's speaking *more*. A lot of this is conversations with "Mommy," some of them little more than babbling, others that make some sense. If some kids have imaginary playmates, I can see no harm in him having an imaginary mother, especially if it makes him happy. That's the big change in Kenny. He seems happier. He fusses less, laughs and smiles more. He's getting to be a lovable kid. In fact, he's already there.

Howard Levine lives with his family in Maryland, where he teaches special education. In his free time he writes, bicycles, and hikes.